THE RETURN OF
THE ADONI

THE RETURN OF
THE ADONI

[The Final Book of
The DULAN ARCHIVES]

DENNIS KNOTTS

COVER AND MAP BY
RONALD G. PATTERSON

Strategic Book Publishing and Rights Co.

Strategic Book Publishing & Rights Co., LLC
USA | Singapore
www.sbpra.net

For information about special discounts for bulk purchases, please contact Strategic Book Publishing and Rights Co. Special Sales, at bookorder@sbpra.net.

ISBN: 978-1-949483-00-0

DEDICATION

Dedicated to Tanya, the daughter whom
God brought home,
To David, the son we never had,
And to Jayme, my inspiration for Tanya.

THE RETURN OF THE ADONI

TABLE OF CONTENTS

"And other sheep I have which are not of this fold, them also I must bring and they shall hear my voice and there shall be one fold and one shepherd"

—Jesus—

(John 10:16)

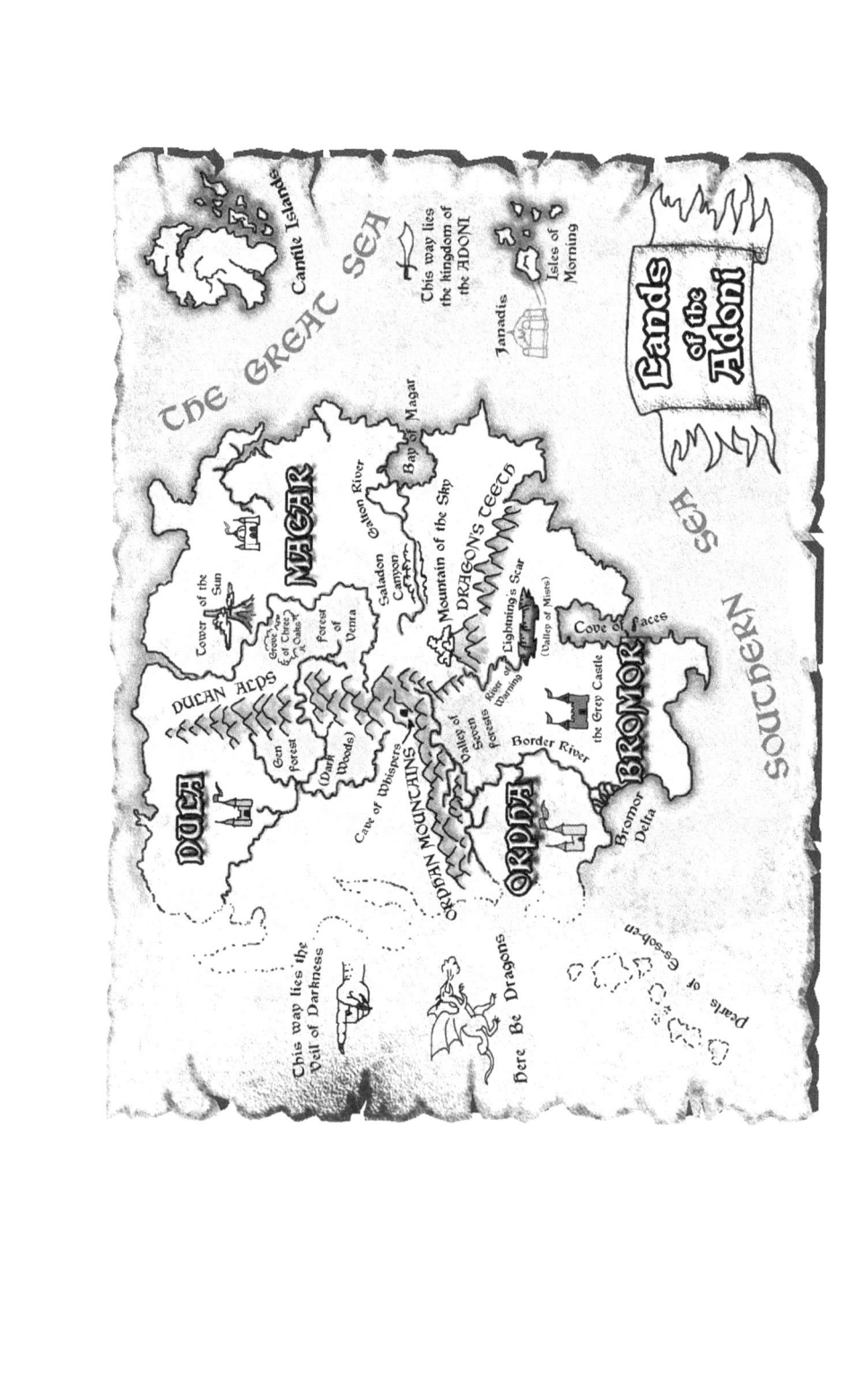

INTRODUCTION

THE BIRTH OF DULA

Welcome to the final book of *The Dulan Archives*. What began as a dream when I was only ten years old, grew into a collection of science fiction short stories in junior high school, became a barbarian-versus-civilization story in junior college, and then had its infancy as a fantasy story in 1977; has now come to its maturity. And it's only taken forty-two years.

As I discussed in the introduction to *The Battle of Es-Soh-En* this all began as a dream. We had just moved from Baltimore, Maryland to Woodland Hills, California. In Maryland I had played in the fields and woods around my parent's home; but even though it had been named Woodland Hills, there were no woods where we lived, and only one hill. It was a private hill, too, with a house on the top of it. So in order to climb the one hill, I had to make sure I didn't get caught. Maybe it was the desire to go back to Maryland which prompted the dream – at least that's what psychologists would probably tell me; but I think God was getting me started.

In the dream I was climbing the lone hill in Woodland Hills. I came to the top of the hill, and for the first time, I made it all the way over to the other side. The house was no longer there in my dream. As I came down the previously-unexplored side of the hill, I found myself wandering into a kind of golden fog. The further I went, the thicker the fog grew. At one point, everything was blocked from view. I should have been terrified, but I remember a strange, calm, relaxing feeling flooding me. It was like the golden fog was a soft blanket, wrapping itself around me the way a mother would wrap her child in a blanket, cuddle the child, and rock the child to sleep.

When the fog faded away, I was in a clearing with trees all around. Tied to one tree was a woman, out of the damsel-in-distress category, complete with the outfit. As I tried to untie her, a knight in full armor – the face plate pulled over the face so I couldn't make out any features – charged me on horseback. In the dream I was run through by the lance, and I woke up as I died.

The dream stayed with me for many years. It wasn't that the dream frightened me, or was a kind of recurring nightmare. The truth is that I have never had the dream again in my entire life. What kept coming back to me in my waking hours was that sense of complete peace I had walking through the golden fog.

In ninth grade I tried my hand at being a writer and did a collection of science fiction short stories about the planet Dula and the planet Magar. I called the collection *The Thunderers*. Several names were also pulled from that collection for my fantasy series. Unfortunately, the manuscript was lost many years ago. (If found, please return…)

In 1977, I died – literally. I was in an auto accident where the driver of the other car was drinking and driving on the opposite side of the four-lane highway. He pulled out to pass, lost control of his car, and came right in front of us. We couldn't stop, and struck his vehicle at fifty-five miles an hour. My friend and I spent a few weeks in the hospital. The passengers in the other car were not so lucky. While recovering at home I had this vision of the workers pulling my body out of the back of the van. This surprised me because I thought I had been pulled through the windshield, which was completely gone. Even more surprising was the fact that as I watched them work on my body, there was a voice behind me that said, "You're not done yet."

During the recovery time I began to type. I wanted to re-do *The Thunderers*, but it never came together. Instead, the story was coming together as a fantasy story. I remember thinking how stupid I was being as I wrote the title page. I had always had trouble writing any story much longer than twenty or thirty pages. This is why *The Thunderers* was a collection of short stories. But I knew that this was going to be more than a short story. What I couldn't believe I was doing was giving *The Search for Logos* a subtitle, and the subtitle was: *Book One of the Dulan Archives.*

I wasn't planning for series, but as I wrote *The Search for Logos* the characters all kept asking about something called, the *Battle of Es-Soh-En* and with so many questions, that became the title/topic of the second book. I wrapped it all up with *The Return of the Adoni* and thought I was done. But God had other ideas. He gave me *The Song of Es-Soh-En* and for many years I thought it was a four-book series. In the last couple of years He gave me *The Ballad of Pentra* and *The Silence of the Sword*. Now God is bringing me back to *The Return of the Adoni* and letting me finally publish the final book of the series.

The Dulan Archives is a *What If?* Series. It was written to answer a question in my mind: *What if God created another Creation; and that Creation fell into sin? What steps would God take to redeem that Creation?* This is why there are parallels between the Bible and *The Dulan Archives*.

As I wrote each of the books for *The Dulan Archives* I tried to take the teachings of the Bible and re-think each one. I had to go back to the Bible, and read the passages without thinking in

terms of current beliefs, traditional thoughts, or religious structure. I had to think in terms of *"what was God truly trying to say
here?"*

When *The Return of the Adoni* came together, there were
parallels to the Rapture, Tribulation, Second Coming and other
themes, but it was not identical. This is not an attempt to tell the
book of Revelation in fantasy form. It's another world, with different Laws in place. This is why it is a fantasy because I needed
to change the Laws God had set down for our world. I did not
feel comfortable changing God's Law for our world, so I created
a different world – a fantasy world.

There are different characters following the paths set down
for them. I had planned to make Gib-ron the Antichrist, even
down to the blindness in the right eye, and useless right arm;
but it never went any further than that. The story was too developed along other lines, and I suddenly found myself unable to
use Gib-ron the way the Antichrist will be used in our world. I
wanted to, but I had to tell the story of Dula, and not Earth; and
as much as I wanted to, Dula has its own history, its own laws,
and its own destiny; and even I couldn't change that.

It's only been forty years since *The Dulan Archives* began
to evolve into a fantasy story. There have been a lot of changes
along the way. I freely admit that I loved C. S. Lewis' *Chronicles of
Narnia* and J. R. R. Tolkien's *Lord of the Rings*. However, I could
spend twenty pages telling you where the ideas and names came
from, and it was not from either series. There are similarities
because Lewis, Tolkien and I were telling variations of the most
epic adventure of all: the Redemption of a World. The Bible,
more than Lewis or Tolkien, was my template to work from.

For those who missed the imagery, Dianna was my representation of the nation of Israel under its Messiah. Janadis was
my representation of the Church. And in this final story, David

James and Tanya are the Two Witnesses from Revelation. Outside of that, there was no intentional representation with this book.

One last observation. There are those who read *The Chronicles of Narnia* and do not see the Christian messages hidden there. I felt led to write an eighth addition to *The Chronicle of Narnia*. It is called *Return to Narnia*. It is the story of Susan's adventure that brings her back into the service of Aslan and eventually into Narnia. I wrote to Douglas Gresham about getting permission to publish it. He was not happy, but the book was already complete. He did not even want to read it.

But with *Return to Narnia* and *The Dulan Archives* I revealed the man behind the curtain – or the Savior of both series. I know Lewis kept reference to Jesus directly out of his books, but his subtle references are lost on today's readers. They literally know nothing of the Bible. I chose to make it clear that the Adoni of the Lands of the Adoni and Jesus, God the Father and God the Holy Spirit were the same. All worlds are the same, only the names are different. As I mentioned earlier, my series was following a simple question – just like Lewis. If God made another universe and it fell into sin; what steps would He take there to redeem it?

Hopefully, with the addition of *The Return of the Adoni* this question has been finally answered; both in Dula and in our world as well.

Dennis Knotts
First draft 12/31/1997

INTRODUCTION TO 2019 PRINTING

Yes, I know the introduction is getting a bit carried away. My apologies. I wrote a trilogy back in the 1977 – 1980. There was *The Search for Logos*, *The Battle of Es-Soh-En*, and *The Return of the Adoni*.

Then God gave me *The Song of Es-Soh-En* and I change the subtitle for *The Return of the Adoni* from the Third Book to the Final Book. I did this because I had no idea how many books God wanted to give me. He gave me two more: *The Ballad of Pentra* and *The Silence of the Sword*. So this book has sat untouched since 1980, and it is now 2019 – thirty-nine years since I finished it. The dream came when I was ten years old. I am now sixty-six.

What amazed me when I came back to make any revisions to include details from the last two books, is that *The Agenda of Magar* was written thirty-nine years ago. I was trying to picture how bad America could get and turn Dula into that. When I came to this chapter thirty-nine years later, it read like a Fox News Commentary today.

I was surprised that there was no need for a major revision. That chapter pretty much reads as it did thirty-nine years ago; but I do not profess to be a prophet. The book, as a whole, needed little revision other than to add changes and characters added in

The Ballad of Pentra and *The Silence of the Sword*. But other than that; the story survived with very few changes.

So now it is complete; and I release it to God to use as He releases it to the world. Enjoy!

Dennis Knotts
2/3/2019

CHAPTER ONE

THE SUMMONING

David brushed the strand of brown hair which kept hanging annoyingly in his hazel eyes. He noted that his breath had become a visible puff in the chilled air. It was colder this year than normal. He stared at the tired sun; now too weak to hurt his eyes. His mind pulled up all the different theories he had heard which attempted to explain the change in the weather. It was everything from a weather front in the Pacific Ocean, to the ozone hole, to a theory that this *was* normal weather. Of course, *Global Warming* was always on everyone lips these days.

He smiled, and the cold made the scar which now creased his right cheek ache. He raised his hand, pulling it out of the warm coat pocket where he had kept it since parking his car several lots away, and touched the wound. A sardonic laugh escaped his lips. The scar had been the only thing which had followed him home from Dula.

Each time he had visited the mythical world of the Lands of the Adoni, he had returned as he had left, even down to his original weight, size, and clothing. It would amaze him because on several visits they had been gone so long, they had forgotten where they were, what they were doing, and what they had been wearing when they left earth, and were transported to Dula via a golden mist. One time he had been gone for over two years.

It was as if he were a citizen of Dula, and was no longer was a Child of Earth. He noted that more of his life had been lived in the Lands of the Adoni than here on earth – so which was his true home?

The Knight of Es-Soh-En smiled softly with the term, *Child of Earth*. When Queen Dianna had called Tanya and him by that title on their first visit, he felt his temper flair. He was too old to be considered a child. Then when he had witnessed the birth of Dula, and the creation of Ish, he came to understand that the title had nothing to do with his age, but the fact that he – and his entire race – had been formed from earth, the dust of the ground. The emphasis of this title was the word *earth*, not the word *child*. He no longer tensed when it was applied to either himself, or his sister.

The memory of Dianna brought his hand to the scar once more. He had obtained this reminder fighting to save Queen Dianna from an attacking Bat Creature. It had been his last visit to her world, only four or five months ago. It was on that visit that he had finally faced the feelings he had for the Queen of Dula. He had professed his love for her, begged her to marry him.

She had been kind, polite; but very firm. She was the betrothed of Teacher, the Rightful King of Dula. Teacher who was the human incarnation of Es-Soh-En, the Great Hobber, the Son of the Adoni, One of the Three Who Were One, The Creator and Savior of the Lands of the Adoni. The titles were endless. His anger had flared that day. He was actually jealous of the Creator of the Lands of the Adoni. He had sought to steal what rightfully – and lawfully – belonged to another. He ran away from the queen out of anger, and even more so out of embarrassment for letting his feelings show. He was sure his actions had cost him his standing as a Knight of Es-Soh-En. He had betrayed a most sacred trust. He thought for a moment of Lancelot and Camelot. He did not like the similarity.

In his desperation, his self-exile brought him to the Cantile Islands, the furthest land mass from the Kingdom of Dula. He had hidden himself there for long months, suppressing all evidence of who and what he was; even more so, suppressing all feelings for his queen. He had removed his Knight of Es-Soh-En garb, and hidden it in a cave. He had even placed Gennerroth, his sword, in the cave and vowed to never take it up again. It would mean that his mission – whatever it had been – would remain unfulfilled. It would also mean he would never return to earth.

David had lived as a shepherd for almost a year. He wandered in the high mountains of the Cantile Islands, drank of the cold crystal streams which were fed by melting snow. He was old enough by then to grow a full beard; and although his hair was normally long, he gave up trimming or cutting it so it was more shaggy than normal. Then he came upon Kya. She had been outcast from her tribe. When he had found her, she was near death; exhausted, starved, and frozen. He took her to his shelter, and spent weeks nursing her back to health.

It was through Kya that he forgot all about Dianna, Dula, and the Knights of Es-Soh-En. They made a home together, working as a team to care for the herds of sheep and goats, harvesting small crops they tended in the spring and summer. Kya had worked the wool of their sheep, dying it, weaving it, and turning it into a blue sash. It was the same shade of bright topaz as the eyes of the Great Hobber. When the black lion stood before David that first time years ago, and His golden mane had flashed with sparks of light from the sun; it was the topaz-blue eyes that caught, and held his attention.

David took the sash, lovingly from his Kya, and that night confessed his hidden past. Kya then confessed that she had been outcast because she had dared to declare that she accepted Teacher. She had sworn allegiance to this man and the doctrines He and His followers taught. At that moment she was dead to her family. She was driven from the tribe. She had feared to say anything else about her feelings for Teacher out of fear of further rejection.

It had only been a few days later when David stood before the mouth of their shelter, watching the sunrise over the mountain tops in the east. Suddenly, Es-Soh-En stood next to him. David's throat tightened and he could not find words to speak. He had sought to steal Es-Soh-En's bride away. He was filled with shame for his feelings and his action.

As the Child of Earth struggled to find the words, the Great Hobber leaned against him, rubbed His golden mane on David's side, and made eye contact. The topaz-blue eyes of the Great Hobber held only love and forgiveness for the wayward knight. Even more than that, the eyes held what David needed most: understanding. The Knight of Es-Soh-En broke, threw his arms around the Adoni, and sobbed with all the pain in his heart. Kya heard the sounds, and came outside, only to find David embracing the Great Hobber. She had never met Es-Soh-En. She had heard the many lessons about Teacher, but never knew that They were one-in-the-same.

The Adoni had come to call David back into service. Dianna was in danger. She had sought to travel through the Forest of Venra to find him, and bring him back. She had forgiven him of his actions. She would not entrust the message to anyone else, but wanted to tell it to him face-to-face. Her journey was going to bring her into a swarm of Bat Creatures.

The moment Es-Soh-En spoke of the danger, David's eyes were clear, and eager. The Hobber nodded, and the Child of Earth stood before Kya dressed in the attire of a Knight of

Es-Soh-En, Gennerroth fasten at his hip. The only difference was that the topaz blue sash she had woven for him was now wrapped around his waist in place of the leather belt he had previously worn.

Es-Soh-En breathed into the air, and the golden mist appeared. The Adoni stepped back, and as David plunged through. He found himself in the Forest of Venra just as the first of the Bat Creatures dropped from the sky.

Instantly Gennerroth was in hand, hacking and cutting at the sky. The death wails of the creatures tore the stillness of the forest. The Knight of Es-Soh-En positioned himself between his queen and her attackers. It was a gory battle. For each one that David tore from the sky, three more seemed to appear. Several times one or another grabbed his arm, or fell upon him. He had to constantly shift sword hands to free his blade to continue the battle. It must have been hours, but finally the last dropped to the ground with a sickening thud. The Child of Earth stepped back out of the carnage, working his way out from among the twitching bodies. Dianna was safe, unharmed. They had not gotten past him to her. His body burned from all the talon cuts and clawing it had endured. The poisons from the creatures' fangs and talons had worked their way into his blood stream. His arms became like lead. His knees went weak. His eyes rolled back and he fell at Dianna's feet, thankful that he had given his life to save her; hoping that this would somehow redeem him in her sight.

How long it had been he could not tell, but he came to with Dianna, Kya and Es-Soh-En looking over him. The pod needed to cure the Bat Creature venom lay on the ground next to him, and a plant – which he was sure had not been there when he collapsed – was sprouting new pods even as he woke. Kya threw her arms around him, kissing the wound on his cheek. All had healed except that one.

When David went home, he had left Kya in the care of Dianna. The friendship between the queen and knight was restored. No dishonor remained to deal with. Only the heartache of leaving Kya behind marred his return to earth.

The cry of a hawk high overhead reminded him of the war cry of Glidon, the Great Eagle: the Third of the Three. Glidon was another of the Adoni who had appeared through their journeys to Dula. This, however, was not a golden eagle soaring in the air, but a red-tailed hawk. It hovered on the cold winter wind, fluttering its wings ever so softly to hold its position as it searched the hillside for prey. The buildings he sought had been built on hills that had once been its home. The hawk adapted and learned to search for its prey among this piece of civilization that had intruded upon its world.

David pushed the memories from his mind, and focused on where he was. He had parked on the far side of the college in order to save on the parking expense. Everything cost these days. He now realized that he was lost. He caught the attention of a passing student, "Excuse me, miss?" She turned to give him her attention. "I'm looking for a girl…"

"Oh?" she replied, suddenly interested. David realized her intentions, blushed and stammered.

"Yes, I'm looking for a specific girl." Her smile faded as he spoke. "Actually, she's my sister. I was supposed to meet her in Johnson's Hall." Her eyes twinkled once she realized that there still might be a chance. "That is the woman's dorm, isn't it?" he added trying to defuse the situation.

"Woman's dorm?" she echoed and then smiled. "You *are* innocent, aren't you? There are no women or men's dorms here anymore. It's all co-ed." She saw the concern crossing David's face, and then softened. "Of course, Johnson Hall does have an all-female floor. She's probably on that one. Johnson Hall is the brick building over there."

David thanked her with a faint smile. He did not want to hurt her feelings, but he didn't want to encourage her either. He knew that the odds were that Kya would be long-dead when he next traveled to Dula. Each time the Adoni called them from their world into the Lands of the Adoni; it was a different time in Dula's history. Their second visit had been two hundred years after their first, although only two months had passed by earth time. Their third visit took them thousands of years into the past to witness the creation of the world. They had then appeared at various points along the timeline of that world. Each return had been at least two or three generations' difference. When he would return to Dula, Kya would be lost to him. He knew that when he left her behind and returned to earth. It was now the reason why he did not want to return to Dula. As long as he could pretend she was still there, waiting for him, he could go on with each day. Once he would go back to Dula that illusion – that comfort – would be forever lost to him. He now understood the actions of his sister.

That had been the reason why Tanya had not gone with him on the last visit. The golden mist had appeared, but she refused to go. As she refused, the mist faded from her view, and only David could still see it. She had lost Jensen. That was two visits ago, a year by earth time. It had been the talk of the palace. The romance was on everyone's lips, and if they had not returned to earth at the end of that mission, Tanya would have wed the poet. He had a way with words. He had spent his entire life expressing his love for Tanya, even though she was gone, and would not return in his lifetime. David had seen the collection of poems he had written. They were the most passionate and popular poems in the entire kingdom. Other poets would use them as models on how to write great poems. When David returned, and told Tanya about them, she sat and wept for over a week. It had been hard for her, even though the time frame since she had been with him had been shorter. She knew he would not be alive on the next visit, and so she had refused to go.

David felt the cold through his boots. It had actually snowed here a month ago according to Tanya. "It never snows here," he declared to no one in particular.

His mind pulled up the changes in the weather once more. It cross-referenced the increase in earthquakes, tornadoes, and floods. Already the government was declaring that such disasters were putting a strain on the country's resources. Without realizing it, his thoughts then slipped over to a class in environmental science he had taken just last year.

"We have set forces into motion which cannot be undone. Even if we were to stop our actions today, over one-third of the world's population will die." The unbidden thought bothered DJ. It had always been an abstract thought. If one-third of the world died, it didn't matter unless you, or someone you liked, were part of that one-third. There always seemed to be enough problems to go around. He had worked all summer trying to get enough money to continue college, but he had ended up using all of it just to find a place to live, and so he was forced to attend a single night class at the local college.

His journeys to Dula had nearly cost him his job; not that he had missed any time from work, it's just that when he came back, he had trouble remembering which task he had been working on when he left. It was also hard to shift from the mentality of a Knight of Es-Soh-En, to factory worker. He had been warned about insubordination when he would tell his boss or lead man that they were doing something wrong. They said he kept acting like he was the one in charge.

David felt the tension in his jaw muscle; one of the signs of stress. He drew in a long breath, pulled it deep into his chest, held it a little longer than was comfortable, and then slowly exhaled; letting the tension leave his body with the swirls of smoky breath. He wasn't going to be depressed when he met his sister. He had made that promise to himself.

David completed the trek to Johnson's Hall without any further problems, but when he found the all-woman floor; he had waited almost half-an-hour in the lobby for someone to pass by. When a woman came out of the wing, he asked her about the proper procedures for contacting someone on the floor. The student gave him a disgusted look, and told him to just go and knock on the door.

To say that Tanya was surprised to see him was an understatement. She had nearly crushed his rib cage, and dragged him into the room before he could even greet her. The hug produced a crumpling sound from inside his jacket, and he broke off the welcome before more damage was done. He unsnapped the top three fasteners of the coat, reached inside, secured a package with a now-crushed bow, and handed it to his sister, "Happy birthday!"

"You shouldn't have," she declared tucking a rebellious strand of her reddish-brown hair behind her left ear. She had been about to mention the fact that he was struggling with his finances and couldn't afford to buy anything extra, but she stopped. She had been the lucky one. She had collected several scholarships to help her through college. David, although doing well in school, and athletic in sports, just never seemed to work with the right people who could have submitted his name for the financial support. She had been proud of him going on to college, working odd jobs and nights to make it, but money had always been a sore spot between them.

"If I can't get a present for my favorite sister, then who can I spend my money on?" David joked.

"I'm your only sister," Tanya reminded as she snapped the ribbon, and peeled back the red wrapping paper. The actions revealed a black, hardbound book. She opened it to see sketches of characters and places they had visited on their journeys to Dula. The last entry was a collection of drawings of Jensen. The final addition was one of the poems the poet had written to Tanya after she had left Dula. David had illustrated the poem with Jensen and Tanya's faces smiling in love. Tears began to swell in Tanya's deep blue eyes before she could fight down the memory.

"I'm sorry, Tanya. I thought you might like it…" David began to apologize, but she hugged him as hard as she could, and cut him off.

"I love it. It's beautiful. I didn't know you could draw."

"I never had that much time for it before. It just seems that so many places and faces have been slipping into my head, especially just before I go to sleep. I used to stay up long hours just trying to get back to sleep."

"I remember. It would drive mom and dad crazy because you were up and around all hours of the night. They were afraid you were up to something."

"Parents always worry about things like that," David noted. "Then one night, instead of trying to get the image out of my mind, I took a piece of paper and a pencil, and set to work creating what was so vivid in my mind. It was strange. I've never had any art lessons. I just saw these faces and places from so many directions that I could draw them from any angle."

"When you came back last time, you said that Jensen had become one of the great poets of Dula. Tell me more about it," asked Tanya. It had been a tender subject when David had first mentioned it months ago, now she felt that she could deal with it. She was hungry for some word, any word about her beloved.

It must have been over an hour later when Tanya finally confessed to DJ that she had taken up writing poems. "It's something Jensen taught me when I was in Dula. He would have me think about something that I really felt strongly about – a concept, an event, a person; and then to work it in my mind. The key is to find the right image or phrase. The rest is just a skill in putting it down on paper."

"Kind of the same thing with my drawings," David suggested. Tanya opened a drawer, pulled out a battered spiral-bound notebook, and trembled as she handed it to her brother.

"No one has ever seen these before," she admitted. David opened the first page, and found his sister's cursive script as the first poem unfolded. It was a passionate poem, speaking of her love for the Dulan poet. Several other poems dealt with her anger and her grief. Then the pained poetry was replaced by memories of characters, deeds and events in Dula.

"These are great!" David declared. "You've got more than just a skill. There's real talent here." The conversation was suddenly broken off by the appearance of two students: Tanya's roommate, Sally, and Sally's current love-interest. The couple took no time in letting David and Tanya know that they had plans, and the Children of Earth were in the way. It caught David off guard to realize the moral conditions Tanya had been forced to live in on the college campus.

"When's the last time you ate?" asked Tanya, grabbing her coat, and ushering her brother to the door.

"I ate this morning, but you know I never turn down food," he quipped.

"Good, there's a cafe in town…" The look on her brother's face made her break off and laugh. "Don't worry. We can walk. So, how many times did you get lost before you found a parking place?" The Knight of Es-Soh-En made a pathetic puppy-dog face, and held up three fingers. "The first time I came here it was five, so don't feel…" Her voice broke off in mid-sentence. David's attention was instantly fixed on the scene before them. The hallway was filled with the swirling golden mist which had always transported them to Dula.

"Do you see it, too?" Tanya asked cautiously. There was actually a trembling in her voice.

"I'd have to be blind not to." He scanned the area, but no one seemed to notice the occurrence but the two of them. "Are you coming this time?"

"But DJ, every time we've gone to Dula, we had been looking for the doorway. This is the first time since our first visit that it's come looking for us."

"So…?" his voice trailed.

"Don't you recall the warning by Es-Soh-En? *Beware the time the golden mists seeks you. You shall not return, and one of you shall taste of death.* Is this the time?"

"If it is; then what of it? Outside of you, mom and dad, there's nothing in this world to hold me. I've always thought that I got born in the wrong world anyway."

"David James!" his sister's voice was severe. "You know the Adoni do not make mistakes."

"I know, but I've waited my whole life to get out of this world and stay out. When I see a movie, if I don't like it, I leave. Only every time I leave this place, I seem to keep ending up back in it. If it means that I'm going to die this time, so be it. I've seen…we've seen what lies beyond death's door. What's so horrible about it?"

"But what if I'm to be the one who dies?" suggested Tanya. She was not afraid of death, but she wanted to sober her brother up with the thought. It struck him square in the face.

"It can't be you. It would have to be me," he insisted.

"Any hidden message from the Adoni on that point?" Tanya teased, but David wasn't in the mood to joke about such a concept. "I'm as ready as you to face my own death, but are you ready to accept that it might be me?"

"No," came David's weak response. "That was something I never considered. I've always believed that I would be beside you. That if death came, I could throw myself between you and it so that I could make sure I was the one to die."

"I've known you were always more reckless in battle than I. You took chances to protect me which left you in greater danger. David, I'm a Knight of Es-Soh-En, too. I'm not a delicate female who needs protecting. Give me the chance to serve the Adoni as intensely as you."

"So are we going?" asked David. They both knew that their loved-ones would not be waiting on the other side of the mist for them. A student came around the corner, did not seem to see them, and actually walked through the brother and sister as if they were only shadows or ghosts. Tanya cried out at the experience, but no one in the hall noticed. She swallowed hard to gain control and replied, "It seems that the decision about going is no longer ours." She offered her arm to her brother, and David ushered them into the swirling mists. The golden cloud became thicker around them so that they were blotted from view, if any had been able to see them. The fog then dissipated; removing any trace of its, or the Knights of Es-Soh-En, ever having being there.

From high overhead, there came a shout, like the single note of a golden trumpet on the highest parapet of Heaven, calling its citizens home. Its voice spread across the world, lingering for a moment, and then it was gone taking the last beauty of earth with it. As the last wisp of golden mist evaporated along the baseboards of the hallway, a dark shadow began to stretch across the face of the sun, squeezing the light from it, and claiming the earth as its own.

CHAPTER TWO

CRISIS IN DULA

The harsh light of summer burned down on DJ and Tanya forcing them to shield their eyes with their hands. It was a drastic change from the winter's day inside, to the brilliant glare outside. The full heat of the Dulan summer descended upon them. Even though they were now filled with the Power of the Adoni, and their senses and abilities were enhanced to a level higher than normal, it was more than they could comfortably endure. Tanya could feel her face flush. David tore off his jacket. As he held it in his hand, it suddenly struck him.

"We're still wearing earth clothes. Where's our Dulan attire?" Tanya made the mental command to transform to her battle garb, but nothing happened. She raised her hand, and called Sy-lar, her eagle-sword, from its place of waiting; but it never appeared.

"Something is wrong. Very wrong," she declared. The pair scanned their surroundings to try and determine where they were; if not in time, then at least in location.

"This is the palace of Dula," David noted.

"It can't be," Tanya challenged. "Look at the grass and vegetation. It looks dry and brittle. The lawns and fields around Dula were always some of the most beautiful in the entire world. This is spotty. Look at the weeds!"

"The weeds aren't that old. It could just be a little neglect," suggested David. He, too, had noticed the differences. The sun beat down hotter than had been normal for even the warmest summer days. The air was thick with some kind of pollution. Dula had never displayed air pollution on any of the Children's previous visits. The Lands of the Adoni had rejected technology because wise men had brought the Curse upon the land. But David could feel a thin layer of grit settle on his skin even as they stood in the courtyard. The light was filtered through the grime, giving the impression of a sun which had grown tired of looking down upon the tainted world. For a brief, fleeting moment, David half-hoped to turn, and see that the golden fog was still available to take them back to Earth.

Dula had always been the place where he could escape all of this. Now it was in this world as well. He felt depression seeping into every pore, and instantly realized it was the influence of the Dark One.

"No!" he shouted, and threw his coat onto the ground. He mentally commanded the Dark One to leave. He called upon the Power of the Adoni to protect him. The depression faded. He looked up, and saw that Tanya had just endured a similar battle. The resolve in their eyes was easy to read when their gazes locked.

"Dula is dying," Tanya whispered in disbelief, more to herself than to her brother. She had always been better at reading plants than he. Their third visit to Dula had given him a brief taste of her rapport with plant life, and he had always envied her for it, until now. She was feeling the cries of the plants around her. They were suffering, withering, calling out for someone to care for them. David could see the pain of the plants mirrored in his sister's eyes. She looked quickly around for any signs of water to meet the needs thrust upon her. There was none. Tanya had to fight down her desire, and focus on those things she could control.

"Glidon told us that we would always be brought to the point in Dulan history where we would be needed most. I guess this is when – and where – we're really needed," David suggested.

"We must find Dianna." The thought struck them both, but Tanya was the first to give it voice. The Knights of Es-Soh-En bounded out of the courtyard, and up the steps which led into the palace. Although Dianna had kept her palace opened to her people since their second visit, there should have at least been ceremonial guards on either side of the portal. Their absence sped the Children of Earth all the more. In the hallways, shouts were echoing. When the words became recognizable, David and Tanya put on a greater burst of speed.

"The Queen!" wailed one of the voices. "Somebody find the Queen!"

"We're doomed!" cried another. David and Tanya entered the throne room. Their enhanced senses captured the details instantly. All the guards were surrounding the throne, which sat empty. Others were tearing down tapestries, or pounding on sections of the walls and floor. Ministers and counselors stood dumbfounded. Several had dropped papers, but only one had collected enough of his wits to stoop down and pick them up. An older man, almost in a stupor, stumbled back when they filled the doorway to the throne room. He staggered to go around them, fell into a suit of armor, and it crashed with harsh sounds to the floor.

The clanging made the entire room stop. David lifted the man bodily from the floor, gripping the facing of his robes. The man's feet actually dangled in mid-air. The Knight of Es-Soh-En shook the man, and David's eyes took on the appearance of smoldering embers, "Where's the queen?"

Tanya wished that he wouldn't shake the poor man so, and she placed a hand on her brother's shoulder. The motion woke him from his intense focus. He lowered the man, released his hold, and the now-free advisor bolted from the room. David turned his attention to the throne, noted that ten guards had abandoned their search, and now blocked their way into the room. The sounds of scuffling boots on tile floors behind them told the Children of Earth that any retreat down the hall had just been blocked.

"Where is Queen Dianna?" David demanded taking the initiative. The troops stared back with blank expressions, holding their positions. After long moments one of the advisors, broke through their line to confront the Children of Earth.

"And who are you?" There was arrogance dripping from his voice. He studied their clothes, made a sniffing sound as if he found a stench about them.

"I am David James, Knight of Es-Soh-En. This is Lady Tanya, also a Knight of Es-Soh-En. I repeat my question: *Where is the queen?*"

"*You?*" the man snorted with disbelief. "*The Children of Earth?* Your clothing is completely wrong. You had better go back, and research further before you try and pull off this charade." He waved his right hand with his wrist going limp as if to dismiss them. David caught it in an iron grip, bending the man over so he was off balance. The Knight of Es-Soh-En positioned his face until his eyes were only a few centimeters from his captive's.

"This is the attire we wear in our world. Now I will repeat this question only once more. As Protector of the Queen of Dula, as Representative of the Adoni, as Knight of Es-Soh-En and Steward of the Throne of Dula..." the last title came to his mind suddenly as he recalled Es-Soh-En granting him that title on their first visit when they met the Great Hobber on the Mountain of the Sky. "...*Where is the queen?*"

A soldier swung his sword at David. It never finished its journey. Tanya had stepped in, caught the soldier in the tender point along the side where the breast plate was missing. As she drove her fingers like a knife into his ribs, he cried out, dropped to the floor, and his sword clattered on the tiles next to him. A quick blow to the neck rendered him unconscious. Tanya could see the concern of the guards that now a weapon was available to her. Her look of disdain caught them off-guard as she intentionally kicked the sword away from her. There were mixed emotions among the soldiers as they tried to interpret the action. Either Tanya was foolish in discarding the weapon; or she was so good, she didn't need it to defeat all of them.

A second guard moved forward, and Tanya clipped the back of his knee, sending the man to a kneeling position. She raised her knee quickly, slamming hard into the soldier's jaw. A moment later, he lay on the floor next to the first attacker. The soldiers now knew she had discarded the weapon because she did not feel she needed it to defeat them. Each guard became a little nervous at the realization that she might be right. The Knight of Es-Soh-En then positioned herself between her brother and the remaining troops, crouched like a tiger ready to spring into action.

"She's gone!" blurted the counselor held by David.

"What do you mean, *gone?*" David demanded. "Has she left the kingdom? Is she out of the palace?" He applied more pressure against the man's wrist joint. The counselor cried out. Guards sought to move forward, but Tanya repositioned her weight on the balls of her feet, indicating her ability – and determination – to protect her brother.

"*She's gone!*" repeated the advisor once it was clear that no help was coming to his aid. "One moment she was on the throne attending to state business. I turned to cough, looked back, and she was gone." David released the man. "She just disappeared. Vanished…in the twinkling of an eye. Without a trace." As he spoke the man continued to rub his abused wrist, and stumble slowly away from his attacker. Once he was out of danger, one of the other guards hurled his spear. The action was more to force David to step back into the waiting arms of other soldiers than to kill the Knight of Es-Soh-En.

David moved faster than eye could follow. Soldiers had moved in to secure the Knight of Es-Soh-En when he would fall back to protect himself. The Child of Earth defied the danger, and stepped directly into the path of the spear instead of trying to avoid it as the soldiers had expected. The guards were now inside the Knight of Es-Soh-En's attack area, and too surprised to respond to this new plan of action.

David threw his left arm up across his face, clenched his right fist, and snapped it down against his right side to add momentum to the motion of the left arm. The added benefit of the movement drove David's right elbow into the midsection of the closest guard. The attacker fell back with a large dent in the abdomen area of the breastplate. As David's left arm rose, his forearm connected with the shaft of the spear just behind the head while the razor edge of the projectile was only an inch away from his face. At the moment of impact, David tensed and locked every muscle and joint in his body, sending the full weight of his body into the point of contact with the spear. The movement *bumped* the projectile so that it flipped up. It now was about to pierce his forehead instead of his cheek.

The Knight of Es-Soh-En continued to follow through, relaxing his body and opening his fist so that the wrist twisted, and the palm locked onto the weapon in mid-flight. David tilted his head slightly to the right to avoid impact with the spear's head. The Child of Earth then plucked the spear out of mid air. He took the momentum of the spear's original flight, redirected it, and spun the shaft of the weapon around his own body several times, using the hard shaft to knock several opponents to the ground. When only one guard remained standing, David snatched the man by his breastplate, making escape impossible. The entire motion took only three or four seconds, and it ended with the motion that brought the point of the spear fixed firmly against the throat of the final guard.

"End this now!" demanded David with all the menace in his voice that he could muster. It had the desired effect of causing the others to step back. "If Dianna is gone, our first priority is to find her. Each minute you spend delaying us from our task makes her safe recovery more difficult."

"I am Tanya, Child of Earth, Knight of Es-Soh-En, Dancer in the Garden of Tangar, Singer of the Lesser Song, Stewardess of the Throne of Dula." Tanya announced, calling attention away from her brother in an effort to defuse the situation. She noted that one of the guards who was rising to his feet was glancing over her head. Expecting to see another attack coming from the balcony area of the throne room, she glanced in the same direction, and saw a tapestry hanging high overhead. It bore the likeness of her and her brother.

"What further proof do you need?" she added, pointing toward the tapestry. "The Adoni have sent us to you in your time of need. Fighting us is fighting the Adoni. It is not in the best interests of the kingdom. Our first concern is to find Dianna. Work with us in this effort."

"My lord?" began one of the advisors, detaching himself from the wall where the other non-combatants had taken refuge. "I wonder if your appearance is not more than a coincidence." He motioned, and the soldiers got to their feet and backed away. David released his captive, but still held onto the spear.

"Queen Dianna was on the throne. All was as it had been each day for many years. She held court here to address the needs of her kingdom. I was staring directly at the throne when it happened. I had not looked away. I was not distracted. She was there, and the next moment the throne stood empty. The objects she was holding fell to the ground as if they had been suddenly released by the one holding them. The hands which held them were there one moment, and gone the next.

"If you are the Children of Earth, then you are also the Steward and Stewardess of the Throne of Dula. Those titles would empower you to rule the kingdom in her absence. Become the king and queen of Dula until she returns," the speaker offered. The other advisors nodded their agreement.

"We are not here to assume the throne. That is for Dianna, and Dianna alone. But our first concern is for the safety of Dianna. We will assume the role of steward and stewardess as assigned us by the Adoni, but we will *never* assume the title of king or queen. Those are not titles you are empowered to give, nor are we empowered to accept," David declared.

"We must seek the guidance of the Adoni in this matter. Even in times when it seems clear to others, we must always test the spirit," Tanya advised. "It's obvious that Dianna is no longer in this room. Have the soldiers bring in all the guards and expand the search. Contact those in the outer posts, and have them split their forces. Half should work towards the palace; the other half should work outward away from the palace. Everyone who was in this room when she disappeared is to meet back here in half an hour to offer what information and observations he or she can. We will make further plans at that time."

David and Tanya relaxed their defensive posture, but remained battle ready. David returned the spear to the soldier who had hurled it. It had been the same soldier he had held by the top of the breastplate, and threatened moments ago. The look of disbelief in the guard's eyes told David that he had accomplished a seeming miracle with his action. As they left the room, several guards offered a military bow to the couple. It was only the nodding of the head; anything more would have weakened their battle readiness, but it symbolized their allegiance to the Children of Earth. David and Tanya both noted that some of the soldiers did not give the courtesy as they passed.

The brother and sister made their way up the stairs to their own quarters. Dianna had set these chambers aside for them to use on their various visits. Due to the extended time frames between their visits, and the unexpected appearances and disappearances in their service to the Adoni, Dianna had ordered the rooms constantly ready for their return, and would not allow any changes to be made other than routine maintenance. Dianna had done this so as to give the Children of Earth some sense of stability in an otherwise unstable life style.

"Well?" asked David as he closed the hallway door, separating their quarters from listening ears.

"Well what?" Tanya snapped. She felt the anger in her voice, and tried to control it. David knew the feeling. It was when you were angry about something, weren't sure why you were angry, and were stalling to explore your own thoughts and feelings. It had been a position he had been in many times before. It was not a common position for his sister. He chose to wait until she was ready to speak.

"I don't feel right about it!" she finally blurted out, after pacing the length of the room several times. She dropped into the high-back, padded chair which faced the fireplace.

"I can tell that," observed David, handing her a goblet of refreshment. "What doesn't feel right about it? The disappearance of Dianna? Our missing clothes and swords?"

"It's him!" she snapped when she finally found the focus of her anger.

"Him who?" David teased to calm her temper. It was a trick she had played too often on him. He was almost enjoying the reversal of roles. If Dianna had not been missing, it would have been entertaining.

"That man down there. That politician offered us Dianna's throne!" she stormed. "It wasn't his to give. He wasn't talking about us assuming leadership, and keeping things going until Dianna returned. He basically was trying to remove Dianna as queen. It was like the throne was some sort of door prize that had just been forfeited because the person with the winning ticket had left the party early. Es-Soh-En died to establish that throne!" She struck the arm of the chair. "He has declared that Dianna is to be His chosen queen. He gave her Unending Life to ensure that she would always be the one to sit on that throne, and this man wants to give it away before the cushions are even cool!"

"I guess you're right," David admitted. "I don't know of any changes since our last visit, but I don't know what legal argument he is using that gives him the right to declare a new king and queen. We must address the people in this time of crisis. If Dianna is not found, and found soon, the people will need someone to speak to them or panic will ensue. If…" and here David paused, and placed emphasis on the *if*. "If she does not return, we must put it to the people if they want us to guide in her absence."

"And if they don't want us to fill in?" Tanya probed.

"Then we leave the kingdom in whatever hands the Adoni permit, and the two of us conduct our own search."

"Us?" echoed Tanya.

"Yes, us. We're a team. I do the leg work, you do the research. That's what we're both good at," David offered.

"I'm pretty good at the leg work part myself," Tanya declared; her anger now gone.

"Yes, that was a pretty good counter defense you threw in the path of the guards downstairs. I think both of those men will give you a wide berth whenever they see you again. Not bad for being unarmed."

"*Unarmed simply means that you have both hands free to fight.*" Tanya quoted the ancient minotaur proverb.

"Now, let's find some clothes more fitting our current positions. We have a meeting in fifteen minutes," David reminded.

"David?" Tanya suddenly interrupted. "I was wrong."

"About what?" he asked pulling out a black tunic which bore the likeness of Es-Soh-En embroidered on the breast and a clean blue silk shirt.

"Es-Soh-En did not intend for Dianna to always be the one to sit on the throne."

"Of course He did. That's why He gave her the gift of Unending Life," David reminded his sister.

"Then why did the Adoni assign us the titles of Steward and Stewardess of the Throne?"

CHAPTER THREE

SEVERING THE TIES

David stood on the high tower of the Western Wall of the castle. It had been this location where he had stood for hours looking for the return of Teacher from the Veil. It had been here that he had stood waiting for Gandra's message regarding the voyage by sea to the Cantile Islands. He had found himself on this wall many times waiting. Sometimes he wasn't sure what he had been waiting for. He looked at the parapet. In his mind he remembered when the blocks were fresh and new. He could recall the actual smell of the fresh-hewn rock as the pieces were fitted together. He recalled the newness of the stones. They seemed so smooth when they were lifted into place. Now he touched the one closest to him. It had been polished from centuries of touching, generations of walking upon. The blocks seemed as worn and tired as he felt in his soul.

He smiled as he recalled that it had been several visits to Dula ago when Dianna had informed him that this section of the castle wall had been dubbed *David's Perch* by several guards. Many had noted his frequent appearances. It was said the farmers to the west of the castle would look in the direction of the castle, focus on this very spot to see if the Children of Earth had returned to Dula. If they saw a lone figure standing here, they would actually send someone to the castle to inquire if David

James and Tanya had returned. He never used to think of himself as being that predictable.

Had it only been two weeks since they had returned to Dula? It seemed like a lifetime. The initial meeting had failed to produce any results or information. Everyone told the same story from a different view. Dianna had been on the throne one moment, and gone the next. The patrols and search parties covered from the castle outward for a length of twenty miles. There were no tracks, there were no traces; there were no clues. He and Tanya had spoken to the people after a week of searching. The people spoke back, and declared them the Steward and Stewardess of the Throne. It seemed that all the titles Es-Soh-En had bequeathed to them on their first journey had now been fulfilled. There might be another one tucked in there somewhere, but he couldn't recall any. Maybe there was an obscure one, one that had only been mentioned in passing, under someone's breath; but if there was, he couldn't remember it. David closed his eyes to focus internally rather than externally as he considered the Adoni.

That had seemed to be the way of the Adoni. They were famous for placing clues in prophecies and what appeared to be irrelevant passages, names, or titles. The Adoni worded everything in such a way that it seemed unimportant, and then They would catch everyone off-guard by fulfilling prophecy in such a way that what seemed obscure was actually the most important piece of information in the entire passage. It was a form of *hiding in plain sight* which the Adoni used to speak the truth without revealing more than Their followers needed to know. That seemed to be the way with prophecies and destinies. They were rarely what you thought them to be, but they were always what the Adoni intended.

"*A most creative and imaginative Hobber...no wonder I bear Him such a love.*" David quoted to himself. He had not been present when Kal spoke those words on their first visit, but Tanya had told him about the phrase, and the Knight of Es-Soh-En liked it. It seemed a perfect description of the actions of the Adoni.

David had no idea how hungry the people were for something…anything from the Adoni. They had accepted him and his sister as the Children of Earth simply because of their looks, and because of their claim. On other visits, the people had asked for a sign. It had normally involved the presenting of Sy-lar and/or Gennerroth as a sign of their office. This day they asked for no sign. This time they sought no proof. They did not test the spirits. Their ears were that *itchy* to hear from the Adoni. It was that desperate hunger of the people which made David uncomfortable.

The Knight of Es-Soh-En could feel his back growing warmer. He opened his eyes and turned to see the sun climbing over the distant horizon of the Dulan Alps. He studied the orb pulling itself up from its rest. He thought for a moment that even the sun gave the impression of being weary of its endless job. He closed his eyes once more and let the warmth drive the chill from his bones. The morning breeze played with his hair. He could even feel the coolness of the chain mail links in his shirt fade to be replaced with a warmer sensation.

He heard the sounds of Tanya climbing steps toward him. Even with his eyes closed, he could see how worn those steps had become. There had been talk about the need to replace the blocks in the steps because the bevel in their center was so great it might be unsafe to climb them. The discussion had been ten visits ago. When a Magarian spy was captured by his slipping on those steps since he was unfamiliar with them, the discussion of replacement ended, and Dianna ordered everyone to learn all the quirks of the castle rather than to change them.

"Good morning, Tanya," David spoke without opening his eyes. She had a very distinctive walk. She carried herself with the grace of a Knight of Es-Soh-En. There was a blend to her movements: that of a woman mixed with that of a warrior. It had something to do with how she carried her center of balance. He knew she would later accuse him of showing off, but for now she simply smiled at him. "Is it time for the morning Council meeting already?"

"*Those old bags of bones?*" she quoted him. He opened his eyes to make contact with her. "It's sunrise. The only people who are up at sunrise in this palace are the guards and servants...and the Children of Earth. I think it's making the Council members nervous that we get up so early. It makes them look bad when the meeting doesn't start until after lunch."

"It used to start after lunch. We had it changed to halfway between breakfast and lunch," David reminded her.

"They're still grumbling about that. If you ask them, they're too busy in the morning to come to meetings, but when you want the details of their business it all revolves around sleeping in and having a leisurely breakfast. No, I stopped by your chambers on the way up here, and was informed by your servants that you forgot this." She handed him a crown. He took it, gave a look of disgust, and instead of placing it on his brow, hung it over the hilt of the sword he now carried.

"You know that people expect you to wear it. You're the king now."

"The Steward," David snapped. He didn't mean to put so much feeling into his voice, but it was there, and there was no hiding it. "There is only one King in Dula, and we both know Who that is. I tried to take what was His the last time I was here. I won't make that mistake again." He noted that Tanya wore the delicate crown given to her as her sign of office. It was made of silver wires, braided together and studded with small diamonds, emeralds, and rubies. She had been able to make the craftsmen go easy on the precious stones. They were scattered evenly throughout the work. David's crown was a simple band, and held only one gem: a topaz set in the middle of the forehead. His, too, was made of silver. It had annoyed the Council when David ordered the face of Es-Soh-En embossed on either side of the stone, and insisted on silver, not gold as the material, but he wanted a lesser crown to remind him – and the people – that he only held the throne for another.

"Politics: the war without allies, the weapons without warning." Tanya quoted the centaur proverb. David laughed at the serious tone she used to quote the saying. It had been the effect she desired. "You mustn't forget how to laugh. Once you get to that level, the next loss is hope."

"Still," David added. "You shouldn't make fun of all those proverbs from the centaurs and minotaurs. If I recall, you were the one who pushed them into becoming warriors."

"I had no idea I could influence the entire races by just yelling at them," she defended.

"Yelling at them?" David joked. "The pitch of your voice would decalcify any spine within twenty yards. And then to take up sword and humiliate them by fighting when they refused, and you *a female of the species*." David quoted. "It's been several thousand years, and they still haven't gotten over the insult. They became a warrior race to prove to you that they weren't...now what did you call them?" David continued. "...*Bags of bones not worth the effort of insulting*. Did I quote you right on that one?"

"Perhaps I should inform the Council of your pet expression for them?" teased Tanya.

"But I never called them that to their face, nor did I ever talk about their mothers..." David replied.

"Wait a minute. I never spoke about their mothers…They were the first of their races. They had no mothers," Tanya added with a twinkle in her eye. "No, it's not time for the morning meeting, as they are now calling it. I just wanted to spend some time up here away from prying eyes."

"Then you've come to the wrong place. Te-far has his spies that monitor everything that goes on up here," noted David.

"Are they already up and out?" asked Tanya looking towards the spies' hiding place, smiling and waving. "He must be paying them extra to get up this early."

Two men came out in the open, looked suddenly awkward, returned the wave, and pretended to be involved in some other business, and then move on.

"They hate it when you do that. It blows their entire cover," David observed.

"Why do you think I do it? It's definitely not because I like them. So what brings you to *David's Perch* this morning?"

"Don't tell me you're using that term, too?" David groaned.

"It's common knowledge you come here, and come here often. I'm the only one who knows you come here when something is bothering you. You really shouldn't be so predictable."

"It's Gib-ron." He spat the name out as if it left a bad taste in his mouth.

"Is he still giving you trouble?" asked Tanya

"He isn't exactly giving me trouble. He knows the boundaries, he knows the limits, and he plays them like an expert. It's nothing obvious. He's always the first to speak. He's the first to suggest. He's the first to find fault with anything we present. This man can keep more from being done than anyone I've met in seven thousand years!"

"Are we really that old?" asked Tanya trying to ease the tension.

"I one time started calculating how many years we have lived if you added Dulan and Earth years together. When I realized I would have been eligible for social security benefits twenty visits ago, I stopped calculating. It's just that if Gib-ron doesn't stop pushing, it's going to lead to a showdown between us."

"The kingdom is unsteady as it is. We don't want to make it any more unstable. The idea is to keep the kingdom intact while Dianna is gone. She is going to need a kingdom to come back to," Tanya suggested.

"But, if we don't address it now; then…" David let his voice trail off.

"…He might be too powerful a foe to stop later on," Tanya completed. They had both noted that Gib-ron had tried to sway the Council to make David and Tanya figureheads only for the sake of the people, and to have the Council assume control, and elect one of its own to lead. They had little doubt who would be the one chosen.

***

David drew back the large wooden doors of the Council chamber. He could feel the thirty eyes pressing in upon him even though several seemed more ready for sleep than to transact business. It had been the same business for two weeks. *Where was Dianna? How long would the Children of Earth rule?* He let his eyes rest on each member of the Council and acknowledged their existence. He had learned long ago that it had an unnerving affect with a foe and a bonding affect with a friend. Eye contact would either force someone to throw up defenses, or to open up and invite you in. Either way, by being the one to initiate the eye contact it gave him the advantage he needed.

Together the Knights of Es-Soh-En entered the room, came to their place at the head of the long walnut table, and with a fluid motion seated themselves in the larger padded chairs.

"*What is the state of the kingdom this day?*" David asked – trying to make sure he used the traditional invitation Dianna had used when she started the meetings.

"The people want to know what's being done to find Queen Dianna!" declared Gib-ron. He had actually cut into David's last word. It was a breech of protocol, but could easily be mistaken for thinking the speaker had finished. Gib-ron had also timed his response so that his topic would be the first order of business since no one would have dared to interrupt the Head of the Council. This was Gib-ron's style.

"We've done as much as can be done for the time we've been in command!" David snapped. He felt his tempter beginning to flare. He took a breath, and held it to bring himself under control. The Knight of Es-Soh-En looked out at the sea of plastic faces; none revealing what was actually hidden or felt behind those blank eyes. David continued. "We have sent messages to Janadis, but there has been no response. Troops have gone as far as the Veil of Darkness, but there have been no clues. We have begun to search the ancient scrolls and records to see if Tra or Kal left any evidence hidden there regarding this matter."

"*Tra and Kal!*" mocked Gib-ron, again cutting into David's words before he was actually through. "Those fanatics?! This sounds like just a delaying tactic..." This time it was David who interrupted.

"Enough!" the Head of the Council lashed out, slamming the gavel on the table. "They are not fanatics. I know them both, and will not stand by and allow you to insult them. They are not fanatics..." Here David realized he was speaking of figures who had been dead for centuries as if they were still alive. He recalled his brief visit to the Lesser Kingdom when he had spoken with them. To him, they were still alive with a life which could never die. He chose to continue speaking of them in the present tense. "They are not fanatics, but good and honest citizens," he completed with only a moment's pause which seemed to the Council to be a public speaking technique to add emphasis to his words instead of the brief moment of self-doubt which it truly was.

"And I am not?" charged Gib-ron, his voice thick with arrogance.

"They were involved in the freeing of Dula from the traitor Dragnock's hold," David continued, ignoring the comment from Gib-ron. "They were given charge of Logos, the Talking Sword, and had the Curse lifted from their ears. Only they could hear the voice of the Sword, and they took great care in recording everything the Sword told them. Their entire life was dedicated to the good of the kingdom and the Queen. What have you done for this kingdom other than to disrupt Council meetings and display your ignorance?" David turned his attention back to Gib-ron with the last phrase. The tension hit a new high, even for a Council meeting as the opponents locked stares.

The mood was suddenly broken by the sound of applause. David looked at the source and found Pentra, standing and applauding David's words. He made no pretense of hiding his approval that someone had finally spoken what he truly felt. If Pentra had spoken the words himself in Council, he would have been censured; but to endorse what was spoken by the Steward would not lead to open political attack.

The Council member had been named for the hero of legend who had gone into the Veil of Darkness, and saved Dula from an earlier attack by Cronis, the Dark Lord. Pentra was of military background, and the only member of the military to sit on the Council. It had been said of Pentra that he was the youngest member to sit on the Council. When David had first heard that, he envisioned a man in his twenties, but when he was introduced to Pentra, he found an older man, easily in his late forties, possibly early fifties. The warrior had graying salt and pepper hair, and his steel-blue eyes were entrenched with years of wrinkles. The Knight of Es-Soh-En knew he was old for a military man, and wondered how he could be the youngest to sit on the Council. When the first Council meeting had convened, David then realized that the average age for a Council member was in the mid-sixties. Only Gib-ron was the exception. He was in his fifties, but probably a few years older than Pentra.

Even though there were only a few years difference between Pentra and Gib-ron, it was obvious that Gib-ron was the more seasoned warrior when it came to the battlefield of politics. Where Pentra's eyes betrayed his weary spirit, Gib-ron's eyes were still full of cold fire. They had been disciplined to show no emotion except the one necessary for the moment. Gib-ron's eyes were one of his greatest weapons. He had practiced the kinds of expressions and stares which could warm an enemy's heart, or melt ice with a glance. His voice was a velvet sword, soft, but able to cut deeper than any blade. Add these to his vast hidden army of those he owned or had terrorized into obedience, and he was obviously the unspoken ruler of the Council. He may have even held that position when Queen Dianna sat where David now sat. Gib-ron had seen and endured more wars of words than Pentra, and was now prepared to match his skills and resources against the Knight of Es-Soh-En. To Gib-ron, Pentra was, at the most, a gnat which has momentarily distracted him; a gnat which would have to be dealt with later as Gib-ron's gaze spoke the unvoiced promise to his victim.

The military Council member was a follower of the Adoni, that was obvious. He had not learned to hide any such beliefs as the other members had done. However, even though a Follower, Pentra was not strong in his beliefs. David could sense that at one time the military leader had stood firm, spoken out, and lived according to the instructions of Teacher; but he had been beaten down in this arena. He had learned to keep quiet, and not to speak his true feelings in order to survive.

It was now obvious to David that Pentra was re-inspired by the words of the Knight of Es-Soh-En. Pentra had been looking for some role model to help him make the right decisions, but had never found one with the wisdom, skill, and power that David portrayed. For this brief moment, Pentra was his old self; full of fire, and daring to side with the right and throw political career to the winds. His reaction defused the situation. Not that the situation was resolved, but Pentra was now an instant enemy of Gib-ron. Gib-ron had simply paused in his attack on the Steward of the Throne of Dula in order to refocus his anger towards the military leader. David cleared his throat to bring the attention back to himself, knowing that it was like a deer calling attention to itself to a pack of jackals looking for a prey.

"If these actions are not enough; then the Council is opened..." David began, but Gib-ron cut him off once more.

"There is one method which has been very effective in the past, and which you have not considered. I want to know why you haven't used it," demanded Gib-ron.

"And what is that method?" asked David.

"The crystal eye," Gib-ron responded. "It has been in wide use throughout the kingdom. We have conducted tests into its effectiveness. There are people certified in its use. It's a proven tool in finding things which were lost. Why have you not considered using *that* for a change?" Gib-ron had risen as he spoke to focus the attention of the entire Council on himself. As he threw the challenge back at the Knights of Es-Soh-En, he dropped smugly into his chair.

"Such a thing is mere legend. It's a fable we use to tell our children at night," declared Fen-ton from the far side of the table. Gib-ron was annoyed that someone other than David or Tanya had chosen to reply to his suggestion.

"Not so!" Gib-ron declared, waving aside the man's opinion as if less than worthless. "I can produce test results made over the last several years showing that it does work."

"It is a thing of Cronis! We should not touch it. How can you suggest such a thing in Council?" attacked Pentra.

It's not a thing of Cronis!" bellowed Gib-ron as if the volume of his objection would carry more weight than fact. "I have used it myself. It's a science!" David saw that Gib-ron was not completely supported by the Council.

"It *is* a thing of Cronis!" David declared. Although his voice was much softer, the tone of it carried greater weight than Gib-ron's. "It belongs to the devil-god, and is used by the Dark Lord to deceive and misdirect. The records speak clearly that it is something which should not be allowed. We cannot, we will not, use it!"

"It's a science!" shouted Gib-ron on his feet once more. "We must use it. I suggest that we call it to a vote. Do we use the crystal eye to find Dianna, or do we continue to let these two usurp the throne…" This time Gib-ron was interrupted by a loud crash. David had sprung to his feet, and in one fluid motion drawn his sword from its sheath, and imbedded it deep into the once-smooth surface of the table. The Head of the Council pointed an accusing finger at the Council member who had dropped back into his chair, astonished that any would draw sword in open meeting.

"The Words of the Ancients warn against such a thing, Gib-ron! *That* is all the proof that I need! The Words of the Ancients also tell us that anyone practicing such things, or encouraging practice of such things should be put to death. I will not kill you because the kingdom is still dealing with the loss of its queen; but I will not sit by, and let you pollute the minds of the Council with your talk of Cronis-worship. I dismiss you from the Council, and banish you from Dula. If you ever return again, it will be reason to put you to death." The Knight of Es-Soh-En wrenched the blade from the polished wood, and let its slamming back into its sheath finish his comment. David did not sit, but Tanya rose to stand by his side.

"I reject your ruling!" spat Gib-ron, now on his feet. "I have power with this Council. I got you appointed king. Now you throw me out because of an out-dated tradition…a silly superstition? You are closed-minded, and that closed mind will be the undoing of the kingdom. This decision is unfair, and I will fight it!"

"It is fair, Gib-ron. It is more than fair. By your own mouth you have testified that you have used the crystal eye. That very evidence places you under an automatic sentence of death. I suggest that you take what is left of your life, and think on the Adoni. Only They can protect you now," Tanya replied.

"*The Adoni*?" Gib-ron sneered. He spat upon the table. "That is what I think of the Adoni." David was already bounding across the table, springing from it to slam Gib-ron into the stone wall. No one came to the aid of the ex-Council member. The Knight of Es-Soh-En felt the Presence of the Adoni swelling up inside of him, and it gave him the control he needed. He lifted Gib-ron off the floor, hurled him into the hands of guards who had entered at the sounds of the commotion.

"None may speak so of the Adoni in my presence!" declared David. "The crystal eye may seem like a small thing to you, but

I have seen what the Dark One can do. I have looked into his eyes, and know that his only goal is the destruction of all the Lands of the Adoni. Everything he does is to that end. Even when he offers help, it is only to help us destroy ourselves. The Dark Lord already has you, Gib-ron. Your actions this day prove it. One who is owned, and guided by the Dark Lord can never sit on Council."

David redirected his speech from Gib-ron to the entire Council. "This is the message *this* Council will send: We stand for the Adoni. We reject the teachings and practices of Cronis. We will cleanse the kingdom if we have to, but these lapses in proper respect for the Adoni will no longer be tolerated. If any of the Council do not agree with this policy, I suggest you leave now, or be thrown out the way Gib-ron will be when I have finished."

"But the laws state…" Gib-ron began, but David cut him off.

"You are no longer of this Council. You do not have the right to speak your poison. If laws are contrary to the Laws of the Adoni, they are now null and void!" David waved Gib-ron out of his presence. The two guards dragged him from the room. Two other Council members left the room.

"Your orders, sir?" asked the captain of the guard.

"Escort Gib-ron and the others to their homes. Help them pack what is theirs, and escort them to the boundaries between Dula and Magar. Once they have crossed over, make sure that they understand that if they return, they are to be put to death." The captain saluted, turned, and left the room. Pentra then rose and spoke.

"I have been waiting a long time for someone to do that. I, for one, will support you with my heart, my mind, and my sword." All of the others rose to give voice to their support. David smiled at Tanya, who squeezed his arm. He then noticed the gash in the surface of the meeting table. He wished he had not scarred the wood so. He then looked up and asked, "I accept your support. We will not be ruthless in the application of the Laws of Es-Soh-En. We will try to win them back to the ways of the Adoni. If not, then they will have to leave. I will not turn this into a chance for others to bear false witness against neighbors to gain revenge, but the kingdom will be ruled as the Adoni have directed. Is there any more business before we adjourn?"

"Perhaps you would like to order the table repaired?" suggested Pentra.

"No. Let it be a reminder for each of us, and for those who might come after us that we are severing any ties with Cronis as of this day. We will support the Adoni completely..." David then smiled and added. "It will also remind me not to lose my temper in meetings. I am sorry, my friends. I am a warrior, not a politician." The others laughed as they ushered him out of the chambers and to the dinning hall for the mid-day meal.

CHAPTER FOUR

THE FORGOTTEN SCROLL

David reached up, and drew the cobwebs back like a drape. He noticed that several still clung to his hand, wiped his hands together, rolled the strands into a ball, and discarded them. He made the observation that if the fibers could still cling in such a fashion that there had to be spiders still here, and that the creatures had only abandoned their webs recently. He made a mental note to contact the keepers of the library, and have them add spraying for pests as part of the clean-up program. The smell of dust hung more thickly in the room than the cobwebs, and David's nose began to itch as he breathed in the disturbed layers.

The servants had informed him that Tanya had been here most of the morning. She had risen before sunrise, eaten only a meager breakfast, and then had come straight here. He had thought she would have waited until the cleaning had been done; but he also knew his sister, and she had been determined to begin her research.

It had been late last night when their discussions with others revealed that there had been an old wing of the palace which had been used to store the older manuscripts and tomes. When an older work would be transcribed and bound in a newer volume which was easier to store, the older documents would simply be stored away in a separate library. The moment the location of the collection had been revealed, Tanya's eyes had lighted up, and David knew that she wanted to go right then and begin her research. He had always found her among her books. Several times when he came to see her, he would discover her at some library or old book store, buried in the back where the rarely-read books always ended up. This was where she had always found her greatest treasures: forgotten poets, undiscovered novelists who had self-published – but never marketed their works, anthologies of writers who never produced enough material for a book of their own. As soon as she became aware of this forgotten collection in the palace, it was all her brother could do to get her to sleep before beginning her studies.

David ran a finger along a stack of scrolls. It came back thick with dust. He squinted to make out what information he could from the scrolls and books stored along the entrance way, but there was no rhyme or reason to the order. Apparently whoever had been given the task of storing the manuscripts had simply taken the least amount of effort to deposit them and leave.

As his eyes grew accustomed to the faint light of the room, he began to realize the enormity of the task ahead. He could now make out the back wall, fifteen or twenty feet away. It was easily twenty feet tall, and comprised entirely of built-in book cases and shelves. He looked at the other walls, and saw the same vast storage space, all of it filled to capacity – and then some. The room itself was a maze of aisle ways and bookcases. He could easily get lost in here, but not in the same way his sister would lose herself in a book store. He saw a faint flicker of a light to the left, stepped forward, and knocked over a stack of books which had simply been dumped closest to the entrance.

"Over here," Tanya's voice called out. David worked his way through the twists and turns of the aisles. Twice he turned down a row of bookcases only to find a dead end, and had to come back and start again."

"How did you find your way in here?" He finally called out to her.

"This world is right-handed, just like our own. Since it was designed by someone who was right-handed, I assumed the proper paths would have to be to the right," her voice echoed in the faint gloom.

"But you're left-handed," David observed.

"Which simply means I'm smarter than any right-handed person, and so I figured out the pattern that much quicker."

"Is that a left-handed compliment?" he quipped finally finding a pathway which went deeper into the room than any other had previously led him.

"It wasn't even close," came her retort. Her voice was clearer now which told David he was getting closer. He rounded one more bookcase, and found her hunched over a make-shift desk of several cases of books which had been stacked to fill the void. The scuff marks in the dust, told him that she had rearranged several to create her own little cubicle. He noted the small lamp flickering about eye level. It struggled to hold back the gloom, and its feeble efforts were barely rewarded.

"Is that all the light you have in here?" he asked. "You'll ruin your eyes for sure trying to read by that." He leaned back on a stack of crates, tested its strength before committing his full weight, and sat down behind her. She never looked up from her volume as she spoke.

"It's enough. Don't worry. I never knew there was so much information written down in any one place. There are complete works telling of our visits to Dula. Some written by witnesses, others written by writers who wanted to embellish our exploits. I even came across one where someone wrote the adventure as if he were me. Not very good at grasping my motivation." She made a sour expression.

"There also several collections of historical works filling in the various gaps between our visits. I could easily know everything that ever happened in Dula without ever leaving this room."

"But still no information regarding Dianna?" he probed.

Her expression saddened, and she shook her head slowly. "Anything from Janadis?" she asked.

"No. We've sent several messages, but there is no response from the undersea city. I've sent another messenger this morning instructing him to go to the Isle of Morning, and see if there is any clue as to why the city refuses to answer."

"I was sure that they would know something," Tanya exclaimed. Her eyes were red from the long hours of reading she had put herself through that morning. As she raised her face to meet David's eyes, he saw it for the first time in the glow from the small lamp she had carried into the room with her. Her brother knew better than to challenge her directly when she was set upon a course of action, but he knew he had to do something before she dropped from exhaustion. She stretched her back, arching it like a feline. David heard several vertebrae popping back into place.

"I think it's time to get more people involved in this search. I'm going back to the palace, and sending in servants to clean and air this room out. Then I'll have proper lighting fitted throughout the chamber. I'll let you pick the best scholars in the kingdom to help you in your work, but it's clearly more than one person can handle," he announced.

"Oh no!" The cry of the Knight of Es-Soh-En was genuine. She looked about her at the mountains of books, parchments, scrolls and sheets of paper. "Don't air the room out. Any sudden change in air moisture can damage the older works. And we can't just throw open the windows and set up bright lights. Some of the ink in these texts is faint enough as it is, and bright light may cause the last of it to fade. And an army of cleaners…" She continued. "Have you seen how brittle some of these scrolls are? A swipe with a cleaning rag or pressure from a duster could cause it to crumble. No. We have to approach this as if it were some kind of archeological dig. Everything must be carefully examined and protected. I've already sent several scrolls over to the palace to begin the process of remoisturizing them so they can be unrolled without destroying them."

"What about all this dust? Can't we get rid of some of it?" he offered.

"Dust is the only filing system this room has," said Tanya, modifying comments made by her favorite detective. "The amount of dust tells us how long something has lain in here undisturbed. That bit of information can make it easier to detect the older works from the more recent additions to the room."

"Alright, but I *am* going to have you interview several scholars, and pick some to help you in this search." Tanya was about to protest, but David cut her off, "We don't have the luxury of time in this matter. We need results quickly. You can make sure all the scholars are properly trained in the way the room should be treated, but you are going to need help. The people have been patient with us long enough. They want some kind of progress report other than, *We still don't know.*"

"Okay, I'll let some others in, but I pick the ones, and they have to be trained before they touch anything in here."

"Good!" David declared. There was something about the tone of his voice, as if he had just been set free from a concern which had weighed heavily upon him. She knew the tone, and knew something else was hidden there.

"And what are you going to be doing while I'm in here pouring over old manuscripts?" she challenged. The look in his eyes told her that she had guessed right, and now he was trapped.

"I've got a few ideas I want to check out on my own," he admitted.

"But they're ideas you don't want to share with me?" she pushed.

"It will just make you worry," he offered. The expression on her face told him it was the wrong thing to say. Now she would worry. Finally he opened up. "We've done everything physically possible to track Dianna's exit from the throne room, and from the kingdom."

"And everything came up empty. Nobody saw her leave. Nothing was found to mark her passing: no footprints, no pieces of cloth; no broken twigs, scuffed rocks, or trail of bread crumbs." She added the last clue to lighten the mood which was descending upon the room.

"And so we have to face what we don't want to face," David began. "When you've eliminated all the possibilities, whatever is left, no matter how impossible is the most likely explanation," David could tell quoting from her favorite mystery books was irritating his sister. He decided to avoid it until she was more receptive.

"There is no physical evidence of Dianna ever leaving the throne room. There is no evidence of Dianna passing out of the gate, over the walls, or through hidden passages to leave the palace. Everything says that she should still be here."

"Which leads us to believe she either hid her trail, or was taken by someone who was an expert in kidnapping royalty," Tanya interrupted.

"Actually, I was thinking of a simpler explanation," David offered.

"Such as…"

"Everything about the disappearance of Dianna does not seem natural. There is no physical evidence we have found. If it doesn't fall under the natural, then that only leaves…"

"The supernatural!" Tanya completed.

"And if we're dealing with the supernatural, we have only two sources." He paused to let Tanya identify the options.

"The Adoni or the Dark Lord," she finished – refusing to mention their enemy by name.

"Exactly! If she's with the Adoni, then we have nothing to fear, but if she's with the Dark Lord, we need to rescue her as soon as possible."

"So what are you planning?" she inquired.

"If she is being held by the Dark Lord, he would hold her where she would be the most secured…"

"The Veil of Darkness!" Tanya interrupted. "But David, no one has ever gone into that realm and come out alive." Up to the point where she said, *come out alive* he was going to counter with Gaylord and Yeesha returning with Teacher, but all three had died in the Veil. He sought his memories, and could not find a single example to counter her argument. Even Pentra had died there. The memory of his and Tanya's brief visit to bring back the body of Pentra was blocked from his mind.

"If Dianna is there, I am sworn to protect her. I must go in, even if there is little chance of coming back out again. I'm more of an action person, Tanya. I can't sit here while you read old books. I'm not good at long hours of research myself. I need to *do* something!" The urgency in her brother's voice told her he was right. She knew he would not react well to waiting and search-ing. He was a warrior, with warrior's blood burning in his veins. She also knew that he had gone into situations before where she was sure he would never return, but somehow he had always made it out. The thought of the warning about one of them tasting of death hovered just in the back of her mind. She refused to think that this might be the time.

"Are you going alone?" she asked. The tone in her voice told David she would support his decision, even though she was frightened for him.

"An army would never enter the Veil and have any chance of coming out. Secrecy is the best way."

"So you're going into the Veil alone?" she pressed.

"Actually, Pentra learned of my plan. He's adamant that he must go with me."

"Pentra?" Tanya was surprised to hear that one of the Council members was asking to go.

"He's named for the original Pentra who first went into the Veil to stop the spread of the Veil of Darkness. When he heard of my plan, he came to me in private, and begged to go. He believes that it is his destiny to do what the original Pentra did," David explained.

"The original Pentra died in the Veil. Is that his intention?" Tanya challenged. "Make it very clear to him that I fully expect him to survive, and to bring you out of the Veil in one piece. I will not give my blessing to a suicide mission."

"I have no intention of making this a suicide mission. If we can't come back with our findings, then the mission is worthless. We should be back in a week or so. I'll notify the scholars before I leave that they are to report directly to you for interviews and instructions. Try not to work too hard until help arrives."

"I will if you will." she quipped. It had become the standard response between the two of them. In all their visits to Dula, they had faced many dangers. Each had stared death in the face, and refused to give up. They had tried countless times to keep the other from taking risks or confronting those dangers, but they knew it was their job. Either one could be called upon to risk life and limb; whether at home, or on the battlefield. Several times the safe decision to stay behind while the other went into battle had unfolded into some of the closest calls they had ever encountered. They had finally adopted the pet expression to recognize that being a Knight of Es-Soh-En was anything but safe. Both knew the other would do what had to be done, and so no further arguments could be raised to elicit promises to be careful. David began to turn and leave the chamber. Tanya called him back.

"David," Tanya suggested. "Have you ever noticed our division of labor?"

"What? I do the action, and you do the research? I would agree except I have seen you in battle, and would never question your lack of action."

"No; but there is a division. Describe the hilt of Gennerroth to me," she asked.

"You know what it looks like. It is the head of Es-Soh-En."

"So why is your Adoni blade a picture of Es-Soh-En; and mine is a picture of Glidon?"

It suddenly dawned upon David that her Adoni blade was called *the Eagle Sword.*

"Also," Tanya continued, "at the Creation of the Lands of the Adoni you were sent to Es-Soh-En and I was carried by Glidon to complete *the Lesser Song.* I am beginning to suspect that even though the Three Are One, our division of labor may be more related to your service to Es-Soh-En and mine to service of Glidon."

"Where did you get this crazy idea?" David challenged.

"It was a theory someone wrote a few hundred years ago. I found it this morning. I was just wanting to get your thoughts," she admitted.

"We serve both of Them – all of Them," David corrected. His voice was firm.

"I would suggest that we wait to see which One shows up to save you in the Veil of Darkness, but since Es-Soh-En is now Teacher; Glidon is the logical One to respond."

"So you are entrusting me to the Adoni?" David smiled.

"Always have; always will," she admitted.

"I wouldn't have it any other way."

Once David was out of the chamber, Tanya dropped her head into her hands and wept. She wasn't sure if she wept for her brother and the dangers he was about to face, or if she wept for Dianna who was still missing. She had even considered that she wept because she no longer had the energy to hold it back. It felt good to weep. Her pent-up anxiety, fears, and frustrations were washed away by her tears. When there were no more tears left, she slumped over the stack of books, and drifted into a welcomed sleep.

Tanya had no way of knowing just how long she had slept. From her vantage point, she could not see the door, and all the windows were closed. It might have been minutes or hours. She was sure her sleep could not have been a full day as no scholars had entered the room to speak with her. As she lifted her head, she noted that the lamp was half-empty of its fuel. She didn't know how quickly it would burn, but she knew it must have been a few hours since she had fallen asleep.

As Tanya returned her attention to the page she had been reading when David had interrupted her, she saw tear stains covering the parchment. Several had dripped onto words, and the letters had smeared and run together. As Tanya touched the first smeared letter, trying to keep it from smearing further, the dust on her index finger mixed with the ink and the tears. There was a sudden *puff* of smoke. Tanya's fear that the book was going to burst into flames made her jump back; but no sparks, embers, nor fire appeared. The puff of smoke turned into a twisting wisp of smoke, rising off of the book's page. The Knight of Es-Soh-En followed its path. It came to rest in front of the higher shelves where several scrolls had been stored. Like a worm, the strand of smoke entered one particular scroll. The parchment of the scroll glowed for a brief second, and then all evidence of the smoke and the glow were gone.

Tanya stretched to reach the scroll, pulled it from the stack, and noticed that it was a blue parchment. She had not seen blue parchment during any of her visits to Dula. All the scrolls and pages in the room were an aged-yellow color. The scroll was held together by a red ribbon, and protected with a drop of gold sealing wax. Embedded in the wax was the imprint of the Clan of Sword Keepers. Only Kal, Tra, and Dig Gen had belonged to the clan. It had been a short-lived clan, covering the time directly after their first visit to Dula. The clan had been entrusted with the care of Logos, the Talking Sword, once it had been returned by the Quest for the Sword. Tanya thought back, and could not remember any actual document bearing this seal. Books which were the collected writings of the clan had this seal on the cover, but she never recalled any individual scroll.

The fact that Tra and Kal had been set free of the Curse, and were allowed to hear the voice of Logos when all the other Lands of the Adoni were still deaf to its words and songs, made Tanya breathe faster. The minotaur and centaur had written down everything the Sword had told them. They had asked questions, and recorded the answers. She had read the work on previous visits as it had been the only link with the Sword. Tanya's hands trembled slightly. She had never had trouble with her hands before. It was the surge of adrenaline as her heartbeat increased. She blew ever so gently on the dust that covered the scroll. Most of the dust was caught in the breath, but some still clung stubbornly to the paper. She saw the distinctive cursive writing which belonged to Tra the Skeptic as the centaur had come to be called since he had resisted following the Adoni for so many years. Tra had a very precise way of capitalizing and curling the first letter of each word. It made his hand-writing easy to recognize.

"To be read by the Steward…" she read. There was a smudge of dust still clinging to the edge of the scroll. The writing dropped down to the next line. "…Of Dula," Tanya completed. As she turned the scroll over in her hands, she saw another inscription below the last line. It was a bolder print, but she could read it easily: *"AND NONE OTHER!"*

Tanya had been about to open the scroll, and read it there; but it clearly indicated that only the Steward of Dula was to open and read the scroll. She had been declared the Stewardess of the Throne, and so even though ever fiber of her being cried out to read the scroll for herself she knew it belonged to David.

She suddenly thought that he might still be in the palace since the scholars he had promised to send had not appeared. She clutched the scroll, doused the lamp, and ran for the door-way. As she rounded the last stack of books in the darkness and came to the steps leading up to the door, she had a nagging feeling that she was forgetting something, but couldn't recall what it was. As her foot struck a book lying in the path, she suddenly remembered that David had spilled a stack of books when he came in. It was too late. She tried to regain her footing, stepped on another book, slipped, and fell forward. As she tucked and tried to roll with the fall, her head struck hard against the first stair. She was lost in blackness before her body slumped to the flagstone floor.

CHAPTER FIVE

BATTLE IN THE VEIL

David and his companions reined their horses in as they cleared the last hill. Before them the western sky appeared to be a stain of black ink on a blue background. The upper edges of the stain were smudged, blending the black and the blue. David thought of a thick black cloud of smog when he saw it. The upper edge of the Veil had been visible for the last several hours. David motioned for the other two to dismount.

"We need to rest the horses. When we get into the Veil, they will be our only escape, and if they are tired or weary it reduces any chance of our coming back out."

"I have heard tales of the Veil, but never seen it for myself," noted Handar.

"Perhaps you're having second thoughts about insisting you come with us," joked Pentra referring to the fact that Handar had waited outside of the city to join the pair since it would be more difficult to turn back someone already prepared and on the road.

"My ancestor, Gen, went into danger with Sir David. When I heard he was back, and going to search for the Queen, I could do no less," Handar replied.

"The gnome-made-man," Pentra noted of Handar's ancestor.

"A good gnome. He fought well in battle. His heart was that of a warrior. I had often wondered what had become of him and

Leah," observed David as he poured some of his water into a sack for his horse to drink.

"He became captain of the guard for Queen Dianna. Had many children with Leah, and lived happily ever after." Handar laughed. "I believe that the gnomes still tell the tale to their children over firelight on the summer evenings."

"I don't like the looks of it," Pentra noted nodding toward the Veil.

"Having second thoughts?" countered Handar. David had noted that Handar was still young. He had not been tested in battle so he was full of idealistic dreams of grand adventures. This was a trait which could prove either dangerous or helpful depending upon the mettle of the warrior. He had hoped that Handar would turn back the closer they came to the Veil, but the young novice had never shown any sign of wavering since he joined them.

"It is not fear, ax-blade," Pentra retorted, referring to the warrior by the name of the short handled, great-bladed weapon Handar preferred to use. The ax had been a point of confrontation between Handar and his superiors on many occasions since it was not an assigned military weapon. "I have concerns. Concerns need to be addressed in order to be successful in battle. Learn this, and you might survive your first battle."

David had to credit Handar with the way he took the rebuff. He did not let anger take hold, but considered the words of the more-seasoned warrior. Pentra, to his credit, did not bring up the matter again.

"If the Dark Lord has taken Dianna, this is where he will keep her. This is the only place in all the Lands of the Adoni where he is free to act. This is where all his forces have gathered. This is where he is strongest," David observed.

"I note that you always refer to Cronis by title and rarely by name," noted Handar.

"It is a practice which we should try to follow," advised David. "There is power in a name. When you call someone by name, it gives you power over them, it also gives them the right to respond. Use of the Dark Lord's name is an opened window he uses to gain access to a person's life. Once he is in, his servants will follow. Use of a title gives less right to the person spoken of."

"Do you really believe all this talk of the Dark Lord and his servants?" queried Handar.

"What sort of talk?" asked the Knight of Es-Soh-En.

"That there really is such a creature. That there really are shadow creatures. That there is power in all this mumbo-jumbo." The tone of Gen's descendent was sarcastic, bordering on the insolent.

"I have seen both. I have battled both. Yes, I believe. And I suggest that you believe as well. This is not a foe to be taken lightly. Keep in mind that there is one law which still applies."

"Which law is that?" Pentra asked.

"That if the Dark Lord is real, so is the Adoni; and vice-versa. You cannot believe in one without believing in the other. I take care not to spend too much time dwelling on the Dark One. The more my thoughts are on him; the more likely he is to be attracted. I will not confront him without the Adoni surrounding me. Even I cannot win such a battle."

The horses rested, David motioned for them to mount, and begin the descent into the Veil of Darkness. "We cannot use torches or lights to guide our way into the Veil."

"Then how will we see?"" Pentra asked.

"When Gaylord and Yeesha entered the Veil to come to Teacher's aid, they found their path lighted for them by glowing footprints. I suspect we will find the same. Those footprints will lead to the Ring of Fire. That is the heart of the Dark Lord's domain. If Dianna is in the Veil, she will probably be found there."

"You have an advantage on us." suggested Handar.

"What advantage is that?" David replied.

"Aside from being a Knight of Es-Soh-En, having lived for centuries in our world, having been through countless battles, you have the advantage of having actually seen these characters which are only names in history books. You can sift through what is fact and what is myth. I had always heard about the glowing path through the Veil, but I always thought it was just a myth which grew up after the fact. I also put very little stock in talking horses helping Teacher during the Battle of Es-Soh-En. You speak as if it is fact which cannot be disputed."

"Did the sun come up this morning?" David asked. The question seemed to change the subject completely, and it caught Handar completely off guard.

"Yes, it did." he replied, wondering what significance that fact had to do with the conversation at hand.

"How do you know the sun came up this morning?" David continued.

"I saw it."

"What if I were to tell you that you were wrong? What if I told you that it really wasn't the sun coming up, but some other body in the heavens passing through, and once it had finished passing, this world would freeze?"

"Not very likely," muttered Handar.

"Why? What if I told you I knew something that you did not? Maybe you actually slept all day, and this is now the night; and the sun came up in the night. Maybe it's no longer coming up during the day."

"I wouldn't believe it."

"Even if I told you it was so?" pressed the Knight of Es-Soh-En.

"Even then," admitted Handar. Pentra sat quietly in the saddle watching the exchange.

"Why?" David asked once more.

"Because I saw it for myself," he finally replied after long moments of thought.

"That is the way it is with me," David announced. "You speak of things that I saw happen as if they didn't really happen. You give other explanations to what I know to be true. I saw it. No one told me, I saw it for myself. I am a witness to these events. When others try to convince me that they did not happen, or that they did not happen that way; I have to stand up. I have to tell what I know to be the truth."

"But there are so many versions running around. How can I know which ones to believe? Very knowledgeable men are supporting the stories I have spoken of," Handar added in his defense.

"You have the Words of the Ancients. You have the New Words. You have the testimony of Gaylord and Yeesha. These works are true. All other revelations must be tested against them. Any revelation which contradicts these teachings is false. Any counsel that tells us not to refer to these writings is false. We must have a standard by which all other lessons are judged. The standard is those words that we know to be from the Adoni. These will not change. The moment we accept some other as the authority over these, we are doomed to fall into ignorance."

"But they sound so intelligent. They're logical. They make sense."

"What if I were to prove to you that you did not exist?"

"That would be quite a trick," Handar admitted.

"You say that you are a descendent of Gen," David probed.

"Yes I am."

"Can you prove it?" Then to the dismay of the other two, Handar spent fully thirty minutes reciting his family history. He finally came to the reference to Gen.

"But Gen did not exist," David declared.

"What do you mean, Gen did not exist?" challenged Handar.

"If the story of the Quest for the Sword is only a legend, a myth, a fictitious story given to us to teach us an abstract lesson, as your teachers suggest; then I must make the assumption that Gen is also a fictitious character. He was created by someone to give the story a love interest. If Gen is fictitious, and you are descended from a fictional character, then I must assume that you do not exist."

Handar sputtered a few times trying to find a response, finally Pentra announced, "I think he has you."

"But I know I exist!" was Handar's defense.

"Exactly!" declared David. "But if you let teachers stray from the standard by which all others should be judged, and permit them to discard and discount references because they do not fit into their concept of how the universe should work, then you are doomed to cease to exist. You cannot have it both ways!" The Knight of Es-Soh-En paused to let the thought sink in before continuing.

"The Veil is right before you. It proves the Dark Lord is real. I am beside you. That proves the legends concerning my sister and I are true. We are about to confront the greatest evil in the entire universe. Have no illusions that strength of arm or cunning of mind will see us through this mission. The only force which will get us out alive is the Adoni. If you have any doubts regarding Their existence, or if you are not fully committed to Them; then stay here, outside of the Veil. Your body and soul are the lawful prey of the Dark Lord. The only thing which keeps him from claiming them is that he is in there, and you are out here. If I let you follow us into the Veil, I would be taking you to your own slaughter."

Handar sat for long moments, not moving. David's words had humbled him. He finally raised his eyes to meet those of the Knight of Es-Soh-En. "What must I do?"

"Accept what Teacher has done for you. Swear allegiance to the Adoni, and commit your body, mind, and soul to Their care," Pentra announced. David was comforted with the knowledge that his comrade knew the requirements, and was obviously a follower of Teacher. When Handar looked toward David for confirmation, the Knight of Es-Soh-En nodded in agreement.

The trio drew rein, dismounted, and there in the shadow of the Veil of Darkness, Handar drew forth his sword, raised it point first into the sky.

"Let those present witness this oath. This day I declare my need for Teacher in my life. I invite Him to claim me as His own. I swear allegiance to Him, and to His cause. I now pledge my life and my death to His service." When Handar had completed his vow, his companions acknowledged his oath, and vowed to support him in his efforts.

"Nothing like walking into death with a clear heart, is there?" joked Pentra.

"I do not think of it as death, nor as life; only as service," David declared.

"I wish I had your years of service. You make it seem so easy," noted Handar.

"And I envy you," David replied. Handar's only response was a quizzical stare. David finally added, "Don't let my legends fool you. It is never easy. Each day when I rise, I have to question my actions to make sure that I am on the right path. The longer the years of service; the greater the burden. Those outside see that you have done it right for all those years. They look to you to continue to do it right, to give them an example. If you blow it now it will hurt more than you. This is your first day as part of the Following. No one expects you to be the warrior everyone looks up to already. You are still free to make mistakes. I am not. And so, I envy you."

As David spoke, he felt uneasy. He finally came to realize that the feeling was centered on the fact that he was going into battle without Gennerroth. The sword he had chosen to use had a similar weight and balance as his own blade; it was a subtle difference, but a difference all the same. He had spent hours working with it so that the difference in the feel would not prove fatal in combat. He had sharpened the blade, applied a thin coat of oil so it would slide quickly and silently out of the sheath. He half-laughed to himself when he recalled all the movies back on earth which had menacing sounds created by blades being drawn for battle. A true warrior would never announce his intentions in such a way. He slipped the hook loose on his sword so it would be free to draw when needed. It bothered him that the blade had no history, it had no name. He was about to put his life to the test with an untried blade. He then calmed his fears by reminding himself that it wasn't the blade he trusted.

As they were swallowed by the gathering gloom of the Veil, David broke the silence by speaking in a low battle voice. Had he been with centaurs or minotaurs, he would have simply extended his hand. The warrior directly behind him would have wrapped both hands around David's to feel the battle sign language, and then pass the message down the line to the others. However, these were humans, and not trained in this level of stealth. Although it made David uncomfortable, he spoke as softly as he could. "We had better be careful, even on the outer edge of the Veil. When

Teacher came here, the Dark One spotted him immediately…of course he was expecting Teacher to come."

"And he's not expecting us?" quipped Pentra. The trio had no illusions about eyes already focusing on their actions.

True to David's prediction, as the light faded, the glow of footprints marked their path through the ocean bed. It was like riding at midnight with a new moon. The glowing prints became the focus of their efforts. As their eyes adjusted to the darkness, there was still little they could see. They were crossing into the great skeleton of the whale before they actually saw it. David thought briefly that he should know the name of the great sea beast. Was he more than an unknown victim of the Dark Lord's power? But try as he might, no name came to mind.

Once they had passed through, David signaled for them to dismount. He led the band off to the right where there was a shadow darker than the rest. As they came up the gentle slope, a faint glow emanated from the rubble of broken rock. David brought his horse through a crack in the cliff wall, and found himself in a cave that was filled with a green light generated by a fungus that grew on the walls. Near the back was a pool of water, still fresh and flowing, and watering a patch of grass where the horses could feed.

"What is this place?" asked Handar.

"This is where the body of Teacher lay for three days. As He lay here, Gaylord and Yeesha stood guard against all the forces of the Dark One."

"Then there really is such a place. It all happened just the way the witnesses said?" exclaimed Handar. "I could not believe that if the Veil was as our legends said that there could be a haven so deep inside its darkness. Yet here it is: the sanctuary I refused to believe in."

"Yes." replied David. "I thought it best to rest for a moment, let the horses refresh themselves before we make the last part of our journey. I also thought it might be good for you to see some of the places spoken of in the *legends* so you could see them for yourself. The first thing the Dark Lord will try to do is to make you doubt. Therefore, let this cave remind you how true the death and resurrection of Teacher is. That will be the only thing which will stand against the Dark Lord."

Once they had finished refreshing the horses and resting, David led them back out and further into the Veil. After several minutes, a glow began to be noticed in the distance. Pentra tapped David, and motioned toward the phenomena.

"*Ring of Fire,*" David breathed softly. It was the soft voice used by the centaur and minotaur when battle language failed to communicate the information needed. Pentra knew the story of the Ring of Fire. It was reported to be the very center of the Veil of Darkness. It was close to the throne of the Dark Lord. It was also the site of the Battle of Es-Soh-En where Teacher and the Dark One met in physical combat to resolve the issue concerning the title deed of the Lands of the Adoni. It was here where Teacher had been killed by the Dark Lord. During the battle, the Dark Lord had produced Logos, the Talking Sword, even though weapons were forbidden in the battle. The Dark Lord then thrust the blade through Teacher's back, piercing His heart. It was the shedding of this blood that broke the power of the Sword. What the Evil One had never realized was that he was in control of the Sword, and so it was his power that was broken. The Fallen One had defeated himself.

"What causes the glow?" whispered Handar.

"It is the blood of Teacher that was shed there," David replied. "Even the power of the Dark Lord cannot quench the power of Teacher's blood."

They drew rein at the edge of the Ring. Dismounting the horses, David began a careful search of the area. There was nothing to indicate that anyone had been to this site since Teacher had left it on the back of Gaylord and the redeemed horses flew on their newly-gained wings. The group spread out from the Ring, leaving it behind them as a point of reference. After long minutes, a black shadow, darker than the darkness of the Veil passed between them and the faint glow of the Ring of Fire.

As David moved in on the creature, he was surprised that the creature did not seem aware of them. It was as if its mind was somewhere else, focused on some other task. It was actually muttering to itself as it passed by.

David was thankful that the creature was between him and the Ring. He was still cloaked in the darkness. David moved without sound, stepping right behind the creature, lifting his knee to the level of the small of its back. The Knight of Es-Soh-En then hooked one elbow around the creature's throat, and clapped his gauntlet-hand over its mouth before it could make a sound. As he slammed the shadow creature to the ground, Pentra and Handar were at his side.

In the faint glow of the Ring of Fire, the creature's lidless eyes grew larger with fear. Its slick membrane skin was difficult for David to hold in place, but he used the weight of his body to pin his captive to the ground. The many fangs of the upper teeth had slipped out from under his gauntlet, and the creature tried to sink them into warm flesh. The unyielding metal protected David, and he pressed harder. Pentra placed the edge of his sword against the creature's throat, applying enough pressure to draw blood from the captive. It squirmed against the unyielding rock.

"If you wish to live, then tell me what I want to know." David sought to make his voice sound its most menacing.

The talon claws tore at the hand that held the demon creature. The long claws found several places where the metal of the gauntlet over-lapped, slipped its talons underneath the metal, dug through the leather underneath, pierced the skin of David's hand and tore the flesh. The Knight of Es-Soh-En felt the pain as the blood begin to flow, but he never blinked. He gave no indication that the creature had hurt him in any way. In response to the creature's effort, David tightened his grip, and he feared that the bones he clutched would splinter from the effort. Finally the creature surrendered, and nodded its agreement.

"Where is Queen Dianna?" David hissed.

"I don't know," croaked the creature through David's still clenched fingers. "Nobody seems to know. We've all heard that she was gone, but no one knows. Spare me. Spare me," wailed the creature. Its voice was becoming too loud for David's comfort. He slammed one fist against its head, and the captive went limp, collapsing under David's weight

"She's not here," Pentra echoed. "Then where could she be?"

"I don't know. I was sure this would be the place," David admitted.

"It could be lying. Maybe we should look further," urged Handar.

"Look all you want. She's not here," came the hissing voice from behind them. The trio spun about only to find the darkness filled with thousands of pairs of yellow or red lidless eyes glowing back at them from the darkness. Stepping into the Ring of Fire so the glow could illuminate his features from below was the hideous form of Cronis the demon-god.

"Believe me. If I knew where she was, I would have sent my servants after her to bring her here, but even we can't find her. You," Cronis paused for dramatic effect; "however, are another story."

"Don't stare, CHARGE!" the harsh voice of the Knight of Es-Soh-En in the stillness of the Veil shocked Pentra and Handar out of their fear. They responded with reflex actions, drawing sword and ax before hurling themselves into the midst of their foes. David had torn his sword from its sheath, and slashed at Cronis. The Dark One held up one taloned hand, and caught the sword in mid-air. However, instead of letting the action unnerve him, David followed through with a side-thrust kick into Cronis' midsection. The Dark Lord released his grasp, and doubled over. David slammed the hilt of his sword into the back of Cronis' head, driving his foe into the dust. As Cronis lashed out with his claws, David sprang into the air, rolling over several creatures to put distance between himself and the Dark One.

David tried to find their horses in the darkness. Their cries of fear told him the direction he needed to go. There were no cries of pain at this point, and so the Knight of Es-Soh-En knew that he and his companions were the focus of the attack. The demon things did not see the horses as any threat to their goal or they would have already attacked and slain them.

"If we can just make it to them, then one of us might just make it out alive," he told himself. His mind then began to formulate a plan so either Pentra or Handar could run for the light. He had no intention of saving himself. This would be his Death Song; and he would take as many as he could as he sang it.

Realizing survival was no longer an option for him freed David's mind. It was now one less thing to worry about. The Knight of Es-Soh-En was clawed, torn, and pulled from every side. He spun his sword about him as best he could. Wails and howls of pain pierced the Veil as limbs were torn or severed by the blade. One creature threw itself onto the blade, driving it all the way through its body. Before it died, it tore at David's hands forcing him to release his hold on the hilt. With its last breath, the creature rolled away with the sword still in its chest. David noted that the forces of Cronis seemed more dedicated than they had on previous occasions.

With his sword torn from his grasp, David recalled the minotaur proverb, "*unarmed means you have two hands to fight with*;" and began to punch, kick, jab, and bash any creature that was in range. He gained several more feet with his efforts. He could see Handar had his ax torn from him, and was going down amid the sea of servants. Pentra still had his blade, but three creatures held his sword arm while two more pinned his other arm to his side. The Knight of Es-Soh-En could tell that a wall of shadow creatures was preparing to throw themselves on top of Pentra, and drive him to the ground.

David did the unexpected, fell back over ground he had already captured, spotted the dead creature with his sword still protruding from its chest. The Knight of Es-Soh-En tore it from the carcass, swung it around three times, and hacked a path toward Pentra. The shadow creatures were cut down from behind. Killing three other creatures which still clung to Pentra was a bit more difficult so as not to injure his companion. Once Pentra was free, the warriors stood back to back, and carved their way to where Handar had fallen. They stood guard over him, giving him the chance to recover. Once he had his breath, he rose, retrieved his double-bladed ax, and the three formed a circle within the midst of the servants of Cronis.

David had no idea how long the trio fought in this position. It might have been minutes, or it might have been hours. The attacks were taking their toll on all three. Sweat drenched their bodies and stung their eyes. As they were shoulder-to-shoulder and back-to-back they did not need to see where they slashed. It was an arch of death in front of any of the warriors. Cronis kept sending his forces to the slaughter. After a while the bodies had to be pulled away so that others could attack.

Another shadow creature threw itself onto David's sword. This time, however, it twisted its body as it died, and snapped the blade. A quick glance told David other servants had performed the same attack on Pentra. A third creature had fallen on Handar's ax, wrapped its body around the blades, and as it died, fell to the ground tearing it from the warrior's grasp. David began to pummel and kick. He even resorted to biting when his hands were too busy to hold off the wave of attackers. He blocked the taste of foul slime from his mind as he did.

The sheer weight of their foes washed over them, driving them to the ground, pinning them, and all but crushing them. David's body was one searing scar, burning like fire from hundreds of wounds. His arms were like lead, his chest heaving, his vision blurred. He tired to push the bodies off of him, but it was too much. What little strength he had failed him. As the darkness swam into his eyes, he thought he heard the cry of an eagle amid the screams and cheers of their foes. Then he fell into the darkness which had tried to claim him.

As the three warriors went limp under the pile of creatures, the war cry of the Golden Eagle tore the Veil. Those on top of David and his companions scrambled over each other, and clawed their own to escape their dreaded foe. Those creatures pressed between the upper layer of attackers and the warriors were killed or wounded by the retreat. Cronis had already fled with the first sighting of their hated foe.

Within minutes, the Veil was still and deserted. The only sounds were that of the dying. Glidon lighted in the Ring of

Fire where the battle had finally ended. He plucked those still on top of the trio with His beak, and flung them to one side. The demons and shadow creatures slithered off into the darkness, seeking the safety of their slime pits and caves. In only moments, the only figures still left in the Ring of Fire were the unconscious warriors and the Golden Eagle.

CHAPTER SIX

MEETINGS AND RUMORS

Slowly David became aware of his own body. It was as if his consciousness had been tucked away in some hip pocket, and was just now being taken out and examined. He realized he was in darkness; he wasn't registering any other observations, but he knew it was darkness. The next level allowed him to feel his own body. It was a weight that clung to his soul at first; then it was a womb in which he felt safe. He then experienced a dull, aching pain in all of his joints. As each level of consciousness passed, he had the sensation of being at the bottom of a well full of water, or on the bottom of the ocean, and he was floating closer to the surface. He felt the ground beneath his back, the weight of his clothes, and the warmth of the sun over-head. Somehow that wasn't right. There shouldn't be any sun in the...It was then that he realized he didn't know where he should be. He couldn't recall the events that led to this moment.

It was almost as if David turned about in this floating state, pushed back into the darkness to look for his missing memory. As the darkness grew deeper, he recalled a phrase: *the Veil of Darkness*. It was a Dulan phrase, and so he knew he was in the Lands of the Adoni. Slowly bits and pieces of the battle in the Veil were recovered, floating in the darkness around him. He knew what had transpired, and so now he let himself resume the *floating* to the surface. He was surprised at how little time the trip to the surface of consciousness took this time.

There was grass underneath his body; well, maybe not green grass. It felt dry, bristly, and poked him in the back; but it told him that there was vegetation under him. He wasn't sure how, but he was no longer in the Veil of Darkness. The warmth of sunlight on his face seemed to confirm his suspicions. He lay motionless, trying to keep his breathing rhythmic as if he were still unconscious. Long ago he had found it wise not to announce his recovery from unconsciousness too soon. It gave him a distinct advantage to collect information before developing a plan of action.

A shadow passed between him and the source of light. Something was making contact with his face. David determined that the advantage of a quick attack with his foe so close was preferable to remaining unconscious and losing the advantage. He shot his hand up, clamped down on the wrist close to his face, and twisted it so that the person he now held cried out in both shock and pain. He pressed the advantage, pulling his foe off balance, onto the ground. In a fluid motion he flipped up, pressing his knee into the throat of his captive, applying pressure to the wrist he still held, and reaching to draw his sword from its sheath.

"Peace master! PEACE!!" croaked the voice of his captive. It was then that the Knight of Es-Soh-En recognized his victim as one of the palace servants. Running sounds to his right drew his attention in that direction. He completed pulling his sword free, and swung it in the direction of his attackers. As he spun in that direction, he saw Pentra and Handar running towards him. He slowly relaxed his grip on the palace servant, rocked back on the balls of his feet, and rose to his full height, keeping his sword at the ready. His eyes examined his surroundings.

They were outside of the Veil; its black smear on the skyscape several miles behind them. Their horses were tethered to the left; a small fire was burning, with food cooking over its open flames. No one else was around. Pentra and Handar held their positions until David's eyes and mind were clear.

"I'm sorry El-ton. I thought you were a demon thing. Forgive me." He reached down, and helped the servant to his feet. Pentra and Handar now knew it was safe to approach their leader.

"So what happened?" David asked of his companions.

"We thought you might know, sire," began Handar. "One minute we were fighting in the Veil. The enemy had disarmed us, and was pouring over us. I tried to fight back, but every arm and leg was held by several creatures. Something slammed me onto the ground. I lost my breath and the next thing I knew..."

"The next thing we knew," interrupted Pentra, "we came to laying here. All of our wounds healed, our horses tethered nearby, and our weapons restored. If not for the tattered clothing, I would have believed it all was just a dream."

The Knight of Es-Soh-En touched his face. The old scar was still there; however, all the fresh wounds were completely healed. He studied his arms and hands. There had been hundreds of claw marks when they were in the Veil; now, there was nothing. He looked down at his attire, and found it slashed, torn and shredded. The wounds he should have received from such an attack made him tremble in his soul.

"Did any of you hear anything above the sounds of battle?" David asked.

"How could we hear anything? The screams of those creatures was enough to freeze your blood," Handar confessed. The innocence of battle was gone from his eyes.

"I thought I heard one sound above all the rest. It was a screech of some kind. It didn't sound like any of the cries of the demon things. Before I could look up to see what made the sound, I was battered senseless," related Pentra.

"I, too, heard the sound. It was the cry of an eagle…" his voice trailed off.

"There are no eagles in the Veil," observed Handar.

"Nor would any eagles enter the Veil," added Pentra.

"There is One," David announced. With the mention of this One, David felt new strength filling him. His eyes took on a new light. His companions noted the difference, and whispered the name, "*Glidon*!" Both Handar and Pentra spoke the name in hushed tones of reverence. Handar then seemed to free himself from the magic of the moment and added, "It's impossible! Our wise men tell us that with the Battle of Es-Soh-En, the Great Eagle returned to the Kingdom of the Adoni. His role is complete. He shall not return!" His final line was so matter of fact that he was surprised when someone dared to challenge it.

"Then your wise men are not as wise as they should be," noted David. "I have seen the Great Eagle many times. I have spoken with Him, eaten with Him, learned from Him. Many of those times were after the Battle of Es-Soh-En. I don't know why He removed us from the Veil, and did not stay to speak with us, but He must have His reasons." The Knight of Es-Soh-En noticed that El-ton was dancing impatiently. He wanted to speak, but he did not know how to interrupt the Steward of Dula. David nodded to the servant, who blurted out, "Your sister, sire…" but before he could say another word David cut him off, "Has she found the answer? Did the records tell us where Dianna is?"

"Let the man speak," joked Pentra. He had bonded with the Knight of Es-Soh-En as comrades-in-arms should. He was comfortable speaking casually with the Steward of the Throne.

Handar was shocked at the familiarity with which Pentra spoke. He waited for David to reprimand his fellow warrior, but the Knight of Es-Soh-En laughed in response. David then motioned for El-ton to continue.

"The scholars went to the Chamber of Records, and found her unconscious on the floor. She spoke your name several times, but she has not recovered. I was sent to find you," the servant stammered. Before he could even finish his report, the Knight of Es-Soh-En had spun on his heels, bounded to the nearest horse, mounted it in a single motion which placed him in the saddle, and pulled the reins free of the bush that held them. He drew the reins in, the horse rose on its hind legs, turning around in the direction of the kingdom. David stood in the stirrups, leaning forward as the horse completed its maneuver.

"Follow me as best you can!" he shouted. "I'll see you in Dula." As the front hooves touched down, David repositioned himself in the saddle, spurred the horse, and it leaped into the air, coming down with front and hind hooves tearing the ground as it burst into speed.

"Is it that serious?" asked Pentra. As he spoke, he handed the half-cooked food to Handar, kicked the campfire, and soaked it with water from his canteen. He then moved the party towards the remaining horses. "Will she recover?"

"The healers are not sure. It does not seem serious. They hope she will recover in a day or two, but as they say: *with head injuries you can never tell.*" El-ton replied adding the proper gloom to his voice as he quoted the healers. He brought his own horse to join the others. As they mounted, El-ton added, "The healers wanted the Steward to return as soon as possible."

"Well, I guess he's doing that." observed Handar nibbling on the unfinished meal. There was no trace of David or his horse on the horizon. "It's just that he took *my* horse."

"We can give him back his horse and his gear when we reach the castle," noted Pentra. They turned their horses around, and followed the Knight of Es-Soh-En at a much slower pace.

***

David rode as hard as he could. The darkness was coming, and the moon and stars gave some light. He hated to slow his pace, but the horse was weary, and there were still potholes in the road from time to time. The horse would need to rest soon. He recalled a small water hole not far from where he was. He slowed the horse, and guided it off the road to the pool. He slipped out of the saddle, released the reins, and let the horse drink its fill. The night air was chilly, and he recalled the red cape he had packed in his saddlebags. He opened the left one, and found dried meat and hard bread. He checked the other, and found more supplies. It was then that he realized he had taken the wrong horse.

The Knight of Es-Soh-En gritted his teeth against the crisp night air. The breeze must have been coming from off the Dulan Alps to the east for the sudden gusts had the feel of snow and ice in them. David's teeth chattered; as the continuing night breeze cut through the tattered garments he wore. He finally took the horse's reins, and walked it in the direction of Dula. He waited as long as he could before mounting the steed and driving it through the darkness towards the kingdom. As he realized this was not his own horse, he was more cautious; not because he cared less for his own mount, but he knew the limits of his own horse. This horse was untried, and so he was more cautious about trusting it. The Steward of Dula used the chill of the night to keep him alert. He almost nodded off several times during the night, but the cold would not let him sleep for long.

As the long night wore on, even the cold was losing its effect. He stopped at another water hole for the horse to drink. He thought about it for a moment, and then mumbled to himself, "This will probably give me pneumonia, but it should keep me awake. He pulled off the shirt of chain mail with its numerous snapped links. He then pulled off the slashed leather vest. With only his shirt, tunic and pants, he waded into the cold waters. His legs felt numb, and he had trouble feeling his way into the waters. As the chilled waters touched his stomach and back, he took a deep breath, dipped under the surface, and held himself there for as long as he dared. His face and arms were numb as he dragged himself out of the pool. As sensation returned to his body, he was tormented with a burning "pins and needles" sensation throughout his entire frame. He rose, shook off the excess water, and combed his fingers through his hair to pull it out of his eyes. By now his entire body shivered and trembled. He clutched the reins of the horse, pulled himself into the saddle, and spurred it on. The galloping through the crisp night air only made it that much more difficult to stop the shaking his body was experiencing to fight off the cold. He thought about hyperthermia, and how it would slow down the body functions. He also recalled conversations about frost-bite and numerous respiratory illnesses which came from exposure to the cold like this. He pushed them from his mind, fought to control the trembling and convulsions that now threatened to topple him from the horse.

"Well, at least I'm awake," he comforted himself.

It was two days after David had separated from Pentra and Handar that he saw the spires of the castle being lit by the early morning sun. There was something about the quality of the first rays of dawn which cast a glow on objects unlike any other time of the day. David thought that this must be one of the reasons why he loved the dawn so much. He had always been the early riser. He shook his head to clear his mind. It had been over forty-eight hours since he had slept. He was almost at the end of his journey, but now he would need to be conscious enough to deal with the situation. He breathed a silent prayer to the Adoni and pushed on.

***

As the first rays of light entered Tanya's room, she mumbled, shifted her weight on the silk sheets, groaned, and opened her eyes. Her nurse immediately called for the healers. Three of them burst into the room before the cry had escaped the attendant's lips. Once they were sure that she was waking up, they began to minister to her. They poured several bitter-tasting teas down her throat before she was even aware they were in the room. She shook her head several times to clear her thoughts. Everything was jumbled. She tried to recall where she was, and what was happening; but her surroundings were so different than she had recalled them, that parts of her mind and memory refused to respond. She called forth her battle attire and sword, but when they did not appear, she half-believed she wasn't in the Lands of the Adoni. Then she saw the surroundings, and knew it wasn't Earth. All of this kept adding to her confusion.

One healer shoved a nasty-smelling ointment under her nose. Her nostril burned, and her eyes began to tear. Before she could hold her breath, her lungs felt like they were or fire. She began to cough and wheeze, pushing the healer and the foul-smelling jar away from her.

"I think it's working," the healer announced.

"Working?" came Tanya's sarcasm. "It's about to kill me off. What is that stuff?" She rose from her bed; several ladies in waiting threw robes over her, tried to put slippers on her feet, and attempted to maneuver her back into bed. The Stewardess of Dula reached the window of her room despite the efforts of a small army to usher her back under the covers. She threw open the shutters, and took several deep breaths of fresh air. After a few moments the burning in her lungs stopped. She coughed a few more times to clear them; then noted a lone figure riding at break-neck speed and coming from the west.

"David!" she called out with her voice cracking as another coughing fit took over. The healers were now pulling her physically back to the bed. When the healer produced the jar once more, she caught his wrist, wrenched the medicine from him, and hurled it against the wall where it shattered.

"I guess she's getting stronger," noted the second healer.

"She still needs to rest," announced the third.

"But that was takard!" whined the first healer who had administered the foul-smelling ointment. "Do you know how rare that is?"

"Takard!" snapped Tanya. She recalled the potion from several years ago when Es-Soh-En taught her and David about potions, herbs and healing leaves. "Takard!" she echoed. "That stuff can kill you!"

"If it's used the wrong way, but I assure you Lady Tanya, I took great care..."

"Takard is used to kill infections. You never inhale its fumes!" she bellowed.

"Well, if my Lady thinks she knows more about medicine than a healer..." began the indignant voice, but Tanya cut him off.

"If you give takard to someone who has a head injury, then you're right! I do know more about medicine than you. Get me pava leaves, willow bark, or dandelion seeds for this headache; but keep that takard away from me." Her ladies in waiting were trying to manipulate her back into bed. Tanya waved them back with a motion and waited for the healers to leave and find the supplies she asked for. The sounds of boot heels clicking on the stone hallways, and the rattle of battle gear caught everyone's attention. Moments later the door burst open, and David barged into the room.

When David saw that Tanya was awake and out of bed, he breathed a sigh of relief. The two days of stress over her health drained from his face. He crossed the room, healers and ladies in waiting darting out of his path, took her in his arms, and hugged as tightly as he dared. When they had clung to each other long enough to be sure the other was alright, David held her at arm's-length, and started asking questions as quickly as he could think of them.

"What happened? Are you alright? How long had you been unconscious? The last time I saw you was in the record chamber…"

The mention of the record chamber caused something in Tanya's mind to click into place.

"The Record Chamber!" she shouted, and cut David off. Her mind was quickly putting all the pieces back into place. "I found a scroll. It was written by Tra. It was addressed to the Steward of Dula. That would have to be you. There never has been a Steward of Dula until now. It was in my hand." She held up her hand as if the scroll should still be there for all to see. "Books were scattered on the floor. I feel over them. The stairs were coming up at me. That's the last thing I remember. Where's the scroll." She started searching her bed clothes as if it might have pockets, and the scroll was tucked away in one of them. She instantly realized it couldn't be there. "Where are my clothes? The ones I was wearing that day?"

The ladies in waiting brought the clothes to her, but even after a careful search, the scroll was nowhere to be found. Those who took care of Lady Tanya when she was first brought to her room were questioned, but no one recalled any scroll. Tanya dropped down onto her bed, letting out a long groan of frustration.

"Maybe it's still in the records chamber. You could have dropped it when you fell," offered David. Several servants were dispatched instantly to the records chamber, but after an hour's search, the scroll still remained missing.

"I had it in my hand when I ran from the chamber," Tanya insisted. She snatched her coat, and bolted for the door.

"My lady!" exclaimed one of the healers. "You're still weak. You need rest." He then began to list numerous concerns, symptoms, potentially fatal complications. David could tell that Tanya would not be put off. He stepped between her and the door, blocking her escape.

"If you're determined to go, at least get dressed. How would it look to the people if you go running around in your night gown?" he joked.

"Speaking of looking…what happened to you?" He glanced down, and saw the tattered, muddy, clothes. Even his boots still "squished" when he moved. Suddenly Tanya recalled his own mission. "You went to the Veil!"

Apparently it had not been common knowledge as several servants let out gasps, and one even dropped a ceramic cup and it shattered on the floor. David tried to discount the sudden intensity of the room by down-playing his mission.

"She wasn't there. We made it all the way to the Ring of Fire, but Queen Dianna wasn't there. The Dark Lord doesn't have her."

"How do you know?" asked one of the healers. Before he considered his words, David replied, "Because if he did have her, he would have shown her to us before his army attacked. He was sure we would never escape alive."

"You saw the Dark One?!" exclaimed another healer.

"The army of Cronis attacked you?!" exclaimed the other. The energy in the room rose several more levels. Everyone wanted the details of the mission. Tanya slipped out of the room and to the chamber of records while everyone fired question after question at her brother. It took him over an hour to get away from them, and another twenty minutes to realize that Tanya had slipped out in the confusion. He found her sitting on a stack of books in the center of the chamber; head down, eyes red from tears.

"It was in my hand," she insisted.

"I'm not denying it," he offered for what consolation it was worth.

"So where did it go?" she demanded of no one in particular.

"How did you find the scroll?" he asked, and Tanya related the story of the tears on the page, the swirling smoke, and how it led her right to the scroll. "And so you figured a few more tears might lead you back to it?" he added wiping them from her cheeks.

"Not really. I was just so frustrated."

"Look!" he began. "The Adoni led you to the scroll the first time. They must have allowed it to become hidden once more. Perhaps now is not the time to open it and read it. When the time is right, They can bring it back to us."

"But what if it's fallen into other hands?" she suggested.

"Then the Adoni are powerful enough to protect it until we do need to read it. If it is lost or destroyed, then I'm sure They can always get the information to us some other way. Don't put Them in a box. We can't limit Them with our own expectations or fears."

Tanya nodded, dried her eyes, and motioned for David to sit on a stack of books next to her. "So tell me about the Veil."

David took over an hour relating all the information he could remember about the Veil, the meeting with Cronis, the battle with the Dark Lord's servants, the cry of Glidon, and their coming to outside of the Veil.

"I don't understand. If the Dark Lord didn't steal her away, then who else has the power?" she pondered out loud.

"We both know *Who* has the power," David observed.

"But why would the Adoni snatch her away?" Tanya probed.

"We may not know. However, if she is with the Adoni, then she is safe; and we must focus on the reason for our being here," suggested David.

"You know the people. If we told them: *Dianna's with Es-Soh-En; don't worry.* Do you think they would believe us? This kingdom has little or no faith left in it," Tanya declared.

"I know. It seems that *wise men* have risen up explaining away the Adoni, making it all seem like ignorant superstition. Whenever anyone speaks of the Adoni, it's either to curse someone, make a joke, or show their ignorance."

"Then maybe it's up to us to restore honor to the Adoni's name," Tanya proposed.

"Since when did the Adoni need us to protect Their honor? That's when problems always start. People try to protect or defend the Adoni on their own, instead of letting the Adoni protect Themselves."

"I'm not talking about passing laws, starting wars, or putting people in prison. It's just that we take as common in our lives what others see as miracles. We have a great storehouse of lessons, experiences and memories that these people are hungry to hear. They want to believe, but no one has allowed them to believe. Dianna was only one person, and the *wise men* had tried to explain away her long life, but we are different. They never explained away our long life, just our existence. Now we've disproved their theories. We're here in the flesh. I think it's time to press the advantage."

The meeting moved back to her chambers where meals were ordered, warm drinks, fresh clothes for David, and the latest information available as to what was going on in the kingdom. The Children of Earth wondered what had happened to the Fibbergee family. They would have felt more at ease trusting the loyalty of that family of mice to scurry through the palace and the city with their many eyes, hungry ears, and superb memories than the written reports which always looked as if they have been edited before they came before the Knights of Es-Soh-En.

"We have to have a celebration," Tanya insisted.

"About what?" David argued.

"You, Pentra and Handar went into the Veil to search for Dianna. You fought the armies of The Evil One. You came back out alive."

"The only reason we made it back out was because Glidon saved us. It wasn't because we were great warriors."

"That's the whole point. We have to let the people know that Glidon is still here. Glidon has taken a hand in the search for Dianna. Besides, don't you think Pentra and Handar deserve some honor for even going into the Veil?"

"Well...yes. It took a great deal of courage for them." He pondered the value of getting the message out concerning Glidon. He also thought his comrades should be honored for their deeds. He finally agreed to support the celebration so long as it centered on Pentra and Handar, and allowed him to stay in the background. As they eased back into the high-back chairs with the extra padding, Tanya noted the look in her brother's eyes. It had been two days since he had slept, another six hours that they had been at the planning phase. She deliberately turned the direction of conversation away from the important matters of the kingdom. As she focused on less important topics, minor events, casual gossip, and then mundane observations, she watched his eyes grow heavy. The adrenaline that had kept him going this long dissipated. The need was no longer there. Within moments he was deep in sleep. She rose, crossed over, and covered him with a warm blanket.

When she tucked the blanket under his chin, she recalled her first visit to Dula. It had been on that mission that she had met Dianna, tied to a tree, fearing for her life from Dragnock the usurper. Kal the minotaur had brought her and Dianna to his cottage, provided food and drink for them while he went to prepare for David's rescue from the dungeon. That night, as Dianna had related the history of the Sword, and the events of the kingdom, Tanya had fallen asleep in similar fashion. Dianna had covered her, and when Kal returned, the minotaur had carried her to bed where she had awaken the next morning to the most beautiful song she had ever heard, the Song of Morning sung by Logos.

She knew she would not hear the songs again. Ever since the Battle of Es-Soh-En the voice of the Sword was gone. Logos was now an empty shell. Its power had been broken when it had shed the innocent blood of Teacher in the Veil. Cronis did not realize that when he took control of the Sword, he became the power of the Sword. Thus, when the power of the Sword was broken, it was the power of Cronis which broke. The intelligence that lived in the Sword was set free by Teacher. An empty, powerless, blood-stained sword was all that Teacher brought back from the Veil. Dianna had clung to it as a reminder of what once was. She had tried over the years to release her hold on the past, and to look to the future. During the last several visits, she had made great strides in that direction. She no longer needed the sword by her side. She would speak of it casually, and the passion which was once in her voice was gone. It no longer controlled her life. Unfortunately, it no longer sang to the Children of Earth, either.

Tanya went into her adjoining chamber and prepared herself for the meetings which lay ahead. She would have the streets decorated and the people ready to praise Pentra and Handar as they came through the gate. By her estimation, she only had a few more hours left.

***

The two warriors were caught completely off-guard as they rode through the main gate with El-ton six hours later. The flag of Dula hung from hundreds of flagpoles placed along the main route, people lined the street, and well-wishers sang, cheered, and tossed flower petals along their path. When Pentra and Handar arrived at the palace, all the guards were at attention, in full armor, and formed a line on either side of the walkway. The soldiers had drawn their swords, and raised them so the points touched over-head, giving the effect of steel arches for the honored guests to pass through. When they came into the throne room, David and Tanya were present, in their best attire. The townspeople had been invited into the palace to hear the praises of these warriors who had dared the dangers of the Veil to search for their beloved queen. Medals were bestowed, and a great banquet had been prepared.

"Not a bad party," joked Handar with David when they were off to one side.

"I can't believe that Tanya had all this put together in less than six hours," he noted.

"So, what is the punishment for stealing a horse?" asked Pentra with a twinkle in his eyes as he joined them.

"The punishment is having to wear these stiff clothes, meet with boring politicians who have never held sword in hand, and look happy about it all evening," quipped David.

"Sounds like the same punishment for riding into the Veil and getting beat up," added Handar.

"So why didn't they make a big fuss over you?" observed Pentra.

"I'm a Knight of Es-Soh-En. The people expect more of me. If I hadn't done this, then they would have demanded to know why. You, on the other hand, do not have legends to live up to. Keep that in mind when you volunteer for any future missions," countered David with a laugh.

The trio continued to joke throughout the evening. Several times they had to break up and meet with others, but eventually they found their way back to a small oasis from the crowds and the confusion.

The Council met the following morning for the first time since David had left for the Veil.

"The kingdom has been growing uneasy these last few days," reported Pentra. He produced several reports sent by his men from around the kingdom. The copies of the reports were distributed while Pentra continued. "It appears that with David gone into the Veil, and Lady Tanya in bed after her accident, Gib-ron has taken the initiative. According to sources, he has been gathering an army outside of Dula. He is not strong enough to attack, but he has sent in various spies. These agents have begun to spread various versions of how and why Gib-ron was expelled. His version is that he stood up for personal freedoms, and was driven out by the Children of Earth. His forces are trying to build a platform for a rebellion under the guise of restoring lost freedoms."

"It seems that expelling Gib-ron may have been a mistake, but it seemed more humane to exile him rather than to imprison or execute him." Several Council members seemed awkward with reference to capital punishment. Tanya took note of who they were for future reference. Apparently the Council was not as solid behind them as she had thought.

"It's too late to worry over that. The point is that if we make any move against Gib-ron, he will simply claim that it was because he was protecting free speech. If we arrest him, attack him, or begin to hunt for him, he will become a martyr to the people. The last thing we need right now is a martyr," David observed. "Perhaps the best method is to be opened about this. It's time the people knew the truth about his expulsion from the Council, and his exile from Dula."

"But if we open up the minutes of a Council meeting, we may be subject to legal action." Lendar interrupted.

"Legal action?" queried David.

"The meetings of the Council are always private. We cannot make them public knowledge without permission of all those present. If we did, those members which protested opening the records to the public could bring legal action to stop us."

"WHAT?" shouted David, nearly coming out of his chair. "That's absurd. Who ever heard of such a thing?"

"When the Council assumed certain duties many years ago, a law was passed to protect the members of the Council. All records of the meetings were kept sealed. This way a member could speak openly and freely without fearing public opinion. This has been our most protected right. The events of Council meetings can never be made public, only the decisions of the Council can be announced."

"Wait a minute. You mean that the people of Dula have no idea what goes on in these meetings? That they can never find out what happens inside these walls?" Tanya challenged.

"That is the basis of the Council. We meet to discuss the business of the kingdom. However, we must be free to explore all issues, opinions, and positions. The members of the Council ordered the records sealed so that no one could be damaged by his or her personal comments during the meetings.

"We meet, pass new laws, make decisions, and then announce them to the kingdom; but the actual meetings are always kept secret for reasons of state security," Lendar declared.

"It sounds more like reasons of job security. No wonder the people suspect us!" Tanya observed. "They have no idea what we do in here or why. The only things they see are the final results."

"I believe it is time to change the law. The people have the right to know," David announced.

"Change the law?!" the terror on several of the member's faces was obvious. "That can only be done if the majority votes in favor of opening the meetings to the public."

"As Steward and Stewardess of Dula, we can make those changes we deem necessary for the kingdom. The only purpose this secrecy serves is to make the Council members unaccountable for their actions. They can do and say what they want in private, affect the entire kingdom publicly, and then hide behind a law which keeps the population in ignorance."

"It must be called to a vote," Lendar stammered, sweat already forming on his brow.

"Is there some reason that you do not want the people to know what you support and what you attack in Council meetings?" The ice in Tanya voice caught even David off-guard. "If Gib-ron is going to use the platform of freedom of speech as his springboard to attack our kingdom, then we must make it very clear that freedom of speech is practiced at all levels of the kingdom. If the people see that they are free to speak, and that they are free to learn what was said, Gib-ron will not gain any support."

"But then you have another problem," noted Ki-el. "Gib-ron was expelled from the Council for speaking his mind. Where do you draw the line between free speech and blasphemy?" There was something almost smug about Ki-el's voice which made David take new stock of the Council member. He was no longer sure if he could trust him to the level he had previously.

"We will not draw the line. The Adoni have set down their Laws for us. We will use them to guide us. We are free to speak our minds. We have the right to express our opinions, but when the person speaking is trying to use that freedom to deceive, or mislead others into doing what is harmful to themselves or others; then at that point the protection and safety of others limits the right of others to speak.

"We cannot allow people to be free to lie to others in order to steal their savings. The right to free speech does not give others the right to lie about threats or dangers, to terrify individuals or the public when there is no danger. The right of free speech does not give others the power to serve Dark Lord and seek to lead others away from the Adoni." David noted the various exceptions to free speech which had existed for many years before the Battle of Es-Soh-En. He called upon the Words of the Ancients, the Words of the Clan, and the lessons he had been taught by Es-Soh-En on this matter. When the meeting was over, the Council had a platform on free speech which would be published for all to see and hear. Once it was in place, the Knights of Es-Soh-En announced that the records of the Council meetings would soon be made public.

As they worked their way back to their private chambers, Tanya noted to David, "I think this is just the beginning."

"Of course. The only question now is what will Gib-ron and his men do."

"I think I liked it better when the enemy was more obvious, and battle was out in the open," Tanya admitted.

"They say that politics is a war of a different kind. We will just have to trust Es-Soh-En to train us in this kind of warfare as well." David agreed to meet with Tanya for dinner, went into his room, pulled off his tunic, shirt and boots, then collapsed on his bed, and drifted into a welcomed sleep.

CHAPTER SEVEN

THE QUEEN'S MESSENGER

Word that Sir David had been one of the three who had gone into the Veil of Darkness to search for Queen Dianna spread throughout the kingdom. The fact that he had kept his name out of the official announcements seemed to have the opposite affect than he desired. Where he had sought to remain in the background, he was now more honored than ever. The fact that he was one of the Children of Earth had allowed him to win the hearts of the kingdom. When they learned he had taken a stand for the Adoni further endeared him. When it was discovered that he had gone into the Veil, met with Cronis, battled the armies of the Dark Lord, came out with the help of Glidon, and then tried to keep it quiet in order to give greater glory to his companions made him the most popular person in the kingdom.

The news that the Council was going to put the right of freedom of speech in writing to guarantee this to the people, and the records of the Council were going to be opened for all to see were also attributed to his leadership. Tanya was still in her room, reading over books which had been brought to her by servants. Books were brought to her instead of her traveling to the records chamber because for some reason, she had been having continued difficulty recovering from her fall. David had stopped by to see how she was doing.

"They always like a leader of action," noted Tanya as her brother paced the floor. He wore the red cape he had left in his saddlebags. It trailed behind him, and hung in the air momentarily when he turned abruptly. "Nice cape, by the way," she added.

David pulled it loose, tossed it on the bed, crossed over to the large table filled with books, and dropped into the empty chair.

"That wasn't nice!"

"Look, when Handar mentioned that the cape was with you in the Veil, and wasn't torn like the rest of the clothes you all wore, it became a symbol to the people," she noted.

"But now I have to wear it everywhere I go. If I appear in public without it, the first question is: *what happened to the cape?!*" He slammed his fist on the table. Several books shifted and slid to new positions.

"I know it's tough," Tanya consoled. "At least you are still popular."

"And you aren't?" he challenged.

"The *tyrant of the castle?*" she quoted. "That's just one of the nicer terms they use to describe me."

"They don't mean it," began David, but his sister cut him off.

"Yes, they do." When she had his attention, she continued. "I am an anomaly in this world. A female Knight of Es-Soh-En. Do you know that after several thousand years, I am still the only one?" she announced. "The people remember the tales of my love for Jensen. They see me as a romantic figure. They are confused. Am I a warrior, or am I a woman?"

"Can't you be both?" offered David.

"*I* can, yes! But will they let me? No!" She caught herself before she began to vent. "If I come to the forefront in leadership, it frightens them. If I stay in the background, they suspect me. If I smile and act properly, they don't respect me. If I do what has to be done, they attack me."

Her brother rose from his chair, crossed over, and placed a supportive hand on her shoulder. She reached up, squeezed it. "We are what we are," David offered. "We are Knights of Es-Soh-En. The Adoni do not work with molds to create people. They are artists Who sculpt us into the images They choose. The path you trod has never been trod before. It makes it lonely, but you aren't alone. I am with you, and the Adoni are with us. There are no untried paths with Them. We can try to follow the people's expectations and fail, or we can be ourselves, and let the Adoni use us and succeed."

"I know, but it doesn't stop the pain when you hear the rumors and the gossip which fills this castle like a foul odor." She took a deep breath, and pushed the problems away. David could feel the tension in her neck and shoulders, and began to massage them. Tanya closed her eyes, sat up, and let him work the stress from her muscles. The fact that she even let him do that much told him she was more frustrated than she would let on.

"Thanks," she finally replied, stretching her neck, and rolling her shoulders to complete the relaxation process.

"I won't say that I know what it means to be in your place," David offered. "I fit into the image the people want. You do not. It is not because there is anything wrong with you; it's just that you are serving the Adoni in ways that most people can barely imagine. While it may be a man's world, even with Dianna on the throne, the Adoni select and use whom They will regardless of the expectation or prejudices of others."

"Some of these books have been very informative," she replied, shifting the conversation away from the present topic.

"How so?" he asked resuming his seat once he saw that she had gained control of her frustration.

"Did you know that there were those who claimed that Glidon was taking an active part in the kingdom several years ago?" He shook his head, and Tanya continued. "Seems that there was almost a split in the kingdom at that time. Several insisted that Glidon was still active in the affairs of Dula, while others argued He no longer served any purpose. The factions almost came to blows."

"So what happened?"

"They met with Dianna, and sought her blessing to leave the kingdom in order to maintain the peace."

"Where did they go?"

"According to this text," she began as she hefted the large volume and plopped it down before her, "*The Great Migration of Glidonites.* That's what they called those who believed the Great Eagle still worked in the ways of man. It was eight years ago, and they sold all their possessions, packed everything up, and moved to Janadis. According to reports, Janadis was still very active in support of the Adoni. Their beliefs actually caused several confrontations with the Council. There were so many people who packed up and went to Janadis that the Council tried to pass laws making it illegal to immigrate there. They warned Dianna that Janadis was stealing away the citizens of Dula, and would eventually have the entire kingdom following them. There were hostile debates in the Council meetings. Several laws were passed without Dianna's knowledge or permission."

"How could that have been possible? She attended all the meetings," David challenged.

"All the *weekly* meetings. It turns out that the Council members were secretly having *supplementary* meetings. Only enough to form a quorum came to these meetings. Those who would not support the laws they made weren't invited. Those who favored a certain new law or regulation would contact only those who also supported the proposition. They would call a special meeting outside of the regularly-scheduled Council meetings, and pass the law. When the next weekly meeting was held, those who had passed the laws announced that they were already in effect. As a law could be created by a simple majority, they had complied with the law. However, once a law was made, it took a unanimous vote to repeal it. The Council even met that way to draw some of Dianna's authority away from the throne and assigned it to the Council."

"Anyone notice any private meetings lately?" David asked with only a half-joking tone in his voice.

"Dianna tried to put a stop to it, but it was a pretty hostile battle. The Council accused her of becoming a despot. The Council members turned it into a real smear campaign. There was even talk of dissolving the monarchy, and setting up a pure democracy."

"They would dare to remove the throne Es-Soh-En established?!!" David was almost on his feet. His anger was obvious. It took a few moments to catch himself, and to be able to sit down and calm himself enough to where he could give Tanya his full attention.

"It gets even more involved. Apparently Gib-ron, Lendar, and Ki-el were the ring leaders."

"And Ki-el and Lendar still serve on the Council. I think it's time they found other occupations," suggested her brother.

"They have the people's ears. If we throw them off the Council, it will cause additional problems. As long as they are in favor with the people, we can't just dismiss them. Our efforts with Gib-ron seem to be working. When people began to learn that he was teaching the ways of the Dark Lord in open Council meetings, it turned the people against him. His forces are still growing, but he has to recruit from outside of Dula."

"We will have to keep a close eye on them," David promised. He rose, and went back to his room. Tanya rubbed her eyes. They were itchy and teary from the long hours of reading she had done. She broke proper protocol by not summoning her servants, prepared herself for bed, crawled under the covers, and was soon fast asleep.

She wasn't sure how long she had been asleep, but something seemed to intrude on her dreams. It was a voice calling to her. She slowly opened one eye. There, standing on the pillow right next to her face was a large brown mouse. He was leaning close to her, and the angle of his stance and posture told her that he had been studying her. He had a tunic opened on both sides draped over his head and covering his chest and back. It was held in place by a black belt, and the crest of Dula was embroidered on the chest of the garment. He had a wide belt which draped over one shoulder, across his chest, and held a small blade, just the right size for his height. In his hands he held a black, wide-brimmed hat. Protruding from the side of the hat was a rather larger, fluffy blue feather.

The tilt of the mouse's head shifted slowly, and Tanya moved with her visitor. In a moment she was face to face; literally nose-to-nose with the intruder.

"I see by your feather that you must be of the Fibbergee family," she finally whispered. The fact that she had not sat up-right immediately, screamed or shouted for help had impressed the mouse. He nodded in agreement.

"Very good, my lady. You are correct." He spoke in very soft tones as if he did not want anyone to hear their conversation. "I am Hentery, last of the Fibbergee family. I trust that you are Lady Tanya of Earth?" He extended his small right paw to shake hands with her. She carefully pressed it between her thumb and forefinger so as not to crush the limb.

"Yes, I am," she replied in just as hushed tones. "What brings you to the castle? According to public records, your family has been absent for many years. I was wondering how the family of our old friend was faring."

"Well, I came to warn you of a danger," he offered.

"A danger?" she echoed in whispered voice. The whispers made it all seem more menacing, but neither she, nor Hentery seemed the least bit worried.

"It seems that someone has paid a large sum to have you killed."

"Once I would have asked who, but now I feel like asking: *who wouldn't?*"

"Yes," the mouse smiled. "Your actions have not made you the most popular person in the kingdom," he offered. He then held up his index finger to his pressed lips to quite her. He bounded over the pillow and off the bed. In a moment he was back in view. The mouse motioned for her to follow him quietly as he moved towards a large tapestry. The image woven was of the New Forest. It had been a section just outside the castle where Es-Soh-En had cleansed the ground and given it the power to heal itself of the evil that had tainted it. Instantly great trees and brush sprang from the ground. It was a forest like the great forests she had walked through in the Garden of Tangar. It was a reminder of that time when the Lands of the Adoni were young, and free of the stain of the Dark Lord.

Those who had never seen the New Forest before it gradually became tainted over the years would stand in awe of the beauty captured there in the weaving. The craftsman had been a true artist. However, Tanya had not only walked through the original New Forest before its glory faded, but had spent several months in the Garden of Tangar. It really failed to do either of them justice. Hentery scampered over to the tapestry, drew his sword from its sheath, and jabbed at the hanging just above his head.

A flailing figure protruded from the tapestry, pulled part of it loose from the wall as he cradled his left calf in both hands, lost his balance, and fell to the floor. Before he could move, Tanya had obtained the largest volume from the near-by table and swung it with great precision so that it slammed hard against the side of the man's head. He collapsed in a heap on the floor. Within moments, David was at her door.

"How did you know?" she asked lighting several candles. A grey mouse popped around David's neck, and perched on his shoulder. "Oh," she added.

Tanya brought the candles over to the man. David turned him over and pried a knife from his hand.

"It's no use questioning him, sire," the mouse on David's shoulder observed. "I know the man. He's a mute. By the time you figure out any way to communicate with him, his accomplices will be half-way back to Magar. Oh...a thousands pardons, Lady Tanya. I am Beech." He doffed his small hat.

"Beech is one of my captains," offered Hentery. "I am Hentery, last of the Fibbergee family." the brown mouse came to David's boots, and raised his hand to greet the Knight of Es-Soh-En while he still knelt over the fallen assassin.

When David had summoned the guards, Beech and Hentery moved back out of sight. They had asked Tanya and David to keep their presence a secret as they may have to return to Magar to gather more information. Once the assassin was in custody, and on his way to the prison, Hentery positioned himself on the table, and prepared his report.

"This may take a while," the brown mouse offered. His companion pulled several small scrolls from his shirt, and shifted a book around so it would serve as a table for Hentery and him to work from. "I suggest that you have Unter the Healer arrested before we continue. Word of the assassin's failure and arrest will probably reach him within the hour; and he will flee the city. According to our sources, he was feeding Lady Tanya takard along with other medications to keep her dysfunctional. They had hoped he could have continued such mistreatment, and eventually she would have died, and her death would have been blamed on her fall in the records chamber; but it seems that his only supply of takard was destroyed."

David called one of the guard from the hallway, gave the order for Unter's arrest, and then the Knight of Es-Soh-En resumed the small gathering at the table.

"Sit with me for a spell," offered Hentery. "I will make a full report of these last ten years, but I must warn my Lady and Lord that there is an evil spreading in Dula which may eventually bring about an end to the worship of the Adoni in Dula."

CHAPTER EIGHT

THE AGENDA OF MAGAR

"You might want to order food and drink, for the report I have is a detailed report, and will not be done in one sitting," suggested Hentery. El-ton arrived at the request of David, and spread several plates before the Children of Earth. Hentery and Beech chose to hide from the servants as they had done when the assassin had been taken away. As El-ton arranged the plates, drinks and place settings, another servant came in with a supply of Gen Wood for the fireplace. There was something special about certain trees that grew in the Gen Forest. When the branches were cut for firewood, they gave off one of the most desirable aromas ever imagined. As the wood burned it gave off the smell of pine, cinnamon, and several spices. When David had asked the gnomes about it many visits ago, they claimed it was a combination of the kind of wood, and the type of fertilizers used to grow these unique trees. The gnomes had made an agreement to provide this wood for Queen Dianna so long as the trees lasted and she still sat on the throne. It had crossed David's mind suddenly that he had not seen any gnomes in the castle since they had arrived.

El-ton had finished laying out a small banquet, and had departed. The mice returned to the table.

"It was ten years ago when my father, Kendery had finally chosen to retire. He had grown old, and his bones ached to the point where he could no longer climb the various steps of the castle. Queen Dianna approached me at that time, but stated she did not want me to assume the role of royal messenger. She had greater fears which she wanted me to help calm.

"I was sent to Magar to develop a spy system, collect data, and return the information to the Queen. Over the last ten years, I have been faithful to that calling, sending messages back and forth between Dula and Magar. Queen Dianna saw several common place events as a signal for a hidden agenda. She did not want to voice her concerns out loud as when she had mentioned them casually in Council; she had been all but laughed at by several members."

"They would dare to laugh at the Queen?!" came David's incredulous response.

"The authority and prestige of the throne is not as it was in older times. Over the years there has been a gradual chipping away of Queen Dianna's power. The Council now rules in Dula; Queen Dianna is now little more than a figurehead," Hentery apologized.

"It had begun with several books and plays that appeared in Dula. The books were all very well-written. They were popular with the people, and the plays were performing to sell-out crowds. Queen Dianna's concern was over the subtle message they were presenting. The topic was something which has come to be called *situational ethics*." Hentery stopped to see if he needed to explain the phrase to his audience.

"We have heard the term before. I did not know that it was taking place in Dula as well as it had on Earth," offered Tanya.

"Then you know the concerns which this can cause. It takes an extreme situation, presents it in a way that the reader or viewer must accept or feel foolish. Very few people like to feel foolish. The situation is one in which the guidelines set down by the Adoni have been challenged, and to follow the Adoni would be stupid. It would hurt others; be unusually cruel. These kinds of settings."

"When it was just one or two books or plays," Beech began, taking up the story; "it did not seem to be a dangerous thing, but the number of books and plays seemed to increase. Over a period of several years, all the great works were set aside, and replaced with this new way of thinking. It became very popular with the people because it made them feel intellectual. They would set aside the standards set down by the Adoni, see the individual situation, and rule that the Adoni were harsh, cruel, uncaring, or no longer in fashion.

"When Queen Dianna tried to address the problem in Council, the Council all but implied that she was closed-minded – narrow in her way of thinking. They equated her with concepts and beliefs which were out of date, and claimed that no intelligent person would even consider such teachings, laws, or guidelines. These books and plays made the teachings of the Adoni appear to be unreasonable. The works made the Adoni seem like tyrants. Little-by-little over the years the teachings of the Adoni were replaced with acceptance of all ways of life, new thoughts; new ethics. When Queen Dianna could no longer keep silent about these changes, the Council literally began to pass laws without her being present!"

"I have read the reports in these books," confirmed Tanya. "So what did she do?"

"She began by trying to reestablish the original works. She funded publishing companies to put out the classic works. She sponsored plays and schools to provide examples set down by the Adoni of how we should live, and work, and act. All of this failed to return the people to the ways of the Adoni. Even the works of Teacher were being set aside by the younger generation," Hentery explained.

"Queen Dianna first had me to investigate the sources of these books and plays. They did not seem to be all they should. My first assignment was for Beech and I to go to the publishing companies and the theaters, and to see who was sponsoring these works. That was when we found that Magar was sending the money to keep these books in print, and to keep the plays opened. We had even found in some cases where large numbers of Magarians had slipped over the borders and into Dula for the expressed purpose of making the plays and books appear to be sell-outs and best-sellers."

"But Magar is a warring nation. Each time they sought to attack, it was on the open field of battle. They sought to shed the blood of Dula. Why send so much money and effort in these areas?" challenged David.

"Magar has a new policy. It is a war of the mind. They do not declare war. They move against their enemies without their enemies even knowing that they are in battle. They submit information in a slightly altered form at first. When their enemies have become comfortable with the small changes, they move on to the next level. They have a plan so that within sixty years, they believe all the Lands of the Adoni will follow them freely because they will all come to believe as Magar does now. When your ideas, desires, and goals are the same; then it is a small step – even a desirable step – to join forces to reach those goals.

"Magar now is in the war for the long-term. They no longer see the battlefield as a desirable thing. They believe that with this approach, they can take over all the Lands of the Adoni without ever lifting another sword," Hentery declared.

"It was to this end that Queen Dianna sent us to Magar," Beech explained. "We have been studying their methods. They have already taken over Orpha and Bromor with these tactics. These other countries fell much quicker because they already had beliefs similar to Magar. The only thing that kept Dula from following was its strong belief in the Adoni and the guidelines of the Adoni.

"Magar has spent a great deal of money and effort to weaken the position of Queen Dianna, and to build up that of the Council. When they heard that the Children of Earth had returned, and had taken such a stand for the Adoni, they saw several years of work instantly undone. Gib-ron was one of their main operatives."

"A member of the Council in league with Magar?!" bellowed David.

"We knew he worked for Magar, but we could never gather the information we needed to remove him. Under the old laws and guidelines set down by the Adoni, we could have dismissed him from the Council, but he and his allies have set aside those laws. It was behind these new laws that he was able to hide and function."

"And when we took control, we did not recognize these new laws. We dismissed him based upon the original guidelines set down by the Adoni," observed Tanya.

"Magar has determined that both of you need to be removed from office. It was the only way to put Gib-ron back into a position where he could continue to mislead the people. He had already made several practices of Cronis-worship acceptable in Dula."

"Such as the Seeing Eye." suggested David.

"He is difficult to fight. Queen Dianna tried several times to oppose him, but he would always flash some study, some poll, or some research to disprove her position. The Council would always vote with Gib-ron, and she was losing control," Hentery added.

"But what about the other races?" noted Tanya. "The minotaurs, the centaurs, the Water People, the gnomes? These races would not fall for such teachings," Tanya insisted.

"It did not matter. Gib-ron worked to alienate the other races from Queen Dianna. It seems ironic that Gib-ron would use the Words of the Ancients when it suited his own purposes. He found a reference that the Dark Lord would only have a limited control over the other races. The gage for how much influence the Dark One could exert on the non-humans was the level to which they associated with humans. Few people realized that Gib-ron played both sides against each other. His own people began to emphasize that doctrine. As the other races saw changes taking place among the humans, and how they were moving away from the teachings of the Adoni; they were also reminded of the fact that close association with humans would open the other races up to the influence of Cronis. The other races began to appear less frequently in Dula. They separated themselves, and soon they were gone from Dulan society," Beech related.

The mice spread out several scrolls they had with them. They pointed to several events in the recent history of Dula and Magar. Following careful charts, the mice were able to show a direct relation to forces in Magar. Money had changed hands from Magar to Dulan when these events took place. What had once been minor careers as writers or performers had suddenly become opportunities for instant wealth. However, only certain books or plays were providing the wealth. Those who wanted to become rich, had to produce what Magar wanted produced. If the writers, performers, or directors sought to create some other work, it went unaccepted, unnoticed, or ridiculed to extinction.

"You can see a direct relation in the increase of crime to the setting aside of the teaching of the Adoni," explained Hentery comparing several charts he had created. "As crime increased, other social problems began to grow in Dula. Economic problems added to the decline of Queen Dianna's power. We can show where forces outside of Dula worked to undermine everything Queen Dianna did to help her people. Agents of Magar held key positions; and delayed, misdirected, or ignored the changes Queen Dianna sought to bring about. If these changes had been put into action, they would have relieved much of the burden on the people; but they were sabotaged, and caused to fail. When it was made public that the actions Queen Dianna took had failed to help the people, the agents of Magar took her suggestions, altered them enough to make them look new, and then had those same agents which sabotaged Queen Dianna's efforts intervene, and bring aid to the people."

"So in just a few years Magar will control all the Lands of the Adoni. Why didn't Dianna take more forceful action?" Tanya asked.

"It was because she could not take forceful action that she called me into service. As crime had begun to increase, there were numerous accounts of people being attacked in the Gen Forest. The non-human races had acted as a buffer between Dula and Magar, but as they came less and less often to the castle, Queen Dianna was uninformed of the actual events. Those passing through the Gen Forest were becoming easy targets for bands of robbers. They would capture travelers, steal from them, beat them, and release them. They literally had no fear of being arrested or punished. As the practice continued, the attackers became more brazen, and would actually kill their victims, and leave their unburied bodies lying in the roadway for others to find.

"Queen Dianna became very concerned about this, and sent troops into the Gen Forest to make a show of force – to arrest the bandits or to drive them out. It was on one such policing action that everything got out of hand." Hentery motioned for Beech to take over the story as he took a drink and rested his voice.

"When the troops moved into the area of high criminal activity, they found not just robbers, but a fully equipped army. They wore quality chain mail. They carried weapons that could fire bolts that pierced shields and armor. Instead of a disorganized band, it was a well-trained military action. The Dulan troops fought for their lives. If not for the help provided by the minotaurs and centaurs who heard the sounds of battle, the Dulan troops would have been massacred.

"Our troops drove them back, but after several days of tracking them deeper into the forest, it was as if they had simply disappeared. The troops had to return for supplies and to report to Queen Dianna. She sent them back with a much larger show of force. There was no word from them for over a week. After two weeks, one straggler came to the gates of Dula. He was the sole survivor of a battle fought in the Gen Forest. His armor was gone; he had been badly beaten and battered. His clothes were torn, and his sword blade broken. As he pounded on the gates for help, several shafts fired out of hiding and pinned him to the gates, killing him at the same time. The marking on the shafts were clearly Magarian."

"It was then that Queen Dianna met with the Council to declare war on Magar, and to drive them out of our borders," Hentery resumed. "When she came to the Council, they refused to agree to go to war. There had been many years of peace, and no one wanted to destroy that peace. She went to the people for support, but they refused to believe that the soldier had been killed by an invading Magarian force. She had sent me and several others to investigate. It seems that the public opinion was that most travelers who had been robbed or attacked had been gnomes, centaurs or minotaurs. Everyone seemed to have forgotten about the others who had been robbed, beaten or killed. When Queen Dianna tried to call attention to it, the Council censored her for trying to incite the people. They kept the number hidden, and admitted only a *few* had actually be attacked. The Council convinced the people we could not get involved with the non-human races. We had too many problems of our own to deal with."

"It was conveniently over-looked that twelve centaur, fifteen minotaur, and thirty-five gnomes gave their lives to save our troops during the first attack," spat Beech. "Because we treated their sacrifice with dishonor, they broke all ties with the castle. They still owed allegiance to Queen Dianna, but they would have nothing else to do with the people of her kingdom.

"There were tales passing around the city that the Magarian shafts which had killed the lone soldier were not from Magar at all, but had probably been stolen from Magarian troops by the same thieves who attacked our troops. Numerous other tales surfaced. All of them defusing the anger of the people. When I identified those who seemed to have originally suggested the new version, they couldn't really give me any reason for why they believed it. It was just that it seemed like a good idea. It made sense. The odd thing was that each of the people who started the rumors had come into sudden money: a rich uncle here, a good investment there, someone wanting what they had and being willing to pay a very great price."

"Magarian agents!" Beech declared. "But we couldn't prove it!"

"Then as if in response to her request to go to war, the Council censored her for trying to increase the borders of Dula beyond what had been assigned by the Adoni. It was one of the few times the Council ever supported any action of the Adoni. Taxes went up just after that. The raises were due to the Council's secret meetings, but the people saw it as Queen Dianna's revenge for not letting her go to war. Her popularity fell drastically. There was a crisis at that point, and the Council tried to have her removed from office. That was when the attempt was made to dissolve the monarchy. It failed, but not by much," Hentery observed.

"The attacks continued, but this time only the non-human races were the victims," Beech noted.

"Not because the bandits were more selective, but because humans stayed out of the Gen Forest. Queen Dianna prepared another military action, but the Council vetoed her. She was told that any attempt to protect non-humans with human lives would be challenged."

"What became of the power which once was Dula?" David exclaimed. "This was the most powerful nation in all the Lands of the Adoni! When Dianna spoke, the people listened. When she asked, they gave without thinking. When she led, they followed. Now we stand and bicker about personal interests, Council rulings, and popular opinion!"

Hentery cleared his throat, drained his cup, set it down, and took a deep breath which sounded very much like a sigh, "We have fallen, my lord. Once all those things you claim were possible, but that was a time when we had seen Es-Soh-En. We had heard the words of Teacher back then, remembered the Battle of Es-Soh-En, looked upon the Band of Betrothal with hope. In those days it seemed that the Great Eagle had spread His wings from one side of our kingdom to the other. People still spoke of the songs sung by Logos. Those days have been lost to us."

"How were they lost?" Tanya pressed.

"It was subtle at first," Beech began. "The people wanted freedoms."

"Freedom is not a dangerous thing," suggested David.

"In and of itself, no," admitted Beech. "It is what people did with freedom that caused the problem. There were those who came forward and tried to claim that Teacher was not Es-Soh-En. Since Teacher was not the incarnation of the Adoni, the Battle of Es-Soh-En never took place. Others rose up trying to claim that they were Teacher's replacement. Somehow the Adoni had failed with Teacher, and so Glidon had called these others to fulfill Teacher's destiny."

David snorted his opinion of the folly of such words.

"That was how we all felt...at first," admitted Hentery. "Those who taught such things were considered the town idiots. People made fun of them. No one took them seriously. Several were even treated for sickness of the mind. Then over the years, a new wave of thinkers rose up. They rejected the Words of the Ancients; something no one had ever done before. They had new truths, new messages, and new insights. Some of the insights actually took the Words of the Ancients and twisted them for their own use, most just disregarded them completely.

"The basis for their teachings was that we had been lied to. The Words of the Ancients were written to serve some political end. They were not inspired by the Adoni. After a while, this group of new thinkers removed the Words of the Adoni from all forms of education. They taught that there must be a separation between what we believe, and how we are ruled. Queen Dianna was actually silenced by court orders not to speak of what she knew of Teacher, Es-Soh-En, or the Adoni. The basis for these orders was that if the Words of the Ancients were written for political ends, then any efforts on the part of the ruling class to cite these Words to support their own position is delusion.

"Those in power could never cite the Words of the Ancients to support any of their decisions. The result was that those who denounced the Words of the Ancients eventually made the rules and came to power. After some time all the great leaders who had followed the Words of the Ancients in their decision-making went on to the Kingdom. All save Queen Dianna. Most figured it would have been only a matter of time until she, too, went to the Kingdom; but she confounded them. They would not believe that she had Unending Life from a promise made by Es-Soh-En centuries ago. They accused her of having discovered the secret of long life years ago, and keeping it to herself. Some even tried to challenge her right to rule." At this point Hentery's voice seemed to crack. Beech took up the story for his leader.

"When she came forward with Logos to display the blade as her divine right to rule, the people laughed at her. They refused to recognize it as proof of her right to the throne. Fortunately, she had kept very careful records over the centuries. When those trying to remove her from office challenged her, she came before an impartial Council, and displayed volumes of genealogies that could be carefully traced. None of those trying to usurp her throne could come anywhere close to the documentation she had. Those who had challenged her slipped off to other countries, and have not been heard from since."

"But tell me," interrupted Tanya. "These new thinkers proposed many theories, but I do not see where they ever sustained the proof of their new ideas."

"They never did," Hentery replied. "But they said it loud enough, long enough, and often enough that the people began to listen. If anyone challenged them in public, the new thinkers would attack the person, not the position. The new thinkers used standards which were so strict that even Teacher would have a difficult time meeting them all. However, they did not use the same standards to judge themselves. They were actually proud of their infidelities and vices. They told the people that it put them more in tune with the common man."

"So these new positions were never proven, only accepted by popular opinion?" Tanya noted.

"Exactly!" Beech declared.

"So they suggest a theory, never prove the theory, but then quote that theory to support all of their other actions," Tanya concluded. "Didn't the courts stop such stupidity?"

"At first, but as time went on; there were strange decisions being handed down. It was not because the person who won was right, but the persons challenging them were not allowed to speak," Beech explained.

"Not allowed to speak in court? That's absurd!!" David thundered.

"It was a game of words. When the new thinkers came to court, they would stop the other side from using arguments, again by attacking their character and not the logic behind the position. The new thinkers would ban documents from coming into evidence, have witnesses dismissed, evidence barred from the court. Before the followers of Es-Soh-En and Teacher could find a new way of presenting their position, the new thinkers already had decisions handed down in their favor. They then kept using these flawed decisions to keep anyone else from raising the same arguments they had previously silenced. When we finally saw where all of this was going, we were powerless to stop it." There was defeat in Hentery's voice.

"How did Dianna take all these defeats?" asked Tanya.

"It was strange," Hentery began. "She was angry. She was upset and frustrated, but after a while she would take on a look as if she were seeing something in her mind's eye, something we could not see. She would then say *My Beloved is coming*."

"*My Beloved is coming?*" Tanya repeated. "That could only be a reference to Teacher, but what does it mean?"

"Apparently, she saw many things when she looked into the Portal of Ages on the Mountain of the Sky. She spoke how some of the scenes made no sense to her then, but as time passed by and various events took place, it was like pieces of a puzzle that were falling into place. There was something about her experience on the Mountain of the Sky which gave her the hope that kept her going. She would tell us that all this was according to Plan. She was often referring to *The PLAN*, but would never mention more than that. Finally she sent me and my spies to Magar to see what they were doing, and when we should expect an attack."

"Was it wise to send you into the castle of Magar? The Magarians hate the followers of Teacher. They would kill you if they had the chance and count it an honor to do so," David observed.

"My lord forgets, only Dula still has talking animals. So long as we go about them…naked," Hentery was a bit awkward with the image and the confession, and Tanya motioned him to move on. "So long as we do not act any differently than other animals in Magar, they do not suspect. For ten years we sent messages back and forth with talking birds that were still loyal to the Queen. Our contact came back only a month ago rather distressed because Queen Dianna was no longer available, and no one knew where she had gone. The bird told us the Children of Earth had returned, but the Queen had commanded our messenger to speak with only her and no one else. I sent her back to report to you, and she came back to say you were ill, and Sir David was in the Veil of Darkness. I had prepared to leave Magar and come back to make a formal report when I stumbled onto something by accident. Passing guards in the palace mentioned a speaker coming to their Council meeting that night.

"I went to the meeting in order to gather some last-minute information before returning to Dula. You can imagine my surprise when Gib-ron was ushered into the meeting with all pomp and ceremony. He was a guest of honor. They gave him the head of the Council table, poured and drank wine in his honor." A look of disgust crossed the mouse's face.

Beech picked up the tale. "It was learned that he had been one of their most trusted agents. He, and several of his fathers before him, had laid much of the ground work for the undermining of the Adoni and Queen Dianna. We also found out that he was using the Seeing Eye, a crystal globe used by servants of Cronis to see and hear things from great distances.

"He reported having trouble seeing what was happening in the palace of Dula. He accused both of you of using your own dark arts to block his power…" Hentery paused, and David realized that the mouse still was uncomfortable with the accusation.

"No friend mouse," David comforted. "We do not use black arts. I expelled Gib-ron from the Council for even suggesting we do such a thing. If his Seeing Eye cannot pierce our castle, it is because Glidon is protecting us."

The thought of the Great Eagle taking an active part in the current events of the day, excited Hentery. He downed his cup of drink, and poured another before continuing. "As the meeting continued, Gib-ron revealed his own plan to use his crystal eye to find Queen Dianna so they could capture her, and hold her hostage. With her as bait, he would force you to turn the throne over to him. If you refused to comply, he would let the people know that Queen Dianna had been discovered, but you still held the throne. Using her only as a *front* he would have rallied the people against you, stormed the castle, and removed you by force. Of course, he realized that Queen Dianna would die in the battle, and so the Council would have to take full control."

"Queen Dianna is not in this world," offered Tanya. "Her method of disappearance was beyond the laws of science. It could only have been done through the supernatural. We have already confronted one source of supernatural power. If any of his followers had stolen Queen Dianna, the Dark One would have taken possession of her; and used her for his own ends. So we know she was not taken by the Dark Lord or Gib-ron. That leaves only the Adoni. If she is with the Adoni, she is safe; and we must direct our efforts to the protection of the kingdom."

"Then what are our plans?" asked Beech, becoming more confident than when he had first heard the news of Queen Dianna's disappearance.

"It is time to take back what should never have been lost," declared David as he rose from the table.

"How?' asked Hentery.

"In the courts if we must, in the streets if we can," the Knight of Es-Soh-En announced. "Who is loyal to the Adoni?"

"There are many, but they do not speak for fear of ridicule," Beech admitted.

"Then the time has come to call them forth; to give them strength and encouragement. If they crumple because of ridicule, they will never survive the battle."

"*Battle?*" Hentery and Beech both echoed.

"Battle!" David James confirmed. His jaw was tight, his eyes clear. The determination on his face demanded immediate attention from his audience. "Lady Tanya had said that *politics was a war without weapons, a war without allies.* That may not be completely correct. The weapons are hidden, subtle; but just as deadly. Tonight we change the rules of combat. Politics and corruption are wars of a different kind. They work best when none know they are in battle. Once the foe has been alerted, the war must either end, or return to conventional methods.

"You do not think that Gib-ron and Magar will sit quietly by while we undo generations of planning and preparation? They have invested too much into their agenda," David declared. "Tonight they attacked my sister. I will be next. They will not stop until we are gone, and Gib-ron is able to worm his way back into favor with the people. I suspect that we will find the army of Magar has been massing outside the Gen Forest for many years in preparation for this next phase of their attack.

"For the good of the people, for the safety of Dula, we must force Magar's hand. The people must know that the actions of Magar, although not drawing blood, are still acts of war. Magar must know that they have lost this war of ideas, and now they must meet us on the open field of battle. Before this day is done, we will declare open war on Magar, and may the Adoni guide us to victory!"

CHAPTER NINE

CONFRONTATIONS AND MURDER

David James eyed each member of the Council as they sat before him for the emergency session he had called. It was too early in the morning for most of them. He could see it in their eyes. Several large mugs of hot drink were spread around the table, and the members nursed the drink to stimulate them enough to get through the morning session. Several seemed anxious about a sudden meeting called without warning; others were sluggish, and their heads nodded as they fought to stay awake while waiting for the servants to provide them their own hot drink. Most were surprised to find every one of the Council members had been invited to the special session since in the past only those who would support a new law would have been invited. That had been the only real reason anyone called an emergency session of the Council.

David wondered if any of them knew what he was about to do. He had no illusions about spies in the palace. It was a fact of life that he had come to learn long ago. When one was in a position of power, those wanting that power would watch. If they could not watch personally, they would find those who would watch for them for a price. They always watched, looking for the first sign of weakness. They plied their trade to find some way to tap into or steal the power they all wanted. David found it ironic that he did not necessarily want the power which had been thrust upon him, but he would not abdicate it because he knew to do so would destroy the kingdom. He determined to take the bull by the horns and press on.

"Gentlemen and lords of Dula, for such you are. I would like to call you friends as well, but certain sources I have been in contact with have proven that not all of you are friend, either to myself, my sister, or to the kingdom. During the night, there was an attack upon my sister's life while she lay sleeping in her bed." There was surprise on some faces. David noted one or two which did not seem genuine. "We have captured the assassin, and we are holding the assassin in the dungeon."

"Has he spoken?" asked Lendar. David let a smile play at the corners of his mouth.

"I don't recall ever mentioning if the assassin was man or woman," David suggested. Beads of sweat broke out of Lendar's forehead.

"An assassin would have to be a man," the head of the silver-smith guild stammered.

"With your reputation for women, Lendar, I would have thought that you had more sense than to underestimate what a woman can and will do. I suggest you take greater care, for you would make an easy target if someone sought to assassi-nate you." A ripple of laughter floated around the room. David could tell he was pushing harder than the opposition liked. He thought about clarifying that the assassin was a man, but then chose better of it.

"In addition to the attempt on my sister's life, we also learned that one of the healers caring for her was in league with the assassin, and had been giving her the wrong medication. Her life is no longer in danger from either of these sources." He paused to let the facts sink in.

"In addition to these two attempts on my sister's life, we have reason to believe that Magar is amassing an army, and is preparing to attack the castle directly. I believe the attack will come quickly since the attempts on my sister's life failed," The Knight of Es-Soh-En was cut off by Ki-el of the stone-cutters guild.

"Council members! This is terrible news indeed. We are not prepared to wage war, especially with Magar. We have been at peace for so many generations. I move that we send representatives to Magar immediately and sue for peace, before they can enter our lands."

The other Council members began to voice their agreement with Ki-el. He had placed his allies in all the key positions in the Council meeting. No two members who would support David's motion were together. Each had one of Ki-el followers between them, and they urged approval of Ki-el's recommendation.

"They are already in our lands," David interrupted. The news froze the Council members in their tracks. "They have been in our lands for over ten years. They are the bands of robbers in the Gen Forest. They are the bandits the Dulan troops encountered in the forest and were nearly beaten by. They are the same ones who pinned the sole survivor of the campaign to the city gates with Magarian arrows."

"Those were not Magarian arrows. The reports are false…" Lendar began trying to regain control, but David's fist slammed hard onto the table top, jarring the drinks and terrifying the Council members.

"Those *were* Magarian arrows, and any attempt to spread lies that they had been stolen by thieves in the woods is treason, and will be treated as such. Our country has been under attack by Magar for years. It has been a war of the minds, and Magar has won because we never knew we were at war. As of this day, that war is now recognized, and it will be countered. We will be a united people, and we will resist their efforts to undermine our society and take control.

"With the attempt on my sister's life, the war moved from the mental manipulation into the physical realm. Their attempt to kill the Stewardess of Dula is an act of war, and will be recognized as such. Since they have chosen to begin the war, we will bring the war out into the open, and meet them on the field of battle. This is not a battle that we will walk away from. Magar is determined to take over this country. If you sue for peace, you might as well open the gates and invite them inside."

"But this kingdom has not fought a war in our lifetime. We have no idea how to fight," Ki-el began, but David cut him off.

"Then it is time that this kingdom remembers how to fight! If Magar assumes control of the kingdom, they will not rest until they have slaughtered all those who follow the Adoni. I will not sit by, and allow you to sacrifice the population for your own personal gains. I will not let this stewardship pass from me until Dianna returns or until I die. I owe that much to Dianna."

"But you cannot go to war without the approval of the Council," Lendar began.

"Understand this Lendar," and David set his most fierce gaze upon the Council member. "When Queen Dianna disappeared, more took place than my sister and I assuming the stewardship of the throne. Read the laws that you wrote during one of your own secret meetings. If Queen Dianna ever disappeared, the kingdom would automatically go under marshal law. That means all laws, rights and privileges are suspended. Even decisions handed down by the courts will be suspended until the new ruler(s) reactivate them. Even the Council is dissolved, and surrenders all of its powers to whoever takes over. I did not declare marshal law, it happened automatically, and it was that action which gave you the authority to offer my sister and I the stewardship we now have. I suspect whoever wrote that law, and recruited the secret conclave to pass it without Dianna's presence meant to use it as a means to steal the throne. I am now using it as a means to protect that throne.

"Let the people know that Dula is declaring war on Magar in response to the acts of war perpetrated by that country against its citizens. A messenger, at this very moment is delivering that written declaration to the king of Magar. I do not need the Council's approval to do this. I am not here to seek the Council's approval to do this. I am here to inform the Council that this is the action I am taking. Any who try to undermine this effort, try to contact Magar for peace, try to incite the people against this action will be charged with treason against the realm.

"Also, until the return of Queen Dianna, any law made or passed without my sister and I being present will be null and void, and those who seek to pass laws without our knowledge will also be guilty of treason against the throne. Have I made myself very clear?"

All nodded, mumbled or shifted their gaze from the Knight of Es-Soh-En. He rose and left the meeting, motioning for Pentra to join him.

"A little harsh there, weren't you?" cautioned Pentra as they walked down the hall together.

"I had to be. According to reports, Gib-ron is not just offering his services to Magar, but he and his family have been agents of that kingdom for several generations. Two of his closest allies still sit on the Council. Before they recruit any naive Council members to join their cause, they need to know that it isn't going to be safe. What is the condition of the army?"

"Been trying to put that together since you sent the request over this morning. Here's a list of the divisions we have and where they are located. We also have these supplies, these kinds of weapons, horses, wagons and equipment." As he spoke, he turned several pages in the report, and pointed to tallies of each subject.

"I am sure Magar will have more than these to bring against us. The key will be in making them uncomfortable using them. Have we had any word from the centaurs, minotaurs, gnomes or water communities?"

"Messengers went to see them this morning. Our preliminary reports seem like they are willing to meet with you and your sister, but they will not commit until they do."

"Sounds like the centaurs I know," David quipped. "I will be by later to see how the men are doing at their training sessions. Do me a favor, and don't make them look better than they are. I'm not coming to find fault and punish, but to see our true status and determine how we can improve it. If we hide our weak links instead of improving them, then Magar will cut through us like we weren't even there."

"Understood," Pentra snapped. He broke off down the west wing toward the barracks. David continued on looking for his sister. She wasn't in her room, and so he stopped by the records chamber. Since they had discovered what Unter had been giving her in her food and drinks, the other healers had been able to counter the reaction. Already her cheeks had more color, her eyes were brighter, and she moved with more grace and determination than before.

"So, did they give you their approval?" Tanya asked.

"I didn't give them the chance to say no," David announced.

"That's a dangerous move," she suggested looking up from the books she was poring over. "Their next move will be to go to the courts to stop you."

"They can't," her brother countered.

"Can't?" her voice was incredulous. "Are we talking about the same people?"

"Yes we are, but this is where a snare they set for Dianna backfired on them."

"Then fill me in," she suggested, and set aside the book on her lap.

"Not much to fill in. It turns out that the Council had been planning on getting rid of Dianna for some time. They just couldn't find a way to do it. They had passed a law during the midnight meeting marathon which stated that if Queen Dianna ever disappeared, Dula automatically fell under marshal law. Whoever took her throne had complete control over the kingdom. All governing bodies were subject to the new ruler(s), and they did not have to adhere to any law or court of law until Queen Dianna was returned. You're not the only one who can read books at night, you know."

"Especially when Hentery points you in the right direction?" Tanya suggested.

"Well, I never said I found it all by myself. Thanks for the help." David aimed his last remark to Hentery who appeared over the top of one of the books which lay opened on the table.

"So, how did your search go this morning?" David asked, shifting the attention away from himself.

"Nothing!" and the tone of his sister's voice told him more than her words ever could. "I've gone over ever inch of the chamber. Hentery and Beech looked in places where I couldn't. It's not in this room."

"So we then move to the next phase of the investigation," David suggested. "Now that we're sure you don't have it, and we're also sure it isn't lost in the chamber of records; we start eliminating everyone who came into contact with you from the time you fell until the time you woke up. Who found you?"

"I'm not sure. It was several scholars coming into the room after you left," Tanya replied.

"Then let's get a list of who they were."

The investigation began with El-ton who had carried the message from David to the scholars to meet Lady Tanya in the records chamber. El-ton had provided the names of seven scholars who were in the room when he gave the message. The Children of Earth had interviewed four of them when they finally determined which scholar was the first to enter the chamber.

"So you were the first to come into the chamber of records and find Lady Tanya, Jol-dar?" David asked as they relaxed around a table in one of the smaller rooms. David and Tanya had chosen a neutral place so those they met with could be more relaxed and comfortable. Food and drinks had been provided, and the investigation had been much more in the form of visiting than interrogating.

"Not really, my lord and lady," Jol-dar replied. Several warning signs went off in David and Tanya's mind. They had been sure he had been the first to find Tanya according to the meetings with the other scholars. David determined it best to present all the information they had in order to press Jol-dar for the truth.

"According to the other scholars on the project, you were the first one among them to come into the chamber, and to find Lady Tanya unconscious on the floor," David pressed.

"Oh, I was the first one among all the scholars to enter the chamber. I thought you meant I was the first one to find her," Jol-dar replied with a slight laugh in his voice, delighted that he had found the error in the conversation.

"There was someone already in the chamber when you came in?" Tanya continued.

"Oh of course. There was you, my lady." He literally giggled at the thought of the obvious.

"You don't get out very much, do you?" David interposed.

"*Get out much?*" Jol-dar echoed. "Get out where?"

"It was a rhetorical question," David suggested.

"Oh, those can be the most distracting of all. You see, language is a precise art. Communication is a science in and of itself. Many times people ask one question, but are actually seeking completely different information. This can delay conversations forever. And then when you throw in the rhetorical question… well, any chance of an intelligent exchange of information becomes nil." David groaned in the back of his mind. The last thing he needed was someone who took so much delight in his own knowledge.

"Besides yourself, and Lady Tanya, was there anyone else in the chamber of records when you entered?" David redirected the focus of the conversation.

"But of course. There was Unter the Healer. He was already caring for Lady Tanya…"

Even as Jol-dar finished responding to the question David and Tanya were calling out the name of the Magarian spy, slamming their chairs back so quickly that they fell over, and bounding from the room, leaving Jol-dar continuing to talk to the empty room. The surprising thing was that it didn't seem to matter that no one else was there to listen.

"Tanya!" David called as they came to a split in the hallway.

"I'm way ahead of you. I'll take his house, you go to the dungeon." The two moved like a well-oiled machine; each knowing the role they needed to perform. Tanya drafted two of the guards at the door of the castle to follow her into the streets and to Unter's home. David bounded down the stone steps to the lower level of the castle. As he rounded a bend in the corridor, he nearly bowled over one of the guards standing watch.

"Grab the keys and follow me!" he shouted as he caught his weight on the ball of his left foot, pivoted around the guard, and then bounded back in his original direction without breaking pace. It took the guard a second to realize who had given the order, snatch the keys, and fall into line behind the Steward of Dula.

They came to a thick wooden door along the hallway. David stopped and scooped the keys from the guard's hand and fumbled for a moment to find the right one. The guard carefully reclaimed the keys, identified the proper one for this door, and unlocked the mechanism. As David slid back the bolt which held the door fast in the block wall, an ear-piercing screech tore at the air. Something big and black filled the doorway, and David reacted involuntarily to pull the guard back and draw his own sword. To his surprise, the guard had already stepped out of range, drawn his own sword, and swung at the shadow creature as it passed them. Both David and the guard had managed to wound the creature, but it was not enough to stop its escape.

David tore a torch from the place where it flickered on the wall, and dove into the cell. The guard, never missing a beat, was right behind him. The limp form of Unter the Healer hung in the air as they entered. David glanced to see if any ropes connected Unter to the rafters or ceiling above. There was nothing to explain his being motionless in mid air. The guard behind him must have also noticed the lack of support for he whispered a quick *"Teacher preserve us!"*

As the Knight of Es-Soh-En stepped forward, whatever held Unter suspended in the air was removed, and the form crumpled into David's arms. The Steward of Dula caught the healer and eased him onto the floor, sliding several handfuls of straw under the healer's head.

"Should I call for a healer?" the guard inquired almost to the door as he spoke.

"I don't think any healer can help him now. He's dead." David leaned back so the guard could see Unter's face. The healer's eyes had rolled back in their sockets; his skin was a pasty white; his lips were purple. Blood oozed out of two puncture marks above the jugular in his neck.

"Send for someone to prepare the body for burial. Then come back. I'll want you to come with me and make a full report." As the guard left the cell, David stood up and let the torchlight illuminate the walls. Smeared in a reddish-brown substance were symbols on the walls. Unless someone physically came into the cell they would not have been able to have enough light to see them. As David studied them, he recognized them as various symbols used in the worship of Cronis. As the Child of Earth studied the symbols, the guard returned. David leaned forward at one symbol in particular.

"See if he still has his left index finger," David instructed. The guard was suddenly nervous as he saw the markings on the wall. He knelt down over the body, pulled back the long sleeve of the healer's robe. The sudden exclamation by the guard told David what he wanted to know.

"How could he have done that to himself?" the guard stammered, trying to regain his control.

"He had to. This symbol here requires the sacrifice of one body part for the incantation to work," David noted as he touched the torch to the wall. The symbol sizzled from the heat which told David it had only been recently drawn, and the blood used to make the symbol had not completely dried. The smell made David turn up his nose. Bring me oil." David instructed. "Lots of it."

The guard darted out of the cell. David suspected the smell was as much the cause for his speed as the order. When he came back, David took the buckets of oil and used straw to paint every inch of the walls with the oil. The Steward of the Throne then took several buckets and poured them on the floor of the cell until a layer completely covered the floor. He took the last of the oil, and soaked the body of Unter.

"Now get outside." As soon as the guard was in the corridor, David stepped outside the cell and threw the torch in on the floor. Both men had to throw themselves against the wall to avoid the fireball and intense heat that erupted from the room. In their minds, both heard the wail of some lost soul. It was only a moment of the scream, and it was felt more than heard; but it would haunt both of them forever.

As they stood watching the flames burn the symbols off the wall and consume the body of Unter, several men arrived to prepare the body for burial.

"There won't be a body," David announced. "Nothing is to be removed from this room."

"Not even the ashes of the healer?" asked the man who would normally take care of burial and funeral arrangements.

"Nothing!" David's voice was firm on this matter. "Are you followers of Teacher?" The question caught everyone off guard. It was not the sort of questioning they were used to in their line of work.

"Of course not!" the head man finally exclaimed when he regained his composure.

"Are any of you followers of Teacher?" Finally one man near the back of the small gathering raised his trembling hand. No one else seemed to notice as they were all watching David. David thought it best to protect the man since it was obvious this was not something he wanted to be widely known. "Alright, get out of here. All of you."

"But the body must be buried," the leader of the group insisted. "Dulan law requires everyone the right to a burial."

"You are not a follower of Teacher, are you?" David asked again.

"No!' the man declared.

"And you're not a follower of Es-Soh-En, either, are you?"

"Of course not."

"And what about the Adoni?"

"What about them?"

"You don't follow Them, either?"

"Absolutely not. I am a man of considerable education."

"Then why is it so important to bury a dead body?" David asked.

"To avoid disease," the man replied.

"What kind of disease will come from a pile of ashes?" David pressed.

"But the law…" the man began again, but David cut him off.

"The law is based upon the Law handed down by Es-Soh-En. If you do not believe in Him, then why are you so adamant about keeping His Law?" The anger was obvious in the Knight of Es-Soh-En's voice. "Es-Soh-En gave the Law in the Garden of Tangar. No body should be left unburied because it pollutes the land. This body shall be taken care of, but not to avoid disease. It shall be taken care of to comply with the Law of Es-Soh-En!" As the crew began to leave, David called out, pointing to the man who had raised his hand so none could see. "You, stay behind. I'll have you take care of the body. The rest, get out of here."

There was a great deal of grumbling as the others left the dungeon area. Once it was just David, the guard, and the worker; David turned to the man and asked him more directly, "Are you a follower of Teacher?"

The man seemed suddenly uncomfortable and nervous. David pressed harder. "Are you a follower of Teacher? Your very life will depend upon your answer."

The color drained from the man's face. Then he seemed to find some inner strength. There was a sparkle in his eyes which had not been there moments before. He had made a decision, and the decision now gave him confidence and peace. When he spoke, it was not the trembling voice of a down-and-out worker. It was the voice of a man who was confident and sure, perhaps for the first time in his life. "Yes! I am a follower of Teacher. Kill me if you want to, but I won't forsake Him."

"Who said anything about killing you?" David retorted.

"You said my life depended on it," the worker challenged.

"Not that I would kill you," David laughed when he realized the impression the worker had. "No, I would never kill a follower of Teacher. I am a Knight of Es-Soh-En I serve the Adoni. I could never kill one of my own. No, I need you to complete the process in this room. It was in this room that Unter the Healer committed acts against what is natural to open a portal of communication through the power of the Dark Lord. Inside this room, the Dark One still has power. You must go inside, after the flames have died down, you must remove the door, burn it in the same fashion, and then brick up the doorway. None must enter this room for a period of seven years. If you had not been a follower of Teacher, then the Dark One could have claimed you, but your faith in Teacher will protect you. Hold onto it, and never let go."

"I have been foolish, my lord. I always followed Teacher from afar. I would only claim Him when it was safe or convenient. I would denounce Him if it was expected by those I was with. I will not let that happen, ever again."

"Then some good has come of this after all," David suddenly realized that he didn't know the man's name. "What is your name?"

"Gart!" the worker replied. David extended his hand to greet the man. It was obvious Gart was impressed and nervous at the same time. He clutched David's hand and shook vigorously. Then he seemed to have something on his mind. "My lord?"

"Yes?"

"I don't mean to be so bold, and I apologize if I am, but you are the Child of Earth who went with Queen Dianna on the Quest for the Sword?"

"GART!" the guard challenged as if the worker had just insulted the Knight of Es-Soh-En.

"It's alright." David said, coming between the two. "Yes. I am the Child of Earth who went with Queen Dianna on the Quest for the Sword."

"I didn't mean to doubt you, it's just that that was quite some time ago," Gart stammered.

"I know. It's hard for many to believe." David admitted.

"The reason I was asking was I wondered if you could remember an ancestor of mine?"

"If I can," David offered.

"His name was Tonru," Gart began.

"Tonru and Yeema?" David exclaimed. "The shop keepers?"

"Then you know them?" Gart cried out.

"Yes! They were the ones who supplied Kal and Tra during the occupation. Their store was the starting point to hide the followers of Es-Soh-En from the Magarians."

"Then it is true?" Gart began to weep. "I had heard so many stories, but the wise men told me they were only myths and legends. I always wanted to believe, but each time I mentioned my ancestors, people would laugh and make fun of me…or them." Gart wiped the tears from his eyes.

"Tonru and Yeema stood for the Adoni when it was not safe. They gave when they really could not afford to. Kal told me a brief tale when we ate at the Feast of the Sword…"

"The very first Feast?' Gart asked

"Yes. We left after that Feast, and we didn't make it back for two hundred years. It's been a long time since I had the chance to visit with Kal and Tra. But during the feast Kal told me that once Tonru gave all the fresh fruit he had to Kal to feed the followers. Fruit was scarce then because Magar confiscated it for their own tables. Someone came in and wanted to buy fruit; had a lot of gold to pay for it, but Tonru didn't have any left. The man begged Tonru to go and look to see if even one piece of fruit might be left.

"Tonru went back into the storage room, and found it filled to the brim with the best fruit of any crop in all of Dula. He ran back out to sell the man what he wanted, but the man was gone. His purse of gold was on the counter with a brief note: *For the Following*. Tonru and Yeema contacted Tra and Kal, and transferred all the fruit to the Cave of Whispers." David related the story with joy as he saw the excitement in the eyes of Gart as the worker listened, hungry for every word.

"There is also a story among my family that even after the Sword was returned, Tonru and Yeema kept finding fruit in that storage room, and even if it took months to sell it all, it never went bad. People would always come to them first because their fruit was the best in all the land," Gart added. He waited a moment; then looked into the eyes of the Knight of Es-Soh-En with true joy. "Thank you."

"I suggest you find a soldier named Handar. He is a descendent of Gen who also lived at the time of Tonru and Yeema. I think you will have much in common. Tell him I sent you. Oh, and if anyone gives you any problems about my instructions, have them come and see me," David advised. He then motioned for the guard to follow him as he returned to the upper levels.

CHAPTER TEN

AN ALLY IN THE RANKS

As the pair walked out of the castle and into the streets, David turned to the guard at his side.

"So what's your name? I can't keep calling you *guard* all the time."

"Agron," the guard replied. He did not seem prepared to offer much more information, and so David felt it best to strike a conversation in order to gain more knowledge about his companion.

"You seem to be a man who has been tested in battle," the Knight of Es-Soh-En observed.

"Thank you, my lord, but you are being more than kind," Agron replied. He almost relaxed, but pulled his protection about him.

"No, I'm serious. When we opened the door to Unter's cell, I fully expected to have to protect you. Instead, you are already acting, moving to a position of defense, drawing your sword, and attacking before most soldiers would have realized what they were dealing with."

"Thank you, my lord," was all Agron would say.

"You do realize that I'm trying to have a conversation here, don't you?" David joked.

"My lord, you are the Steward of the Throne of Dula. You are a Knight of Es-Soh-En. You are a Child of Earth. You are the Air-Walker..."

"*Air-walker?*" David cut in. "Are they still using that title? It's been so many years."

"It's just that it is not my place to speak freely with one in your position. There are reasons why we have ranks in the army. There are reasons why troops do not associate with those who give the commands," Agron observed.

"And what would those reasons be?" David probed.

"We are the ones who go into battle. We are the ones who give our lives. You stay behind and determine who is to live and who is to die. It is best that I remain only a guard to you so that you are free to make the right decisions."

"Agron?" David began. "When have I ever stayed behind and sent others to battle for me?"

"Not you personally, sir," Agron stammered. "I did not mean to be disrespectful to you, sir. It's just that this is the way it is between soldiers and officers."

"Then it is not a good way," David noted. "If all my troops are nameless faces who pass before me and out into battle, then I am a foolish leader. I do not know the strengths or weaknesses of these men. I might deploy the wrong man to the wrong place. I might send too few men to hold an important area. I might send someone into battle before he or she is ready."

The reference to a woman being sent into battle brought a reaction from Agron. David smiled and continued.

"A woman going into battle seems strange to you, Agron?"

"It's just that they would not do well in battle, sir. They are not as strong as a man. They do not know how to handle a sword like a man. The other men would be worrying about her, become distracted in battle, and might be injured or killed," Agron offered.

"Yes, I've heard all of those reasons before, too. The surprising thing is, every time I hear them, I turn to my sister and ask her what she thinks about them."

"I am sorry, my lord. I did not mean to insult Lady Tanya." It was obvious that Agron was having a very difficult time conversing with the Steward of Dula.

"That's alright. I won't tell her you said that. But the point is that we can't make generalities. There are exceptions to most opinions. I would send my sister into battle without concern because I know she is able to handle it. There are some men I would not send into battle unless there was no other choice because I know that they could not handle it. This is not just about women, but it is also about men. This is why I am going to be training with the troops this afternoon. I want to stand across from the troops I am sending into battle, cross swords with them, and see what they can do."

"It is not safe for the Steward of Dula to engage in such combat," Agron declared.

"Oh, I'll be careful. I don't want to wound anyone by accident. We will need all the men we can."

"I was thinking of your safety, my lord."

"You know, I do have a name," David suggested.

"I know that, my lord. However, you also have a great many titles. Most of which are unique to all the Lands of the Adoni. I know of no one else who is *Friend of the Unicorn*, *Air-Walker*, or *Steward of the Throne of Dula*. Only one other holds the title of *Child of Earth*, and only twenty or thirty hold the title of *Knight of Es-Soh-En*."

"Actually, there are one hundred and forty-four who hold that title," David corrected. Agron's expression told David that so much had been lost concerning those who serve the Adoni. He paused for a moment and then changed his approach. "Yes, I see your point. As long as you don't start trying to determine which title is more important that the others, you'll do fine." David joked recalling a visit he and Teacher had to the undersea city of Janadis. The humor was lost on the soldier, and so David continued. "The point is, a title is simply a way of recognizing what some has done or is going to do. The name is the person. We have just been in battle together. Admittedly it was only one sword stroke each, but we stood against a Shadow Thing and drove it off. We went into a room where the Dark Lord held power, and came out alive. I would think that what we have been through together would give us some sense of camaraderie."

"But to call a commanding officer by name instead of rank is a break down in discipline. It shows disrespect."

"Let me be the judge of when I feel you are being disrespectful. When we are not in battle, or not among the troops, I would like for you to call me *David*. That is my name."

"Very well...David." The word was stuck in his mouth, and Agron had a difficult time speaking it comfortably.

"Agron? Agron?" David mused for a moment. "It seems to me that I once knew of a Captain Agron who served Dianna many years ago. It was on my last visit to Dula."

"I am named for him," Agron confessed. "He was my great, great, great..." here he seemed to lose count of the number of generations involved, and tried to recall them all on his fingers. He finally gave up and simply said, "He is several generations removed. He served Queen Dianna with honor, and when I was born, my father prayed to the Adoni that I, too, would one day serve with such honor."

"And how did someone who comes from a family with so much honor end up serving in the lowly position of dungeon guard?" David had hoped he had worded it right, but he knew it still hurt Agron's pride. It showed only for a moment in the man's eyes, and then he reverted to his sense of duty, and moved on.

"I serve where I am needed," he offered in his defense.

"And you serve very well. But I can tell that your abilities are far beyond that of those needed to guard prisoners. Who did you tick off?" David meant the comment as a joke, but it struck home more accurately than he realized.

"It was Lord Ki-el." Agron finally confessed. David did not know that the man's position was the result of offending someone in power. The Knight of Es-Soh-En was about to explain that to Agron, and then thought better of it. The soldier had opened up to David. This was something he had been trying to get his companion to do. To tell him now that it was a joke, would have destroyed what progress he had made.

"I was one of the ones who cried out for war when Tondar was pinned to the castle gates by Magarian arrows. I know the story better than most. Tondar was a close friend. We had grown up together, trained together, served together. Queen Dianna had asked me to speak at the Council meeting when she sought permission to go to war. A week later I was broken from my rank and assigned to the prisons. Lord Ki-el caught me alone one day, and warned that if I spoke out once more, or if I attracted Queen Dianna's attention to my punishment, not only myself, but my family would suffer."

"My lord…David. I…I need to say something. If you truly seek the truth, then let me speak of a greater truth; one that has been silenced by the Council."

"Something silenced by the Council? Now that's an idea I haven't considered before." The sudden pale color on Agron's face told David his companion had missed the attempt at humor once more. "That was a joke Agron. Get to know me, and you will find I use humor a lot to deal with situations. The real surprise is when the Council doesn't hide something from the people. Go ahead and speak freely."

Agron stammered for a moment trying to find the best way to start his revelation. Finally he seized the moment, and simply blurted it out, "The thieves in the Gen Forest are really Magarian troops!"

"That wasn't too painful now, was it?" David asked.

"My lord, I knew most of the men who went into battle against the thieves. They were under my command. I led the first attack. We found the thieves, but they were too well-armed. They were too-well disciplined. It was an army, not a band of thieves that we fought in the forest. Because I had been injured, Queen Dianna had sent another officer to lead the second police action in the Gen Forest. When the second force was wiped out, and one of our own pinned to the door with Magarian arrows, I knew – we all knew it wasn't just thieves in the woods."

"And what if I told you that I believed you?" David offered.

"Then all these years as a prison guard would have been worth it since it gave me the chance to speak freely with you."

"The Adoni have a way of doing that, don't They?" David joked.

"There is something else," Agron pressed.

"Well, I have news as well, but I will let you finish before I speak."

"As long as I have your ear, my lord. There are many among the troops who believe as I do."

"Who follow the words of Teacher?" David asked.

"Is it that obvious?" Agron asked.

"I wouldn't have allowed you back into the cell once I saw the symbols unless I was sure," David confessed.

"Thank you my lord. Yes, there are many who secretly follow the words of Teacher among the army; but I was speaking of my belief that the thieves in the forest are actually Magarian troops.

We all believe that it is only a matter of time before they attack, and we will have to go into battle."

"Then they are wiser than those who sit on the Council," David suggested.

"The point is, my lord. I have been secretly training many of them for the last few years. No one knows of this except those who are part of it. We have an army, a small army that's true – maybe three or four hundred; but we have been preparing for war. If my superiors were to know of this, we could all be brought up on charges. But I tell you this to try and emphasize to you how serious I believe the danger to Dula to be."

"Then let me speak and put your mind at rest Agron. This morning I met with the Council." The look in Agron's eyes told him he had been this route before, and had found that the Council had convinced those he spoke with that all was well. What hope had been in the soldier's eyes was staring to die. David stopped in the streets, placed a hand on the soldier's shoulder to comfort and encourage him. "It's not what you think. The same reports you just gave me were brought to my attention last night. I met with the Council this morning to inform them that we have sent a Declaration of War to Magar. It is my intention to drive the forces of Magar out of the forest, and out of our kingdom."

"My lord?" Agron stammered. Tears were already in his eyes. "We will fight for Dula?"

"We fight for Dula." David agreed. "Now give me your report on Unter."

It was difficult for Agron to focus on the report as his mind was racing with various details to be addressed in preparation for the coming battles. David finally felt it best to ask the questions he needed specifically answered in order to move his investigation along.

"Who was the last person to see Unter?" David asked.

"I was, my lord. I had checked in on him about an hour before you came. It was part of my rounds. He was sitting there on the floor, mumbling, chanting and rocking back and forth. If I had known that it had something to do with the Dark Lord I would have stopped him immediately. I thought that it was all part of the strange rituals of being a healer."

"You couldn't have known. Few have seen such rituals and lived to tell of them," David noted. "Who was his last visitor?"

"His servant came to visit him just after he had been arrested. They spoke for some time. Unter gave him numerous instructions regarding patients and care. He told him that certain medicines were to be found in his home, and to take them to other healers to give to his patients."

"Still caring for the ill all the time," David noted.

"I found that strange, my lord." Agron admitted.

"How so?"

"Well, he spoke of various patients, but his servant had to keep asking him who it was he was talking about. At first the servant seemed shocked that Unter had any patients except for those at the royal court. At one point the servant made some comment that made me think all this concern for the ill was new for Unter, and the servant was surprised by the change in his master."

Something seemed to click in David's mind. "Did Unter give anything to his servant?"

"Mostly the instructions were verbal. He made the servant recite them several times to make sure he had it right. It had to be word-for-word. All the medicines were in his home in various places that almost sounded like they were hidden away. Some were behind bookcases; others were in drawers which had false backs. A couple were even inside books that had been hollowed out. He did give the servant some written instructions. He said it was a special case he had been working on."

"Written instructions?" Every alarm in David's mind went off. "Was it a piece of paper, or more of a scroll?"

"I guess you could call it a scroll. It looked like a piece of parchment which had been rolled up and tied with a ribbon."

"Agron?" David broke in trying to keep his excitement under control. "I need a favor of you."

"Merely ask, my lord and it shall be done."

"Pentra is even now reviewing the troops for battle. Go to him and tell him that I sent you. Tell him to seal the city, and find Unter's servant. If he needs to send patrols out to search the roads between here and the Gen Forest do it at once. Give him a detailed description of Unter's servant. Oh," David paused. "What was your rank before you spoke to the Council?"

"I was a captain," Agron admitted.

"Tell Pentra that I have given you a promotion, and I will be by later to confirm it."

"A promotion?" Agron stammered.

"Yes, tell him that you are in command of the army only under him. What's that called? Second-in-command, isn't it? Think you can handle it?"

"My lord," Agron began.

"Enough with the *my lords*. Get moving. I have to find Lady Tanya. I'll be there in about two hours."

With those instructions David slapped Agron on the shoulder, squeezed for encouragement, and sped off down the street towards Unter's home leaving a befuddled Agron running in the other direction toward the barracks.

CHAPTER ELEVEN

THE PRICE WHICH WAS PAID

Tanya took her index finger and made as little contact as possible with the drawer in order to slide it tightly closed; turning up her nose, and gagging as she did. It had been an hour of searching, and all Tanya found were things which disgusted her further, or things which she had no desire to find. To say that Unter was disorganized would have been a massive understatement. Filth, dust and clutter were the only kinds of interior decoration he knew how to maintain. While she had been going through stacks on a desk, she came across one large leather-bound volume with bright silver lettering. She could not make out the language of the title. She opened it, and had to control her own reaction. The pages were a mass of symbols used in the worship of Cronis. Several were symbols of human sacrifice, and it was obvious the lettering was penned in blood. Even now a small fire burned in the hearth, fueled by the remnants of the book. She was wiping her hands again on a cloth she had found when David came in.

"Unter gave the scroll to his servant!" he announced as he entered the room. The smell caught him off-guard, and he nearly choked on its power.

"Ray-ton?" Tanya replied. "Oh, you'll get used to it," she added in reference to the overpowering odor.

"I doubt it." He worked his way past the debris littering the floor and doorway to come down to the sunken level where Tanya was still searching. "His servant's name was Ray-ton?"

"I found it among several notes." She motioned to the stack of papers on the table. "I imagine the smell is what made him feel safe about leaving things lying about. No one would come in here on purpose"

"I was speaking with Agron, and he over-heard a conversation between Unter and Ray-ton," David began.

"Agron? Have I met him?" she asked.

"No. He was a guard in the prison, but I found out a lot more about him. I made him second-in-command of the army."

"I guess he impressed you," Tanya exclaimed.

"I'll fill you in later. It looks like things are going our way. He was the captain who led the first attack in the Gen Forest ten years ago. He was wounded and missed the second campaign. The man who was killed at the gates by Magarian arrows was a friend of his named Tondar. When Agron spoke at a Council meeting to support war with Magar, he was broken in rank, sent to guard the dungeons, and Ki-el threatened him to keep him quiet about it."

"It's nice to know Ki-el is abusive to everyone. I thought it was just us at first," Tanya noted.

"Well, turns out Agron believed it would eventually come to war, whether the Council wanted it or not, so it turns out that he's been training about three or four hundred soldiers secretly so they'll be ready."

"I can see why you're impressed."

"I also found out he's a follower of Teacher."

"That's another point in his favor. So what did he hear during this conversation with Unter and Ray-ton?"

"Unter made it sound like he was giving his servant instructions to care for several patients, but Agron told me it sounded like Ray-ton had no idea Unter was treating people outside the palace, namely you. Unter told him about something behind the bookcase, a drawer with a false back, and something inside of a hollowed-out book. He then had Ray-ton memorize certain instructions word-for-word, and then handed him a small piece of parchment rolled up and tied with a ribbon."

"Sounds like the scroll," Tanya agreed.

"I've ordered the city sealed, and a search made for Ray-ton. Agron went to Pentra with the order and the description."

"How did Unter take the news that we knew where the scroll was?"

"Hard to say. It seems he's dead."

"Dead!" Tanya responded. "How could he be dead? He's in the dungeon."

"Seems he was practicing the black arts to contact someone. What he got was a shadow thing. Agron and I wounded it, but it still got away."

"So what did you do?"

"I burned the body and cleansed the cell with fire. I've ordered it sealed for seven years."

"I'm sure the Council will love to hear this one," Tanya suggested.

"You did know about the symbols on the cell wall?" David offered in his defense.

"Symbols? Written blood?" she probed.

"Those are the ones."

"Where'd he get the – let me guess. Missing a finger?"

"You don't seem very surprised," David observed.

"Actually I found one of the books he wrote on the subject. If you want to take a look, I think there's a few ashes left in the fireplace. Ah! Here we go." She pulled the drawer all the way out of the dresser, and slid open the back of the drawer to reveal a small compartment. She reached into the small area and pulled out a key.

"I take it that Ray-ton hasn't made it back here since he spoke with Unter," David observed.

"Now if we just knew what this went to." Tanya mused. David had been pulling every book from each shelf, flipping them opened, dropping them in a pile, and moving on all the while Tanya had been exploring the dresser drawers.

"Got it!" he announced. He held a large volume opened, revealing its hollowed-out center, and produced a smaller book. He tossed it to Tanya as he quickly examined those books left on the shelf. "That's the only one," he declared.

"So all that's left now is to see what's behind the book case," Tanya suggested. The two tested several bookcases, but most seemed fastened firmly to the wall. The last one they checked swung out on a concealed hinge. There was a door built flush to the wall. Tanya found the lock, tested the key; and was rewarded with the sounds of tumblers moving into position. There was a hand hold embedded in the door, and Tanya pulled it opened.

The Children of Earth discovered an entire room built behind the bookcase. When David brought a lamp into it, they could see that it was filled with documents, charts, maps, books, and other resources and equipment. Notes were strewn over several tabletops. They were reports on her condition, bits and pieces of information about the palace and the people in power. None of the notes had been sent. Tanya even came across one which had recommended that Magar attack immediately since everything was in place.

She found another stack of documents which seemed to be more organized than the others. Tanya picked up the first one.

"It doesn't make any sense," she noted.

"Code?" her brother suggested.

"It would have to be. Now if we just knew how to crack it."

"Don't have to," David replied. She looked up and saw he was going over a document rather quickly, referring to the small book they had found inside the large book on the bookcase. "This is the code book right here." He let out a long whistle.

"What is it?" she asked coming over to see the document he was reading.

"This is a complete organizational chart of the entire Magarian spy ring here in Dula. Names, positions, code references. There's also a complete listing of where all their supplies are stored, and what those supplies and weapons are."

Tanya took the document and the book from her brother. She then gave the entire room with its vast collection of documents a long look. "This," she declared, "is going to take a while."

"Then I will leave you to your research. I promised to meet with Pentra to confirm the messages I sent through Agron," David announced. As he ducked back into the streets, he noted how bright the glare was on his eyes, and he then realized how dark the interior of Unter's home had been. The servants of Cronis always seemed to have a desire for darkness.

As the Knight of Es-Soh-En made his way through the streets to the barracks, he passed through the market place. It was alive with bustle and hawking. Each merchant shouted out for customers to see their wares. One would begin to shout the prices trying to get a passer-by's attention. Another vendor selling a similar or identical item would then shout out a cheaper price. Not a lot cheaper, just enough to frustrate his competition. It wouldn't be long until the vendors were no longer shouting for customers, but were screaming at each other. As they bartered, begged, and manipulated; he was glad he had been in common clothes. If it had been known that he had money, power, or position, they would have swarmed over him like locust on a field of ripe grain. This was why the upper class always sent their servants to the marketplace for them. He paused with that thought. Unter must have sent Ray-ton to the market. Perhaps not all the trips were to purchase food or wares.

David made a mental note to have Pentra check the merchants who made regular trips to other countries. Unter may have been using them to carry messages. Obviously the price of the spell to make direct contact was a little too high to perform except in extreme emergencies. The normal route would have been to send Ray-ton to the marketplace to meet with the contact merchant, pass the messages to him or her; and then the merchant could send the messages on under the guise of a business trip. If that were the case, then the messages still on the tables in the hidden room would be a good indicator as to when the last batch of messages had been sent.

***

The barracks was its own fortress. Here the army was housed. Here they trained and drilled. It also served as an armory and a supply post. The Knight of Es-Soh-En could hear steel striking steel from inside. It was the standard three-step sparing practice. One soldier would advance for three steps, striking with each step. The other soldier would retreat for three steps blocking the attack. The positions would then be reversed allowing both partners to practice the attacking motions and the defensive motions. As David came to the gates, a sharp voice cried out.

"Hold! Who goes there?" came the crisp cry from the senior sentry. David noted the crossed spears blocking his way.

"David James, Steward of the Throne of Dula!" he replied back. He had to stifle a laugh when he saw the color drain from the guards' faces. They did not know what the Steward of the Throne of Dula looked like. They were suddenly faced with the choice of trusting this stranger and letting him in, or of endangering their careers but refusing entry until he could prove who he was. To the respect of the senior officer on duty, the decision was made to send for Pentra to verify the identity of the visitor. The captain had also chosen to move additional guards around so that any chance David had of retreating at the last moment were cut off.

Pentra arrived, saw the situation, and was about to tear into the captain for detaining the Steward; but David discretely cleared his throat before the first word could be said. Pentra was sharp enough to catch the clue before he took action.

"I'll speak with you later," Pentra promised, and motioned for the guards to let David through.

"I apologize, sire. I will see that the man shall be punished for his insolence."

"Really, I was going to suggest that you reward his diligence, and encourage such actions in the future," David replied.

"My lord?" Pentra was caught off guard.

"Too many people have used their titles to get what they want around here. From reports I have heard and things I have seen – And I mean no disrespect, friend Pentra, for you have a good army. It's just that some soldiers have been beaten into submission by those in power. The fear of punishment for doing their jobs has made some more concerned about their own careers than the safety of the kingdom. Your captain had no way of knowing if I was the Steward. He chose to endanger his career than to let a possible spy into the fortress. That kind of dedication to duty should always be encouraged and rewarded."

"I had not considered it in that light, David," Pentra replied. "You are right about those in power bullying my men; but the Council seemed to always favor their own, and I was ordered to enforce their desires," Pentra offered by way of apology.

"The Council will not have that kind of power over the army again while I'm the Steward. Proper protocol shall be followed. If someone claims to be of high rank or position, they will be treated with the respect due that rank or position, but no one is to break the security of the fortress, palace, or city until their identity and authority is proven…Speaking of such. Have you spoken with Agron?"

"Yes. He arrived a little while ago."

"I don't want to cause a conflict with you, but I have seen him in action. I have seen his heart. His love for the Adoni and the kingdom are commendable. I also found he has been taking action to protect the kingdom when the Council sought to punish him for putting the safety of the kingdom first. I want him to be your second-in-command. You will find he is a valuable resource, and even filled with a few surprises."

"That is quite an announcement," Pentra noted.

"*Announcement?*" David replied.

"Agron simply told me you had sent orders to seal the city and find Ray-ton. He also said you would come by later to confirm the order, and would have an announcement."

"It's nice to know he is still discrete. Do you see any problem with his promotion? Speak honestly to me. If I am misreading him, I want to know."

"It is a good choice," Pentra answered without hesitation. "When he was captain, I knew he would make a fine officer and leader. He was able to command respect from his men. He had the highest success record of any other. When I was given the order to break him in rank and transfer him, I fought it before the Council, and only my own position on the Council protected me. I will call the troops together and announce his promotion."

"I want this to be your decision as well, friend. The safety of the kingdom depends on us making the right decisions. I would rather disappoint him and protect the kingdom, than to press someone on you that you are not comfortable with."

"I have no regrets about it, David. If I were to have a second-in-command, then Agron would have been my first choice. It's just I've never had a second-in-command before."

"*No second-in-command?!*" David was shocked. "There's always someone who is second-in-command. That's just the way an army is."

"I know that, and you know that. The Council would not allow any one to be appointed to such a position. They saw it as a political structure in the army, and felt it would weaken the military."

"But if something were to happen to you, then who would lead the troops?"

"The very point I made to the Council when they announced the restructuring of my army. They told me the law now forbids such a political structure in the military; and that if I needed to be replaced, they would convene and appoint someone."

David stopped in their tracks. "As of this moment, the army is under your control, Pentra. Ignore all the laws set down by the Council. Make those decisions to restructure the military so that it is efficient and effective. When you have everything in place, bring it to me for final approval. We don't have time to fight the Council on this matter."

As they came into the practice yard, David used his enhanced eyesight to take in all the details before him. There were several hundred men before him, but he could see each one clearly. He noticed the way they stood, how they moved. He could tell which ones held their swords too tight or too loose. He noted the ones who were focused on the drill, and those who were simply going through the motions.

Pentra called the troops together, and while they stood in formation, he called Agron out of the ranks. He then announced to the entire army that Agron was promoted to second-in-command of the entire army. Pentra then called Wen-Gar forward. He was the captain of the guard over the gates who had halted David's entrance. The soldier looked as if he believed he was about to be executed, and when Pentra promoted him to third-in-command, it was an obvious shock. Pentra used the promotion of Wen-Gar to drive home the point that duty and honor would be rewarded while self-interests and favoritism would not. When the troops were sent back to their training, there were congratulations all around.

"Looks like good choices," David noted.

"I think so," Pentra laughed.

"There's something else you ought to know about your second-in-command," David continued.

"What's that?"

"He's believed the thieves in the forest were an advanced strike force from Magar. He's also believed it was only a matter of time before there would be war, even if the Council did not want war."

"Many of the troops feel that way."

"Yes, well, he's the only one I know of who did something about it."

"He has?" The shock in Pentra' voice was genuine.

"He told me that he has been secretly training an army to fight when the time came."

"WHAT?!"

"I thought that would get a reaction from you," David laughed.

"That would save us months" Pentra declared. "How big a force? Who is involved? How far along are they?"

"As for size, he said about three to four hundred. As to how far along they are, and who they are, he didn't tell me; but I think I can spot the ones who are here now."

"That would be quite a feat," Pentra declared.

"Not if you know what to look for. I saw Agron in a brief battle. I've watched how he moves. When we came into the yard, I studied him as he practiced the three-step drill. From there it was easy to look for others who performed the drill the way he did."

"You can tell all of that?" Pentra was truly impressed.

"Walk with me, and I'll show you." As the pair moved among the men, David pointed to the way Agron stood. It was a very strong stance. The legs were spread so they were in line with the hips and shoulders; no further apart nor closer together whether the legs were front-and-back or side-to-side. When they moved, they made a fluid motion to bring the feet together directly under the body to support the weight, then back out as they stepped forward or back. At any point in the movement, the balance was centered, and the soldier could resist any attack. The body also remained at the same height throughout the motion, never rising or falling.

"Agron knows the value of a solid foundation," the Knight of Es-Soh-En observed. "I would suspect it was an expensive lesson for it's emphasized in every motion. Nothing flashy. Nothing fancy. Just good posture and solid footing. That attention to such a small detail would lead me to believe that some event called attention to the importance of it, and was an event of life-changing proportions."

"You read more in people's motions than most would find in a book. I shall be interested in speaking with Agron to see how precise your observations are."

As they continued their inspection, David pointed to arm motions, body language and posture throughout each of the drills. Pentra would comment on each detail. He, too, had a great store of knowledge about battle posture, but even he had not considered some of the details David showed him.

When they had finished studying the troops, Pentra called Agron to his side.

"I understand you've been keeping something from me," he offered.

"I'm sorry sir. I was afraid the Council would disapprove."

"Oh they would. They will…but who cares. Call your troops together Agron. Let's see what you've got."

"Heart Company, front and center!" Agron called out across the practice yard. True to David's prediction, all of these who used the same style as Agron removed themselves from their partners, came to the front of the yard, and stood perfect formation. Wen Gar stood at the head of Heart Company as he had been Agron's second-in-command. Pentra looked at David and laughed, slapping him on the shoulder.

"Nothing gets past those eyes of yours," he declared. "Now, let's review the troops, commanders." Wen Gar joined them, and the four walked the ranks, commenting on what they saw. To Agron's pride, each of his men was perfect in their posture, weapon care, and attire. After the review the men were dismissed from practice as a reward for their hard work. To Pentra's surprise, they requested to stay on, and train with the others as long as the other troops practiced.

"On one condition," Pentra told the men. "Break up and select a partner from those not of your company. Work with them. Teach them what you know. Dismissed!"

As the company broke formation and returned to the drills, Wen Gar took command of the troops. David and Pentra walked with Agron to the armory to inspect the weapons and the construction of weapons.

"So why is it called the *Heart Company?*" Pentra asked.

"You may think me a fool, sir, but it came from something that happened to me several years ago."

"I hope I don't start thinking my second-in-command is a fool," Pentra joked.

"It's just that when I spoke of it to others, they laughed at me. I finally chose not to tell the story openly, only to those I could trust."

"I hope you feel comfortable trusting us," David offered. He lifted a sword and studied its blade, testing it for balance and craftsmanship.

"My brother and I served together," Agron began.

"Yes...good man. I was sorry to hear about his accident."

"*Accident?*" David enquired.

"We were practicing the three-step drill. I was still learning, he was still teaching. He insisted I be more aggressive in the drill. As we continued, his foot slipped as he stepped back. I couldn't stop in time, and stuck him down. The blow was fatal." Agron was struggling with the memory. As David and Pentra waited for Agron to collect himself and continue, Pentra shot a knowing look at the Knight of Es-Soh-En, amazed that he had been right in his estimation that the lesson about stance had been a costly one.

"I was with him in the infirmary. He was struggling with his breathing. Bleeding a great deal. All the while he told me it wasn't my fault. He then died as I knelt beside him. At that point I was still young. I did not understand the ways of the Adoni. I did not know how to accept death. I grabbed his hand and prayed. I prayed harder than I ever did before. I prayed that in the name of the Adoni he would come back to life. I prayed it like an incantation over and over again because I didn't know what else to do."

"*In the name of the Adoni* is a powerful term," David noted as he recalled that those very words had been the ones which brought the Curse over all the Lands of the Adoni.

"After several minutes, my brother's free hand clasped my own. I was filled with terror and joy. Somehow the Adoni had heard my cry. My brother was no longer dead." Agron's eyes contained the same joy of which he spoke.

"Back from the dead?" Pentra's voice was incredulous.

"You'd be surprised at what can be done in the name of the Adoni," David suggested.

"That wasn't the point," Agron continued. "My brother grasped my hand, and spoke to me. His eyes tore my soul as he pleaded with me to set him free. He told me that he had found himself upon the path to the Kingdom. Teacher had come to him. Teacher had welcomed him, embraced him. He told me that Teacher had parted his robes, and showed him the scar over His heart. *This is the price I paid for you.* Teacher told him. Then my prayers drew him back. He didn't want to stay. He wanted to go with Teacher, but I had to release him. I had to accept that this was all part of the PLAN. I closed my eyes, wept, and nodded my agreement. When I opened them, he was dead, just as before.

"I would have thought the whole thing but a dream except for the fact his hand still grasped mine. I created a shield that pictured the sword-pierced heart. It became the crest of my family. A few weeks later, Lendar saw the shield. It obviously disturbed him. The next day an order came down telling me to get rid of the shield and the symbol. I figured that as long as I was disobeying one order from the Council to forget about the threat by Magar, I might as well disobey the one that meant the most to me. I came to call my troops the Heart Company after the sword-pierced heart. It is the standard of the company. Each one has vowed allegiance to the throne and to Teacher. They have pledged their lives to His service. I vowed that that would be the first criteria by which I would select those I wanted to train."

It was quiet for long moments when Agron finished his tale. Obviously Pentra had taken several steps closer to the Adoni as the story had been told. He had been humbled for his own casual beliefs, even after the Battle in the Veil. His heart was sore from his grief, and he vowed to walk closer than ever before. The commander of the army, gripped Agron's shoulder, pulled him into a massive bear hug, and then released him. "Reactivate that shield commander. It's time we stood for something worthwhile once more."

David threw an arm over each of their shoulders, moving them back to the practice field. "I think I could use with a little exercise. Think you can find me a troop to spar with?"

"You, my lord?" Agron exclaimed.

"I've found the best way to grow is by doing – and I think it's time to let the Adoni teach us how to grow."

CHAPTER TWELVE

ASSAULT IN THE DARK

When David James left the training field, it was already evening. He had spent long hours pushing his body to its limits. Several partners had to be taken back to the very basics of how to grip a sword, how to stand, or how to swing. The Knight of Es-Soh-En had worked with several as a group in order to speed the training process along. He would have each one in the group come to the center of the work area, and then have them block his blow. If they had taken the wrong stance, he added the full weight of his body to the blow, knocking them to their knees. If they were not properly gripping their swords, he would slam his own blade against theirs so it would make their hands smart from the force of the impact. If they held the sword improperly, he would use several techniques he knew to knock it from their grasp.

The Steward of the Throne of Dula had to be careful not to discourage his students, but he had to make his point. When they realized that their very lives would depend on the basics of sword play, they gave him their full attention. He would show each one where they were wrong, and then run them through the drill a second time. This time it was harder to knock the sword from their hands, drive them to their knees, or make their hands smart from the blow. As they improved, he would praise them, let them tell the others how it felt, or what they experienced by doing it just a little bit differently. The students began to try new ideas. Several times David had to draw them back to the basics. One or two would have some new method they wanted to use because it looked impressive and was designed to demoralize the foe. Each time, they would come at David spinning their bodies around, whirling their swords, screaming, and leaping into the air. Each time the Knight of Es-Soh-En stood his ground, waited until the proper moment, and then countered their attack.

What was the most frustrating for those showing off their skills was that David defeated them with such ease. When the first attacker came in with spinning body, kicking legs, and whirling blade; David simply stepped inside the attack, and took a firm stance. The attacker slammed into David's body, lost his balance, and fell to the ground. Another time David merely raised his blade with a firm grip and proper angle. The attacker's force was blocked, and the attacker dropped his sword, and cried out in pain as the force of the block traveled back up the blade into his hands.

The most outrageous of the attackers suffered the most humiliation. This warrior was sure his flying death blow would be unstoppable. As the soldier flew through the air, David simply waited until the last possible second, and stepped aside. The soldier then had to flail his arms to regain control before he fell to the ground. David had considered following through with the side-step by slamming the air-borne attacker to the ground, but it seemed like over-kill.

"As you can see," David explained as he helped the fallen soldier to his feet, "These all sound good. They look impressive, but only to an amateur. A seasoned warrior will not flinch like you expect. A veteran of numerous campaigns will not freeze with a flurry of motions and jabs. Those who have been in war and survived, survived not because they were flashy. They survived because they were careful. They did not use any more energy than was needed to accomplish their task. They did not sacrifice the tried–and–true defenses for something that would make the ladies cheer. They had two goals: *stay alive* and *complete the mission.*"

David then took them back to the basics of stance, swing, and grip. "Always keep one foot on the ground. Two feet are better, but as long as you have one foot on the ground, you have contact with earth, and can change your direction. The moment someone else has both feet off the ground, they are committed, and cannot change. This gives you the advantage."

The training then continued with the three-step drills. Those who had thought such training was a waste of time had come to see it differently. Those who had seen such training as a waste of time were also the ones aching from their defeat at the hands of the Knight of Es-Soh-En.

"A little humbling can go a long way," Pentra noted to David as the three-step drill began once more.

"Not good as a general rule, but better to be humbled and survive than to be proud and dead," David observed. David left the group to the direction of Pentra, and moved to the next group. The practice continued for several hours. The Heart Company had already made several strides with the others since they had been recognized as a special breed of soldier. Before, they had been reluctant to give advice to their partners without being asked since they had no distinction. Now their partners wanted to know how to fight, how to defend. The Heart Company was able to speak with authority since they had been given the respect of both Pentra and the Steward of the Throne of Dula.

Now David left the gates of the fortress behind. He was drenched in sweat from the long hard hours they had worked.

He was bone-weary, but it was a satisfying weariness. His hair hung about his face. Even though it was long by most standards of fashion, he had kept it trimmed so it never fell into his eyes. He did not want to find himself at that disadvantage during a battle.

As he moved through the night-time darkness of the side streets, his sharp ears caught several signals. The first was the faint rustle of cloth as it moved behind him. There was labored breathing as if the person moving against him was not used to such physical effort. There came a faint ring of steel as it was pulled free and raised. There came the odor of some sweet oil which nearly gagged the Knight of Es-Soh-En. He recognized the stench from Council meetings. It was a full three seconds before Ki-el stepped on the loose gravel and made the *crunching* sound that he thought had betrayed him. But David already knew he was being attacked, by whom, and from which direction.

There was a swishing sound in the air as the flat of the blade passed through the still night air. A seasoned warrior would have turned the blade so the edge would cut the air in preparation for attack. Everything about the incident told David he was dealing with a rank amateur at the very least, and an incompetent at the very best. He told himself not to get confident. Many times such an attack was successful, not because the attacker was skillful, but because the assailant got lucky.

David timed the motion in the air. He judged the intensity of the cologne, and the body heat being generated by such a plump individual. He waited, ducked under the blow, and let the steel slam into the brick wall behind him. The ring of steel on stone and Ki-el's scream of pain as the sharp vibrations assailed his palms could be heard all the way back to the fortress. David noted that it was probably more painful for the head of the stone-cutters guild since he had noticed the lack of calluses on Ki-el's hands in previous Council meetings. David had wondered to himself what kind of work the head of the stone-cutters guild would do.

To Ki-el's credit, he recovered quickly, shifted the weight of the sword in his hand, and resumed the attack with a downward slash. David stepped in so close that the blade was behind him, As he stepped in, he crouched with his feet firmly planted, one slightly ahead, one slightly behind, no further apart than the width of his hips. He pulled his left hand down and across his chest, balling it into a fist as it was forcefully twisted palm-side-up and tucked at his side. Using the momentum of that motion like a spring to increase the speed of his other arm, David threw his right arm up towards his shoulder, twisting it up over his head, clenching his right fist, locking his wrist, elbow, shoulder; and tightening all the muscles in his body at the precise moment of impact with Ki-el's forearm. The effect was Ki-el's arm slamming into a rock-hard structure, nearly shattering the bones in the Council member's forearm. The force of the sword's momentum tore it from the stone-cutter's grasp, and it clattered to the pavement.

After deflecting the impact of Ki-el attack, David extended his body to its full height, knocking Ki-el back and off balance. Before the attacker could think to recover, David dropped to a crouching position, balanced on his fingers and one foot as he shot his left foot out in a sweeping motion that knocked Ki-el's feet out from under him. The assailant screamed out, and slammed hard on the flagstones. He landed square on his back, and the air was knocked from his lungs. His head slammed hard with the impact knocking him senseless. Within moments, torches were lighting the alleyway.

"It's Lord Ki-el!" came the guards' voices. They moved forward to capture the one whom they thought had attacked the

Council member. David side-stepped the first, tripped him as he moved past, and slammed his elbow in the guard's back driving him to the ground. The second guard dropped his torch, plunging the alley back into darkness. A few moments later an entire patrol responded to the sounds of battle and the cry of the watchmen. Agron was in the lead.

To Agron's credit, he took in the situation before he committed any men. He saw Lord Ki-el dazed and gasping for air on his back in the alley. One guard was facedown, trying to get up, and shaking his head to clear it. The third had been slammed into the block wall, and was in a crumpled heap. David stood in the middle of the carnage without even breathing hard.

"Sir David!" Agron called out, directing his men to identify the one they were about to attack. "Are you all right?"

"I'll be fine," David declared. Several troops moved in to help their fallen comrades. It took three men to prop Ki-el in a sitting position. He had lapsed into unconsciousness once he had managed to get his lungs to work.

"What shall my report show, my lord?" Agron asked. It was a polite way of trying to get information from a superior officer. David decided it was best to let all know the events. Ki-el did not deserve diplomatic immunity for trying to kill him in the alley.

"Lord Ki-el attacked me in the dark. Have him taken to the throne room of the palace so he can be questioned," David directed. Two of the strongest guards hefted Ki-el between them. They were unable to lift his entire weight, and so his feet dragged along the street as they carried out David's order. The two guards had been helped to their feet, and taken back to the barracks to rest and be treated. "Don't be too hard on them. They didn't know it was me."

"You took them out?" Agron was surprised. "I suppose I should reprimand them for acting before they took stock of the situation, but if you request it, all will be forgotten; at least by us."

"Your sword, my lord." One of the other troops had picked up Ki-el's sword, and offered it to David.

"Thanks, but that's not mine. It was Lord Ki-el's," David explained.

"Then where is your sword? We only found this one, and the two belonging to the guards." The soldier was not meaning to be insolent, but he was truly perplexed since the alley way was relatively clean, and there was no other place for a sword to be.

"That's alright. I didn't have a sword with me. Mine is being cleaned and sharpened." As soon as David had replied, he realized that he had just accomplished a major miracle in the eyes of the troops. "Perhaps you can keep it for evidence," David suggested passing it on to Agron.

David excused himself from the scene wanting to get back to the throne room before Ki-el's mind cleared. As he bounded up the palace steps, Tanya was coming from Unter's home.

"You won't believe what I've found." she declared catching up to her brother.

"It'll have to wait unless it deals with Ki-el. He's in the throne room to be interrogated for trying to kill me in a sneak attack."

"Sneak attack? Him? With that cologne he wears! The man's living in a fool's paradise."

The brother and sister made it into the room just as Ki-el was shaking his head and trying to figure out where he was. David had sent the guards to the back of the room out of sight. The room was intentionally left poorly lit. The walls and ceiling were lost in the darkness giving Ki-el the impression of being insignificantly small in such a vast and unending hall. A torch light had been placed at the foot of the throne, lighting David and Tanya's features from below. The Steward of the Throne of Dula used his deepest, most menacing voice to begin the interrogation.

"Why did you try to kill me, Ki-el?" David deliberately left off the stone-cutter's title to let the head of the guild know that he was without rank or protection in the session. Beads of sweat were forming Ki-el's forehead. His eyes darted back and forth trying to see what was in the darkness beyond his sight. The attacker licked his lips several times, and seemed to be having difficulty getting his dry mouth to become moist. "Why did you try to kill me, traitor?!" David pressed.

"For the good of Dula!" he blurted out. His voice cracked and trembled with even those few words. He was trying to regain control of himself. David knew he couldn't give his prey the time to regroup or think.

"How is killing me for the good of Dula?"

"You were going to take us into a war. I had to kill you to avoid the death and bloodshed."

"You lie!" David charged. "Killing me would not stop the war. My sister would have taken up the cause. Were you planning on killing her as well?"

"If I had to," the stone-cutter squealed.

"You would kill the Steward and the Stewardess of the Throne of Dula for the good of Dula?" David made his voice sound incredulous. "That would have solved nothing. Magar is already moving against us. Kill us both and they would have broken down the gates, and slaughtered everyone inside. How is that for the good of the kingdom?"

"It would stop the war!"

"It would destroy the kingdom. How is that good for the kingdom?" David kept pressing the point. Ki-el no longer had the nobility in his voice. The words were without conviction. He spoke about the good of the kingdom as if it were mantra to be recited without thought. Ki-el stopped, took a deep breath as if he were about to speak. David moved in for the kill to cut him off.

"NO! There is no way this could be for the good of the king-dom. This was for your own good. This is about greed. This is about yourself. Why did you try to kill me?"

"My lord..." he stammered, but David interrupted.

"Do not call me your *lord*. I am not your *lord*. You tried to cut me down in a dark alley. You struck at me from behind. You're a liar and a coward. Why did you try to kill me? Was it the greed? Was it for money?"

"It was for the Eye!" Ki-el finally broke.

"The Crystal Eye?" David was confused. He did not see how the Crystal Eye would play into all of this. However, the first rule of interrogation is to keep the person off-balance; make them tell you what you don't know without letting them know you don't know.

"No, the Eye of Suma," Ki-el corrected. As Ki-el spoke of the jewel, David recalled the great sky ship that would float upon the winds. It was shaped like the Great Eagle, with gold-spun sails, and twin topaz blue jewels minded from deep in the earth served as the eyes of the eagle head. Those jewels were living jewels, full of life; so full of life that they actually glowed on their own, even when no light was around. During the testing of Teacher by Queen Dianna, Teacher had given one of the jewels to Tray-ton to pay the debt he incurred for accidentally killing Giban. David had wondered what had ever happened to the stone. The moment the Steward of the Throne of Dula had taken to reflect on the history of the jewel had been an empty silence which fur-ther pressured Ki-el. Ki-el continued to ramble. He wasn't sure if he rambled because he thought David had paused waiting for him to continue; or if he rambled to fill the dreaded silence of the room.

"Do you know what that stone has done to me?" he wailed. David felt it best to remain silent, and let Ki-el's own fears continue their work. "I work with stones. I am the master of my craft. There is nothing I cannot make, shape or form. Nothing except for that jewel. It has burned in me, haunted me ever since I saw it. I knew that it had to be mine.

"Trayton never sold the jewel. He charged people to come and see it. He made more than enough money to pay his debt, and so the stone has been with his family for generations. Once their debts were paid, and they had enough money to live on; they locked it away. People could no longer come and see it. As head of the stone-cutters guild I managed to convince them to let me see it. The moment I looked into its depths, my soul was lost. Every time I close my eyes, I see that swirling glow. I feel the warmth of its inner fire. I can hear it singing its own kind of song. I had to have it, but they refused to sell it.

"Then one night, I had a dream. In that dream I was carried into the Veil of Darkness. I feared for my life, but a figure of pure light came to rescue me. I had never believed in those tales until then, but as the shadow things closed in about me, the figure of light drove them back. His wings were enormous. They were filled with the colors of the rainbows. Even his eyes were a blood red.

"I thought that Dianna was insane for believing those old fables, but that night, I was ready to believe. The figure of light brought me out of the Veil of Darkness, back to my own room. He opened his robes, and showed me the Eye of Suma. He told me that it could be mine. All I had to do was forsake the Adoni completely, and to prevent Dula from going to war at any cost. I had never followed the religion of the Adoni, and so it was little to ask of me. I gladly forsook any allegiance to the Adoni. As for the second part of the bargain, it was in everyone's best interests to keep Dula out of war. I would have given my soul to have that gem, and instead, it would be mine for so much less. I swore on my own blood that night to do as the figure of light asked. As soon as the deal was closed, I awoke in my own bed.

"A week later I saw Agron with that pathetic shield of his. I don't know why, but it disturbed me; so much so I couldn't even come near Agron while he carried it. I told Lendar about it, and asked him to confront Agron for me. Lendar went to see Agron for himself. We pulled some strings, and had the shield removed. As soon as the shield was gone, I heard guards speaking of Teacher. People in the street spoke of the Adoni. We had those intolerable *Glidonites* everywhere you turned. I couldn't forsake the Adoni without tearing my ears from my head, and plucking my eyes from their sockets. The Adoni was everywhere in Dula. The Adoni *was* Dula!

"Then came reports of robbers in the Gen Forest becoming more aggressive. Dula was considering war. Agron spoke to the Council about the robbers in the woods. The Council was about to believe him, and go to war. We sent Agron to guard the dungeon where he wouldn't be seen by any of the Council members. We believed that if he was out of sight, the others would soon forget his passionate speeches. Gib-ron and I passed rumors about the arrows from Magar. Slowly we were able to defuse the situation. Members of the Council who believed as I did began to call meetings at night, and to pass laws to remove the power from Dianna to declare war. It was all going so well until you came along. I would kill you and your sister for the Eye of Suma, and it would be a very small price to pay indeed." The head of the stone-cutters guild was ranting. He was delirious in his greed.

"You have paid a price which even you cannot comprehend," David replied softly. He no longer needed to intimidate the attacker. There was nothing left for him to tell. David now felt it best to give the stone-cutter what little chance there was of redemption. "The figure of light you saw in the Veil of Darkness was none other than Cronis," David breathed a silent prayer of protection as he used the Dark Lord's true name this one time – something he tried very hard to avoid. "You made a pact with the Dark Lord. You forsook the Adoni. In short, the price for the stone has been the price of your soul.

"What is equally unfortunate is the fact that the jewel does not belong to the Dark One. It was given by Teacher, and protected by the Adoni. The Dark One cannot overcome the Adoni. He has swayed you with empty lies and promises. Your soul has died within you for a lie."

"No!" screamed Ki-el. "I saw it in his hands. He has it in his possession. He will give it to me! He will!"

"He lied. The stone is still with Trayton's family. The Dark One does not have the power to possess it. He has, however, come to possess you. You have sold yourself for an illusion."

The truth began to dawn on Ki-el. He began to weep and wail. He tore at the guards which David motioned to take him away. All the way down the hallway his pitiful voice tore at David's soul. When the doors to the dungeon area were closed behind him there was silence in the throne room. Tanya spoke, softly, and to no one in particular.

"I wonder how many others have sold themselves to the Dark Lord for nothing more than an illusion?"

CHAPTER THIRTEEN

A GATHERING OF FORCES

David cinched the wide black leather belt about his waist. He wore a black tunic over a short-sleeved steel-grey chain mail shirt. Under the chain mail, a topaz blue shirt was visible only because of the wide collar and the long bell-sleeves. On the black tunic was embroidered the glistening form of the Great Hobber, Es-Soh-En. Tanya had it made for her brother using spun gold thread. The eyes of Es-Soh-En were matching topaz jewels. It looked, for all intents and purposes, like his traditional Dulan garb. Even though they had been in Dula for some time, they had not been able to learn why their clothes had not changed. Tanya felt at a disadvantage. She had always been comfortable with her attire knowing that she could will it to transform into battle garb, and Sy-lar would appear. Now she would have to either wear her battle attire, take the time to physically change her clothes, or battle in whatever she was wearing. She also missed Sy-lar. She had tried numerous other swords, even some that were copies of her own sword, but it wasn't the same. There was always something different about the feel, or the weight, or the way it moved in her hand.

"You're regretting again," David noted as he held out his hand for his sword belt. Tanya crinkled her nose to make a face at him. It annoyed her that he found her so easy to read. Jenson had not been as keen as her brother in knowing her moods and expressions.

She passed the sword belt to her brother. It was a wide leather belt that hung a little lower than the one he had just fastened. The sword belt had over-lapping silver plates fastened to the outer side of the leather. Each silver plate held a matching red ruby. David slipped the leather end through the buckle, fastened it in place, and the adjusted it so that it hung at an angle, dropping the sword a little lower on the hip so he could pull it free for battle.

"Let me guess," David continued. "You're either pouting because you can't call Sy-lar, you have to change your clothes for battle, or you're staying behind while I go into battle."

"Actually, it was only the first two, but now that you mention it, maybe I should go into battle," Tanya offered.

"I would love to have you fighting by my side, but someone has to watch the fort. I'm taking most of the troops with me, and there's only going to be a handful left here to protect the palace. If Magar gets past us, or if Gib-ron's men try anything, you're our last hope." David drew the sword from its sheath, and eyed the edge of the blade.

"That's the third time you've done that," Tanya observed.

"I never had to check when I had Gennerroth. Its blade was all-but-indestructible; but this is a sword forged by man. It has a tendency to get nicks and chips in the blade – and you know how superstitious warriors are about their blades."

"*A blade which has a nick should never be taken into battle. Each nick reminds the blade of sometime when it missed the mark. If the blade is demoralized, the wielder will be too,*" Tanya quoted. "So they grind the blade down until all the nicks and the chips are gone. The fact the broadsword becomes a foil doesn't seem to bother them."

"I still think the sword belt is a bit much," David noted as he slid the blade into its sheath, and fastened the small hook which held it in place.

"So do I, but it was a present from the gnomes many years ago. They worked hard on it, and wearing it will remind them of their previous support," Tanya suggested.

"It sounds like politics to me," He brother mumbled.

"Politics is only the art of making people act as if they like you when they want to stab you in the back," Tanya replied.

"So the gnomes are out to get me, too?" David joked recalling the attack by Ki-el. The stonecutter was still in the dungeon for the assault. Word of David being able to disarm, and defeat a man of Ki-el size even when the Knight of Es-Soh-En was unarmed further promoted David to living legend. The public had cheered his action when the news came out the following day. "Have the guards doubled around the gates while we're gone."

"You expecting something?" she asked. It had not been the first time their intuition had saved them from a surprise attack.

"Not really, but while we're gone is the perfect time for Ray-ton to try and slip out of the city."

As David descended the stairs from the palace to the courtyard, he saw the Heart Company at the head of the army. Each one was precise in their attire. Their gear was identical to that worn by the others in the company. They sat straight in the saddle, unblinking, staring straight ahead. Each one held a shield. This was the only difference in their appearance. Each shield was of various shapes and sizes, but they all had some rendition of the sword-pierced-heart logo. Some had large designs painted on their shields. Some had the design engraved or etched in silver or gold. Some had designs that covered the entire shield's face, while others had smaller designs in the very center of the shield. All depicted a heart, pierced from behind by a sword with an upward thrust. Some had taken great care to research the picture of Logos, and it was obvious this was the sword piercing the heart. Other had just any sword depicted. Some had blood sprayed on the shield, others did not.

David noted Agron's shield. Agron was one of those who had researched the sword to its minute details. The unicorn horn handle of Logos was made from some kind of spiraling bone material. The white locks of unicorn hair used for the cross piece was raised and painted. The sword on the shield was missing the hilt jewel. The long tapered blade pierced the heart from behind with an upward thrust, and the blood had stained the blade where it had passed through the heart. Beneath the design was a banner with a word in the ancient Dulan embossed in red. On either side of the sword-pierced heart, and standing with their hind legs resting on the top of the banner, with the front hooves raised with one touching the side of the heart, and the other resting on the edge of the stained blade were Gaylord and Yeesha. Their wings were spread out filling the upper portion of the shield. David smiled when he translated the ancient word on the banner.

"*Redeemed?*" David asked.

"My lord, very few can still read the old language," Agron complimented.

"It's not that hard for me. I've been reading it, and hundreds of variations of it all my life."

"How does that work?" Agron asked, and then thought better of being so bold. "If I might ask, my lord?"

"I'm not really sure. Each time we come to Dula, we just seem to know what people are saying. When we speak to them, it's as if the Adoni are translating for us. When we see words, we understand them. After a few days of being back in Dula, then we begin to realize the differences in the wording, the pronunciation, the manner of speech. It's like a gift of knowledge. We learn all the changes in only a few short hours. Then we practice those changes. By the time we leave, we've become quite fluent in them."

"I was wondering," Agron continued. "I've heard that the Lady Tanya has spent long hours reading the ancient manuscripts and books in the Record Chamber. Several people have tried, and found the changes in the meaning of words, the rules of spelling and grammar, even the sentence structure was so different it was almost impossible to decipher."

"I believe Tanya and I are the only ones, next to Queen Dianna, who could read all the books in there." It then dawned on him why Tanya had been doing most of the research while those assigned to help her had seemed to move at such a slow pace. He smiled to himself turned to review the troops. As he noted the sword-pierced-heart emblem on each shield, he added, "It seems that Teacher rides with us today."

"He rides with most of us," Agron replied. There was caution in his voice as if he suddenly realized he may have said something which would offend the Steward of the Throne of Dula. Agron's eyes were focused on the design on David's tunic.

"He rides with me as well," David offered. "I am a Knight of Es-Soh-En. Es-Soh-En is Teacher. I knew Him first, and best, as the Great Hobber. Where you see the Adoni become man, I see the Son of the Adoni." David smiled to himself once more as he recalled how Es-Soh-En had received that very title for His name in this world.

"Are they not two different people?" asked Handar reigning up his horse next to Agron's. His popularity for the Battle in the Veil had earned him the easy familiarity with the Steward of the Throne. Handar had become so comfortable with it, that he had responded this way with both Pentra and Agron. Fortunately for him, neither officer chose to be offended by his ease at speaking his thoughts in their presence.

"They are one-in-the-same," David declared.

"It's just hard to picture. Es-Soh-En has always been. Teacher was born and raised here in Dula. It just seems like they would have been two different people," Handar noted.

"Es-Soh-En was before the world was formed. He sang it into existence. Before there was anything else, He was there. When the time came, He cause Himself to be born into human flesh. He did not enter into someone else's body," David explained, recalling how on several visits there had been those who taught Teacher was only an ordinary man blessed by the spirit of Es-Soh-En for His dedication. "Es-Soh-En had the body formed in His mother's womb. He transformed Himself, became that baby, grew as a child, and taught as a man. He was the Adoni-made-flesh. He was the blend of Adoni and man. If He were any less-or any more, then He could not redeem this world."

"But after the Battle of Es-Soh-En, He was reported to have been Es-Soh-En, and then changed back to Teacher. Does He have two bodies, and they keep switching back and forth? When He's not using one, does it just sit in the corner?"

Agron was becoming annoyed with the questions. He said nothing, but cleared his throat. David noted the displeasure and added in Handar's defense.

"He is new to the Following," David observed, using the term which had once referred to followers of Es-Soh-En, and now referred to those who followed the instructions of Teacher. "I don't believe he means any disrespect." Then in response to Handar's question David added, "There is only one body. Es-Soh-En transformed His entire being into Teacher as a babe in the womb. He does not set aside one body and put on another. He transforms into whichever He chooses to be. Those who trusted Him before the Battle of Es-Soh-En see Him as the Great Hobber-made-flesh. Those who came to trust Him after the Battle of Es-Soh-En see Him as Teacher the One-who-always-was. I see Him as both."

"I should have listened more to my mother when I was a child, and she spoke of the stories of Teacher. There was a magic dancing in her eyes when she shared them with us, but I was young, full of energy and pride. I have lost many years to such misdirection. But I have seen the Veil. If the Veil is real, then all else must be real. There are really three of Them?"

The troops were all mounted. David motioned to Agron to move them out. Pentra sat on horseback, next to Lady Tanya to see them off. Pentra had protested at being left behind, but he had been entrusted with the safety of the kingdom in the army's absence, and would serve where needed. The Steward of the Throne of Dula saluted Pentra and his sister. The entire army, including Agron and Handar followed suit. Once they were out of the gate, David decided to use the time riding to the Gen Forest to teach Handar about the Adoni.

"There are three of Them," David responded once they were underway. "Only three," he added as he recalled other teachings he had heard before. It seemed like such a hassle to have to keep correcting the simple teachings of the Words of the Ancients, but every time he came back to Dula, there was some other *new revelation* making the rounds. "Always test the new revelations by what is taught in the earliest revelations. The Adoni do not change." And so the discussion was underway. David allowed the army to break formation and ride in several lines instead of a single line. He had allowed this so that the troops could take turns riding close enough to him to hear what he taught. They were hungry for more information. They were like men dying of thirst in a desert to hear words that could confirm or deny what they had heard. It concerned David that the ones who had come forward to hear the lessons were mostly those of Heart Company; however, those who rode to the front had an honest desire to learn more.

As he spoke, David could see the thoughts churning in the eyes of the Heart Company. They were full of questions, and after several hours of David's sharing, they fell into two lines to allow him time to rest his voice. Even then, the Heart Company began to sing songs of praise to Teacher and the Adoni.

"Not exactly the way of the warrior," noted Handar as the sound of the praises filled the dales between the castle and the Gen Forest. "If the enemy were looking for us, I think they might know we were coming."

"Yes, they would," David observed, and then he smiled, "but even more important, they would know we fight in the name of the Adoni. We do not come in our own strength, but in the strength of the Three."

"Still, it would be nice to act like an army," suggested Handar.

"Let me tell you a secret," David offered, leaning to the side as if it was the greatest secret in the world, and only for Handar's ears. The warrior leaned over to hear. "We aren't going to win this war because we're good warriors."

"WHAT?!" Handar exclaimed, sitting back up in his saddle.

"The Adoni determine who is to win in each battle. They grant the victory. If They have given the victory, then no one can stand against Their army. If They withhold the victory, then nothing we do can succeed."

"That doesn't sound very encouraging," the warrior noted.

"On the contrary," Agron interrupted. "That's the most encouraging news we could have."

That evening they stopped on the shores of Lake Gen to set up camp, and prepare for the meeting with the other races the following day. As they ate, David spoke more of the Adoni, and confirmed or corrected legends which had grown up around his visits to the Lands of the Adoni. David had not realized that there had been so many visits. Each soldier had one that they liked above the rest. They wanted to hear it from David. While many legends had to be corrected, and placed back into perspective, the one everyone thought was a myth David actually confirmed.

"So why do they call you *Air Walker?*" one soldier asked as they sat around the fire after the meal was only a passing memory.

"Because I was crazy enough to ask Es-Soh-En to let me walk on the air," David admitted.

"But did you?" came another voice in the back.

"Actually, yes…but only half-way across the chasm on the Mountain of the Sky."

"Half-way?" a voice was incredulous.

"It might sound impressive, but keep in mind; half-way was not all the way. I still fell. As long as I looked into Es-Soh-En's eyes, I believed I could do it. I started walking forward. I kept waiting for the sensation of standing on the air, but there wasn't any change. It felt like I was still on the pathway. Finally, I wondered how far I had to go until I was on the air. I took my eyes off Es-Soh-En, looked down, and realized I was right in the middle of the chasm. There was nothing but empty air below me, for several thousand feet. I panicked, and the next thing I knew, I was falling. I was screaming for Es-Soh-En to help me. Not the most dignified of screams I must admit, but He heard me. He was suddenly underneath me, breaking my fall, and carrying me to the other side."

There was a silence over the camp as they all sought to absorb the tale. Finally, David broke the silence, "It wasn't anything that I did, or was, that let me walk on the air. It was all Es-Soh-En's doing. When I looked away, I was cut off from His Power. I was only myself once more, and so I fell. When we look to Es-Soh-En, when we trust in the Adoni; then we are far more than we think we are."

"If that's the case, then we should be able to win this battle without having to lift a single sword," someone in the back declared. David couldn't tell if it was a serious remark, or someone heckling; but it came from the direction where those not of Heart Company had gathered throughout the evening. The Knight of Es-Soh-En could hear faint laughter and whispered comments which were not complimentary being passed among the rest of that group.

"If that is the will of the Adoni, then They can bring it to happen. I will not speak for Them without Their clear guidance. Yes, They could do it. Do They plan to do it? I don't know. I suggest you *trust in the Adoni, but keep your sword at hand* all the same." David quoted an old proverb which had come to be more of a joke in the last few generations. It had once been used to call attention to the need to trust the Adoni, but at the same time not to presume to know Their will for your own life. This trusting and lack of knowledge would require that you act in a prudent manner, do what was needed to complete a task, but trust the Adoni for the results. It had once been good advice, now it was a humorous cliché. A ripple of laughter drifted over the camp. The moment had passed. David could sense the Adoni had closed whatever door of opportunity had been opened to him a few minutes ago. He dismissed the men to sleep, or prayers, or watch. Those who stood watch sang soft songs of praise to the Adoni throughout the night.

"I know You're there, Glidon. I don't know why You are keeping Your distance, nor what You have planned for tomorrow, but I know You're there." He rolled over on his blanket, closed his eyes, listened to the songs of praise, and was soon fast asleep.

***

The following morning, David rose before the sun even hinted of the false dawn on the eastern sky. The twin moons were settling in behind the western horizon. There was a full sky of stars. David looked up at the constellations. He called each one by name, reciting them in their proper order, and thought about the legends that were associated with each collection of stars. Ish and Issha had heard the stories and names many centuries ago. They had all learned them from Es-Soh-En in the Garden of Tangar. Now centuries later, David could see how they told the tale of the creation of Dula, the Fall, the Battle of Es-Soh-En, and the lessons of Teacher. It wasn't that they had been altered to tell the tales, but the tales had been told when the stars were first named by the Adoni. Somehow people had just forgotten along the way.

David stretched, rolled his blanket up, and was surprised at how refreshed he had felt given the lateness of their meeting the night before, and the earliness with which he had risen. Somehow it was not the sleep which had invigorated him. It had been the long hours of sharing about the Adoni, and the songs of praise that had continued all the while he had slept.

Something touched his mind. The Knight of Es-Soh-En smiled.

"I am here," he said to the unheard voice. It was Deenara, the Steward of the Unicorns. The ancient one served as head of the herd in place of Lendara who had given his life to save Ish and

Issha. David was warmed by the sense of presence of the entire herd. They were everywhere around his camp, but none would be allowed to see them. Rentara's voice joined David's mind, and the Friend of the Unicorn was glad. There had been a special bond between he and Rentara since the night they had battled the evil sent by the Dark Lord. The battle had lasted the entire night, and had actually created the Valley of Seven Forests. They had failed to stop the Demon Cloud, but they had slowed it long enough for Lendara and Deenara to prepare for their own battle with the cloud creature.

David thought about slipping away from the camp to visit with his brothers of the herd. He alone had been bonded to the minds of the unicorn. They had chosen to remain pure when the Lands of the Adoni fell. This choice made it impossible for any but him to see or hear them. Deenara knew his thoughts and added, "We desire to see you, as well, but there is work which must be done. You must follow our instructions for the Adoni have sent word to you."

"That's strange," David replied in his mind. "Is there some reason why the Adoni cannot speak directly to me?" For a moment, David thought about his own counsel: *test the spirits*, and ran a mental check to make sure he was speaking with Deenara, and not a servant of the Dark Lord trying to misguide him. The unicorn waited for him, knowing what he was doing, and praised him for his carefulness. They spoke the names of the Adoni, and swore allegiance to Them without David really needing to ask. The Friend of the Unicorn thanked his brothers for their understanding. "What is the message?"

"You have too many men," Deenara instructed.

"*Too many men*," David almost spoke the words aloud, but caught himself. "The army is small enough as it is," he observed.

"We have 5,000 to what may be two or three times those sent by Magar."

"If you were to win this battle by force of arm, that is correct. But as you told your men yesterday, this is not to be a force of arms battle. The Adoni has already decreed that you are to win. They want to make it very clear that They have given the victory into your hands. For this reason, only those who are truly devoted to Them are to be on the battlefield. All others would seek the glory for themselves, and this would cause problems in the future."

"Then what am I to do?" David asked. When Deenara had finished with his instructions, David went to the sentry and instructed him to call battle formation. The camp sprang to action in the first light of the false dawn. The eastern sky was beginning to lighten, but it would be another half hour before the actual sun would clear the mountains. Everyone ran about, gathering their clothes and gear, running to their place in the formation. David noted with pride that Heart Company was ready before the rest of the army. They stood in perfect formation while the others came in grumbling and complaining about the darkness of the morning.

"I have a message for you – from the Adoni." He had the full attention of the entire army. Those of Heart Company were eager for the words; others looked on in wonder, suspicion, or hostility. It was then that David understood the need to *weed out* those who were not loyal to the Adoni. "The message is this: *We have too many men!*"

Those in the back, away from Heart Company laughed or made jokes. They were the first ones David cut from the army. He then spoke to the remaining men, "Those of you who have married within the last year, or those of you with children under ten years of age; you have a responsibility at home. I thank you for your service, but I release you this day to return to your homes, and fulfill that sacred duty."

Another fifty or so men broke away from the body, and stood by the sidelines. "Still too many," Deenara advised.

"Those of you who are unsure of the Adoni being able to deliver this battle into our hands with the smaller number are free to leave." This time two hundred moved away.

"There are still too many," Deenara said.

"Then how do I cut the remaining troops?" David asked in his mind.

"They must be those who worship the Adoni, in secret as well as in public. Their habits will tell you what you need to know about them."

David thought for a moment, and then he struck upon the perfect test. "Those of you left will need to pass a final test." The sun was now lighting the world, announcing it would clear the mountains in only a few minutes. David led the rest to the bank of Lake Gen, away from the shore. "Each of you is to drink from the lake, without entering the lake."

Three of Heart Company came to the edge where the shore hung over the water. They pulled off their gauntlets, unfasten their helmets and set them aside. They then laid flat on their stomachs on the bank, and lifted the water to their mouths. Agron was at David's side. Handar was with them as well.

"They won't make the cut," Handar observed.

"And why is that?" David asked.

"They are poor soldiers." As Handar spoke Agron cleared his throat. This time there was anger in his eyes.

"You wish to reply to Handar's comments?" David offered.

"If I may speak freely."

"Then speak as freely as you wish," David replied, humor in his eyes.

"These men are some of the finest soldiers in the army. I think that it is poor of you to cast such dishonor on them without testing your theory!"

"What I meant was that by lying on their stomachs, they have exposed their backs. They make perfect targets. They should kneel. That way when someone attacks, they would be ready to fight," Handar explained. There was no anger in his voice. David smiled.

"Why don't you take Agron's challenge, and test your theory."

"How?"

"You say they are vulnerable to attack. Attack one of them," David offered. Handar, hefted his battle-ax from his belt, and approached the soldier closest to him. He took great care not to make any noise as he came upon his prey. At the last possible minute, the man lying on the ground rolled over on his back; raised up to grab Handar hands where they gripped the ax, placed a foot in Handar's stomach, and sent him flying into the Lake. Laughter erupted from the troops. Handar dragged himself out of the lake; water poured from various compartments in his armor, boots, and gloves.

"So, do you still think they are poor soldiers?" David challenged.

"No…I don't think that anymore. But how did he know I was coming?"

"There were three ways," Agron noted. David motioned for Agron to continue. "First, his entire body was in contact with the ground. He could feel you moving. You made sounds which did not travel by air, but which did vibrate through the ground. A wise soldier knows how to *listen* for these sounds. They can tell of an approaching army, or even a single foe. Second, he could see your reflection, even though distorted, in the water. Lastly, there was a shadow you cast that fell over him. And do not think that one cannot fight in that position. First of all it makes a difficult target for archers; where someone standing, sitting, or kneeling is easier to hit. Also, with a single roll or flip, the soldier is out of position for the attack, and has protected his back. This is also the position where someone can lift the greatest weight."

"Any more questions?" David asked of Handar. The ax-wielder shook his head, and fell silent. "Actually, Handar, I am not testing for the best warriors."

"You aren't?" the water-drenched soldier replied.

"No. This is not a battle of arms this day. I will not win because my men are better than anyone else's. This is a day when the Adoni will show that They can win the battle, no matter how small we are. For this reason, I am not testing battle skills, but loyalty to the Adoni."

Both Agron and Handar fell silent as the Knight of Es-Soh-En continued to observe those who came to drink from the lake. Half-way through the testing, three soldiers of Heart Company unfastened their helmets, and long hair tumbled out. It was braided so that it did not get into their eyes.

"Women?!" came Handar's incredulous voice. David could hear others not of Heart Company make the same or similar comments.

"Yes, women," Agron declared. "I had to do some re-thinking when I spoke with the Steward of the Throne of Dula, and he reminded me that Lady Tanya was unbeatable in battle. There had been several women who have trained with us during our time of training in secret, but were not part of the army. After I considered Sir David's words, I came to see that I was denying myself valuable fighters for no valid reason. They became part of Heart Company the night Ki-el attacked you, sir." His last comment was directed at David.

When the testing was over, David began to separate the soldiers who would go into battle from those who would return to Dula. The group returning to Dula was almost five thousand. Those staying were Heart Company and maybe another hundred soldiers. Handar noted that each of those selected to stay had lain upon their stomachs and drank the water, while those returning to Dula had knelt and drank.

"So if you weren't testing for battle ability, how was kneeling versus laying down a test of loyalty to the Adoni?" He inquired.

"Quite simply. I had to think of what those who worshipped the Adoni did differently than those who worshiped the Dark Lord."

"Cronis?!" Agron spat the name out of his mouth as if it had left a bad taste.

"Yes. It seems that people have become prone to worshipping the Dark Lord. They may not realize they are worshipping him, but their actions show it. Each of the rituals involved in other religions, practices, and other ceremonies which are not designed to bring honor to the Adoni involved bending the knees and kneeling. Those who come before the Adoni in true submission fall face-down before Them. Whichever one the person is most used to doing will be the position he or she becomes comfortable with, and will use that method automatically, without thinking. Those who bent their knee have been involved in some form of worship of the Dark Lord; maybe indirectly, but they have been touched by the Dark One. They are not comfortable coming to the Adoni in true prayer. Thus, those who are left are the ones who come often to prayer before the Adoni."

"But I would have knelt," noted Handar.

"Which is why I did not test you. I know you are new to this, but your heart is right. I can vouch for you, but I could not vouch for all the others. You have chosen your Heart Company wisely," David noted to Agron who swelled with pride. He, too, had noted that none of Heart Company had been cut during the process.

As the other troops broke camp and returned to Dula, Heart Company and the others selected to go into battle traveled to the other side of the lake. After they had established their new base of operations David felt the thoughts of Deenara once more. He had chosen well, but there was still another matter to deal with when they met the other races.

David moved the men into position, and called everyone to attention. Deenara informed him that the other races were only a few minutes away. True to Deenara's estimation, the centaurs were galloping into the camp a few minutes later. They came in formation: three abreast. Those on the outsides carried the war bow of the centaur race. The centaur in the middle carried two swords. David was familiar with this variation. Those on the outsides could move away to swing the double-bladed war bow without injuring his comrades. The middle centaur did not have that option; and so while he wore the war bow across his back, he carried two swords so he could swing and attack without injuring those on either side of him.

The centaurs wound their way around the camp, encircling it three deep. The man-horses continued to circle until the head of the centaur clan was directly in front of David. The circle parted, and revealed that the minotaur had been hidden among the centaur as a concealed inner circle. The man-bull warriors now created a fourth circle of allies. When all were in place, the head of the clans came to greet David. The Knight of Es-Soh-En stood in battle-ready position, advising his allies that he was trained in the art of war. Agron and Handar stood on either side of him, a step behind.

"I am David James, Child of Earth, Knight of Es-Soh-En, Steward of the Throne of Dula," he declared in a firm, crisp voice. He listened to the voice of Deenara advising him of another detail that most seemed to have forgotten.

"I ask Fin Den and Wil Den to come forward, and speak on behalf of the gnome clans." As soon as David spoke, the shrubs and brush came to life. Each one carefully concealed a gnome. No one had noticed the sudden growth of brush which had appeared in the compound when the centaurs had circled the camp as part of their entrance. David had noted, and found their disguises impressive. Deenara had only given him the names of the heads of the clan.

"You are everything the legends say of you," exclaimed Fin Den as he discarded his disguise, and stood before the Knight of Es-Soh-En in the traditional gnomish garb. His brother, Wil Den joined the other allies as they introduced themselves to David and his war council.

"I am Han." announced the centaur. He stood before them, clean shaven, tall and proud.

"Es-Tra" David pronounced in greeting. The centaur smiled.

"Es-tra, to you as well, Sir David. I am of the Clan of Tra, and I wish for you the Peace discovered by Tra through his relationship with Es-Soh-En. You are versed in the ancient battle tongue of my race."

"I have had many teachers…all of them good," David offered in reply.

"We have waited centuries for your return, David James of Earth. Our ancestor, Kal spoke highly of you; and has recorded in the New Words that your final return to the Lands of the Adoni will signal the time when Es-Soh-En will establish His final kingdom. We serve you. I am Ren." The minotaur gave the war bow of his race. Where Kal had been humble enough to bow low enough for his horns to touch the ground, this man-bull race was prepared for battle, and so their bow was a simple tilt of the horns which protruded from either side of their bull heads. David returned the same bow to show his allies that he, too, was battle ready.

"Thank you all for coming. This is Agron, my second-in-command for this campaign. He is a loyal follower of Teacher, and serves me well. This is Handar, a veteran of the Battle of the Veil. He and Pentra journeyed with me to the Veil of Darkness to seek for Queen Dianna."

"Then the rumors are true? She is missing?" asked Fin Den.

"She is missing. We have ruled out that she has not been captured by either Magar or the Dark Lord," David explained. "My sister and I serve as stewards of her throne until she returns."

The gnomes all came forward, doffed their green caps, and bowed low enough for their long hair to brush the leather turned-down boots they all wore. The clan as a whole rose, and tucked their hats into the belts which fastened about their leather vests.

"We will go into battle, our heads uncovered. As a race our heads will remain bare until we know her fate," Wil Den declared. David knew it was a great honor they bestowed upon Queen Dianna. A gnome's hair was his glory. He would not cut it, and always wore the traditional cap designed to accent each gnome's hair color. He did not know of any time in all the history of the Lands of the Adoni when the entire race showed such respect. They had gone without head dress among a clan or family, but never as an entire race.

"You do honor to Queen Dianna," David announced. He motioned all of the leaders towards a table prepared for them. Special drinks and food had been transported for each of the races. David instructed them all to dismiss their troops, and let them spend time getting to know each other.

"Is it wise?" asked Ren. "We should have guards posted," he suggested.

"Normally I would agree, but there are guards watching over us which none can see," David replied. There was something in his voice which Han caught.

"Unicorns?" the centaur whispered in disbelief.

"Yes. My brothers stand guard over us. None will see them, and so they cannot hide from them."

"Is that how you knew we were among you?" asked Fen Den.

"Had I not been here, you would have gone undetected. You forget that I trained with Fel Dor many years ago." He paused and Wil Den, Fen Den and David all breathed the proper respect, "*A good gnome. We know and we grieve.*"

After the proper pause of silence, David continued. "It was a well-executed maneuver. I had not seen it used in conjunction with the centaur before. You work very well together. However, the unicorn did not tell me of your presence, only of your names."

"You can speak with the unicorn?" Ren whispered.

"Our minds are joined. I am one of their herd. That is the meaning behind my title, *Friend of the Unicorn.*" David explained. David paused in response to a message from Deenara. "Your wife is well," David instructed. If there had been any evidence of concern on the bull-face, it was gone. "I believe her name is Zon. The unicorn tell me that you have a son, strong and healthy. His name is Gar," David added.

"It must be true. None knew I had to leave her for the battle at a critical time. Thank you, Knight of Es-Soh-En." Ren grasped David's sword hand and touched it to his forehead, between his mighty horns. "If I can serve you, I am yours," Ren added to the vow he had just made to David.

"How many thieves are in the woods?" David asked turning the focus to the business at hand.

"We have counted five, maybe six thousand," Fen Den replied. "You know that they are not just robbers," he added.

"I know that they are the initial attack force of Magar. I also have word that another five thousand troops are coming from Magar, and were expected to have joined them three days ago."

"Your sources are correct," Wil Den replied. "They are like locust in the forest."

"What is our plan?" Han asked. He was a true centaur, always coming to the point of the conversation.

"The plan is this. You and your people have been wronged by Dula. This was not the will of Queen Dianna, but a subversive faction of the Council which had secretly sworn allegiance to Magar. They broke her power, and prevented her from offering you proper aid in your time of need. Their own trap has snared them, and I have been able to restore the power to the throne. We are here to make amends for the years of indifference.

"My troops will go first into battle. We will bear the brunt of the attack. We do this to show you that we will take the vanguard, and never the rear in any battle which is to come. Your races have carried the battle alone too long. Now it is our turn to carry the burden," David explained.

"Where are the rest of your troops?" asked Fen Den.

"These are all we need," David replied.

"We were told you had left the city with five thousand troops," announced Wil Den.

"Yes, but they were not all dedicated to the Adoni. I felt it best to go into battle with only those who were willing to give all for what they believed than to have more troops which had divided loyalties."

"You plan to attack 10,000 troops with an army of..." Ren now did a fast calculation of what he saw. "About 500?"

"Those were my instructions," David admitted. He could see that Agron and Handar were obviously nervous when the final numbers had been tallied for both sides.

"*Instructions?*" Han asked.

"My brother unicorns have given me guidelines from the Adoni. They have told me that the Adoni has already placed the battle into our hands. These will be all that we need."

"And you will go into battle first. What are we to do?" Ren asked.

"If we are turned back, then we will call upon you for help, but I don't see that as happening. I ask you to come and see what the Adoni has in store for us all."

CHAPTER FOURTEEN

BATTLE IN THE FOREST

David stirred in his sleep. He should have been lost in restful slumber because, in addition to the songs of praise being sung by the sentries, the unicorns were singing to him in their own special way. He drifted between this world and the next. He felt as if he were neither awake, nor asleep. It was a comfortable feeling. He wasn't tired. He felt more rested than he had from any such sleep, but somehow the sounds of the camp were slipping away from him. He almost felt as if he were hovering in the air above his bedroll. He finally decided that sleep was going to escape him for several more hours, and so he opened his eyes. Now he was wide awake, but he could no longer hear the sounds of the sentries singing, nor the unicorns echoing the songs of praise to the Adoni. He sat up, and noticed that the camp was still. He could not even feel the evening breeze coming off the lake. There were no sounds of insects, wildlife, or night fowl to be heard. The Knight of Es-Soh-En rolled over, pulled his feet under him into a crouching position, and surveyed the camp. Those who were asleep did not seem to breathe. There was no rhythmic rising and falling of the chest to prove that they were even alive. Those standing did not move. The Steward of the Throne of Dula focused on the night fires. They did not flicker.

The flames seemed frozen between this blinking of an eye and the next.

The Child of Earth moved with the grace of a panther stalking its prey low to the ground. He was still in a crouching position, eyes darting back and forth to see where the foe would attack. He drew his sword from its sheath, glad that the faint coat of oil kept it from making any sounds as he pulled it free. David was near the bushes, and stood slowly to see more of the surroundings. As far as his eyes could pierce through the darkness, nothing was moving. He approached the sentry as he stood, mouth opened in mid-song. The eyes were unblinking. David touched the neck and could not feel any pulse. The Knight of Es-Soh-En tried to push down the guard's hand which held the spear, but it was frozen. He did not make too strong an effort so as not to injure the watchman.

David wasn't sure how long he had moved about the camp checking each of the soldiers. Even the centaurs, minotaurs, and gnomes were like statues in their patrols and sleep. David moved to the lake. The waves were frozen. The crest of the waves stood firm, no evening breeze moved them. David was even able to walk out onto the surface of the lake, and touch the frozen waves; climbing over the large waves closer to shore to inspect the smaller waves further out on the lake. The droplets that hung in the air came lose in his hand; but when he dropped them, they hung in the air, neither dropping into the water, nor merging with the wave. He sat several on the crest of the wave, and pressed them together, but they remained separate objects.

"So if nothing is moving, how come I can still breathe?" David mused out loud. "The air around me should be used up, unable to replace what I inhale. In fact, the air around me should hold me fast and make it impossible for me to even move. This is a selective freezing of objects. This type of selectivity implies great control."

As the Child of Earth made his way back to the shore, he noted something: faces. There were hundreds of faces – male and female – in the waters. He could tell what they were. These were the Water People, still in transition from water to human form. They were all along the shore. As the Knight of Es-Soh-En studied the faces, he had the sense that they were friendly faces. They were not here to attack. They seemed to be *observing* was the only word which seemed to describe what he was seeing.

There came a sound, off in the distance. David's senses were instantly alert. He stepped off the surface of the lake, and moved to the shore. If everything were frozen, then sound should also be frozen. If there was sound, then someone, or something, was unfrozen like himself. The voice came from the east, in the direction the army was to travel. It was hovering right on the edge of his ability to recognize the sound.

The Steward moved down the shore of the lake, into the underbrush. He came up suddenly when he came face-to-face with Deenara. The unicorn, too, was frozen in time. David studied the face of his friend. The blue eyes were a normal color. The swirl of light and dark hues of blue was balanced in the eyes. Whatever froze the unicorn had done so so quickly that the Untarnished had never had time to realize the danger. There was an alertness to the expression on Deenara's face, but not surprise, terror, nor alarm.

The sound was more obvious now. It was louder, but still impossible to recognize. David worked his away around Deenara and further into the brush. The sound was getting louder, but it was not any clearer. This seemed to bother the Knight of Es-Soh-En since logic would follow that the louder a sound became, the easier it would be to identify. There was a quality to the sound, almost melodic. David stopped for a moment, closed his eyes, and concentrated; not on the sound, but on the sensation. It was as if he were in a room, filled with bells made of the purest silver – from the smallest, paper-thin bells to the great bells which could deafen you if they sounded. Something – perhaps an evening breeze – was moving among the bells. They were sounding with faint whispers, but their tones were clear, precise. The notes were more perfect than even the skilled craftsman should have been able to generate after a lifetime of labor. There was only one who had such a voice.

"Glidon!" David called out. He opened his eyes, fully expecting to see the Golden Eagle before him, but the forest was dark and bare. Disappointment settled on his heart. He turned, and nearly collided with the Third of the Adoni. The Child of Earth stumbled back, nearly lost his footing, and then reversed his direction to throw himself onto the breast of the great bird. Glidon folded His wing over David, holding him fast. David had not realized just how frightened he had become since coming to Dula and finding so many things changed. Now that Glidon was here, he felt drained of any strength to press on. He wanted to stop, and stay here forever.

The Golden Eagle waited until David had gained what strength and reassurance he could from such close contact with the Adoni. Finally, Glidon could sense David was recharged, and ready for the task at hand.

"Come, we have a ways to travel," sang the bird. His melodic voice caused David's entire frame to resonate with the notes of the Adoni's voice. Glidon crouched, bent one leg for David to step on, and allowed the Steward of the Throne of Dula to climb onto His back. David perched on Glidon's massive neck, and hooked his legs under the powerful wings which caught the still night air, and launched them into the sky.

"I want to show you the battle," the Great Eagle offered once they were in the air, and skimming along the tree tops. Several leaves slapped David's boots. For a moment David wondered about that because he had no memory of getting dressed before he began his scouting expedition. He also wore his original attire as a Knight of Es-Soh-En. Strapped to his hip was Gennerroth.

"Is this a dream?" he asked.

"More than a dream, less than a vision," Glidon suggested. "We have called you to Us. There was no way, other than to snatch you from between the seconds of time, one grain of the hourglass and the next. When you return, all this would have taken place in the twinkling of an eye.

"We have given you the battle tomorrow. It shall be won without anyone lifting a sword. We know that you believe because you have heard the unicorn's message, but your troops will need to believe, both tomorrow and in the future. They do not have the benefit of your years of faith and trust. We will show you what has transpired, and you will tell them before you break camp. This way they will know the Adoni are with them."

Glidon swooped lower, darting between the trees. He hovered, beating the air with His powerful wings. Before them was a tree with a symbol for the worship of Cronis hacked into its trunk.

"They are that obvious?" David inquired.

"They thought it might be a Tree Druid. They believe that by carving a symbol of the Dark Lord into the Tree Druid while it is in tree form, they will bind the spirit of the druid forever in the form of a tree," Glidon explained.

"I have never heard that? Is it true?"

"Of course not, but it doesn't stop them from trying. There are many trees that bear these marks. You will need to *heal* the trees after the battle. There must be no mark of the Dark One here."

"How will I heal the trees, and how many marks must I look for?" David asked. If it was so important to the Adoni to have the job done, then he needed to know how to do the job, and when to tell the job was complete."

"Take the black soil, at the base of each tree injured. Mix it with water and leaves from the tree. Grind them, and mix them together; then smear the compound on the wound. Cover the entire area. We have promised the trees that this will give them the power to heal themselves. There are twelve hundred and thirty-seven such marks. Do not stop until you have personally accounted for each one."

Glidon pounded the air with His wings, and carried them back above the tree tops. Their flight was faster now. They covered several miles. Suddenly they came over the trees, and saw a vast clearing below. Thousands of trees had ben cut down to make room for the massive camp. Tents and camp fires were sprawled across several miles of opened woods. The scene was not uniform. It did not have the initial appearance of military spacing for a camp. As David's eyes adjusted, he noted that most of the tents were torn, ripped apart, and scattered. Not all the fires were in fire pits. Numerous tents burned, torches lay on the ground. Fires burned wagons, supplies, and bodies. Everywhere there was carnage. Bodies, literally thousands of them, lay dead or dying across the entire campsite.

"What happened? Did You do this?" David asked of the Great Eagle.

"No, We did not have to. The advanced army has been gone from Magar for ten years. They were an army when they left, but they had to assume to role of robbers and thieves. You cannot pretend for so long without becoming what you present yourself to be. When the new soldiers came from Magar, they found an undisciplined mob waiting for them. The advanced army refused to obey orders they did not like. They refused to dress in military fashion. They had grown to like their way of life. It started over something small, but then broke into a full-scale mutiny. They have been killing each other since the gnomes, centaurs, and minotaurs joined you."

"And what of the Water People?" David asked, recalling the fourth race once Glidon had mentioned the other three.

"They are coming to join you. They will not make themselves known until after tomorrow's battle. They want to see if you truly are willing to go into battle for them. They were mistreated the worst of all. Their homes were destroyed without Dianna's knowledge. Their village was burned, their possessions either confiscated or destroyed. If their foes had known of their life stones, they would have been killed. As it was, they chose to hide in the rivers, lakes and water ways rather than to confront their foes."

"And after tomorrow's battle they will join us?" David asked.

"Yes. You recall that they have a unique form of fighting which makes them all but unbeatable. But they need someone to lead them. They need a cause. You will be that cause."

"And what of Dianna?" David asked once Glidon had mentioned the missing queen.

"She is safe. Do not fear for her well-being. Beyond that, I can say no more; but you will see her again, soon." Glidon bolted high into the air. Somewhere David seemed to sense more than hear the phrase, *Beware the time the golden mist seeks you...*

Suddenly he was in free-fall. Glidon was no longer below him. He was about to cry out, to shift his angle of fall to try and catch the trees when he sat up in bed back in the middle of camp.

"Agron! Han! Ren! Fen Den!" He bellowed, pulling his shirt and tunic on, and shoving his feet into his boots as he hopped across the camp. The leaders of the clans came charging to the center of the camp. Sounds were coming from throughout the camp as others heard the call David was making. "Prepare the troops. Break the camp. We have a mission."

"It isn't even light out," Handar mumbled, rubbing the sleep out of his eyes. It was obvious he was not a morning person.

"My lord. If we go into battle so disorganized, it will endanger the mission," Agron offered, trying to buy enough time for his troops of rouse themselves, and make an orderly breaking of camp.

"There will be no battle. The war is already over," David announced.

"Over?" bellowed Ren. "But we haven't even engaged them!"

"They've done themselves in," David announced, fastening his sword to his hip. The men were already breaking camp. Agron had voiced his concerns, but as a true soldier followed-through when the orders remained the same. Beds were hurriedly rolled and tied to saddles, horsed were bridled and loaded.

"Leave the supply wagons. They can follow us later. We travel light, and we travel fast," David ordered, slinging the saddle onto his horse. By the time he was pulling himself onto his steed, most of the troops were already mounted and ready to travel. True, many were still dressing or arranging clothes or armor while they sat on horse-back, but they knew the Steward of the Throne of Dula wanted to travel, and travel fast. They would make adjustments along the way. The centaurs scooped up the gnomes, and swung them onto their backs to make sure that they would not be left behind. The minotaurs were already at the eastern edge of the camp.

"Let's go!' David shouted. He kicked his horse, and it bolted forward. The entire army fell in behind him. The minotaurs kept pace with the horses and centaurs. David noted that they didn't even seem to be breathing hard.

"So what brings about this sudden breaking of camp?" Agron asked when they were on the move, and he was able to pull up alongside of the commanding officer. "Did the unicorn send word?"

"More than a unicorn. I had a visit this night from Glidon. He took me to the battle site."

"Glidon?!" Agron's heart beat faster. "But no one saw Him in the camp."

"It's hard to explain," David admitted. "He told me He had brought me there between the twinklings of an eye. It seemed like hours to us, but it was so quick, no one else in the camp noticed it." The Knight of Es-Soh-En then related the details of his experience during the night. When he finished, Agron's look was grave.

"My lord? I must speak freely concerning this." David nodded, and Agron continued. "How do we know this isn't a trap?"

"A trap?" David echoed.

"Yes, a trap. None but you had the vision. There is no physical evidence that such a trip took place. What if this was the work of the Dark One, tricking us into running pell-mell into a fully prepared army? We are distracted, ill-prepared, and poorly rested. If the Dark Lord has deceived you, we will be unable to defend ourselves in battle."

David nearly pulled up the reins on his horse. It was something he had not considered. He had always insisted that the *spirits be tested* before taking any action. He had just broken his own rule. His mind reached out to the unicorn for guidance before his troops were unable to recover from his lack of discipline.

"We are here David. Be at peace. We were not part of the vision, but the Adoni confirm that this is not the work of the Dark One." The Knight of Es-Soh-En thanked his herd-brothers.

"The unicorn confirm the message, Agron. It was a vision, but it was true all the same. Thank you for your wise counsel." He pressed his horse that much harder. In less than an hour, they came to the edge of the clearing. The scene was as David had seen it in his vision. Thousands of bodies lay strewn throughout the camp. Remnants of tents were tossed in the night breeze. Fires burned everywhere. Arrows protruded from bodies, wagons and animals. There must have been several thousand of them. It had to have been the fiercest part of the battle. The center of the camp was littered with the shafts. Someone had fired from the other side, killing a vast portion of the armies on both sides. When the arrows had run out, they had come at each other with sword, spears and axes. The bodies spreading out from the center were butchered, hacked and slashed. As they rode to the far side of the camp, the bodies became fewer.

"Some of them must have escaped," David observed. As he spoke, the centaur, gnomes, and minotaur broke rank and dispersed into the woods. Whoever had gotten away would be easy prey for them. David pulled reign on his horse, and signaled for the army to gather around him.

"We have two missions here. The first will not be pleasant, but we cannot leave the bodies unburied. To do so would pollute the land. We must bury all these bodies…" he looked around at the scenes of violence, "…and body parts. We will take shifts for the smell will soon become hard to bear. One group will dig mass graves; another group will locate and identify the bodies to be buried. A third group will use liters to transport the bodies to the graves."

Already the army was breaking into groups. They did not grumble about the unpleasant task. David then announced another task.

"I need a fourth group to *heal the trees.*" There was confusion on the faces of the troops. "Glidon spoke to me that there were twelve hundred and thirty-seven trees in the area which now bear a sign of Cronis-worship carved into the bark. Whenever any tree is found with that mark, you must take the black soil from the base of the tree, mix it with ground up leaves from that tree and water. This is to be smeared over the entire symbol. Any area that is missing its bark on the tree must be completely covered. The Great Eagle told me that this would give the trees the power to heal themselves of these wounds. The Adoni were very clear that They felt that this was the most important of the mission. All twelve hundred and thirty-seven symbols must be removed to insure that the Dark One has no power or claim in this area. We will purge his stain from the trees, and bury the bodies to protect the land from pollution."

A fourth group broke from the other three, and met with David to prepare a way to tally all the marks found on the trees. David would then personally inspect the treated trees as Glidon had instructed him. The Heart Company was nothing if not thorough. They would not rest until every trace of Magar and the Dark Lord were gone from their land. As they were getting organized, the minotaurs and centaurs dragged numerous other bodies of Magarian soldiers into the clearing.

"We did not kill them," Han insisted. "The strangest thing happened. We confronted them. We drew swords or bow to fight them, but when they charged us; they fell dead without ever being touched. When we examined the bodies, there wasn't a mark on them." It was obvious that the minotaur, gnomes, and centaurs were uneasy about such events. David nodded and simply said, "The Adoni fight for us this day. None may stand against Them." The reality of the situation suddenly dawned upon both the humans and the other races. They all raised their hands to the sky, and sang a song of praise to the Adoni.

CHAPTER FIFTEEN

AFFAIRS OF THE KINGDOM

Tanya turned over in her bed when she heard the knocking at her door. At first she wasn't sure it was knocking, or if it might even be some kind of soft scratching. It had intruded on her dreams. It had been a late night for the entire kingdom. Three days ago the troops dismissed by David had come to the palace gates. Pentra was angry with them for returning instead of insisting on staying with the Steward of the Throne of Dula and forming a back-up force in case the battle with Magar did not go well. When they told how David had demanded that they leave because he had too many men, Pentra nearly hit the roof. It was all Tanya could do to calm the commander-in-chief so that he did not regroup, and march back out with the troops who had returned along with any other forces he could spare.

"He had to have his reasons," Tanya insisted while Pentra ranted in the private chambers. Neither she, nor her brother, had stood on ceremony; and it was common for those who served them to come in private, and express their true feelings. Free speech was encouraged, but discretion was also mandatory for the event. The Children of Earth had found it better to confront these feelings instead of ignoring them, and hoping they would go away.

"*Too many men!*" he bellowed. It was a good thing that the door and windows were shut. Even this high above the courtyard his voice would have carried. Hentery sat with the Stewardess as Pentra vented. "According to our sources," Pentra motioned towards the mouse as he spoke, "There are ten thousand troops in those woods from Magar. He's going against them with only five hundred! Five Hundred!! They won't stand a chance."

"According to the men who came back, Sir David told them the battle had already been given to him by the Adoni. He was instructed to *weed out* those who were not loyal to the Adoni before going into battle," Hentery explained.

"You can't trust the Adoni like that…It's not…" here Pentra sputtered. He was at a loss for words. True, he was a follower of the Adoni, but he had made many compromises over the last ten years to maintain his power. He found it hard to give up old habits.

"*Practical?*" Tanya offered as the word Pentra was looking for.

"My Lady. I mean no disrespect to yourself, Sir David, or the Adoni. It's just that They haven't worked like this for a long time. Any soldier who would place his life, and the lives of his troops, on such a whim would be slaughtered. If he survived the battle, he would be executed for incompetence. It goes against every rule of warfare."

"Lord Pentra," Tanya began with a soft tone to her voice. She knew that he was having a hard time dealing with faith versus reality. "You have said that the Adoni do not work like that. But you are speaking of those times when the Children of Earth or the Knights of Es-Soh-En were not sent by Them to work in just that sort of way. When we appear, it is because the Adoni have deemed it is time to take physical action in the events of this world. From the moment we appeared outside the castle, nothing has been the same."

"Amen to that," Pentra agreed.

"My brother is not given to rash decisions. He has probably five or six hundred years of battle experience behind him." It surprised Tanya when she realized how long their lives really had been. They were young adults by Earth years, but they would travel to different time lines for the Lands of the Adoni, live months or years here, then return to Earth, and not have aged a second. She had begun to estimate the time they had spent in Dula with all of their visits, and the number surprised her as well. It had obviously caught Pentra and Hentery off guard.

"He has been in every kind of battle: physical, mental, and spiritual that you could think of. He has battled alone, with a team, with a partner; and with armies. He has been outnumbered and out-flanked. He knows more tricks about combat than any army has ever forgotten. If he tells me that he has sent these men home because the Adoni instructed him to do so, then I am sure that he was very sure that those instructions came from the Adoni. If the Adoni promise the battle to you, and then you refuse to do what They tell you to do, you might find yourself on the losing end; or winning may cost more than you bargained for. We need to wait, and see what the outcome will be."

Pentra was not comfortable with such a decision, but he was willing to wait. When several messengers from David's army, and representatives of each of the races had approached the gates yesterday morning, Pentra was hard-pressed to wait for Lady Tanya so the messengers could properly deliver their information. When the results of the war were made known, Pentra had to do a lot of re-thinking about his own concepts of the Adoni. Where he had grown after the Battle of the Veil, he now made even greater strides to change his approach to serving the Adoni.

Word spread quickly throughout the city. Those who returned before the battle had made sure that everyone knew Sir

David had cut his forces before going into battle as part of a plan. It was the decision of the Steward of the Throne of Dula, and not that they had deserted or asked to leave. All of the returning soldiers had insisted that they had followed orders, and so they had returned to the city with honor. They taught that their actions were just as important to the success of the campaign as those who went into the battle. Most did not believe what they said, but felt it important to support Sir David to save face among the townspeople. Their tales had actually build up the coming confrontation more than David would have been comfortable admitting.

The entire city had been waiting, almost holding their breath to hear the results. Sir David had been a legend greater than they could comprehend. Each time he acted, it was some new event, some new accomplishment that the townspeople had believed impossible. For some reason, the impossible always seemed possible when Sir David was involved. Many believed that the army would win, even if they were out-numbered twenty-to-one.

Whoever had made the comment during the evening session with the Knight of Es-Soh-En about winning the coming war without raising a sword had begun to share his comment. Now, instead of it being a sarcastic remark; it was viewed as true faith in the Steward of the Throne of Dula. Tanya knew it was difficult for David. He knew the people always seemed to praise him for what the Adoni did in his life. He tried to redirect their focus, but on this visit it had become impossible. He was there before them. The Adoni were nothing more than names in the wind; concepts forgotten long ago.

When the messengers came to the gates, most of the city had turned out to see them. Everyone noticed that the messengers and the representatives were in good spirits, and bore no wounds or signs of battle. Before the message was ever delivered to Lady Tanya, the city was already convinced their army had been successful, and was already breaking out the drinks and the food to celebrate. By the time the official word was handed down, shops had been closed, schools dismissed, and party clothes donned. They danced in the courtyards, the streets, and the fields. Minstrels gathered impromptu, and played for hours. Everyone brought their dinners out of their homes, and spread them on large tables for all to share. Pentra stood at the courtyard gate, looking up with tears in his eyes as Lady Tanya stood in the window and led everyone in a song of praise to the Adoni.

Now the knocking came a third time. Yes, definitely a knocking. It couldn't be about David. He had sent word that it would take a week to bury the dead, and then the centaurs, minotaurs, and gnomes wanted to have him and the army attend a week-long celebration in the Gen Forest. David had even mentioned that the Water People had met with him, and offered their support.

Tanya kicked the blankets off of her, swung her feet out of bed, and felt the cold stone floor against her bare feet. She couldn't find her robe, as her maids-in-waiting were all still celebrating, or recovering from the celebration in some other part of the city. She grabbed the smaller of the blankets, swung it around her, pulled her hair out of her face, and shuffled to the door.

As she threw back the oak door, the small form of Hentery caught her eye. It had been a trait she had developed long ago. When dealing with inhabitants who could be so small, always scan the entire door when it is opened. It could prevent embarrassment from missing someone important, or injury from ignoring a small assassin. Hentery stepped into the room, pulled off his wide-brimmed hat, bowed before her with a graceful sweep of his hand. As he did so, he motioned discreetly to quickly close the door.

"You have news?" she asked as soon as the door was closed to prying eyes and ears.

"Rayton has been captured," he announced.

"Rayton!" she exclaimed. "Did he have the scroll?" She threw off her blanket, and splashed water into the wash bowl, rubbing her face with the cold liquid, and then hunting for a towel. Hentery bounded up several pieces of furniture to put one within her reach. "Thanks!"

"We don't know if he has the scroll or not. Pentra is with him now, and is conducting a search." As the mouse made his report, Tanya slid behind her dressing screen, and threw off her night clothes, and hurried into her regular clothes. She came around the screen, shoving her feet into shoes, and brushing her hair.

"So what happened?" she asked, lifting him to her shoulder so they could make better time.

"We're just now getting details. Beech was watching the gates since last night .He figured that with all the celebration it would be the best time for Rayton to slip out. He was with a merchant, and tried to pretend to be on business."

"Have the merchant and everything he has – or has been in contact with – searched as well." She bounded down the castle stairs three or four at a time. Hentery was glad she had kicked off her shoes and carried them as she descended; for she was treating the steps more like a cliff than a staircase. She leaped several steps, crouched when she hit, sprang further out to clear a few additional steps, skipped one or two more, and then repeated the process. Hentery clung to her hair for dear life. He wished he had lashed himself to her before she started down.

It had to have been a new record to travel from the upper chambers, where important guests stayed, to the dungeon in such a short time. Lady Tanya entered the holding area still carrying her shoes. She dropped them, and they made a clattering sound on the stone floor. She snatched Hentery from her shoulder, and placed him on the nearest table – much to his relief – as she pushed her feet into the shoes, and addressed Pentra.

"Where's the merchant?" she demanded, assuming that the person standing between two guards near the back of the area was Rayton. Pentra was personally going through a mountain of items scattered on the large table in the center of the room.

"We have him in cell number three," Pentra replied. He was carefully examining a piece of clothing as he spoke, and so he did not look up.

"Are there guards with him?" she asked. "We don't want a repeat of the Unter incident."

"I have three guards in the cell, and two outside the door," Pentra reported. The other cells were filled from the arrests made based on Unter's organizational charts.

"Take a look at this one," came a small voice from the middle of the pile of clothes. A shirt began to wiggle and move on its own. A second later, Beech appeared pulling the shirt he had identified. "I think this one has something in the hem."

The mouse had been digging through the items on the table trying to shorten the search by pulling out those items that seemed suspicious. Already several documents and items had been removed from lining, hidden pockets, and hems in various garments. Tanya cast a side-ways look at Rayton, and the nervous expression in his eyes told her more than anything else. Pentra drew his dagger, and cut the stitching that served to form the hem on the bottom of the shirt. He pulled back the material, and a small rolled scroll of blue parchment emerged from the opening.

"That's it!" Tanya shouted. She took the document from Pentra, rubbing its surface to make sure it was real. "As soon as David returns, we can read this, and see what Tra had to say." She left instructions for Hentery to contact her if they found anything else of major importance. So far the documents were unimportant messages, nothing vital, only regular status reports on activities. She returned to her quarters and took the time to properly prepare herself for the day's events.

Once she was washed and dressed, and in the privacy of her room, she took time to examine the scroll. She had only given it a moment's glance in the Record Chamber before she ran with it and fell. She noted that it had thick dust on it from centuries of sitting on the shelf. She was surprised the paper was not brittle, faded, or crumbling. She wiped the dust from the scroll. There came a sudden tapping at her door. Although it was not a loud tapping, it had an urgency about it. Tanya recalled the last problem she had encountered when she found the scroll, and lifted the top of her dresser up, revealing a hollow space along the lip. It was just enough space to conceal the scroll. Tanya did not believe the dresser had been constructed with a hidden compartment, but once when she moved the furniture, she found the little hiding place, and always kept it in mind if she needed someplace to hide something small. Once the scroll was concealed, she opened the door. Hentery pushed in without ceremony, and pushed the door shut himself. Tanya now knew it was serious.

"Gib-ron has returned!" he declared, leaping on several pieces of furniture to reach the table top. Tanya noted that he didn't even have his hat with him.

"Returned?" Tanya echoed. "He was exiled. Was he arrested by the guards?"

"No, my lady. That's the problem. He's seen as a hero to the people," Hentery explained.

"A hero? That worthless bag of bones?!"

"While the kingdom celebrated last night, Gib-ron's men did their work. They moved among the people, and told them that this was all part of his plan. His spies started by saying Dianna had arranged for him to take over the throne while she went on a trip. It was designed to trick Magar into revealing their hand. His spies told everyone that Dianna had requested that the Adoni send you and David to come as soon as she left, and Gib-ron was instructed to put you both in the public role in order to free Gib-ron up for his undercover work. His stories now say that his exile was all a ruse to get him into the good graces of Magar, and misdirect them. He claims he's the one who gave the victory to Dula by using skills long hidden to those in Dula; the Seeing Eye being just one of them."

Tanya was furious. She looked about her room, half thinking she would find Sy-lar, or some other sword so she could confront the traitor. When she saw nothing she could readily use, she turned, and started towards the door.

"My Lady!!" Hentery called out, stopping her in her tracks. "What are you doing?"

"I'm going to stop him."

"That's the problem. The people have already welcomed him. He came through the gates riding a great war steed only an hour ago. Everyone cheered for him, threw coats and branches in the street before him. He is holding counsel in the throne room even now. Pentra and others are already in jail. Beech and I escaped to warn you. At this point, he seems to have the entire city behind him."

"Then we must tell the people the truth," Tanya suggested.

"There's more…" the tone in the mouse's voice made Tanya stop in her tracks.

"More?" she enquired.

"Sir David is with him."

"WHAT?!!" bellowed Tanya. "What do you mean David is with him?"

"Sir David rode beside him as Gib-ron came through the gates. The Steward has confirmed all that Gib-ron has said."

The shock struck Tanya like cold water in the face. She was stunned. Hentery waited a moment. Tanya raised her bewildered eyes towards the messenger, and waited for the rest of the report.

"Sir David also states that only he had returned to Dula this time. He claims that you remained behind on Earth the same as his last visit. Because you did not come to Dula, Sir David had to find someone who looked like you to play the part. Gib-ron claims you were a serving wench given last minute instructions, but very poor at acting like the Lady Tanya would. You lacked all the social graces she had. This is why you cannot call forth Sy-lar, or change your clothes at will." Hentery waited a moment longer for the new information to sink in. He knew that this was the kind of report which would have to be presented in stages. Each section would build on the previous one. When he could tell that Tanya had prepared herself mentally for the next section he continued.

"The problem is that they claim that you tried to steal the kingdom while Sir David and Gib-ron were away. They claim you found someone who looked like Sir David to go take command of Heart Company when the real Sir David left with Gib-ron. The fake Sir David took command for the purpose of mounting a private army that would take over the throne when they returned." Tanya could take no more. She sprang to her feet, charged the door and roared, "I will have the traitor's head!!"

"It's too late, Hentery continued. He danced on the table, obviously nervous about the delay. "Gib-ron says that you and the imposter David found out where Queen Dianna was staying, and have kidnapped her. He's told the people that you and the imposter Sir David have refused to reveal where Queen Dianna is, but you're holding her hostage in a hidden place. Only you and you partner know where the Queen really is, but neither of you will release her. He's calling for the people to rise up against you and the fake Steward, and force you to tell them where Dianna is and release her. We have to run while there's still time."

"What?!!" Tanya cried out. She could not believe her ears. Suddenly, Gib-ron had twisted everything around, and he was now in charge of Dula, while she was the fugitive. The one point which did not make sense was why David was siding with Gib-ron. She had to confront them in public.

Before she could turn around, the door splintered under the weight of several guards. Tanya noted that they were guards who had been disgraced by the actions of her and David. The first guard stepped into the room, grabbing Tanya by the arm. Instead of resisting the pull as he was expecting, she used his pulling motion to add momentum to her own, slamming into the guard with her full weight. He released her, and fell to the floor. She brought her foot down hard and fast into his groin area, stood up on his body, and kicked the next guard full in the face. The attacker's head snapped back, and he went down without any further sound.

Four more flowed through the doorway. The first two had pikes which they crossed in front of the door to block her escape. Tanya grabbed each pike just under the head, held tight, pulled herself up on them, and swung her feet into the faces of the other two guards still in the doorway. They fell back. The two holding the pikes were surprised by the sudden action, and tried to pull the pikes back out of her grasp. Tanya dropped one foot to the floor to give herself balance, and slammed the blunt metal sides of the pikes into the heads of the owners. They dropped the pikes, and crumpled.

Now with a pike in hand for battle, the Knight of Es-Soh-En cleared the doorway, and found ten more guards in the hallway, and twenty more coming up the stairs. Tanya rushed the guards in the hallway, pike-end first. They stepped back to avoid the deadly blade. She pressed her advantage, drove the point into the floor just as she came to the last two men. She vaulted using the pike, slammed both feet into the last two guards in the hallway, driving them to the ground. Still holding the pike she raced towards the stairs. She repeated the vaulting action at the top of the stairs, but this time slammed into the first row of guards just reaching the top. They fell back with her pushing them. As they fell, they drove the other guards back down the stairs. As they fell, all of the twenty guards became a jumbled heap in the stairway, falling and tumbling back down the staircase. Tanya struggled to keep her balance, wits, and pike as she rode the human wave down the stairs. At the bottom, another fifty men blocked her escape. As she got to her feet, they formed a ring around her.

As they completed the ring, Tanya grabbed the base of the pike, and swung it with such speed, that it was like a buzz saw blade keeping all of them back. She stepped forward, and the guards moved back. They didn't break formation, but they did give ground. When they got to the door, they finally had to attack, break, or die. They chose to break.

"So predictable," she spat as she dove through the door with her pike in hand, rolled down the steps into the courtyard, coming back up on her feet, only to be confronted by a sea of townspeople. She stopped in her tracks. She couldn't bring herself to endanger them, and there was no way out of the courtyard without fighting them. The guards swarmed down the stairs, and several grabbed her by arms, legs, and waist; lifting her off the ground so she wouldn't be able to resist. When one guard grabbed her in a way which she felt was too personal, Tanya proved that she was still in control, and far from helpless as she threw back her head, slamming it into his face, and shattering his nose. He screamed, released her, and fell to the ground. The others fell back, leaving only one guard to hold her.

The crowd parted, and Gib-ron strode to the forefront, Sir David at his side. Something must have happened since he left for the battle because he now wore the proper attire of a Knight of Es-Soh-En, and carried Gennerroth at his side. Everyone cheered for them as they approached Tanya. The Stewardess of the Throne knew that it was best to wait and bide her time.

"What is the meaning of this?" she shouted for all the people to hear. She had hoped for a chance to present her position to the townspeople directly, but a guard shoved a gag into her mouth. She tried to bite his hand, but he wore thick leather gloves. Even though held fast, her spirit told the people she was far from defeated.

"The *meaning of this* is that we have come back to reclaim the throne for Queen Dianna. I hope you and your partner have taken good care of her." There was a menace in his smile. As it grew to cover his entire face, Tanya saw what others could not, and the sight sent a chill down her spine. As Gib-ron sneered at her, his eyes began to display a bright, red glow.

Tanya chose that moment to act. She brought her heel down hard against her captor's knee. There came the snapping of bone as his leg buckled under him. He screamed in pain, released his grip on her. She spun, driving her elbow into his face, shattering his nose. Before he had fallen, Tanya had snatched the sword from his sheath, spun it around once, and came face-to-face with Sir David.

THE RETURN OF THE ADONI

Tanya studied the face before her. The stance was not right. She moved in, and he tried to impale her on Gennerroth. Tanya side-stepped the attack, knocked the blade aside, and slammed her elbow into his midsection. Sir David crumpled to his knees, and then rose to swing Gennerroth in a blinding dance of death. Tanya fell back. The motions were too flashy. It would impress the novice, but not the seasoned warrior. Such a display took a toll on the attacker's energy levels. It was just a matter of finding the right time to act. She stepped back three times. The other guards held back as Gennerroth flailed wildly, and was a danger to any in its path. On the fourth step, Sir David had to lean forward as he pressed the attack. His body was no longer in a direct line with the blade. Tanya thrust her own blade into the whirling arc of steel. Gennerroth shattered, pieces of the blade spun wildly through the crowd. Several people ducked, one or two were cut by the shrapnel.

Sir David roared his anger, vowed the death of Tanya as a traitor, and drew a dagger to lunge at her. Without missing a beat from her last attack, she side-stepped, and plunged her blade deep into Sir David's chest. He was dead before he even struck the ground. Suddenly guards were piling onto her in such numbers that the very press drove her to the ground. Someone's gauntlet slammed into her head, and everything went black.

CHAPTER SIXTEEN

"AND ONE OF YOU SHALL
TASTE OF DEATH"

Tanya looked out over the courtyard. The newly-installed bars over her window only confirmed that even though they had returned her to her room, it was still a prison. Tanya wondered why they had moved her from the dungeon where she had been for the past week-and-a-half. The darkness, lack of food, foul water, and unpleasant company had not been able to make her tell Gib-ron's men what they wanted to know: the location of Queen Dianna. Even though Tanya did not know where Dianna was, she thought it best not to reveal this as it seemed to be the only bargaining chip she had left. So long as they thought she knew, then she would not be killed. It might be better to die given what they had put her through the last few days, but she would not break. Tanya had not seen Gib-ron since the day she had fought and killed David in the square. He had not come to interrogate her in the dungeon, but left that task to his soldiers. The fact Gib-ron had not given any personal attention to her interrogation told her that Gib-ron did not really care if they found Queen Dianna or not.

The sound of a key turning in the lock announced that she was about to have visitors. She scanned the room looking for weapons, and found thirty-five items which could kill her visitor, forty-one which would maim or blind, another ten or twelve which would prevent her guest from ever siring children. She thought about taking her vengeance for her treatment in the dungeon now, but chose to wait. When the time came to act, she would make sure it was the one who most deserved the vengeance. Better to have them think they had removed all the dangerous items from her room, and that she was helpless before them. Her thoughts moved quickly to the many lessons she had learned from her long association with the minotaur and centaur races. They had moved war and personal combat to its highest form of art. Their skill in pain, killing, and maiming an opponent made them feared throughout the Lands of the Adoni, but those were just those things they shared openly. She knew the hidden things that were only taught to warriors of the clan.

As the door opened, she noted that it was Gib-ron who had come to see her. Yes, he was the one who deserved her vengeance, but she still felt that now was not the time to act. This was the time to learn all she could from her *host*.

"Good morning, my lady. I hope you are feeling well this morning. Has your food and clothing been satisfactory?" Gib-ron's voice dripped with honey as he spoke. She determined she liked him better when he tried to sound menacing.

"I doubt if you came to discuss my comfort, *walking dead*. I believe you have more important things to take care of." She used the term that the minotaur and centaur gave to their intended victims to let them know that they had been marked for death, and they had best put their affairs in order. Gib-ron was either ignorant of the expression and its use, or did not believe she posed any real threat to him.

"I am concerned about you, my lady. You have some inner hostility that is driving you mad. I stood by and watched you kill your own brother."

"*That* was not my brother," Tanya challenged. Something played in the back of Gib-ron's mind; his eyes reflected his thought process. He was considering several courses of action, chose one and continued.

"You know it wasn't your brother. I know it wasn't your brother," choosing not to continue the lie he had woven previously. "But the townspeople believe it was. That is all that matters. Even now they line the streets to mourn his passing, and curse your name. They still aren't sure what your true name is, so they curse the name of *Tanya*." Gib-ron paused at this point. He was trying to learn something and had used some idle banter to try and put her off her guard. He wasn't very good at this, Tanya noted. "So how did you know?" Gib-ron pressed.

"That's for me to know, and for you to probably never find out," Tanya taunted.

"It is not wise to mock one who has the power to kill you." Gib-ron's voice was now ice.

"Do not fear those who can only kill the body, and then no more. Fear those who can kill the body, and then cast the soul into hell," Tanya quoted. "You aren't even close to being in that category."

"Perhaps not, but death can take many faces, many of them extremely unpleasant. I can choose between sentencing you to death, or allowing you to live as my personal slave." Tanya fought to hide the emotions which flared in her heart. She decided against a physical attack at this point, but sought to put her captor on the defensive.

"And what of Dianna? She is still the current ruler of Dula," Tanya pressed. She goaded him to learn what he knew.

"Doesn't matter. We will find her eventually, and then kill her; and blame your brother the imposter. Or, she will never be found, will be pronounced dead, mourned by the kingdom, and the blame will still be placed on your brother. As you can see, this is a no-lose scenario for me." The spindly-thin form of Gib-ron shook as he laughed, picked up a flower from the table, and paused to smell it. Tanya recalled three ways to kill with the flower stem held by her captive. She smiled at the thought. Gib-ron misread her expression.

"So the reality of your situation dawns on you does it? I am the power in Dula, now. I can order your death, offer you life, or even make you my queen." He dropped the flower on the floor, moved towards her, crushing the petals under foot without thinking. Tanya made her most disgusted look, side-stepped her captor's effort to touch her, turned her back on Gib-ron in mid-stride, and looked out the window. Gib-ron froze in his tracks, anger burning in his eyes.

"You seem to forget that the throne is not yours to give," she added.

"It's a mere technicality, Tanya. Ownership is nine-tenths of the law."

"Yes, but it's the last ten percent that can kill you," she replied in her most suggestive voice. Gib-ron knew what she was suggesting, and that – mixed with her rejection of his advances – brought him to the boiling point. He caught the corner of the table, and hurled it across the room. It shattered against the door with a thunderous crashing sound. No one came to check in response to the sound.

Bad move on your part, Gib-ron, Tanya thought. *This means that if I kill you now, no one will come to check on you, either.*

She fought down her desire to take action. She would wait until he was about to leave, and provide him with a small *present* to remember her by. She turned back to the window to calm herself. Again, Gib-ron misunderstood her actions.

"Waiting for your brother to come and save you?" he taunted. "Let me put your mind at rest. He has sent word that he will be here this afternoon. Seems things at the battlefield took less time than they thought, and so he was able to make it back early. Of course, the entire town realizes he is the imposter, and sees this as an attempt to take the castle and steal the throne."

"So this is why I was brought to my room?" she questioned.

"Let's just say that this is an added insurance. We want your brother to comply with us when he gets here. And don't think of obtaining any help from inside the castle. There were probably twenty, maybe thirty who were still loyal to..." here Gib-ron cleared his throat. He was suddenly uncomfortable with speaking the name of the Adoni. He caught himself, and changed his declaration, "...to you. They are all in the dungeons below. Even that infernal rat, Hentery. We caught him and his hat. He won't be able to send any more messages for you either.

"Seems like everyone who was loyal to you, was named in the investigation of those plotting to steal Dianna's throne. They all supported you in order to rise in rank or power. No one outside of those in the dungeons believes in you any more. They believe you saw an opportunity to steal the throne and did. I am the only one who was truly loyal to the Queen, and my traveling to Magar to defeat our enemies proves it. Soon you will all be out of the way, and Magar will own Dula without lifting a sword."

"You forget about Heart Company," she played him out. He was in the mood to gloat, and she would let him.

"Heart Company will never make it through the gates. The message waiting for your brother when he approaches is that Dula is now a kingdom of peace. All weapons must be left outside the city."

"He would never agree to that," Tanya baited.

"Of course not. He will have to come in alone. The rest of the army will wait outside. That's what we want."

"Do you really think David will let you have the city?"

"*Let me?* It's not a matter of letting me have anything. I already have it. I am in power, and it will take more than an ancient religion to remove me. The people supported him when they thought he was filling in for Dianna. Now that they believe he's an imposter who has kidnapped the Queen, and is trying to steal the throne for himself, they hate him. They love me. I've showed them the error of their ways."

The usurper moved closer towards her. As he slipped his arm around her the Child of Earth did not evade the advance. Once he was in position, Tanya caught his limb at the wrist, twisted the entire arm against the joint, bending it backwards. Before Gib-ron could even cry out in pain from the strained muscles and torn tendons, the Knight of Es-Soh-En slammed the palm of her free hand hard against the back of his elbow. The sound of shattering bones was drowned out by his own scream of agony. The door flew open immediately. Tanya assumed that any sounds of pain from Gib-ron would bring them running. The guards hurried Gib-ron out of her room screaming in pain with each motion, his right arm hanging limp at his side. He shouted threats and promises of intense pain for her as he wailed out the door, and down the hall. One of the guards drew back his hand to slap her across the face with his metal gauntlet-gloved hand. She caught his elbow, and continued his motion by pushing it with all of her might. The action made the guard spin around. Once his back was to her, she kicked him hard, and then shoved him out the door.

"Tell Gib-ron *I throw back the little ones.*" She closed her door herself, and the hurried sounds of a key in the lock told her the guards were locking it more for their protection than to keep her in.

The moment the guards were gone, Tanya heard a sound at the window. She looked out and found, "Hentery! But I thought they had captured you," she exclaimed. She held her hand out the window bars so he could climb on.

"No, that was Beech. I left him my hat when I came to warn you the last time. I couldn't get to you while you were in the dungeon, or it would have created suspicion. When I heard you were being transferred here, I waited until it was safe."

"Safe as it's ever going to be," she suggested.

The mouse seemed to hesitate before continuing. Tanya could tell he was torn with several possible decisions. "Please be at peace, good mouse. I am the true Tanya of Earth. I don't know why Sy-lar has been denied to me on this trip, but remember that David did not have Gennerroth with him, either."

That piece of information set Hentery's mind at ease. He scrambled off the window ledge and into the room. "I believe you are the true Tanya, but you killed Sir David in battle."

"That was not David. He was an imposter Gib-ron created to support his cause," Tanya declared.

"How did you know that this Sir David was an imposter?" Hentery asked, climbing onto the table.

"Gib-ron should pay more attention to details. All the tapestries, paintings, and drawings of my brother show him as he was on his previous visits. However, on his last visit to Dula, David was wounded in battle, and the cut to his face did not heal. He now wears a scar on his cheek as a reminder of that battle. For some reason, the scar never healed, even when he came back to Earth, or after we returned here. The man I killed wore no scar. That is how I knew it was a fake. Further, the fact that a normal blade could shatter Gennerroth proved it was not the true Gennerroth, but a copy. Lastly, the imposter was too flashy. Those three facts proved to me I was fighting someone Gib-ron was trying to pass off as my brother."

"Well, if you want to save the real Sir David, we need to move quickly. Gib-ron has already ordered his men to move. David came to the gate while you were with Gib-ron. He is making his way to the castle, even as we speak. We have to warn him."

"Warn him? About what?" for the first time Hentery heard fear in Tanya's voice.

"Gib-ron has men waiting to ambush David when he gets inside."

"I thought he was going to try and capture him." Tanya was instantly active, retrieving several objects from around the room, and moving to the door. It only took her a second to by-pass the lock mechanism, and to force the door open.

Two guards were stationed outside her door. The first began to draw his sword. Tanya caught his arm, added her momentum to the motion of drawing the sword free of its sheath. By the time the guard realized he was not controlling his arm, the sword was free. His reaction was exactly the one Tanya had been waiting for. He tried to break her grip by resisting, and pulling his arm back down. In his determination, he locked his hand that much tighter on the hilt of his sword. The instant the Knight of Es-Soh-En felt the resistance and change of direction, she pulled down hard on the arm before the guard could stop, and the motion caused the guard to drive his own blade into himself. The first guard was dead before he hit the floor.

Tanya then withdrew the sword so quickly, the hilt slammed into the face of the other guard, catching him where the helmet was opened to allow him to see out. He moaned, and fell to the floor.

Tanya snatched the fallen blade, and darted down the hallway to the stairs. Hentery tried as best he could to keep up with her, but she was little more than a blur charging down the stairs.

***

David had ridden up on his horse when they came to the city almost half-an-hour before. He wasn't sure why, but there was something about the city that did not seem *right*. Agron and Handar came up beside him.

"What is it, sire?" Agron asked.

"It's a *feel* to the air. The gates are closed, even though it's mid-day. There are no sounds of trade or sellers drifting over the walls. I don't hear any of the sounds which normally come from a city. It's almost as if the entire city was asleep or empty."

"Ho there!" Handar shouted at the gates. A lone soldier appeared over the top of the city walls. "Sir David has returned. Open the gates."

"I can't do that," the soldier called back.

"Open the gates!" Agron ordered.

"I'm sorry. But I have my orders," the soldier replied.

"Who gave those orders?" David inquired.

"It was Lord Pentra. He sent orders that the gates were not to be opened for the army."

"Any special reason for these orders?" David continued.

"I didn't ask. I just do what I'm told," the soldier replied.

"Is your commanding officer there?" Agron bellowed. He was quickly losing his patience with the guard.

"Yes, he is."

"Then let me speak with him," David offered.

"He says that the city is closed to the army. This is now a city of peace. No weapons are allowed. If you want to come in, you will have to leave all your weapons outside the city." It was obvious that someone was telling the man what to say.

"Does your commanding officer have a name?" Agron demanded. The guard was obviously nervous. Someone said something to him from the inside courtyard.

"If Sir David wants to come in the city unarmed, he will be allowed in. The rest have to stay outside." Someone said something else to the guard. "Sir David is requested in the throne room to make his report. Until his report is delivered, none of the other soldiers or officers will be allowed in."

"It's a trap," Handar declared.

"Really?" came Agron's flippant reply.

"All was in order when our messengers gave their report and came back. They did not see anything amiss. What could have happened in two weeks to change everything?" Handar replied.

"There's only one way to find out," David offered. He took his sword, and passed it to Agron. "Keep this for me."

"My lord,' Agron protested. "If you go in, you may not be allowed to come out."

"When I go through that gate, move back out of sight. If they attack me, the army must be safe. They will be the only hope of regaining the city. I'll get word to you somehow." David spurred his horse to the gate. A smaller door opened which allowed just him inside. Once through, he eyed the guard who had spoken with them, and the officer who told him what to say. Neither one could make eye contact with him. That told the Child of Earth all he needed to know.

The Knight of Es-Soh-En galloped along the streets, keeping an eye out for any other soldiers or guards. There were no people in the streets or market place. All the doors and windows were closed as he passed. When he saw no signs of resistance, he determined the battle would have to be in the palace.

David leaped off his horse in the outer court, and did not bother to tie it up. The horse moved away, and was soon down a side street. No guards stood their post in front of the main doors. David threw them opened, half-expecting to find the enemy waiting on the other side. The entrance way was deserted. The Knight of Es-Soh-En's boot heels clicked on the marble floor. He marched with determination towards the throne room.

Tanya heard the sounds of David's boots on the marble floor as she came around the corner. She slid low in order to be out of the line of fire. As she came sliding in front of him, she shouted, "Get down!!"

Before the words were even out of her mouth, several shafts came hurtling from hiding. Three of them spat into his back, snapping the chain mail links which had protected him in battle. Tanya screamed as the sight unfolded before her. She lost control of her skid, slammed hard into the wall. The last thing she saw before blackness washed over her was the sight of three shafts still quivering in the back of her brother as he fell face-down on the floor.

CHAPTER SEVENTEEN

"THE PRICE THAT WAS PAID FOR YOU"

David heard Tanya's scream just as she slid across the floor in front of him. His mind went instantly into action. He spun on the balls of his feet, and crouched low. Several shafts flew past him on the left and the right. Suddenly his senses seemed sharper than ever before. It was as if he were seeing everything about him with new eyes. It was similar to the experience he had each time he came to Dula and his eye sight, hearing, smell, and taste were enhanced. Now it was as if they had been enhanced still further.

There was a sound directly behind him. He spun back, fully expecting an attack from behind. He saw Tanya losing control of her skid, spin about, and slam hard against the wall. Her shoulders and head took most of the impact. He was about to step forward when he noticed something at his feet. There was a body lying there on the floor. It had three shafts protruding out of the back. From the angle of the impact, and the location of the entrance wound, they must have hit several vital organs.

David suddenly realized that the figure on the ground had not been there moments ago. He knelt down to examine the body, and noticed that it was dressed in clothing similar to his own. He was about to touch the figure, and turn it over for a more detailed examination; when sounds came from behind him. He forgot the body, rose, and assumed a fighting position. Gennerroth was on his hip, and he drew it without realizing the change.

Those who had fired the arrows were coming out of hiding. What surprised David was the number of figures who were in the hiding places. He was sure such a small area would only have held one or two. There were two hiding places, and so he expected only four assassins; but twenty or thirty figures separated themselves from the shadows. It was the way that some of them separated that caught his attention. Two archers in each hiding place came out of the darkness, but the others seemed to have actually *been* the darkness. They had no depth to their shapes. It was a blacker shadow that stepped into the hallway. Once in the hallway, they assumed features, shapes, and depth.

The Knight of Es-Soh-En now understood the effect of what he was seeing. It was the world about him, the hallway, the archers, and the palace; but there seemed to be another world super-imposed on this one. There was new lighting, new details, new aspects which had always been there, but which he had been unable to perceive.

"It's almost as if a line on a cube suddenly became aware that it was part of the cube," he thought. The creatures of shadow were glaring at him, hissing, while at the same time congratulating the archers on their excellent work. They moved towards him. The archers did not seem to see him, actually walked through him; but the shadow figures saw him, and gave him a wide berth.

As the Child of Earth turned around to see what the archers were doing, he saw over thirty other creatures standing guard around Tanya. Even though she was motionless on the floor, they stood watch over her. Where the shadow figures appeared to have been solid darkness with features, these guards had the appearance of solid light. There was a brilliance about them that filled the hallway. Whenever a shadow figure tried to get close to Tanya, three or four creatures of light drew swords to fend it off. There was no way the shadow figures could get through the guards to harm his sister. It made the Knight of Es-Soh-En feel comfortable knowing that she was not alone.

Gib-ron, his entire arm in a splint, in very intense pain – obviously drugged or drunk – and supported by a guard on either side entered the hall. David almost couldn't see Gib-ron at first because the entire hall was filled with shadow figures surrounding the traitor. It was a small army of shadows moving with him. When Gib-ron approached Tanya, the light guards stepped forward. They did not have to make contact with the shadow figures. The very sense of their presence caused the shadow figures intense pain. They squealed, whined, and slithered back. When they were no longer surrounding Gib-ron, David could clearly see that his right arm had been injured, and the injury seemed to be recent. Each motion of the arm, even by accident, was sending waves of pain into Gib-ron's mind. When it was only Gib-ron and his two guards standing before Tanya, the light guards drew swords. They moved forward, and it was obvious that even though Gib-ron did not see them, he was suddenly uncomfortable, almost fearful. He fell back, far enough away from Tanya until the shadow figures could surround him once more.

Safe within the blanket of these shadow figures, Gib-ron's confidence returned. "Take her back to her room, and make sure she doesn't escape. She's the only one now who knows where Dianna is."

The guards who had carried out the assassination moved forward to obey the order. The light guards stood firm. The assassins began their task confident, filled with hatred and anger, but when their shadow companions fell back, the soldiers felt fearful and exposed. By the time the assassins were able to get to Tanya's form, they had lost all anger. Their hearts were filled with fear. One assassin tried to grab Tanya's arm roughly, but two light guards held his arm fast. It took the man several seconds to realize that he could not hurt the unconscious form. If he were going to move her, he would have to do so gently, and with great care.

As the assassins carried Tanya, the light guards formed an honor guard around her, leading the men down the hall which led to the stairs and up to her room. When the light guards were gone from the hallway, it was obvious that Gib-ron and his swarm of shadow figures were more at ease. Gib-ron staggered over to the figure lying on the ground. David had forgotten about him during the exchange between the light and shadow figures. Gib-ron's foot hooked the arm of the figure on the floor, and turned him over. David let out a gasp as he looked into his own face.

"It can't be!" he shouted. But at the same instant, he understood the enhanced senses, and why Gennerroth was suddenly with him. Even his attire was the original garb provided by the Adoni. At the thought of the Creators of Dula, another light began to glow behind him. As David turned, the hallway filled with clouds. They swirled about him, churning like the waves of an angry sea, but there was no anger or fear in David's heart. The clouds continued to swirl and spin. They blocked his view of the hallway and the world it belonged to; and then formed a great tunnel into the sky. At the end of the tunnel was a light so bright, it should have blinded him instantly. But with his new eyes, he could stare full into the brilliance without blinking.

As David stepped forward, he was stepping onto the clouds. They were solid enough to hold his weight. He laughed with a pure joy as he thought of the time he walked half-way across the chasm on the Mountain of the Sky. This was just like then, only now he knew he would not fall.

He wasn't sure how far he had walked, or how long he had climbed, but the light was always before him. He began to notice that the clouds were thinning out. They were like a morning fog, blowing away on a gentle breeze. He could see that there were thousands of stars, nebulas, and galaxies dancing to a song which now coursed through his veins. The clouds he had walked on were replaced with the most brilliant of rainbows. He recalled the time when he had knelt down, and touched a similar rainbow bridge. It was light at rest; solid light was how Teacher had explained it then.

At the thought of Teacher, David recalled the story Agron had related to him about his brother. Teacher had met Agron's brother, and shown him the scar across His heart. It had been the price Teacher had paid for Agron's brother. David noticed a figure moving in the light. It was as if the figure was absorbing all the light, or as if the light were condensing into the shape of a man. David really couldn't tell which. He stepped forward, and the figure detached itself. It took a second for David to recognize the one who approached, but only a second. Even though they were still several hundred yards apart, David cried out, "Teacher!" and ran towards the figure. The figure ran to meet him. They threw their arms around each other, and hugged so tightly that David was surprised his ribs didn't shatter. Then Teacher held the Knight of Es-Soh-En at arm's length, looked at him, laughed, and held him again. There were tears in both their eyes.

"Tears?' David joked.

"There is always a place for tears of joy," Teacher replied. David waited for Teacher to part His robes, and show the scar where Logos pierced His heart. However, Teacher knew David's thoughts. He shook His head, and said, "That was the price I paid to redeem the Lands of the Adoni. *This* is the price I paid for you." With those words, Teacher held out both of His hands. There were terrible wounds in each one as if the flesh had been torn and pierced by some ancient nail.

"You mean that You're..." but Teacher cut him off before he could speak the name.

"*I AM.*" Teacher waited for the title to sink in. It had been one of the titles David had heard on Earth.

"*I AM that I AM... Tell them I AM sent you,*" David quoted. He had known it all along, but somehow it had been unspoken between them. The truth need be unspoken no longer.

"Jesus!" David cried, throwing himself into the carpenter's arms once more. The figure held David, and patted his back with the nail-scared hands. David sobbed great tears. All the pain of life drained from him as he wept. There was no more sorrow, no more pain; no more uncertainty. It all made sense. Even those things which did not make sense in that world, made sense in this one. As David wept the hold that the world once had on him faded. He was free. He was alive. It was as if he had been in a womb in that world. He had been waiting all of his life to be born, and now he was born. He was born anew into the next.

When David could weep no more, because no sin, or guilt, or pain remained in his heart or mind, the figure released him. David looked about, and the towers of the Greater Kingdom were before them. Around the gate was a great throng, most of whom David could recognize even from this distance. They were calling out to him, bidding him to come and join them. The Knight of Es-Soh-En wiped the tears from his eyes. His guide looked at David, clasped him on the shoulder with one hand, and ushered him into the Greater Kingdom with the other.

"Welcome home," his Savior exclaimed.

CHAPTER EIGHTEEN

THE CONTENTS OF THE SCROLL

There was something cold pressing against Tanya's forehead. It was strangely desirable and unpleasant at the same time. It was cooling an area of her head that felt feverish, but the object was too cold; and pressing on an area which was already painful. Tanya had tried to control her reaction to the rag so her benefactor would not know that she was awake, but it was too late. She had moaned, and turned her head away. As she turned her face, she became aware of an odor in the air. It was more pungent when her face was turned this direction. She opened her eyes, and saw a vaporizer sitting next to her bed, steam fluttering out of its main opening. When she turned back, she saw who was by her bed.

"Hentery?" she asked softly. The mouse held a finger to his lips to indicate the need for her to be silent.

"The guards are just outside the door. They have orders to summon Gib-ron the moment you awake. I slipped in, and tried to treat your wound with this rag. It was left by Co-lin the Healer."

"*Co-lin?*" Tanya whispered. Her mind ran through several lists, and she remembered Co-lin. He had shown indications of being a Follower, but she had never had the time to confirm his dedication before the incident with Unter began.

"Gib-ron had him come, and care for you. He's been imprisoned in the dungeons, and so he can't tell anyone what happened." There was a sudden clicking at the door as the bolt was drawn back. Hentery dropped the cloth he held, and darted for cover under Tanya's pillow.

"My lord," came the voice of Co-lin as the door opened, and two figures entered. "She has suffered a severe trauma, both physically, and mentally. If she is awake now, she still needs to rest."

"I will see her," came the voice of the man who ordered her brother's death. Suddenly it all came flooding back. She saw the scene played out several times, all in slow motion. Each detail burned into her mind. She pushed them to the back of her memory, and focused on the meeting before her.

"You have awaken, my lady," Co-lin observed. His voice was soothing. His face revealed no signs of concern or fear. He picked the rag up from where it was on the pillow. Tanya could tell that for one brief instant a puzzled look crossed his mind, but he suppressed it instantly.

"I got the cloth to cool my head. It felt pretty warm," she offered making sure her voice sounded weak and feeble. Co-lin smiled. It was the smile of a kindly father, caring for his child. He tested the cloth, felt it was too cold, and dipped it anew in the basin next to her bed. He squeezed out the excess, and pressed it gingerly against the wound. It did not burn the way it had when Hentery had tried. She also noted that it wasn't as cold as before. Co-lin smiled with his entire face, making her feel comfortable and welcomed.

"If she is well enough to get the rag, then she should be well enough to be moved," Gib-ron declared. The usurper waved with his left arm to add emphasis to his words. Tanya noted with some small satisfaction that his right arm was limp at his side. With the damage she had inflicted, it would probably never function again. A scowl came over Co-lin's face, but it was obvious the anger was directed at Gib-ron, and that the scowl actually told her that the healer was there to protect her. It was amazing how he had mastered expressions to serve as part of his bed-side manner.

"My lord, she did not have to get out of the bed. She rolled over, and could stretch to get the rag. There is a great difference between reaching and walking. She has had a blow to the head. She has been unconscious. There are thousands of minute points of contact between the mind and the body. In order for her to be rendered unconscious, the blow had to damage a number of these. The mind needs time to go through the process of testing each connection to make sure that it still works. To force the mind to control the body with such activities as walking or long conversations can cause a connection to be missed. If enough of these fail, she may go into a coma. Is that what you want?"

The voice of the healer was firm, even when speaking to the one who held power of life and death over them both. When the healer stepped over to the basin once more, Tanya stole another glimpse of her brother's killer. What caught her eye this time was the object which hung naked at his side.

"Logos," she blurted out. Fortunately for her, her voice was hoarse and cracked. It was due to the anger and pain she was fighting to hold back, and not from any illness, but given what Co-lin had said, it seemed to confirm the healer's diagnosis.

"Yes," gloated Gib-ron. "I found it while going through Dianna's chambers. It's not at all like the sword spoken of in legends. It's missing the hilt jewel. It was given to Janadis as a sign of their eternal treaty, but this gaping hole is an eyesore. And look at this blade. I couldn't figure out what was staining it. I tried to clean the stain, even had the blade ground, but the metal is too hard, and the stain too deep. I've been told it's permanent. It's a rather pathetic item all the same, but it does prove I have the divine right to rule, and so I keep it with me. I suppose if you or your brother had carried it while on the throne, the people would have considered you to be the rightful rulers; but since I have it, and you don't; that just supports my position with the people."

"Sire, please. She needs her rest," Co-lin replied. "Is this a conversation which cannot wait?" Co-lin had read her face, but his application was wrong. He had believed she was too weak to deal with the events, when in reality it was taking all of her effort not to spring from the bed, and strangle Gib-ron with her own hands. He had killed her brother, desecrated the sword, and stolen Dianna's throne. Any one of these was an act worth of death. She swallowed hard, fought back tears that were welling in her eyes, and turned away from her captor.

"Very well. I shall wait a little longer, healer. But notice the emphasis on the word *little*. I intend to conclude this matter in only a few days, not weeks. Use your skills to get her up and moving as soon as possible." With those words Gib-ron spun on his heels, and stormed out of the room. The moment he was outside the door, the bolt was thrown into place.

"You can tell Hentery it's safe to come out now," Co-lin noted. Tanya did not acknowledge the comment. She did not confirm or deny the presence of Hentery until she had studied the face of her host. Finally she said, "I thought Hentery was in the dungeons with you."

"No, that is Beech. He told us Hentery was still free. We've been waiting for him to come to the dungeon with word of events, but he hasn't been seen. He was the one using the rag, wasn't he?" The healer's voice was calming and soothing. He had just called the Stewardess of the Throne of Dula a liar, and never made her feel uncomfortable about it.

"How do you do that?" Tanya asked.

"What?" Co-lin replied innocently.

"The voice, the facial expressions. When you speak, it's more than words. Your entire body conveys a message. There are many messages hidden in the tone, your eyes, your expression, the way you stand, or position your body."

"You will find that the mind sees and hears more than the owner realizes," Co-lin replied. "My specialty is injuries of the head. The mind, if you will. There are those injuries caused by physical damage, and there are those injuries caused by shock or danger. Since you had both, it was only logical to send for me. As for the rest, I have learned a great deal about the mind, and how it works. It sends signals people have no intention of sending. The mind desires to be honest. It is uncomfortable with a lie, but no matter how a person conditions himself – or herself – to hide the lie, the mind wants to be truthful. It's like the games children play when they tell a lie. They always do something so it's not really a lie."

"Like on Earth," Tanya noted. "There we cross our fingers before we tell a lie, and if we're discovered, we claim it wasn't really a lie because we crossed our fingers."

"Exactly. There is always something that the mind does with the body to tell people hearing the lie that they shouldn't believe it. In your case, it's your left eye."

"*My left eye?*" Tanya replied.

"Yes. You have a tendency to squint ever so slightly with your left eye whenever you say something that isn't true. Your bother…" Here Co-lin suddenly realized he had embarked upon a painful subject for Tanya. He recognized it instantly and caught himself.

"That's alright." Tanya offered.

"Another lie, my lady. Really. You must be careful about that."

"No, I'd like to know. I've been with him most of my entire life, and I never noticed any signs of when he was lying."

"It's his voice. Your brother would always tighten his throat, just a little when he lied, and it would make his voice sound a little deeper. In Gib-ron's case-and this should prove useful to you – the left corner of his mouth goes up, just a little."

"It seems that you can read people's thoughts," Tanya observed.

"It's not reading their thoughts. It's reading their body. The body is the book of the mind. If one knows where to look, the information is there."

"And what are your signs for lying?" Tanya asked.

"Ah," Co-lin smiled. "It used to be a flaring of the nostrils. I realized that, and stopped it. Then it moved to a muscle in the jaw. I got rid of that. Over the years I've found it appearing all over my body. I finally discovered that a muscle in my low back tightens when I lie. Since no one can see it, then I stopped changing it. The mind has to display the lie somewhere, and so I let it display it where most people will never see."

"Tell me about your faith in the Adoni," Tanya suggested.

"Now you are in an area which has more than one indicator," he offered. "I have been loyal to the Adoni for many years. I would sit with Queen Dianna on many occasions, and learn from her about Teacher, Es-Soh-En, and Glidon. Her stories would make my heart beat faster. Now there's a woman who has forgotten how to lie. I tried to find her warning signal, and never could discover it. I have to surmise that she is very good at what she does, or she never lies. Given her love for the Adoni, I assume she never lies."

"It would make the world a much nicer place, but given the battles we have to wage, there are times when it is best to keep information hidden, or use lies to misdirect the enemy."

"That would be true, but when your enemy knows you are misdirecting him or her; then the point is useless. So, have I passed your test?"

"*Test?*" Tanya replied, and was suddenly aware of her eye squinting ever so slightly.

"You really need to work on that, my lady," Co-lin suggested.

"We are instructed to test the spirits. To make sure the person is loyal to the Adoni."

"And have I convinced you that I am loyal?" Co-lin asked.

"I would like to believe you. It's just that for someone like yourself, with such control over his body signals, I'm not sure how to tell. You've said all the right things. You spoke the name of the Adoni without discomfort, but like you've said, you've had years to practice all the right responses."

"You are a cautious one," Co-lin observed with a smile. "I guess to survive as long as you have in so many situations, you have to be. I could offer to let you test the muscle in my low back when I spoke but…" Co-lin's voice trailed off here as he waited for Tanya to complete his offer.

"But how do I know that's really your signal. You may have said that to mislead me," she noted.

"And so we are at a stalemate. I want you to believe me, but you are not sure if my message is true. You are in a very vulnerable position. You have just lost a close support, you are locked in a room, you are told to trust no one, but you believe the lives of many are in your hands. You would like to believe, but you don't have the luxury of believing. But that is enough for me. I know you would believe if it were only your life involved, but you cannot risk the lives of others. I feel safe putting my faith in your hands. I can accept your desire, and your willingness to hold off making any further judgment until later.

"Gib-ron will want to know when you will be strong enough to question further. I suspect he has something else in mind, not at all pleasant, but I haven't figured out what it is. How much time do you want?" Co-lin asked.

"Are you sure there's no permanent damage?" Tanya asked.

"Physically, no. I've tested various nerves and muscles as we spoke. If the connections from your brain were not in place, you would have trouble with certain words or facial expressions. Your hands and arms move without difficulty. Right now, your physical wound in nothing more than a cut on the head, and a headache – which will last another day or so. Your mental anguish, on the other hand, will not heal until you have mourned the loss of your brother, and taken the vengeance which is burning in your heart. I cannot give a time frame for that. I will let Gib-ron know that he will have to wait three days before you can be moved. That should give you enough time to recover, and make what plans you need. Do not take too long with the plans, though. I suspect that executions will begin in about a week or so."

With those words, Co-lin tapped on the door, and the guards let him out. When the bolt slid back into place Hentery scrambled out of hiding.

"He's good," Hentery noted.

"*Good* as in what he does, or *good* as in he serves the Adoni?"

"I would like to say both, but when you're as good as he is, he has to get used to people suspecting him."

"So what news do you have to report?" Tanya shifted the subject.

"There are thirty-eight people in the dungeons." Hentery rambled off the list of names. Pentra, Co-lin, and Gort were among the ones listed. "In addition to them, I have found another one hundred and two who are loyal to the Adoni, and are hiding in various places around the city."

"And what of my brother's body?" Tanya asked. The business-like tone to her voice caught Hentery off-guard. He was more uncomfortable about the topic than Tanya.

"I grieve for him, Hentery. But grief right now will not save the lives of those who are in danger from Gib-ron. We will move against him when the time is right, but first we must get everyone to safety. This means getting those in the dungeons free, joining those in hiding, and fleeing the city. If I have to leave the city, I have no intentions of leaving my brother's body behind."

"He is in the back of the castle," the mouse noted. "His imposter is being given the *Honor of the Great*." Hentery voice was filled with anger as he relayed this last bit of information.

"*The Honor of the Great?*" Tanya asked.

"It has not been done for many centuries. The last to be given the Honor of the Great was Queen Dianna's father. It is reserved for rulers of Dula. When they pass on to the Kingdom, their body is prepared, and then put on display in the palace with an honor guard. The public comes to pay their respects.

"Your brother should have been given this respect, but he is in the back with only a single guard standing watch."

"That makes it even better for us to retrieve the body," Tanya noted. "Now," she added, swinging her legs out of the bed, "I need to read the scroll."

"But the scroll was addressed to the *Steward of the Throne of Dula*" Hentery noted. "Will you be able to read it if it's been protected all these years?"

"My brother is dead. There is no Steward of the Throne of Dula. I am sure the Adoni knew this when They had Tra write the message. They will work out the details for us."

Tanya crept to the dresser, lifted the top, and revealed the hiding place. She pulled the scroll out, and returned to the bed before examining it. Hentery held the scroll for her as she climbed back under the covers so anyone entering without warning would not know she had been up and about. When she placed her hand out to Hentery for the scroll, he didn't return it immediately. She looked at the mouse, and saw him staring at the writing on the outside of the scroll. His mouth was opened, and he seemed to be in a state of shock. Finally he collected his wits, closed his mouth, and handed the scroll to Tanya.

"I...I don't see how They do that," Hentery stammered. Tanya looked at the scroll, and read the writing out loud.

"*To be opened by the Stewardess/of Dula and none other.*"Tanya was obviously in shock herself. "But it said *Steward*. I distinctly recall it saying *Steward*."Tanya insisted.

"Look at how it is spaced on the edge of the scroll," Hentery observed, pointing to the writing. "The word *Steward* is at the end of the line. It looks like there was a lot of dust around it. Could the last part of the word been covered by dust when you first saw it?"

"It might have," Tanya admitted. She then recalled wiping the dust off the scroll before putting it away the last time. She tested some of the dust still on the parchment. "It's attached pretty tight to some sections." She used her thumbnail to scrape it off.

"I guess that's why it all wasn't wiped off when it was hidden in the shirt by Rayton," Hentery suggested.

Tanya determined enough time had been wasted. She slipped the ribbon off the scroll, and carefully unrolled the blue paper. There was the cursive writing in Tra's own hand. She read the message out loud in a soft whisper for Hentery to hear.

"Dear Tanya:

Yes, I knew it would be you who opened the scroll, even though events would make you all believe it was written for your brother, David. I offer my comfort at the death of your brother. He is with us now in the Greater Kingdom. There are still events which must take place, and your role is very important in each of them.

"If you wonder how I was able to know so much, I am relating most of this, word-for-word from Logos as it dictates the message to you through me. When done, I am instructed to place this scroll in the message chamber without telling anyone about it. It is a message only for you and the Followers in your time. This is why it was not available to you any earlier. Be comforted, all events are going according to plan.

"Although Co-lin says he will give you three days, Gib-ron will not wait. Do not be mislead, Co-lin did not betray you. He is truly loyal to the Adoni. What Gib-ron has in store for you makes him believe it is better to move now while you are still recovering, than to wait until you are well. For this reason, act disjointed and groggy when you are called. Now is not the time for vengeance.

"Gib-ron will try to use the Seeing Eye on you to probe your mind for information as to the location of Queen Dianna. She is with us, here in the Greater Kingdom. However, unlike others, she has not tasted of death to come here.

"When Gib-ron goes into a trance to use the crystal eye, he will be protected. You cannot harm him. He is hoping you will try something, so the attack will be hurled back on you. YOU CANNOT ATTACK HIM PHYSICALLY WHILE HE IS IN THE TRANCE!

THE CONTENTS OF THE SCROLL

"(Please note that I wrote the last instruction in bold, with all the letters capitalized. This is because this is the most important instruction I have to give you. Do not disobey in this area. Gib-ron is not to be attacked physically.)"

"I take it he's seen your work," Hentery suggested. Tanya smiled at the mouse, and continued to read.

"When Gib-ron goes into his trance, wait until the count of thirty. This will give him time to be completely connected with the crystal eye. The eye will not be able to harm you because you have the protection of the Adoni. After counting to thirty, take the crystal eye, and hurl it against the wall. Hurl it hard enough to shatter. This will incapacitate Gib-ron long enough for you to carry out the other instructions. Do not leave the chamber without Logos and its sheath. Go quickly to the dungeon area. Your ability to call Sy-lar forth, and change to battle attire will be restored at this point. It has been withheld to make others feel safe around you."

"I guess he hasn't seen you for a while, has he?" Hentery added once more.

"When you go to the dungeon," Tanya continued, *"free all of those who are there. Recover the body of David James, and meet with those who are hiding in the city. Hentery, the Son of Fibbergee should contact them, and put all in readiness. Flee the city, and meet with the army in the Gen Forest. There you will be met by others. From there, go to the undersea city of Janadis. When you are there, you will know what else to do. 'Es-tra.'"*

As Tanya finished reading the scroll, it began to crumble in her hand as if it were nothing more than ashes.

"I hope you got all of that down," Hentery suggested. "How could Tra know so many details? He mentioned Gib-ron by name. He even knew *my* name! He knew about David and Co-lin. He seemed to know everything. How could such a document be that old? Are you sure it's not a trick?"

"Tra was being given instructions from Logos. He and Kal had the Curse lifted from their ears. Only those two – and my brother and I – could hear the voice of the Sword. The Sword was the voice of the Adoni. It spoke for Them. They know all things, and so it is a simple thing for Them to tell us what to do – even that many centuries ago.

"You had better go now. Contact those who are in the dun-geon. Tell them to expect me to come and free them. Find those who are in hiding. Have them meet us in the back of the palace, near where David's body is being kept. I don't want to take too long to get everyone together. When the crystal eye shatters, we need to start moving."

Hentery bowed to her, and darted out the window to carry out her message. For the first time, in a long time, she leaned back in the bed, and was able to truly rest.

CHAPTER NINETEEN

THE CRYSTAL EYE

Tanya heard the bolt being drawn back even though she was sound asleep. It had been an unusual kind of sleep. Although only for an hour or so, it had given her a sense of complete rest. She had been completely aware of all the sounds and activities going on around her. There had been three brief conversations with the guards in the hall by someone passing by. A seller had made an unusually good purchase in the courtyard outside her window, and several birds had been singing on her window sill. It was a kind of euphoria in which Tanya's mind swam the entire time. In the back of her consciousness she heard first the Song of Rest once sung by Logos when it was still the Talking Sword. The song called all to rest with sweet promises of peace and relaxation. When the song ended, she caught the beginning of the Song of Morning, which would call the Lands of the Adoni from their sleep to face a new day. Again, she knew it could not be the actual sword singing to her, but the songs were real to her all the same. The Song of Morning had just completed its final stanza, warming her heart with promises to return when the bolt slid back.

The guard was obviously hoping to catch her off-guard, and remembering the instructions of Tra, Tanya played the part to its fullest. She appeared groggy to the guards, then acted uncoordinated when they tried to get her to a sitting position. She pretended to have lost most motor control. She slung her arm spasmodically, and struck one guard square on the bridge of the nose. When the guard tried to strike her, she feigned to collapse, and the guard ended up striking the other guard who had come to help him. This resulted in several seconds of delay as the two guards took turns striking each other until the captain entered, struck them both, and threatened them with the dungeon if they delayed carrying out their orders any longer.

When it came time to transport her to Gib-ron, Tanya made her body go limp, which caused further troubles and additional delays. She wanted to make sure that Hentery had the time he needed to make all of his contacts, and move everyone into position. She went limp several times as the guards propped her up between them, and started dragging her out of the room and into the hallway. She made sure to increase her weight on one side, and throw her escorts off balance. She heard one guard cry out about his back when she shifted her weight, and caught him off-guard so that he had to suddenly support more of her than he was expecting. She even managed to slip her feet in between the guard's feet causing them to tumble. When she fell on top of one of the guards, she arranged for her knee to strike a very sensitive part with her full weight, and then her elbow slammed into the other guard's eye as she rolled over. By the time the trio came into the chambers where Gib-ron was waiting, the two guards were battered, bruised, aching, and limping. Gib-ron seemed to take no notice, and motioned for them to drop her into a chair.

"I see Co-lin was not under-stating his diagnosis of you, Lady Tanya. You seem to be having a great deal of difficulty controlling your body." Gib-ron moved away from his guest, and came to stand beside the chair across the table from her. In the middle of the table which was between them sat a crystal eye.

"Unfortunately for you, it is to my advantage to conduct this experiment while you are in this condition. You see, it is not your body that concerns me right now. It's your mind. So long as your mind is struggling to control your body, I believe it will be too weak to stop me from probing it."

"*Probing?*" Tanya slurred, and then let her head drop to one side.

"Yes. You will note the Seeing Eye here on the table." Tanya rolled her head in response to Gib-ron's observation, and so he continued. "With this crystal eye, I will see into your mind. I will know everything that you know. Of course, it may have some lasting side-effects such as you doing everything I ask you to do, and becoming a complete slave to me."

"Are you sure about that?" Tanya mumbled for effect.

"Of course, my lady," Gib-ron gloated. Tanya noted that the corner of his mouth did actually turn up a little. She silently blessed Co-lin for his skill. "I have chosen Dianna's chambers for the interrogation as they are larger than either yours or mine, but after I have finished, we shall make this *our* chamber."

"Aren't you afraid to be alone with me?" she slurred.

"Of course not," he insisted as the corner of his mouth turned up once more.

"But what about the guards?" she continued making sure it sounded as if she were groggy, and having trouble forming her words.

"I have them standing outside. They will burst in at a moment's notice." Tanya let a smile come to her eyes as she noted the up-turned mouth one more time.

"Let me explain a little about the crystal eye." Gib-ron turned his attention to the globe which sat on the table. He was obviously enjoying his time of gloating. "It is called many things: the crystal eye, the seeing eye, the eye of Cronis. It taps into a force which is all around us, but which we lack the ability to use. By letting your mind become opened, and focused on the eye, your mental thoughts are projected into the globe. Once inside the globe, you now have the instrument to connect with this unseen force. It can see into the future. It can see into the past. It can see all around you. It can even see into people's minds."

At this point Tanya let her arm slip off the armrest of the chair, and her body toppled to one side. Gib-ron let a wicked smile play across his face.

"I thought I would have to tie you to the chair, but it's obvious that would only keep you from falling out of it, and hurting yourself." He laughed, and sat down. Tanya glanced out of the corner of her eye, and saw several ropes lying off to one side. Gib-ron sat down opposite her, now all-but-ignoring her. His focus was on the globe. Tanya waited. He focused completely on the crystal eye. His eyes began to take on a glazed expression, his mouth hung limp, and the eyes rolled back into their sockets. He slumped in his chair with his head back. She began to count to herself, "One, two, three, four…" She kept studying her opponent. The globe was actually glowing with a faint light ever since he had slumped. The light grew brighter as she continued counting. As she got to thirty, the globe was at its brightest. She rose in a fluid motion, and snatched the globe from the table. Spinning around to add more momentum to her throw she dashed the Seeing Eye against the stone wall. It exploded, shattering into millions of pieces. The force of the explosion knocked her to the floor. Light and sparks erupted from the orb. Shards of crystal were flung in all directions. If Tanya had not clung to the floor, she would have been cut to ribbons. Gib-ron did not fare as well. Her captor began to scream, and grab his head as if his entire mind was on fire. The room flooded with the light, and energy crackled all around them. When Gib-ron rose screaming his pain, fully extending his body; the crystal shrapnel tore several wounds on his chest and face. However, he did not seem to notice them as his full attention was on the fire in his mind.

"Time to go," Tanya muttered to herself once the sharps of crystal had stopped flying. She scrambled to her feet, turned, and was almost out the door when a voice cried out to her.

"*The sword!*" and Tanya stopped in mid-stride and tried to come back into the room. It was as if there was a solid wall holding her back, keeping her from getting in.

"Es-Soh-En, help me," she whispered. Instantly she was in battle attire, Sy-lar in her hand, and the wall of resistance vanished. She snatched Logos from Gib-ron's belt as he wailed the agony of the damned, rolling on the floor, tearing the hair from his head, and clawing his own face as if trying to dig his way to his brain and pluck it out in order to stop the pain. Tanya caught sight of the sheath for Logos carelessly discarded on the floor. She slid the sword into its proper case, and bolted out of the door.

Just as she had expected from Gib-ron's lies, there were no guards anywhere on the floor. She dashed to the stairs, and began to leap down them even faster than when she had been going to check on Rayton's capture. Just before she got to the door of the holding area, something told her to step back. She dropped into a side passage just as the door flew open.

"It was some kind of explosion," the captain of the guard called out. "It came from Dianna's chambers." A small army rushed past her, still strapping on weapons and pieces of armor. The moment they were passed, Tanya darted into the holding area. Only two guards remained, and they were no match for Sy-lar. Within moments, the prisoners were freed, and moving like an army of their own through the palace to the area where David's body was resting.

The lone guard took one look at the fire burning in Tanya's eyes, dropped to his knees begging for mercy. The Knight of Es-Soh-En motioned to the others who tied him up, and left him unharmed as they carried David's body out of the palace.

"My lady," came a hushed voice. The voice was soft, not because the speaker chose to be quiet, but because it came from a small throat.

"Hentery!" Tanya called back. The mouse led them to a wagon waiting for them. They were able to load David's body in it, and then several other wagons came out of hiding to form a caravan. As they were lining up, Dayton came to Tanya.

"I have to go to my home," he begged. Tanya looked at Hentery who filled her in.

"This is Dayton, an ancestor of Trayton. The Eye of Suma has been in his family for generations."

"Lord Ki-el has been trying to find the Eye for over a week now. He's threatened me and my family. He's torn apart most of our home to find it. I'm the only one who knows where it is. We need to take it with us," Dayton pleaded.

"Because it is worth so much?" Tanya challenged.

"No, because it was a gift from Teacher. It can't be replaced." Dayton insisted. Tanya could see that this urgency was out of true love for Teacher, and not out of material greed.

"Will it take long?" she asked.

"Five minutes, tops," he declared.

"Then you've got it. We'll meet you just inside the eastern gate in five minutes. But be warned, if you're not there; you're on your own." The man grabbed her hand, kissed it, and was leaping onto one of the horses before she could even realize he was gone. "Let's get everything loaded," she shouted.

"How are we going to get through the gates?" Pentra asked as they loaded wagon after wagon with people. "They know I'm a traitor, and this isn't exactly a small group to slip through."

"Then perhaps we can bluff our way through," Co-lin suggested. "I have not been publicly labeled as a traitor. A healer still has a certain amount of influence in the city. Especially if everyone plays along."

The healer quickly relayed his plans to Tanya and the others. Tanya, Pentra, and those who were too visible as public enemies hid in various wagons among those who were not yet wanted by Gib-ron. Those who were still visible tore at their clothes, smeared dirt and mud on their clothes and faces, and began to practice coughing, sneezing, and moaning. The wagons moved out, traveling slowly so as not to attract attention. Tanya prayed that the soldiers in the palace would not spread their search into the city too quickly.

Just before they came to the eastern gate, the wagon train slowed, and Dayton swung on board the same wagon as Tanya.

"Did you get it?' she whispered. In response, he pulled back a corner of the leather case, and let the light from the stone spill out into the darkness. He quickly covered it back up. Tanya told him the plan, and he snuggled down where he would not be too visible. As they came to the gate, one of the guards cried out.

"Hold! What's your business?"

"An epidemic has broken out," Co-lin declared. Tanya could not see his body motions, but his voice alone was convincing. Anyone hearing the healer would believe that Co-lin was fearful of his life. "These are the ones who have come down with the plague. We have to get them out of the city before they expose everyone."

"Is it that bad?" the guard asked. Whatever Co-lin was doing to convince the guard, it was working. He had gone instantly from authoritative to fearful. The coughing and sneezing of the various people on each wagon added to the confusion. On cue, one of the people in the front wagon collapsed. Those closest to her screamed and clawed to get away shouting, "She's dead! She's dead!" The reaction of those in the wagon was more than enough to send the guard over the top. He backed away from the wagons as fast as he could. People were moaning and screaming in each of the wagons.

"Don't send us out to die. Let us stay." The one closest to the guard reached out, and tried to touch him before going into a coughing fit. The terror on the guard's face was obvious as he shouted to the other soldiers to open the gates, and let them out. Those in the wagons wailed that much louder, begging to be spared. Their cries were so pitiful and so convincing that the guard feared they might begin to flee the wagons, and slip back into the city.

He motioned, and several guards surrounded the wagons, spears at-the-ready. For a second, Tanya held her breath. "If anyone makes any move to get off these wagons, you will be killed here and now. Healer! Get these disease-spreaders out of here. Quickly!"

The guard began to shout for the wagons to move faster before anyone escaped. Co-lin shouted, and motioned for the wagons to pick up speed. When they were all outside the gates, Co-lin made as if to return, but the guards blocked his path.

"You've been with them. You might be a carrier. We can't let you in. Go with them into the forest and die!" Co-lin made as if to protest, but the guards slammed the gates of the city shut in his face. The healer turned, and caught up with the wagons. The caravan was moving at top speed into the night, heading in the direction of the Gen Forest before the palace guards made the discovery that the dungeons were now empty.

CHAPTER TWENTY

THE SECRET OF THE UNICORNS

It had been a rough ride. The roads that the wagons had to travel by were far from smooth. The ruts and holes were deep, and the wagons had little or no suspension to insulate from the impacts. Although numerous passengers were bruised and battered from the harsh jostling, the drivers did not dare to slow down. It took almost an hour of breakneck speed to come to the outer edge of the Gen Forest. The forest itself was so vast that it would take two weeks to travel from one side to the other, but right now, all Tanya wanted to do was to get inside its protective covering.

As soon as they were inside the forest, Tanya motioned for the lead wagon to turn off the road, and into the underbrush. When they pulled up to a stop, there was a mixture of groans of pain, and sighs of relief. It had not been a pleasant ride for any of them. As the passengers disentangled themselves from each other, and climbed out of the wagons, each passenger stretched, twisted, tried to adjust the joints of the back and body, and examine for bruises. Muscles were stiff from the cramped quarters.

"How many did we end up with?" Tanya asked Hentery as she helped some small children out of the wagon.

"With all the prisoners in the dungeons, and those in hiding, we came up with one hundred and forty. Add Beech, myself and you, that's one hundred and forty-three," the mouse tallied the numbers in his head.

"Add David to that and you get one hundred and forty-four," she noted.

"Is that number significant?" the mouse inquired.

"It's a dozen dozen. It's also the number of Knight of Es-Soh-En that there are. It seems that this number keeps popping up from time to time in my world. I find it of personal interest that the number which escaped would equal that."

They had pushed all the wagons well off the road, and buried them in branches and leaves. The horses were unhitched, and moved to one side. Tanya took great care to remove any trace of the wagons turning off the road, or passing through the brush.

"You seem very good at that," Hentery noted as she repaired a broken twig.

"It's something I was taught by the minotaur," she admitted.

"They taught you?" Hentery's voice was incredulous. "According to legends, even those among the minotaur and centaur, you are their teacher. Everything they know they learned from you."

"They are being more than generous," Tanya confessed. "For the first few visits, they were trying very hard to impress me. I had said some pretty harsh things to them when we first met…"

"Ah yes, the Fall. I remember reading about that. Seems you insulted them, disowned them, and then shamed them. They did not take kindly to that," Hentery observed.

"So the next few times I came back, they went to great lengths to show me what they had learned. They turned all of their efforts into becoming great warriors. They practiced long hours at hand-to-hand combat. When I suggested they turn their attention to other areas, they then expanded into hunting, tracking, camouflage, and endurance. What I had in mind was more like farming and building; but they took it all wrong.

Each time I came back, they sought me out, and taught me what they had done. They had developed weapons for personal combat. They had developed battle tactics for warfare. They showed me all of their secrets thinking I already knew them, and wanted them to discover on their own what I already knew and was not sharing with them. They kept wanting me to approve of their efforts."

"Did you?"

"Actually, no. I kept trying to turn them from war towards peace. I wanted them to get on with their lives, and live together. I wanted them to focus on growing crops, raising families, working together. All they heard was family honor, team work, and supply sources. Everything in their lives was directed towards trying to prove they were great warriors, and win my approval."

"Did you ever give your approval, my lady?" Hentery probed.

"No, I wanted them to turn to the ways of peace. When I came right out and said that, they thought I was chiding them, and telling them that they weren't good enough to be warriors. They saw that as further proof they needed to work harder to be worthy of the title: warrior. For some reason, no matter what I did with those races, they always took it to be a challenge to become better fighters."

"Well, if they will join with us in our efforts, I'm glad they put such an effort into learning the skill," Hentery admitted.

Tanya had all the old, the ill, and the children placed on the horses. There were still several horses left, and she half-considered putting some women on them; but instantly chose against it.

"It would seem the honorable thing to do," Pentra suggested.

"Everyone in this group will become a warrior. The young will not go into battle, but they will support from behind the lines. The old will teach the young the wisdom they will need in battle. The ill will get well, and learn to fight. If I start now by treating women as if they were incapable of standing side-by-side with the men, they will never become warriors. I'd rather have them uncomfortable now, than to be dead in a battle later."

She used the last horses to carry a litter with her brother's body. Tanya then motioned for the entire gathering to move deeper into the woods, keeping well off the roads and paths. She found herself and Hentery taking the point, and finding the best way to move through all the trees and brush. They traveled this way for another three hours when they caught the sight of fires in the distance.

They were not large fires. In fact, most would have missed them, but Tanya's keen sense of smell caught the smoke in the air. Her eyes scanned the deeper underbrush until she could detect faint flickers in light off to the left. She moved her charges quietly in that direction. Those on horseback were left in the back of the assembly in case they had to flee.

Tanya motioned with three fingers to Pentra. He tapped Gort who was next to him, and they joined Tanya to spy on the camp. Tanya came to the very edge of the man-made clearing, motioned for Pentra to move to the left, and Gort she motioned to the right. She studied the markings in the camp, and once she was sure of the identity, she signaled for Pentra and Gort to hold where they were while she stood, and walked directly into the center of the camp. She used her skills of stealth to keep from attracting any attention to her motions. Those who knew to look for her would see her clearly; but the way she carried herself, and how she suppressed any signals her body might give off made her appear to be invisible to those who did not expect to see her. She was actually able to walk past three sentries and four soldiers in order to get to where Agron and Handar sat making plans.

"My Lady!!" Agron cried out when Tanya released the control she was exerting to remain undetected, and it created the impression as if she had suddenly appeared before them. The fact that she was directly behind Handar put him at the disadvantage. Agron, jumped to his feet, knocking over the make-shift table. Handar tumbled back, and Tanya moved out of his way as he slammed onto the ground, square on his back.

"What word do you have?" Agron asked.

"I have been instructed to flee from Dula with all those loyal to the Adoni. We were told to meet you here. I figured it would be best to send only myself in rather than to bring them all at once. Such a sight might result in someone panicking or attacking by accident."

"By all means, my lady. Bring them all in. We will make arrangements for them," Agron offered. Tanya motioned to Pentra and Gort at the edge of the camp. The pair moved back, and signaled the rest of the refugees to come out of hiding. Agron's mouth nearly dropped when he saw the large number of people swarming into the clearing. He has imagined ten or twenty, but this many was a miracle in itself.

"How did you get all of these out?" he stammered.

"It was the Adoni's guidance, and Co-lin's quick wits. We got as far as the gates, and he convinced the guards we all had the plague. Once they believed that, there was no way to get us out of the city fast enough. By now, those guards are probably in a great deal of trouble for their actions."

"And what of Sir David?" Handar asked.

Tanya fell silent for a moment. Her expression told them more than her words. "He was cut down in ambush."

Anger burned in Agron and Handar's eyes. Tanya recognized it instantly for it was the same look she had seen in her own eyes of late. She placed a hand on each of their shoulders. *"Now is not the time for vengeance.* We have instructions from the Adoni. We are to meet someone else here, and then move on to Janadis."

"As you will, my lady. Still it would be fitting to have Sir David's body in order to give it the proper respect it was due."

"You didn't think that I would leave my brother's body with Gib-ron, did you?"

"You managed to get it out as well?" Handar asked.

"When the Adoni are providing an escape for this many people, what's one more?" she half-joked. The humor was almost there, but she did not feel like joking when it came to her brother. "Set up a place for his honoring, and place this in his hands."

As Tanya spoke, she uncovered Logos, still in its sheath. "Make sure you keep the blade in its proper resting place. He was the last ruler of Dula. It is proper that he should care for the blade."

As soon as Tanya had revealed the blade, there was the sudden thunder of hooves coming from all directions.

"Ambush!!" she shouted, and instantly Sy-lar was in her hand. She shoved Logos out of the way so none would use it in combat by accident. Heart Company moved like a well-oiled machine. They herded all the civilians into the center of the camp, and formed a living wall between the attackers and their charges. The ground shook with the power of the hooves pounding the earth. Dust was filling the outer edge of the camp, obscuring Tanya's line of sight. She moved forward, posting herself half-way between the Heart Company and the cloud of dust. Just when she felt the enemy was close enough for her to begin swinging her blade, the sound stopped.

It was the way that it stopped that unnerved her. There had to have been nearly a thousand hooves pounding the ground, but they all stopped on the exact same beat. Tanya shifted her pose so that she could spring forward the last few feet between herself and her targets. Her hearing sharpened to detect any sounds of movement or threat from the dust cloud which was now settling around them.

The first thing that Tanya saw, were hundreds of long silver spearheads, protruding above the dust cloud as it descended to the earth. As Tanya watched, they did not move forward or back. They were motionless in the dust. As the cloud settled more, Tanya began to realize that they were more than spearheads. As more and more of each weapon came into view, the impression she had was of spiraling pikes, or twisted sword blades. The metal was highly polished, catching the surrounding light, and shattering it into hundreds of small rainbows. As the scene before her became more distinct, she suddenly recognized her opponents. They were not spears, nor pikes, nor swords, but horns; long, spiral silver horns. Attached to each horn Tanya saw, "UNICORNS!!" she shouted, almost throwing Sy-lar from her grasp. Before the camp stood the entire herd of unicorn – the Untarnished. The white stallions stood completely still, waiting for everyone to recognize who they were. The only motion from the entire herd was the swirling of the different hues of blue in the eyes of the creatures, and the occasional fluttering of a mane or beard as the wind passed between Tanya and the visitors.

The largest of the unicorn broke from the herd, and came slowly toward Tanya. She had dreamed of this moment all of her life. From the time that she came to learn that unicorns were real in this world, she had desired nothing else. She had been reprimanded by Es-Soh-En in the Garden of Tangar when she defied Their wishes, and tried to see the creatures against orders. She had finally obeyed, but it had not been easy. Each time she knew that her brother was in contact with these creatures, she prayed that she would be allowed to see at least one. Now, every unicorn in the entire Lands of the Adoni stood before her. She was speechless. The lack of any movement behind her told her that the Heart Company was at a loss as to what to do or say. All eyes were fastened on Tanya, and the lone unicorn who now approached her.

As the creature pranced across the opening, the grace of his movements almost hypnotized Tanya. She couldn't take her eyes off of him. If he had been an enemy, then she could think of no greater honor than to be killed by him. She was lost in those swirling blue eyes. Her hands and arms hung limp at her sides. Sy-lar had been released from her nerveless fingers, but instead of falling to the ground, had returned to its waiting place until she should need it once more.

The wind danced in the mane. The long flowing stands of pure white hair looked soft to the touch. It hung down on both sides of the noble head, curling and flipping at all the right locations to create the impression of a full head of snow-white hair being caught in the breeze. The chin of the unicorn was decorated with similar soft white hair creating a full beard. The hair from the mane, grew shorter at the shoulders, but did not disappear. It covered the shoulders, and spread across the chest. As the hairline came to the middle of the massive chest, the strands grew long and thick once more, filling in the entire chest the way the mane of a lion covered its chest.

As each hoof was raised, Tanya caught sight of polished silver that made up the unicorn's hooves. It was covered with the same kind of white fur that covered the chest. Each motion of the legs made the fur dance in the wind. The tail was made up of pure white strands over a yard long, and it swished with each motion.

Tanya suddenly became aware that the unicorn had stopped only a foot or so from her. The silver horn sprouted out of its forehead. Where the others bore a horn about a yard or so long, this one was easily a yard-and-a-half. It was thick and round where it grew from the forehead. About two inches up, it began to twist and form a spiral shape. The edge of the spiral appeared to be razor sharp, and the indented curve was like a concave mirror in which she could see her own reflection. She dared to lower her gaze to that of the unicorn. His eyes were blue. There was the rich royal blue that swirled in pools of topaz. The moment she made contact, something exploded in her mind.

Hundreds of voices flooded into her thoughts. She was being over-whelmed by all the sounds, noises, emotions, feelings, scenes. Once they were all inside her head, they began to blend, become organized. Words over-lapped with identical words spoken by someone else. After a few moments, all the voices were saying the same thing. A few moments later, one voice spoke for them all.

"We are the *Untarnished*," all the voices sang in her mind. Then the message condensed into a single voice. "I am Deenara, Steward of the Unicorn. I serve in place of Lendara who gave his life to save Ish and Issha." Tanya suddenly realized that the voice had paused to allow her to speak. She was sure that the unicorn already knew her, probably knew more about her than she remembered about herself, but it seemed the proper thing to do to respond to their greeting.

"I am Tanya, Child of Earth, Knight of Es-Soh-En, Dancer in the Garden of Tangar, Singer of the Lesser Song, and Stewardess of the Throne of Dula. I serve in the place of Queen Dianna who is with the Adoni."

As soon as she spoke about Dianna being in the Kingdom with the Adoni, several comments buzzed behind her from those she was now sworn to protect.

"We have been sent to join you, to guide you on your journey to Janadis, and to fight with you when you return to reclaim the kingdom," Deenara spoke. He was now speaking aloud for all to hear.

"So we are to return, and reclaim Dianna's throne?" Tanya asked. She was glad to finally discover someone who had more information about what was going on than she.

"That is the instruction we have received from the Adoni," Deenara announced. He paused for a moment. "Lady Tanya. You are now one of our herd. Our minds are one, our thoughts are one; our goal is one. We have come to mourn the loss of your brother, Sir David, Child of Earth, Knight of Es-Soh-En, Airwalker, Steward of the Throne of Dula, and Friend of the Unicorn. Just as he held that title for many years, so now we call you *Friend of the Unicorn*."

Tanya led Deenara to where David's body was lying on a litter they had made to transport it. The Heart Company had not been able to move it before the unicorn appeared. Once the Steward of the Unicorn saw the body, he lowered his horn. As he kept his head lowered, each of the unicorns came to pass by their fallen brother. They paused, lowered their horn to touch his still form, bid a good-bye, and then move on. When Rentara came to honor the fallen, a simple lowering of the horn did not seem enough. He touched David's body on the left shoulder, then on the right, and then touched the center of the forehead where – if David would have been an actual unicorn – the unicorn horn would have been located.

"We stood together in the Valley of the Seven Forest, battling the evil sent by the Dark One. We battled to save the first Father and Mother throughout the night. He knew the battle would not stop the creature. He knew that eventually he would be defeated, but he battled on anyway. He knew then that even in defeat, a victory could be won." Tanya noticed something. More precisely, she felt something for she was now joined to Rentara in the same way she had been joined to the entire herd. Moisture was in Rentara's eyes, and the tears of the unicorn fell on her brother's body. A sense of great approval flooded her mind as all the herd added their endorsement of the honor Rentara gave their brother. When the last unicorn had paid his respect, Tanya had this sudden grief well up in her soul. It was in danger of tearing her heart apart if she did not express it. As a single voice, the unicorn herd raised their heads, and released the pain of their loss in a single voice. Tanya found herself crying out with her unicorn brothers.

How long or how loud she had screamed, she could not recall. She had been lost in the grief. Her heart released it all, and there was no more hidden anywhere in her heart or mind. She almost dropped, but Agron and Handar were at her side, catching her, and then supporting her. When she turned around to look at Heart Company and the refugees of Dula, she saw the amazement in their eyes. What they had heard would haunt them forever.

"We have one more favor to ask," Deenara continued, coming to stand beside her.

"Name it, and it is yours," she offered.

"You have the sword, Logos with you." It was more of an observation than a question. Tanya nodded. "We would desire to see it."

Tanya went to where she had secured the sword when she believed she was about to go into battle. She brought it to Deenara, and pulled back the cover.

"I ask that you remove it from the sheath, and hold it aloft for us."

"But that is not the proper respect for the sword," Tanya replied.

"In the hands of a human, that is true. But you are more than human now. You are part of our herd. It is proper for you to bare the blade, and raise it." Somehow Tanya knew that he was right. She drew the blade, handed the sheath to Agron, and raised the sword to the air.

"You have asked to learn the *Secret of the Unicorn*, herd-sister. It can now be revealed, both to you, and to all present. The Sword Logos is not just a symbol of the sacrifice of Lendara, it *was* his sacrifice. It is made from his horn. When he charged the Demon Cloud at the River of Warning, he was full of energy which he had collected throughout the night. If David and Rentara had not battled for so long, the charge would not have been enough to injure the creature. When Lendara entered the cloud, his horn caused the creature great pain. The Demon Cloud had believed that we were of the Lands of the Adoni, and being of the Lands of the Adoni, we would not have been able to harm the creature. The cloud was wrong. We are of the Greater Kingdom of the Adoni. Our horns were not forged in this world, but in the next. Lendara released the charge into the Demon Cloud; however, the initial charge was only to prime the horn. As the last of the energy drained from Lendara's body through the horn, he used his horn to draw even more lightning from the sky, and channel it through his horn into the creature. The impact destroyed most of the Demon Cloud. Fearing for its life, it fled back to these woods where it joined with the plant life, and was trapped until *the Battle of the Forest*.

"Lendara was fatally wounded, but his horn was also blown off by the escaping lightning. It had fallen into the Lightning's Scar, and when we carried him away from the Valley of Mists, the horn remained there in the crevice. Es-Soh-En entered the great flames of the crack, secured the horn, and used the heat of the fires from below to reshape the horn into the sword you see before you. No other fires in the Lands of the Adoni would ever be hot enough to shape the metal of the unicorn's horn. Only in the Lightning's Scar, with molten rock bubbling before Him could Es-Soh-En create such a blade. It was more than just a symbol of the sacrifice of the unicorn; it *was* the sacrifice of the unicorn," Deenara repeated once more.

Slowly the entire herd passed by, raised their horns to touch the tip of the sword; then each unicorn tapped their horns once on Tanya's right shoulder, then again on her left shoulder. As each brother passed by, and made contact with the horn of Lendara, she felt the pain. It was a unique kind of pain. Somehow each unicorn was still in contact with Lendara even though he was in the Greater Kingdom. His was the only grief in the entire Kingdom, for he was the only unicorn who had been without his horn. Somehow, by touching the horn for Lendara, the herd tried to ease his suffering. When the last unicorn had passed by, Tanya became aware that her cheeks were wet with tears that she had been weeping for the fallen unicorn. She had never met him, but now she loved him, and grieved for him as much as she had grieved for her brother.

When the Knight of Es-Soh-En composed herself, Deenara approached her once more.

"So why are you telling us the Secret of the Unicorn? It has been guarded for so many centuries," Tanya inquired.

"It was kept secret to protect the honor of Lendara. Only those in the Kingdom knew that he is without horn. Those in this world would never know. We are now revealing the Secret of the Unicorn because according to legends when the Friend of the Unicorn passes on to the Kingdom, and the sword leaves Dula once more, it is a signal that Lendara's shame shall be healed, and the herd shall be united once more."

CHAPTER TWENTY-ONE

LINES OF COMMUNICATION

It had been an eventful two days. In the last forty-eight hours, Tanya had wounded Gib-ron, recovered her ability to change to battle garb and call Sy-lar from its waiting place, freed all the followers of Teacher from the dungeons, fled the city with all those still loyal to the Adoni, joined forces with Agron and the Heart Company, seen unicorns for the first time, been joined to their herd, and learned the Secret of the Unicorn. In her mind, she believed that things had to take a break. It was what she had determined to do. The unicorn had guided the humans to a safer place to camp, set up watch to monitor the movements of Gib-ron's forces, and had now separated themselves for the evening. The Child of Earth lay back on her bed. She had tried to spread out a simple bedroll under the stars, but Pentra and Agron both had protested. She was a lady of the court, she was their current leader, she needed to maintain that appearance for all present, and so she had been ushered into the largest tent they had and given this bed.

"They have got to be kidding," Tanya whispered to herself. She squirmed on the transportable bed, trying to find a place or position that was comfortable. Apparently such a position did not exist, and finally she took her original bedroll and spread it out on the floor. Once she was comfortable, she looked up at the roof of the tent and added, "I miss the stars."

"They are beautiful tonight," it was the voice of Deenara. At the same moment that the thought entered her mind, Deenara looked up at the stars with the eyes of a unicorn, and transferred the vision to the Child of Earth. It nearly caught her off-guard, but then she remembered that when she was joined to the unicorn, she could hear them at any time. The image of the stars was so different when seen as a unicorn. The colors were deeper, the glowing embers brighter. The empty spaces perceived by human eyes were filled with thousands of more stars that non-unicorns could never hope to see. She closed her eyes to bask in the scene lingering there in her mind.

"Just one question?" she asked to her absent companion.

"Yes?" came the voice.

"What happens if I want some privacy? Are you going to be in my head all the time, or just when I make contact?"

"I see your concern." Deenara replied. Tanya had called to mind the few times she had been alone with Jensen. It suddenly dawned upon her that Deenara – and the entire herd – had just seen the image. She did what she had not done for a long time: she blushed.

"Be at peace, my lady. This is something that we had to work through with your brother. Although you have been redeemed, you have not reached that final state. Your brother had many thoughts which he feared would disturb the herd, or which he believed would make us think less of him. We all want to appear at our best to the world, and so we censor what we would say or do; but it is in the mind that all the things we should not say, or should not do first appear, begging for the chance to become actions or words. The mind must recognize such thoughts, such temptations, and make the decision to accept them and make them part of us, or to reject them. Thus the *us* in our minds is always so much less than the *us* we want to be.

"We try very hard to be discreet. It is not our place to judge what you are tempted with, nor even what you seek to do. You will find us a source of strength in those times when you feel too weak to act the way you desire; and we will help you, but only when you contact us.

"As it was with David, so it shall be with you. We will only make contact with you when it is important that we speak with you or guide you. We will only respond when you seek to make contact with us. Be aware that emotions such as anger, fear, concern, or worry do call our attention to your mind. But unless you desire contact, or are in need of us; your mind and thoughts shall be one of the herd, but like one grazing off to one side. No one will seek out your thoughts unless you call attention to yourself."

"I hope I can adjust to this. It's wonderful to not be alone in this anymore, but I'm afraid that it's going to be like living in a room with so many people you can't get away. Not that I mind the company..."

"It is the way of humans," Deenara completed for her. "We understand. We are comfortable with the bonding. We have all had centuries to adjust and adapt to the way we have blended as a herd, and the way we bonded with your brother. It is more difficult for you and your brother to deal with us. You are afraid to close your mind to us. You think it would be rude, or hurt our feelings. This is not the case. There are those among the herd who separate themselves from time to time. There are many reasons. None of us think any less of those who separate. It is the way of our kind."

Tanya suddenly realized something. She wasn't sure if she had walked into an area that was too personal for her to see. She was surprised by it, and then responded before she could catch herself.

"You have never been separate," she observed.

"Not since Lendara went to the Kingdom," Deenara admitted.

"You have been the head of the herd all these long centuries, and have always had to be in contact with others in case you were needed. You could never rest. You could never break the connection." Then another piece of the puzzle fell into place. "You're in contact with Lendara, even as we speak."

"Yes. My mind was with him the moment he died. All others turned away, closed off their minds from him as he died. It would have been too painful a thing. I was the Steward. I could not close off. I had to experience his death, but I was also able to experience his entrance into the Kingdom. It was the only way to maintain contact with him. He is kept informed of the condition of the herd, and I am able to guide the herd as he desires."

"I understand," Tanya whispered. The emotions she had felt when trying to lead in Dianna's place – the insecurities and doubts of leadership – they all came to the surface, and a tear tumbled down her cheek before she could regain control of the images.

"Yes, you do. It is nice to have someone who does understand. We have been entrusted with a great responsibility. We have been given positions of power, but the power is not ours. We rule in the stead of another. We must be true to a greater calling than the one who first ruled, for our actions reflect on their choice of empowering us. Agron is coming to speak with you. Rest well, my lady – my *horn sister*." The contact faded. It was not an abrupt disconnection like an exploding balloon, or severed cable. It was as if someone reached over and slowly lowered the volume. Tanya knew she could use her mind to increase the volume of their thoughts. It would always be available to her, but she knew the choice was hers.

"My lady?" came Agron's voice outside her tent. Tanya jumped up, and kicked her bedroll under the regular bed.

"Enter," Tanya offered.

"I bring the final report of the day," the officer announced. He began to list the various bits of information which the leader might need. He knew how many were in the camp, their physical and mental conditions, the livestock, horses, and equipment. Agron recalled all the various supplies, food, and the resources available in and around the camp. He finished with the roster of who was on guard duty. When he spoke of that it felt as if someone were tapping on the window of Tanya's mind, seeking an audience with her. Tanya's mind increased the volume, and found Deenara there. There was a quick exchange, and then the volume decreased.

"Tell the men on guard duty to get some sleep. The unicorn will stand guard for us this night. We have to all be well-rested for our trip tomorrow."

"As you wish, my lady," There was a little vibration to Agron's voice. She was surprised that she noticed it. What surprised her even more was the way that she knew what it meant.

"It feels strange to make camp in hostile times without a guard you can see, doesn't it?" Tanya asked softly.

"It goes against all my training," Agron stammered, and Tanya believed that he was more shocked by her knowing his thoughts than the lack of guards.

"I understand the feeling. The unicorn stand guard throughout the night. It is simply that we trust in what we can see and hear. I will ask them to make themselves visible in points around the camp, so that you can see them. I would also ask them to sing their songs with their voices, as well as their spirits, so that all can hear their songs of praise to the Adoni throughout the night."

"Thank you, my lady." Agron made as if to turn, but caught himself. "It seems that there have been great events these last few days. Today seemed a time of healing, a healing of sorrows. It was a time of prophecy, and of promises," He offered.

"Yes, it has been a time of healing. Mourning has a way of doing that." As Tanya spoke, she noted that her words caused Agron's eyes to flit in the direction of the tent where David's body had been honored. "He is not there, Agron."

The officer caught himself once more. Tanya could see the tears in his eyes. The loss of David had been intense for him. The Steward of the Throne had been the first in many long years to have faith in Agron. David had been someone who could share the legends, someone who would make it all easier. The fact that Agron had stayed outside the city gates when David was cut down filled the warrior with guilt and self-incrimination.

"What happened to David was part of the Plan," she began.

"It was Teacher's Plan for David to die in ambush? To be cut down when we needed him?" Agron let more emotion into his voice than he had intended. He caught himself, and fell silent.

"Many years ago, David and I came to Dula for the first time. On that trip we were in the undersea city of Janadis. I remember someone asking a question, not really expecting an answer. What surprised us was that we got an answer from the hilt jewel of Logos. The question had to deal with how many more would die before it was all over – *the Quest for the Sword*. The voice of the Sword gave us the number. David and I questioned the voice trying to learn how to decrease the number, and what would increase the number. What we finally learned was that the number had been set. It could not be increased, nor decreased through our actions or inactions. It was the proper number – if such a concept can be grasped.

"It's all part of the Plan: all these little links that lay scattered on the ground before us. They make no sense. We look at the painful ones most, because they seem to demand our attention more than any of the others. We judge these events and declare them good or bad long before it is time to judge. It's like looking at the ingredients for a cake, scattered on the table, and declaring the cake good or bad before it is even baked. We walk up to the table, and see salt sitting there. Something about the salt makes us keep looking at it. We then sprinkle a little into our hand and taste it. We conclude that the entire cake tastes terrible because this one ingredient is unpleasant. This one part of the cake does not appeal to us. However, when you hold off judging, you hold off tasting until it has all come together the way the Adoni have intended, we have something desirable. You forget all those things that did not make sense, for now they do.

"David's death is like picking up baking soda, and eating it all alone. It's not something you want to do. But it was never meant to be taken by itself. It's one of those pieces that fit into its own place. Only when it is in place will it seem right. Until then, we have to trust the Adoni that it is the right thing, even if it is not the desirable thing."

"*Taste and see that the Adoni are good,*" Agron quoted. "That part of the New Words now makes sense."

"Tasting is a way of judging," Tanya confirmed. "It's also a way of making a commitment. Once you have tasted something, it's now a part of you. The good taste lingers on the tongue. The foul taste taints everything else. The mind will always hold that experience, and use it to judge other things yet to come."

"Speaking of things to come, the gnomes have a legend..." Agron suggested.

"The gnomes have many legends. What makes theirs so good is that the gnomes are careful about their legends. They do not share or change a legend without careful research."

"This one is about a great leader. He will be cut down in ambush, but is believed to return when all seems hopeless. Many in the camp believe that it might be David." Agron's throat was suddenly tense, causing his voice to change ever so slightly, but Tanya recognized it as a sign of grief grasping for any sign of hope. Co-lin's words had given her a new way of looking at people.

"Do not forget that Teacher may also fit that legend," Tanya cautioned. "He came when Dula needed Him most, when Queen Dianna was being controlled by the Dark Lord. While it was not an ambush, it was in treachery. I believe the ancient gnomish word is the same for both. While I would not object to David being the one who returns, I must caution you. David is a man. He is a man, just like you, like Co-lin, like Handar, and Pentra. I have seen him through all the years. He was each one of you at some stage in his life: young in his faith, brash in his actions, patient, insecure, and even afraid. You see only the finished product, those things that he chooses to reveal to the world. He does not like to be put on pedestals. He does not like for people to see him as more than he is. He is a man, full of faults like us all; but he is able to hear the Adoni's voice. That is a skill we all can develop. Do not worship him. He is only human like you."

"You speak of him as if he is not dead," Agron noted.

"That is his body over there." Tanya motioned in the direction of the tent. "But he is not there. He is in the Kingdom of the Adoni. The Greater Kingdom. On our second visit, David and I were allowed to enter the Lesser Kingdom. There were many people there. We had not met most of them, but they were all dead at that point in time. If we had gone to any relative or friend still living in the Lands of the Adoni and asked them about someone in the Lesser Kingdom, we would have been told that they were dead. We even met with Tra and Kal, whom we had been told at the beginning of the visit were dead for long years. Everyone treated them like they were dead, and so we treated them as if they were dead. We spoke of them as if they were dead. But when we entered the Lesser Kingdom, we found that they were very much alive. Death had no hold on them.

"To those who trust in Teacher, Death is only a separation, not an ending. It's a separation that is only temporary. It's like David coming to Dula without me, and I have to stay on Earth. We can't communicate, but we know the other is alright. It's like me going to sleep in this tent. I am not available to you. You have to wait until the morning to see me, speak with me; hear my voice. Knowing we cannot visit with someone hurts; but knowing we will be able to visit again makes it easier to deal with."

"I shall keep that in mind, my lady. Your words give me the encouragement, the focus – the point of perspective I needed. Thank you." Agron bade Tanya good night, and went off to relieve the sentries of their duty.

Although Tanya was drained from the many experiences of the last few days, she found it hard to go directly to sleep. She finally rose from her bedroll and paced the tent. Her eyes fell on Logos, sitting in the corner. She picked it up. There was an instant realization that she had the full attention of every unicorn. She wasn't sure what she should do. She had never had the opportunity to examine the sword this closely since the day it had been displayed and described for them by Es-Soh-En after the Fall. Her mind probed the other minds of the unicorn to see if it would be improper to remove it from its sheath for examination.

"If it were anyone else, it would be improper. As you are the Stewardess of the Throne, and the Friend of the Unicorn, we will guide you so that you do not act improperly," came the voice of Deenara.

Tanya drew it slowly out of the sheath. She did not take it all the way out of its protective covering, just enough to see the stain of blood on the blade. It was the blood of Teacher that had stained the once-mirror finish. She looked carefully at the surface to see if Gib-ron had done any damage to it with his efforts to remove the stain. She could not see any. Her thoughts drifted off to Teacher, and how He had given His life to save the Lands of the Adoni. The stain before her spoke of the love He had for this world.

"It is also the love I have for you," came the voice in her head. She knew at once it was not the voice of Deenara or any of the unicorns. It startled her, and she slid the blade back into its case as if she had been caught doing something forbidden. She knew the voice; it was just a surprise to hear it this way.

"Es-Soh-En?" she asked with her mind. There came a warm feeling flooding not just her mind, but her entire body.

"I am here, Child of Earth. It is not just the love I have for the Lands of the Adoni, but it is also My love for you. I could have chosen to work in a different way in this world, but I wanted to draw you and David closer to me. I wanted to give you the opportunity to serve me in a way that none have done before. It is for this reason that I first drew you out of your world, and into this one."

The mention of her brother made Tanya's mind call forth the image of David. However, this time it was different. She was seeing him in a way she had never seen him before. Her mind was accessing information she should not have had. She saw him in a fresh water sea, with the pod of dolphins they had swum with at the creation of the world. On the dolphin next to him sat Kya. Tanya had never seen Kya, but somehow her mind knew who it was. As soon as her mind made contact with the scene, David looked up, stared right into her eyes, and smiled. It was the smile of someone who was finally at peace with himself. All the pain and guilt he had carried for so long was gone from his eyes. He actually laughed; a sound that came from his entire body. He was a person filled to capacity with joy. In her mind she saw him waving at her. He was pointing at Kya to introduce her to Tanya as if he were some love-struck teenager and not the great Knight of Es-Soh-En. Tanya smiled back, and somehow knew that he saw her. She felt as if it was best to leave the two alone, and so the image faded from her mind.

The fact that she felt as if she had actually made contact with the Greater Kingdom triggered a thought of Dianna, and she suddenly saw Dianna, more a queen than she had ever been in Dula. She was not gaudy, or pretentious, but there was a glowing beauty about the Queen that she had never had in this world. She was royalty. It came from within her, and flowed out. She wore a simple white grown, but the majesty of the Queen transformed it into the most elegant dress of the court. Dianna looked up at Tanya and smiled. Tanya smiled in return, nodded, and the image faded.

Without even thinking of the name, the figure of Jensen replaced the image of Queen Dianna. He sat with his lute upon a grassy knoll. There was a great shade tree supporting his back, and he strummed the instrument. A gentle brook ran near-by. It had been the kind of scene Jensen had always dreamed of. He had said that this was where he would be inspired the most. He was in deep concentration, working on some new piece. Tanya chose not to make herself known to him, but listened for several moments to the tune which he played. It would be enough to hold her through the times ahead.

"Es-Soh-En?" she asked, and the form of the great Hobber was there in her mind. His topaz-blue eyes smoldered among the ebony fur of his face and body. The golden mane flowed in some unfelt breeze on the celestial level. He looked upon her and smiled, bowing to her as only He had been able to do.

"Greetings, beloved child. I regret that we cannot meet in person, so this seemed the next best thing to do. Since you have been joined with the unicorn, and Lendara is here, I used that link to speak with you. I must be careful about the links between this world and the next. When the power of Cronis was broken in the Veil of Darkness, his access to this world was severely limited. He can only come in when the actions of one on your side weakens the wall between the worlds, or if I access the Lands of the Adoni in such a way that suspends the Laws We have lain down since the foundation of the world. Thus I work within the system created, and hinder the actions of the Dark One; but the time is upon Us when the Dark Lord will move freely throughout the Lands of the Adoni. Already Gib-ron works his evil spells to give Cronis greater access to your world." Es-Soh-En paused and smiled. It was a strange smile for Tanya. The information just relayed should have caused concern, maybe even fear, but that was not the emotion she saw in those glistening eyes. It almost seemed as if Es-Soh-En were amused by the actions of Gib-ron.

"All is going according to Plan," the Great Hobber offered as His only explanation for the joy she saw in His eyes. "Soon, we will all be together in that LIFE that cannot end."

"Then I am going to die as well?" she asked. There was no fear in her mind as she spoke the question. There was an excitement about coming into the Kingdom, about all the conflicts coming to an end, but then she thought of her charges. "I have work that is still unfinished."

"You will not taste of death, Knight of Es-Soh-En. Your work is about to come to a close, but it will be a closing that you have never imagined. Trust Me in this matter."

Tanya made the promise in her mind, and Es-Soh-En smiled once more.

"With the morning, the time will have come for you to go to the city of Janadis. As you pass through the camps, make the offer to take with you all who would join you. Trust their decisions, for I have laid it upon their hearts. None will go, unless I have called them. I will not call them unless they are Mine. Take them all from among the centaurs, the minotaurs, the gnomes, and the Water People. The Tree Druids will be safe for now, and would otherwise slow your progress. I have explained this to them, and they will wait. When you come to the Isle of Morning, you will find the passage under the sea to the city. I will contact you later, for now, it is time for you to rest. There is a long day ahead of you tomorrow."

Tanya wasn't sure how it happened. She wasn't exactly falling, but by the time she reclined upon the bedroll, she was fast asleep.

CHAPTER TWENTY-TWO

ATTACK IN THE ALPS

Tanya sat up in the saddle, stretched to take the stress off her spine from the long hours of riding. Before them stood the Dulan Alps, looking like broken teeth across the horizon, behind her spread a vast throng. In addition to the hundred and forty-four she had brought out of Dula, and the five hundred of Heart Company; she now led the entire races of gnomes, centaurs, minotaurs, and Water People. She was surprised that none of them had stayed behind. All had desired to follow her. The Child of Earth was glad that Es-Soh-En had prepared her by telling her to take all who wanted to go. Just common sense would have told her that not everyone in such a large group could still follow the Adoni. The odds would have said that some could not be trusted; but the Great Hobber had instructed her that He had called the ones who would go, and to leave none of them behind.

Tanya had wondered about moving such a large group of people through the Gen Forest without being detected, but the gnomes, centaurs, and minotaurs split up; one group leading, the other group following. The first group guided those of the exodus so that as little damage was done to the forest as possible by their passing. The last group *cleaned up* any evidence that anyone had even passed this way. Tanya could tell that they were good. She had studied the path they had traveled, and could not see any evidence of anyone having been by this way.

"Are you sure that this is the best way to travel?" asked Agron as he pulled his mount up next to hers. Pentra came to join them. A moment later Ren and Han were standing next to them.

"The passage through the Valley of Seven Forests is the normal route to take around these peaks," Pentra observed.

"The very reason that we have to come this way. We cannot do what is normally done. We cannot do what is expected. Gibron will send forces after us. He does not know our current size, but he would assume with the number in Heart Company, and those who fled the kingdom, that we would take the easier route. He will send his troops toward the Valley of Seven Forests to block our escape. This is the path the Adoni have set before us," Tanya announced.

"None have gone this way before, especially with so large a group. But if this is the way the Adoni leads; then we shall follow." The voice of Ren was firm, as one would expect from the leader of the minotaurs. Han, the head of the centaurs, nodded his agreement. Agron could see that they did not have any concerns about the path so long as Lady Tanya and the Adoni said it was the way to go.

"Let me ask you something," Agron began. His voice was casual, but his desire to know was sincere.

"Speak," Ren declared.

"You are willing to take this path because it is the way set down by the Adoni. It's the way Lady Tanya tells us to go. What if half of your forces were to die going this way?"

"It does not matter," Han replied. "It is the path of the Adoni."

"And what if all were to die going this way?" Agron pressed.

"It is the will of the Adoni. It is the path They have set before us. We would still go," Ren replied.

"Even if you could save all of your forces by traveling to the south?" Pentra added.

"We have chosen to walk the path of the Adoni, even though it is certain death; rather than to step off that path and live. It is the way of our people," Ren added.

"These are my children," Tanya announced with pride in her voice. She called out loud enough for those not part of the meeting to hear. "These are my children, and the Children of the Adoni. I am pleased they turned out so well."

She could have sworn that both Ren and Han had tears in their eyes, but caught their reactions and regained control. Tanya smiled at both the leaders, extended her hand in the sign of brotherhood to both. "My life is yours," she added.

"And our lives are yours," Ren and Han replied in the sacred oath.

"Perhaps I should learn to think like that," suggested Pentra.

"You cannot lead, until you have learned to follow," Ren offered as advice. Pentra merely nodded.

"Centuries ago, I said some things to your first Fathers," Tanya began, catching the full attention of Ren and Han. "If I were given the opportunity now, I would unspeak the words. Their actions, and the actions of your entire races, especially the actions of you this day, have proven the words false. I will no longer own them, nor endorse them."

"Then this is a day to be praised," Ren added. Han turned towards the vast gathering, and shouted in his loudest voice, "TAN-CEPTS!" Instantly the chant was taken up by the entire race of centaurs and minotaurs. The volume of the cheer worried Agron that if any of Gib-ron's men were anywhere near the

Gen Forest, their location would be given away; but since Tanya chose not to speak, he remained silent.

"There are none to hear," Wilara advised Agron, as if the unicorn had known his thoughts and concerns.

"Does that mean what I think it means?" Tanya asked of Han above the roar.

"It is our battle language for *Tanya accepts us,*" Han admitted.

"You have a special phrase in battle language just for that?" the Child of Earth asked.

"It is a word spoken only in whispers during the training of all warriors. It is never spoken again, but is held silently close to our hearts in anticipation for the day when it will be our battle cry. Today is that day. We, of all the generations of our people, are the generation to shout it aloud. Thank you, First Mother."

Tanya almost blushed at the term. She had been the closest thing the centaur or minotaur race had as a mother since it was her singing the Lesser Song with Glidon, and dancing in the Garden of Tangar that brought them to life. This was the first time they had ever called her that in her presence. She looked out over her *children*, smiled full of pride, and waved to them all. "Thank you Adoni," she whispered as she smiled.

After several minutes, she heard the voice of Deenara in her mind as the Steward of the Unicorns called to her from down the path. It had been tested by the unicorn, and they now called for the others to follow. With the centaurs and the minotaurs still shouting, clapping their hands, dancing, and singing; the entire throng began to move into the Dulan Alps.

***

"There is a break in the trail several miles ahead. We will need to examine everyone in the group individually before they can cross. If they cannot, we will carry them over," Deenara said as they worked their way up the face of one of the highest peaks. It had been three days into the Alps. The last day had been the hardest of the journey. The paths had grown so narrow, that only two could pass at a time, and funneling such a large number of people, creatures, and wagons into two lines had almost stopped the entire progression. Fortunately, the reorganization had been orderly, and now the line was eight to tens times longer than when they had moved as a group.

"It won't be much longer, herd sister," Deenara added seeing the look of concern on her face. "Once we cross this final chasm, the path opens up, and you will see what no human has ever seen before. Those on the other side never travel this direction because of the dangers in the Forest of Venra. Those who get that far, take other paths which are safer to travel. Those coming from the Gen Forest do not come this way because of the chasms, and so it has never been visited before."

The expectation of finally spreading out the gathering and of seeing someplace never seen before lightened Tanya's spirits. She had been worried about so many traveling such rugged paths. There had been several close calls, but the unicorns had been there each time, protecting her *herd* as she had come to call them. It must have been the way she now thought since bonding with the unicorns she told herself.

True to Deenara's observations, the entire army came to a stop at the edge of a chasm. It wasn't the width of the chasm that concerned Tanya, but the depth. She dismounted, stood near the edge, and tossed a stone into the emptiness. She began to count.

"One, two, three, four…" When she got to fifteen, she gave up, and climbed back on her horse. As she turned to study the rest of her followers, she caught the faint sound of the rock clattering off sections of the chasm walls. "Not good," she added to herself.

Deenara, Wilara, Rentara, and the others moved up and down the files. They pulled out the young, the old. They set several horses aside with their riders, and all the gnomes who were not on pony-back. The inspection took hours, but every one stayed in good spirits throughout. As the gathering had done so often in the past when things slowed down, someone would break out in a song, and others would pick it up. Being in two lines, the length of the group caused some adjustment as those at the front or back were ahead of or behind those in the middle as the song began; but everyone was able to adjust, and soon the song was sung at the same time no matter where you were located in the line.

Deenara motioned for those who had been selected to stay out of the way, while the others leaped over the chasm. Tanya and Agron stayed behind, while Pentra, Han, and Ren led the others further down the path on the other side. Several unicorn went with them to lead them to the spot they had picked out to camp for the night.

"So why have these been set aside?" Agron asked.

"These are the ones who could not make the leap," Deenara explained.

"We aren't going to leave them here?" came Agron voice becoming more excited.

"We leave no one behind," Tanya voice was firm in order to calm her commander.

"Those selected are already unloading the horses. We will carry the load for the horses. Without such burdens, they can make the leap. Those who cannot make the leap will cross over on our backs." The words of Deenara calmed Agron's fears.

"No one has seen any unicorn for centuries. Now we see all the unicorn, we talk with the unicorn, work with the unicorn.

Now we are going to ride the unicorn. Will wonders never cease?" Agron spoke more to himself.

"Not on this trip," Tanya suggested with a smile.

***

It was already dinner time when the last of the travelers filed into camp. Tanya, Agron and Deenara were the last ones in the line. As they came around the trail, the sight of the camp caught Tanya's breath away. Even with all the people spread out around it, her mind quickly absorbed all the details.

The mountain peak had been a volcano centuries ago. It had been burned out now for hundreds of years, but the volcanic ash had mixed with the soil, making it rich and fertile. The crater had filled with melting snows becoming a vast lake with a mirror-like surface that reflected the sky and clouds overhead. It was the very top of the Dulan Alps, the highest point. The air was crisp, fresh, and a little thin, but it was an exhilarating feeling all the same. Trees, bushes, plants, and flowers were everywhere. The Water People were already becoming part of the lake.

"It's everything you said it would be," Tanya declared to Deenara. She pulled off her boots and socks, and leaped off her horse to run barefoot in the thick soft grass.

"My Lady!" Agron called after her, shocked that she would act in such an unladylike fashion, but Deenara calmed him.

"She is a Child of the Earth. Let her be close to her mother, and be like a child. It is a medicine for her soul."

Tanya was lying on the grass at the edge of the lake. Her feet had dangled in the water off and on. The water was too cold for swimming, but several people were daring enough to plunge into it, just to wash off the grime of the road. A place had been set up away from the camp so as not to pollute the water supply for others. Many others built fires, drew water in buckets, and heated the water for their baths. Others drew water for drinking and cooking. Agron sat next to Tanya on the bank.

"So tell me about your world," he asked.

"There's not much to tell. We spend all of our time trying to find some way to build machines that will do for us what nature already does."

"That seems like a great waste of time," Agron noted.

"It is, but for some reason my world refuses to trust the Adoni. We cannot trust nature to supply all our needs. We want things better, or sooner than we think nature can provide. So we have spent centuries trying to replace nature with our machines."

"I find it hard to believe that a world that created you and David, could be a world that does not trust the Adoni," Agron observed.

"Our world not only doesn't trust the Adoni, but most deny Their existence. This is why they try to replace nature. They see nature as temporary. It's all going to die out someday. So in order to guarantee that we survive after nature dies out, we build machines. Machines do not die…they just break down; and if they break down, they can be repaired or replaced."

"Our world is suspicious of machines," Agron admitted.

"That is why your world is so much like it was when we first came here," Tanya noted. "It has never advanced in technology." When she saw the bewildered look on Agron's face she defined her word, "Machines."

"The Council of Ancients, which brought the Curse upon the Lands, tried to create and implement machines. The people rejected them." Agron shared.

"I believe that there was much wisdom in your world for making that decision. Our world seems to lack true wisdom," the Stewardess confessed.

"Yours must be a sad world indeed," Agron observed.

"For the most part. Everyone denies the Adoni. They insist that there is no Adoni, yet are quick to serve the Dark Lord," Tanya reflected.

"How can you have one without the other?" Agron asked.

"You can't...Well, you can have the Adoni without the Dark Lord, and we will one day."

"Is such a thing possible?" came Agron's reply.

"Of course it's possible. The Dark One is not equal to the Adoni. He was created like everything else. His power seems great to us because we compare him to us, but when you compare him to the Adoni, he is seen for what he truly is. The day is coming when the lines of battle will be drawn. Those in my world will choose sides: those for the Adoni, those against the Adoni. When that happens, the Dark One will grow as powerful as he can; but it will not be enough. The Adoni will return, defeat all the forces of the Dark Lord, and set up His own Kingdom."

"Such a promise. I can see why you would want to return there."

"I have to return. It's my home. My parents are there. My life is there."

"But your life is also here," suggested Agron.

"Parts of my life are here. Each time we return it is a different time period. Friends we knew are gone to the Kingdom. Places we've been have changed. The only constant in all of this during the last several visits has been Dianna. She knew how hard it was on us with so many changes. That's why she provided rooms for us in the palace. She would not let anyone change those rooms, even to remove something so small as a dish or a blanket. I understand that the fabrics in the rooms have worn out several times since she first gave them to us. She made the craftsmen keep careful records of how they were made, what materials were used, which colors, patterns, and designs were used. When the blankets wore out, she had identical copies made to replace them. When curtains or rugs were old, she had new ones made that were identical.

"We spend a great deal of our lives here, in this world; but it is difficult for us to live in this world." She fell silent, and Argon rose to give her privacy.

"I pray that the time of the return of the Adoni in your world will be soon," he offered as encouragement.

"It will be, for the Adoni of our world, is also the Adoni of this world. Gaylord once told me, *All worlds are the same, only the names are different.* He had no idea how true his words were."

Agron then left Tanya to make preparations for the rest of the camp. She laid her head back on the grass, closed her eyes and took in a deep breath of clean air, holding it in her lungs a little longer than comfortable, then exhaling slowing. She felt herself drifting into a dream world, and was just about to submit when someone called her name. She bolted up to a sitting position, and looked around to see who needed her. Everything was calm in the camp. Agron was making preparations for the meal and the evenings duties with Ren and Han. Since everything seemed so peaceful, she leaned back on the grass, and closed her eyes. It *was* peaceful here. If Es-Soh-En had not directed her to go to Janadis, this would be the place where she would like to stay.

Suddenly she heard her name once more. She bolted up a second time. Still no change in the camp. Tanya reached into that part of her mind, and increased the volume between her and the unicorns.

"No one has called you from among the heard," Deenara observed. Tanya thanked her companion, reduced the contact, and lay back down. This time she was sure she heard the voice calling to her, and now she knew where it was coming from.

"Es-Soh-En?" she asked softly in her mind, still lying on the grass.

"Yes, Child of Earth. It was I who called you. I am going to take you away from the army for a short while. However, the army must travel to meet you. You must tell Agron to meet you at the Grove of Three Oaks in the Forest of Venra. He will find you there. You must tell him that, or he will stay in the Alps looking for you until all is lost, or all are destroyed."

Es-Soh-En's voice faded, and Tanya knew that the message was over. She rose, and was about to tell Agron, but she saw he was now eating. He had not rested for many days, and so Tanya thought better of disturbing him. She caught a passing soldier, and asked him to bring her paper and a quill.

Tanya wrote out a short note, dried the ink, rolled the parchment up, and was about to ask someone to deliver it to Agron when screams and cries from around the camp called her attention to the skies. It was a bat creature; one of the largest she had ever seen. Its wing span was easily twenty feet across. Guards were darting around, gathering weapons, stringing bows. It dropped out of the sky, back-beating the air at the last second. The force of the sudden gusts of wind knocked Tanya to the ground before she could even respond to the attack. As she fell to the ground, the bat thing snatched her as she fell, and beat its wings against the air to climb back into the sky.

Agron, Ren, and Han charged across the camp to the spot where Tanya had just been, only to be too late. Han, with all the skill of his race, drew the great war bow, held the arrow to his ear, sighted the target; but instead of releasing the shaft, he dropped his arm, the arrow still resting in the bow.

"I can't hit it when they are so high. The fall would kill her." Agron could see that it was true.

"Gather the troops!" Agron shouted. "We ride after her. We leave no one behind," he added, recalling the promise Tanya had given to him on the other side of the chasm. His eyes suddenly caught sight of something fluttering in the air, dropping from where Tanya had last been sighted. He plucked the object out of mid air, opened it; and found the message Tanya had intended for him. He turned, and suddenly found himself with face-to-face with Deenara.

"This is the will of the Adoni," the Steward of the Unicorns declared. "We must trust in Them."

"But she's been taken," Agron ranted.

"She was taken by the will of the Adoni. What does the note tell you?" Deenara insisted.

"*Go to the Grove of Three Oaks,*" Agron recited.

"Then we leave her to the Adoni. We must go, as a group, to the Grove of Three Oaks." The swirling blue in the eyes of the unicorn told Agron that he was not going to have any choice in the matter.

CHAPTER TWENTY-THREE

THE GROVE OF THREE OAKS

Tanya felt the wind slam into her face. It was a cold, harsh wind, and it whipped her hair about her face causing it to slap her cheeks, face, and eyes. The Knight of Es-Soh-En had to reach up, and hold her hair with one hand so that she could see her kidnapper. Already the cold gale-force wind had dried her lips causing them to chap and crack. She shivered from the cold this high up, but her sides felt warm. She looked down, and realized that a certain amount of the shivering must be due to shock. The talons of her kidnapper were buried deep into her sides, apparently locking onto the ribs. Once she saw the wounds, the warm feeling in her ribs transformed to a kind of fever and an intense burning sensation. She turned her attention away from her body, as much to see where she was as to take her mind off the claws embedded into her chest.

Off to the north she could make out the faint spindle of the Tower of the Sun. Tanya wondered if Magar still worshiped the Heart of the Sun even though it no longer existed. Had they ever discovered their jewel from the skies had been taken by Teacher many centuries ago? Ahead of them lay the Forest of Venra. At least they weren't going the wrong direction. She hated to lose ground and have to backtrack.

The Knight of Es-Soh-En turned her attention back to the creature which was still beating the wind furiously with its wings. Whatever guided this thing had filled it with terror for it to travel at this breakneck speed once the danger of attack from her army was gone. She noticed that its eyes were the deep red that marked those in service to the Dark Lord. For a bat thing to have come this far while the sun was still in the sky gave her an idea how determined her kidnapper was. The leather wings were a slick membrane. She tested the strength of the claws that held her, and she knew that she didn't have the strength to pry the claws back and get free. She considered several nerve blocks to make the creature release her, but knew that if the bat thing did let go of her from this height, she would fall to her death. She resigned herself to having to wait until they came to land before calling Sy-lar from its waiting place and attacking her captor.

Her kidnapping had taken place in the late evening, and already the sun was dipping behind the horizon. Being on this side of the Dulan Alps cut the world off from its light that much sooner. Tanya noted that Barris and Fenra, the twin moons of Dula, were already high in the sky. As the light from the sun faded, they grew brighter, and soon were the only source of light she had.

Something jolted her. It wasn't her kidnapper shaking her, but something had hit the bat thing. She searched the night skies, and saw something large moving between her and the night sky. Again she was jostled. The bat thing almost relaxed its grip, but then tightened that much harder to hold onto its prey. The increased pressure called her attention to the wounds, and nearly cracked a rib. With the third attack came the battle-cry of the Great Eagle, as the massive bird slammed into the bat thing one more time.

"Glidon!" Tanya called out above the rush of the wind. She had not realized how much altitude they had lost in the first few attacks until she saw tree tops just missing her dangling feet. The latest attack drove the bat thing below the trees. Tanya had the sudden feeling of weightlessness. Her stomach rose in her throat as the bat thing released its grip on her in order to turn on its attacker. The Child of Earth was in free fall. She snatched out with her hand, and found a branch whizzing past. She locked onto it and almost had her shoulder pulled out of joint before the inertia of her fall caused the branch to snap. She reached out again, caught another branch; then a third. When she was about to reach for a fourth something in her mind told her it was too late. She tried to right herself, roll into a ball to absorb the impact, and prayed.

She hit hard, but not nearly as hard as she had expected. Apparently the three broken branches had slowed her descent more than she had realized. Still, she hit square on her back, rolled several times, and sprawled out on a carpet of leaves. Her lungs had the breath knocked out of them, and every muscle and joint screamed with pain. She had to focus. Her first priority was getting her breath back. No sooner had she accomplished that feat, than she heard the voice of Glidon not far over-head, "Run Tanya! Run!"

Even though pain erupted in every joint and muscle with her efforts, she rolled over, drew her feet under her, and ran. She wasn't sure how far she had run, but she knew it wasn't that far when there came a crashing sound, the snapping of branches, some of them were rather large limbs. She turned, and saw wings and talons locked in a death-struggled. Glidon's beak was tearing into the throat of His opponent. The Adoni drove the bat thing to the ground with such force that Tanya could hear the bat thing's spine snap and its ribs shatter. A trail of thick black blood oozed from the spot where she had been moments before. As the blood touched the grass, the blades turned dark and brittle, hissing as they were charred to black. Tanya realized that if she had not moved, the bat thing would have fallen directly on top of her.

There came a sudden swirling of twigs, leaves, and dust as the Great Eagle back-winged in order to land next to Tanya. The mangled form of her captor shivered once, but with the impact of the fall, and a large branch that had impaled it through its chest on the way down, it posed no further threat. Tanya threw herself onto the breast of Glidon, holding as tightly as she could. The Adoni folded one wing over her to comfort her and warm her from the cold. It was then that Tanya realized she had been shivering so hard that it was making it impossible to hold her defender, or even to speak without stuttering. The sensation of Glidon's soft down feathers against her face and body, His rhythmic breathing, and the sweet smell of cinnamon and cloves that permeated His entire frame calmed her enough to stop most of the shaking.

"We were going to take you away from Agron, but not like this, Child of Earth." There was almost humor in the voice of the Adoni. Tanya smiled, rubbed her cheek into the soft feathers, and held that much tighter. "If you would have told Agron We were going to take you away when you first knew, he would have posted guards around you immediately, and this would have been prevented."

"He would have posted guards around me because You were going to take me away?" Tanya pulled back from clinging to Glidon enough to look into His face.

"In his mind, *taking away* had the possibility of being taken away in the same way as your brother. Agron blames himself for not protecting your brother. He will fight anyone – even

Us – to protect you from a similar fate. Had he insisted on entering the palace with Sir David, there would be two bodies cut down in ambush instead of one. If you had followed Our instructions, then he would have protected you, and when We came to speak with you, he would have realized his mistake, and allowed you to go with Us. However, because you delayed, this gave Cronis the opportunity he desired. It was a small rebellion, but a rebellion all the same; and the Dark One will take any opening – no matter how small – and force it into a doorway for his servants."

"I'm sorry. I was going to tell Agron, it's just that he was finally relaxing. He hasn't done that for a long time. I was going to send him a note as soon as he finished."

"Yes, and it was your intent to follow Our instructions that allowed Us to act directly. You have no idea of the numerous conferences Cronis has demanded, and the arguments he has raised over the last few weeks."

"The Dark One is in the Greater Kingdom?" Tanya's voice was incredulous.

"Yes, he comes quite often to weave his webs of lies and misrepresentation. He comes as often as he can, but his own nature makes it extremely painful for him to be in Our presence. The fact that he has come so many times, and argued so long shows just how desperate he truly is. He thinks it shows how strong he is, but We see it for what it truly is."

"Oh!" Tanya suddenly cried out. "Poor Agron! I never got to give him the message. He'll be worried sick."

"We took care of it. Before I left to follow you, I made sure the note fell where he could see and read it. He will join you tomorrow in the Grove of Three Oaks."

"Thank you, Glidon. I'm sorry for not following instructions more carefully."

"You are forgiven. It was a small act of disobedience, and it was done because you were thinking of another's welfare. However, you must learn that We, too, have considered the welfare of those you interact with before We give you instructions." Glidon pulled back so that He was standing before the Child of Earth, and she was no longer resting on His breast.

"Look about My neck, and you will find a chain. Take it off." Tanya was suddenly aware of a necklace hanging from Glidon throat. She didn't see how she could have missed it when she had hugged Him before, but she had never noticed it then. Now it was obvious, even in the moonlight. As she took it from her rescuer, she noted that a large jewel was attached to the chain.

"This is your next task. You have no idea how important it is, and I cannot stress to you the need to obey without hesitation."

"I will," Tanya assured the Adoni. "What am I to do?"

"When you hear My cry three times, no matter where you are, no matter what you are doing – even if it seems impossible for you to hear My voice – you must immediately place this necklace over your brother's head and about his neck. Carry it with you at all times. It must never leave your possession. It has a power that can only be used once, and only at the proper time. Do not act prematurely, nor delay once you hear the signal. To give you some idea as to how important this act is, even now the Dark One is arguing with the Unnamed Adoni that you should not be allowed to do this. He has numerous lies, past mistakes, lapses of faith. He is bringing them all to the table trying to convince the Unnamed Adoni that you be disqualified and that We must find another to perform this task."

"Will the Unnamed Adoni listen to the Dark One?" Tanya asked suddenly recalling all the times she had not been as strong as she would have liked to have been in the service of the Adoni.

"Oh, He will listen. That is what He does. Will He believe the arguments of Cronis and not allow you to perform Our will?" Here a smile broke out over the face of the Great Eagle, "I doubt that even the Dark One could present such an argument. Our Will will be done. This is all according to the Plan. Trust Us."

"What will happen when I put this on David?" Tanya has spoken before thinking, and was suddenly awkward because the Adoni had just asked her to trust Them, and now she sought more information.

"For you it will be good. For your brother, it will bring sorrow. But do not...I repeat, do not fail Us in this task. If you do not respond when you hear the signal, Cronis will use that delay to keep Us from returning for many centuries. We have set up Laws for this world, and even We will not violate them. I must go now. The Grove of Three Oaks is just over there. Wait for Agron there." Glidon smiled at her, spread His great wings, and beat down on the air three times. Dust, twigs, and leaves swirled all around her so that she had to close her eyes. When she opened them, the Great Eagle was gone. She studied the skies in hopes of seeing some last sign of the Great Eagle. There came a sudden flash from miles in the sky where the moonlight reflected off of something golden. Tanya smiled a good-bye to the Great Eagle, slipped the chain over her own neck so that it would always be with her, and headed off in the direction Glidon had indicated.

***

The Child of Earth came to a clearing about an hour later. She was feeling weak and tired. Her wounds were throbbing, and still bleeding. It occurred to her that she should have asked Glidon to heal them, but it was forgotten in the excitement of battle and the importance of the instructions He gave her. Although she did not want to stop, her legs were trembling, and her knees would not support her much longer. She was glad she had put her boots back on while waiting for the paper and quill to write the letter for Agron. If she had been forced to travel through the underbrush bare footed, her feet would have been cut and bleeding by now. She dropped down in the moonlight, and leaned against a tree to rest.

"That's quite a fever you have, my lady." came a deep, slow voice after she had been leaning on the tree trunk for several minutes. Tanya jumped back, and tried to get to her feet for a defensive stance. She couldn't see anyone around. She touched her forehead, it was wet with sweat, and it was hot to the touch. She noted that her hand was trembling.

"Who's there?" she challenged.

"I'm sorry. I didn't mean to startle you," came the deep voice. There was a strange quality about it. Although it was very bass in its tone, it was not loud. If it were possible for someone to whisper and still cause the ground or the trees to vibrate, this would have been the description.

"Who are you? Where are you?" she repeated.

"I am Gantra," came the slow deep tones. Now Tanya noticed something different about them. It wasn't as if they had been made by vocal chords, but it was like the moan of the winds through the tree boughs. It had the resonating tones of great branches moving in the breeze and groaning from the effort. She turned back to the tree she had been leaning on when the voice first came. She stepped closer to see it better in the light of the twin moons. It took her several seconds to make out the features, but the more she studied the trunk of the tree, the more obvious the image became. She finally made out the face of an old man carved in the cracks, indentations, growths, and knotholes on the trunk. The features were the results of highlights from the moonlight and shadows. The face was old, very old. The eyes looked like knotholes where branches had once been, but as she looked closer, the insides of these holes were definitely looking back at her. The nose was a growth of bark, thick and long just below the *eyes*, and the *mouth* was a side-ways crack that gave the impression of a permanent smile. Additional vertical cracks in the trunk gave the impression of a long, flowing beard.

"I take it that you are a Tree Druid?" Tanya asked cautiously.

"Yes, First Mother," groaned the voice. Tanya noted that the *mouth* on the trunk formed a more obvious smile, and then slowly moved as the voice sounded.

"It's just that I've never seen a Tree Druid like you. Most Tree Druids I've known change back and forth between human and tree," Tanya offered as apology.

"You speak of the younger Tree Druids, my lady. They are only several hundred years old. They are full of the wanderlust. They cannot stay in one place long enough to set down a descent set of roots. No, they are always turning into human form, and rushing off. I think they've got *itchy bark* from growing too fast.

"The rest of us grow wiser with age. I remember my wandering days. Never could make up my mind where I wanted to be. After a thousand years or so, we eventually find a spot, settle down, and take root."

"Excuse me, Gantra. I don't mean to stare or to be impolite, but just how old are you?" Tanya asked.

There was a humming-kind of sound, a creaking of the boughs as Gantra thought for a moment, then he replied, "According to my people, I'm about fifty-three years old. Now in human years that would be…" again the groaning and moaning of the branches, "…around forty-six hundred of your years. Of course the others are older."

"*Others?*" Tanya asked, and she looked around. Now that she knew what to look for, she saw faces in two of the other great trees in the clearing. She also noted that the tree druids were all oaks. "Is this the Grove of Three Oaks?" she asked.

"Yes, that is what we are called," Gantra declared. Tanya suddenly realized that if Glidon had healed her, she would have passed the grove in the night. Her condition had forced her to stop at just the right time. It wasn't a lapse of memory on the part of the Adoni that her wounds went untended.

"You are the Tree Druids Sir Crin saved long ago," Tanya suggested.

"Yes, Sir Crin," Gantra acknowledged. "One of the Knights of Es-Soh-En as I recall. He saved many of our brothers and sisters back them. We, however, had been rooted too long; and so moving to a different place was not possible. He made the Magarians believe that we had left, so they no longer come here."

"Forgive my manners," Tanya began. "I am acting like a twig. How are your roots and leaves?"

"Thank you for asking. They are deep and strong. My branches are full. The Adoni has been good to me." Gantra groaned in the night air. "You know, I have a little bit of that *itchy bark* still left to out-grow myself. If I was as mature as the others, I wouldn't even have spoken to you. They won't speak until they've known you for three or four of your years."

"I doubt if anyone would stay around that long without someone speaking," Tanya suggested.

"That might explain why they never talk to anyone." Her knees buckled, and she dropped to the ground.

"Oh! Now where are my manners," Gantra began. "I started talking because of your fever, and here we've ignored the problem. There's a pod bush over by Bendora." Gantra's branches and leaves moved motioning to the left. Tanya crawled over to the second great oak. Next to it was a small bush with three or four pods.

"Excuse me, Bendora," Tanya asked as she had to stop, roll over, and lean against the tree druid for support. She took several deep breaths, wiped the sweat out of her eyes. "What do I do with these?"

"There are several ways of administering the ingredients of the pod. You could break it and mix it with a drink. That's the best way. You can also sprinkle it on food you are eating. If there's nothing else, you pour the powder in your mouth, and try to swallow; but it tastes terrible."

"Is there any water around here?" Tanya asked.

"There a pool from a river several yards behind Wodin. He got here first, and so he took the best spot." This time Gantra's leaves motioned toward the other tree druid. She wasn't sure, but she thought she heard Wodin moaning in his trunk. It was not a pleasant sound, and she wondered if this may not be a touchy subject among the three tree druids.

"*Wodin?*" Tanya thought out loud. "I know you. We danced..."

"...In the Garden of Tangar," Wodin completed for her. There actually came the sound of the tree laughing. "I told you I had danced with her," Wodin declared to the other two Tree Druids.

Tanya took one of the pods, crawled to the pool of water, and drank some water first to wet her already-dry mouth. She filled her mouth with water, tilted her head back without swallowing the liquid, and broke the pod so that the powder fell into her opened mouth. The taste *was* terrible, and she had to fight every instinct to spew it out. She tried twice to swallow, but it was as if her body was rebelling to make the foul-tasting liquid part of her. By the third time, she had forced down the medicine. She buried her face in the pool of water, and drank deep to wash the taste out of her mouth.

When she had filled her belly, she rolled over on the bank, and dropped her hand into the water, dipping it several times, and running it over her fevered brow. She had several sudden waves of nausea, but the thought of having to swallow the powder a second time gave her the strength to fight them off. She wasn't sure how long she had lain there, but when she woke, she heard the sounds of morning birds flitting among the brush, and seeking their breakfast.

She sat up, caught off guard by the stabbing, burning pain in her sides and chest. She had been so sick from the disease the bat things carried, that she had forgotten about the wounds from its claws. Now that the fever and sickness had passed, the gashes in her skin were demanding attention. She managed to get to her feet, and to stagger back into the clearing of the Grove of Three Oaks.

"Good morning," she said out of politeness to her hosts. "Bendora, thank you for your pods. I now recall that you collected healing plants and herbs as you traveled, and spread them throughout the Lands of the Adoni. We met once before the Curse was placed on the Lands of the Adoni."

"Yes, First Mother. You and David shared your knowledge with me. You are welcomed. It is an honor to repay your kindness to me," Bendora groaned.

"How are your branches and roots?" Tanya inquired now practicing the proper etiquette of the Tree Druids since her fever had broken. The Tree Druids and Tanya spent over an hour asking about each other. Gantra finally moved to actual conversation.

"I had no idea that the infection had moved as far as it had, or I would have guided you to the pods much sooner," the younger Tree Druid confessed. "If you had waited much longer, you would have slipped into a coma, and someone else would have had to treat you."

"But there's no one else around…unless you?" she queried.

"I'm sorry. *Once the roots go down, the tree stays down*," Gantra quoted.

Tanya turned and winced in pain. It was then that the Tree Druids realized the markings on her outfit were not for decoration.

"You are wounded!" Bendora declared.

"First Mother, forgive us. Etiquette can wait when you have such need," Wodin declared.

"Here, use some of my leaves," Bendora offered. Tanya was about to reach up, and pluck several but stopped.

"This won't hurt you, will it?" she asked.

"Oh no." There was humor in the Tree Druid's voice now. "It won't hurt any more than you having your hair cut – I've heard about such practices among humans when I was much younger."

Tanya stripped off two handfuls of leaves, rolled them back and forth between her hands as Es-Soh-En had instructed her in the Garden of Tangar. She looked around, and saw the rich black dirt and moss on the other side of Wodin.

"May I?" she asked.

"Of course, First Mother. Help yourself," the elder Tree Druid responded.

"There also some mold pods behind me," Bendora offered.

"It's good seeing both of you again," Tanya offered, stroking Bendora's bark, and patting it gently. She reached up, and rustled Wodin's leaves the way he liked her to do those many centuries ago.

"Oh, you remember," Wodin almost squealed in his Tree Druid voice.

"So you did know her after all?" Gantra asked.

"I told you I did." Bendora chirped.

"Forgive me, Gantra. I do not recall meeting you before." Tanya let her voice trail off to give the younger Tree Druid the opportunity to correct her.

"No, First Mother. I was never so blessed. When you came into our home last evening, it was all I could do to contain my excitement at finally meeting you. Wodin and Bendora keep telling me all about you."

"Which is why he spoke before getting to know you properly," Bendora chided. "Now those leaves aren't going to be enough. There some kendar bushes several yards to the south. Take the berries and leaves to complete the treatment. Mix those with the leaves, and it will have the right mixture.

"Oh, why am I telling you. You're the one who taught me."

"It's nice to see that you remember your lessons," Tanya offered.

The Child of Earth did as she was told. She mixed the dirt, moss, mold, and some berries into a paste. She smeared them generously on her wounds, and the coolness provided an instant relief for her. She then crushed and rolled the kendar leaves with the oak leaves to form a covering, tore her shirt hem to make a bandage to hold it all in place, and wrapped it around her ribs.

"Better?" Bendora asked.

"Yes, thank you. Thank you, all of you. So what have you been doing all these centuries? The last time I spoke with you, Bendora, you were heading into Orpha looking for the Flenda pod. Did you ever find it?"

"Oh yes." Bendora beamed. "I kept seeds or cuttings of all my collections. I planted most of the medicinal plants around here before putting down my roots."

"Wodin, I wish that we could dance one more time," she offered.

"Not quite as young as I was then."

Tanya then asked about some of Gantra's travels before he *planted*, and was rewarded with several tales of his travels into Magar, and even to the Saladon Canyon where the faces of the cliffs were great sheets of jagged crystals. Gantra had spent several years there watching the sunrise and sunset dance on those great cliffs. Each morning and evening found the sun in a different position in the sky, and so there was always a different show displayed for the Tree Druid. Gantra had stayed several years, just to see certain displays more than once. His favorite was the summer solstice, the *morning version* as he referred to the sunrise displays.

Gantra had traveled from there to the west through the Dragon's Teeth, a great mountain range in Southern Magar. The peaks were tall, sharp, and jagged; with several still-active volcanoes that belched smoke and fire into the air. This created the image from afar of looking into the mouth of a dragon, hence the name for the mountain range. Gantra had gone for the experience, but the smoke and fumes played havoc with his leaves. He could only stay a few months, and then had to move on.

As the conversation continued, Wodin suddenly added, "I think the greatest moment of my life was dancing with you in the Garden of Tangar." Wodin then related the story of how he had been called to life by Glidon and Tanya's singing, and how he had been a young tree, a *mere sapling* at the time. He developed a consciousness when the music first began, but it wasn't until Tanya danced around the Garden and touched his limb that he came fully awake and could move. Wodin told the others of the rebellion of Ish and Issha, the Great Fall, and what it was like to lose the ability to communicate with all the species of life that inhabited all the Lands of the Adoni.

"So what do you three do here since you've put down your roots?" Tanya asked. Her wounds were no longer hurting, and she didn't need to keep splitting her attention between the wounds, the pain, and her hosts.

"Mostly now we just listen," Wodin admitted.

"Listen? Listen to the wind? The birds?" Tanya pressed.

"Oh we hear them, but we also listen to the gossip from all over the Lands of the Adoni," Gantra replied.

"From all the Lands of the Adoni?" Tanya asked.

"Yes," Bendora added. "While the ability to speak with plants was lost to you humans by the Fall, we have always still been able to speak with each other."

"*The Music of the Ground*. I had forgotten," Tanya confessed. "I haven't had time to visit with all my children this visit. I forget you and all the plants have your own kind of language."

"We've heard a great deal about you since you've left Dula," Wodin offered.

"What sort of things?" Tanya realized it was poor manners to ask what someone had said, but she was too curious to follow protocol.

"The grass was telling us that you were able to see the unicorns, in fact, you've been joined to their herd," Gantra shared. The reference made Tanya suddenly recall the "*bonding*." She opened her mind up, and found Deenara waiting for her in her mind.

"We will be there in about four hours. I will tell Agron that you are safe," Deenara offered. The connection went back into a *waiting mode* until they needed to discuss anything further.

"Can you tell me what's happening in Dula now?" she asked.

"Not right now. Our information is about five or six hours old. But they have been celebrating."

"Celebrating?" Tanya asked. "What do they have to celebrate?"

"Seems that when you broke the crystal eye while Gibron was still in contact with it; you caused some kind of brain damage." Bendora took up the narrative. "He's blind in his right eye, and his right arm is now useless. Some say it's because of you, others think it was caused by the damage to the brain. He also lost his ability to disguise his actions. Seems the horse he rode into Dula on was actually some sort of demon creature. The minute the people saw it for what it was, they panicked. The people who were left in Dula had not been strong followers of the Adoni. They were like sheep, going whichever way someone pointed them. But when they had evidence of the Dark Lord existing, and being right there in their city, they all had their eyes opened. They've driven Gib-ron out of the city, cleansed it of everything even faintly related to the Dark Lord, and have been working to restore the worship of Teacher and the Adoni as a way of life. They even realize that Teacher and Es-Soh-En are one-in-the-same."

"Then Gib-ron is exiled?" Tanya repeated.

"Right out the city gates," Wodin chuckled. "They tied him to his horse, and drove it out. All of his followers were driven out with him. I understand some people even drove them as far as they could to the west. When it became obvious that the creature was going to carry Gib-ron into the Veil of Darkness, they let it go on its own, and came back to the city."

"And what of the people's reaction to me? To David?" Tanya asked.

"Some had wondered about Sir David when he came in with Gib-ron. They were forced into silence because of the popular opinion. When Gib-ron was exposed as a servant of the Dark Lord, these people came forward and spoke about the missing scar on the David you killed in battle. They reminded everyone that the true Gennerroth could not be broken in battle. The entire city has come to realize that you killed an imposter in order to protect them from Gib-ron's deception. They have repented for the way you were treated. They long for you to return."

"But I can't." Tanya announced.

"Can't?" Wodin asked.

"My orders are to go to Janadis with my forces. Even though Dula now serves the Adoni, my orders have not changed.

The foursome continued to visit until Tanya heard a voice inside her mind.

"We are about to come into sight," Deenara announced. He did not want to be rude, but felt it best to give Tanya some warning about the army coming upon her.

"Has it been that long already?" Tanya asked her companion through her thoughts.

"Yes. It's been almost four hours."

"It's time for me to go," Tanya declared as she rose. She was glad her ribs were not hurting any more.

"Yes, we've heard about the army's approach for the last half-hour from the various plants."

"I hope they weren't too rough on any of them," Tanya offered as an apology.

"No, plants know how to keep out of the way, but thank you for asking. It was nice to visit once more," Bendora replied.

"Yes it was. It was nice meeting you Gantra, and to see you and Wodin once more. There are a lot of memories."

"Yes, perhaps you might stop by when you come back from Janadis, just for a visit," suggested Wodin.

"I'd love to. If the Adoni permit, I'll see you again then. Thanks for your hospitality." She hugged each tree, rustled Wodin's leaves one last time, and then ran to meet her army. She didn't want so many to be passing through the grove in case someone accidentally injured her friends.

"She's been through a lot, hasn't she?" observed Bendora.

"Yes. I'm sure there will be a special place for her in the Greater Kingdom," noted Wodin.

"Probably so, but I pray it is still a long time before she passes into the Kingdom," Gantra replied. The three voices then blended together in a blessing spoken among the Tree Druids, calling for the Adoni to watch over and protect the Child of Earth. Those passing by with untrained ears would have only heard a noise which very much sounded like an unseen wind blowing through their leaves.

CHAPTER TWENTY-FOUR

THE BATTLE OF THE BAY

Agron spent a great deal of time fussing over Tanya's wounds. He insisted that Tanya ride in one of the wagons, and instructed Co-lin to care for the Stewardess. Agron then left Pentra, Ren, and Han to lead the army through the Forest of Venra while he rode alongside of Tanya's wagon. Han had positioned his race through-out the entire throng, war bows at the ready. Stories of entire flocks of bat things dropping out of the skies on travelers were not unfounded rumors. Further, these creatures were known to carry disease in their talons and fangs. A scratch or a bite – no matter how minor – would infect the person attacked with a fatal illness.

Co-lin took great care to remove the bandage Tanya had applied to her wounds. Agron commented on the crude wrap-ping of oak and kendar leaves with the thick mud pack. Co-lin took one look at the first wound, cleaned a little away from the actual gash, applied enough water to moisten the mud, and smeared it back over the wound. The healer then adjusted the oak and kendar leaves, brought out a fresh bandage, and began to re-wrap Tanya's ribs.

"That's it?!" Agron nearly bellowed.

"She has done a better job of tending her wounds than I. Kendar leaves have a healing property that draws poison out of any wound. They will keep the infection down. The moss, mold, and rich black mud keep her pain down. The lacerations have already begun to knit back together. Nothing I could have given her would have done that in three days, let alone one. My oath tells me to *do no harm*, and so by trying to remove her treatment and apply my own I would be harming her."

"But mud, moss, mold, and leaves for a wound?" Agron found it hard to grasp.

"Remember when you asked me about my world, Agron?" Tanya reminded.

"Yes, it was when we rested along the lake," he recalled.

"I told you that in my world we tried to create machines that would do the work of nature. You found that a waste of effort. Here I have used nature to do the work of medicines, creams, and bandages. Wouldn't it be just as much a waste to try to find something else not of nature when the Adoni have already supplied our needs?"

Agron fell silent for several moments. Tanya liked him, not in the same way she like Jensen, but she knew his heart was good. He was trying to deal with his own shame for acting as if he knew more than the Child of Earth. Tanya thought to find some words to ease his guilt.

"Glidon spoke of you," Tanya announced.

"Of me?" Agron was nearly speechless. "What did He say?"

"He said you need to learn to forgive yourself. He said that if you had gone with David into the city, you would have died with my brother. There was nothing you could have done to prevent David's death. I guess the Adoni did not allow you to follow because They have need of you – I have need of you."

"But I seem to make so many mistakes. I am not skilled in all the areas where you and David are skilled." Tanya noted that Agron spoke of her brother as if he were alive. Her lesson must have made a difference.

"You are not a Child of Earth. You are not called to be a Child of Earth. The Adoni do not expect you to perform as a Child of Earth. They expect you to perform as Agron, second-in-command of the army of Dula. You cannot travel a path that has not been set down before you. This is not because you are not worthy. It's not because you are lacking. It's because the Adoni have designed you for your own path. It is a path only you can walk. Neither David, nor I can walk your path and do as well as you. Do not try to walk our path and feel inadequate because you do not walk ours as well as we do.

"You have been entrusted with care of the army. We have been entrusted with the care of the throne. We work well together, but only when we do not seek the job assigned to the other. The Adoni chose you to prepare the army of Dula for war. You worked in secret. You chose well those who follow the Adoni. You taught those under your command. Your army is the best in the world. This is not something the Adoni gave us to do. They called you to do this, and you have done a wonderful job."

Agron's spirit lifted as Tanya spoke. Once she was sure that he had stopped blaming himself, she added, "Gib-ron has been driven out of Dula."

"What?!" It was both Co-lin and Agron who responded this time to the news.

"How?" Co-lin asked.

"Why?" Agron continued.

"It had something to do with the breaking of the Seeing Eye. Gib-ron is now blind in his right eye, and his right arm is now useless," Tanya advised.

"You broke the Seeing Eye while his mind was still joined to it, didn't you?" Co-lin inquired.

"Yes," Tanya admitted.

"If his mind was actually joined to the Seeing Eye, then several connections may have been damaged. Of course, your blow to his elbow would not help his arm, either. You said that he was clawing at his head and hair when you left. That might indicate some kind of brain damage," the healer observed.

"The change in the city has gone beyond just a change in Gib-ron. According to sources, the horse Gib-ron rode into the city was some sort of demon creature he had disguised. When the Seeing Eye broke, the creature was exposed. By the morning, the city had turned against him, tied him to his creature, and driven them and all his followers out of the city and in the direction of the Veil of Darkness."

"So what is the city doing now?" Agron asked.

"They are turning to the Adoni with open hearts. They have moved through the city, taken anything and everything that is even remotely related to the worship of Cronis, and destroyed it. Some people came forward after Gib-ron was driven out, and told the people about the missing scar on the face of the David I killed, and how his sword should not have broken if he had been the true Sir David. The people now believe, and they now wait for us to return and take the throne."

"Then we are going to turn around and return?" Agron asked – excitement in his voice.

"I would love to go back now, but the Adoni have made it clear that my orders are still to travel to Janadis until I am ordered back to Dula. The city will have to continue without a ruler until the Adoni order us back to Dula."

"A kingdom without a ruler? How can the nation survive?" Agron pressed.

"It's all part of the Plan," Tanya repeated. She wasn't sure what the Adoni had in store, but she knew what her instructions were. "The Adoni do not make mistakes. They have

315

ordered us from the city. They have instructed us to continue our journey to Janadis. They opened the eyes of the people of Dula to who was truly ruling them. It is the Adoni who have removed any ruler from the throne of Dula. Logos is with us so none may claim divine right to rule in our absence. This is a time of testing for the kingdom. The Adoni intended for this to happen. If They intended it to happen, then it is part of the Plan."

"We must each follow the Plan." It was the voice of Pentra who had fallen back from the head of the line to join them. "I have learned much from listening to Ren and Han. They have shamed me on several occasions with their level of dedication to the Adoni. You have shamed me with the lack of commitment to Teacher, Agron. I have chosen to be shamed no more. We follow the path the Adoni have set before us. We support the Plan, even if it is our task but to die for the Plan. I have lived in fear too long. I will live in fear no more." He then continued along the line, checking on each of the soldiers, each member of the various races who had accompanied them. When he was gone, Agron broke his silence.

"I have shamed him with my dedication? How? I am not nearly dedicated enough to Teacher." He stammered trying to find the words to express what he was feeling.

"It is as I told you. We all have our own paths. You walked the path set before you, and your dedication inspired Pentra to follow his own."

"But my path was not that difficult. It all came together for me. I was just doing what I believed in. I taught what I knew. I wasn't any different than I was before I began training Heart Company," Agron insisted.

"Which is the time when we serve the Adoni the best. When we try to be what we are not, that is when it is difficult for Them to use us. Don't forget. They made us what we are. They made us that way for a reason. When we fulfill Their calling, it is fulfilling for us as well. Doing what they called us to do is easy for us, but difficult for others. This is why it is difficult for you to serve in the way that David and I serve. It would be difficult for us to serve in the way you have been called. There are jobs for each of us. There are paths for each of us. We work best when we do what we are called to do."

The conversation then moved to other bits of news Tanya had gathered from the Tree Druids concerning Dula. This kept them occupied until it was time to make camp for the evening. The next three days moved without incident. Han commented each morning that they must have the protection of the Adoni to travel this long in the Forest of Venra and not encounter bat things. Their journey kept them in the Forest of Venra for an additional week, following the forest to its south-eastern point which was its closest point to the Bay of Magar.

"We will move at night." Tanya declared to the leaders. Deenara came on behalf of the unicorns, Fin Den and Wil Den represented the gnome community, Ren spoke for the minotaurs, Han stood for the centaurs; and Laton came for the Water People. Pentra and Agron stood on either side of the Knight of Es-Soh-En. Tanya spread the map of the Lands of the Adoni on the table before them.

"We are here, at the south-easterly point of the Forest of Venra. We must cross this section here." She pointed to a stretch of land that was opened between the Forest of Venra and the Bay of Magar. As she traced the route with her finger, her eye caught the reference to the Saladon Canyon a little to the south of their course. She thought for a moment of the stories of Gantra when he stayed there, and she had a fleeting desire to take a side trip and see the walls of crystal shining in the sunrise for herself. She knew such a detour would endanger her *herd*, and so she blocked it from her memory.

"The Dark One seeks to distract you," Deenara cautioned her in her mind. She acknowledged the danger, and focused on the task at hand.

"I estimate this to be about ten miles. Can we move so many in one night?" Tanya asked.

If we concentrate our efforts, it can be done," Ren declared. "We can run and keep pace with the centaurs. Most of your race," he said referring to Pentra and Agron as the humans, "has horses. If we push them, it will only be a few hours ride."

"Those who have no horses, or the young, can be carried by us," Deenara offered.

"My race can carry the gnomes, and cross the same distance in the same time." Han offered.

"We will have to leave our ponies and many of our supplies here in the forest," Wil Den noted.

"What will we do about transportation and supplies at the Bay of Magar?" Fin Den inquired.

"We will have to travel light." Tanya announced. She looked at Pentra and Agron as she spoke. "People will have to carry only what is most important to them. There will be a lot of things left behind."

"What do we use to determine what to take and what to leave?" Pentra asked.

"We will need our weapons." Agron noted. There was a consensus of grunting and nods of agreement. "We will need some light provisions, a day's food and water."

"Personal possessions?" Pentra asked.

"Five pounds is preferable, ten pounds allowed, but no more than that. If we load down our horses, it will slow down our pace. All wagons must be left behind." Tanya noted. "Two things must come with us, however. The first is the body of Sir David." She had waited for any disagreement, but no one voiced or displayed the slightest objection. It spoke of the dedication of the centaurs and minotaurs to Sir David, for in the mind of the two races, bodies of a fallen comrade – although honored – were abandoned when necessary for the safety of the others.

"We will carry our fallen brother." Deenara announced. "Also, if horses or centaurs grow tired during the trip, we can carry their loads," Everyone voiced their agreement.

"The second item we must make sure to take is the Eye of Suma." Again, there was no objection.

"Now, how are we going to transport the Water People?" Her question was directed at Laton.

"There is a stream at this point." His finger marked the map a little north of the place where Tanya had planned to exit the forest. She looked at the map.

"There's no marking on the map for any stream," she noted.

"No, it is too small for the map makers to list, but we know the water ways. It will flow into the Bay of Magar. My people will separate when you ride from the forest. We can make it to the stream in about an hour. From there we will ride the currents to the head of the bay. We can exit before the waters begin to mix with the salt water from the ocean."

"If it takes you an hour to get to the stream, how much longer will it take to get to the bay? We cannot hold the bay for long. Once we have overcome the guards, and boarded the ships, we will be vulnerable until we set sail," Tanya observed.

"We will be on time. None are as quick in the waters as we," Laton declared with a smile. Tanya did not know what the smile was, but she believed that it meant time would not be a problem for the Water People.

The Knight of Es-Soh-En gave her army an hour to get ready. Plans were discussed for hiding the supplies and wagons so they might be available for the return trip. The task fell to the gnomes who were experts at woodcraft. The entire community set about building storage places out of trees, brushes, branches, and other material found in the forest. When they were done, they still had fifteen minutes to go before the deadline. Tanya could not spot any of the supplies, even though she knew where to look.

"We will stay and watch over the wagons and supplies while you are gone," Deenara noted.

She made one last ride up and down the entire length of the refugees. She inquired with each leader, and those appointed as section leaders. Everyone was ready. She reared her horse up, spun around and galloped to the front of the line. She called Sylar forth from its resting place, raised it high enough for everyone to see. As she dropped it, all the horses, centaurs, unicorns, and minotaurs thundered out of the forest, and charged in a straight line for the closest point of the Bay of Magar.

Four hours later Tanya motioned for the army to slow. They had taken six breaks so far, not for the minotaurs or centaurs to rest, but the horses. Even though they had been some of the best in Dula, the pace was too grueling. Each rest stop had been for complete rest, then a walking rest, then back to full gallop. This time Tanya signaled a slowing of the forces because they were coming near the Bay of Magar.

"I need someone to scout the area, report back on forces, and their locations." Fin Den motioned to his people, and ten of his best were already on their way before she had finished asking for volunteers. Twenty minutes later a messenger came running back.

"You're not going to believe this!" he exclaimed while still catching his breath. "There are no guards. Almost a hundred ships are docked there, and they are all stocked and ready to sail."

"A trap?" Tanya inquired. She knew that it was impossible to move as many people and creatures at such a speed for so long without being detected. Even in the darkness, the sounds of their passing, or the vibrations they set off would warn those ahead of them that something large was coming.

"No," gasped the gnome.

"Did they turn and run?" the Knight of Es-Soh-En inquired.

"No," The gnome finally caught enough of his breath to continue. "Water People got there before us. The entire Magarian Navy was docked and there is some kind of celebration in the city. Laton's people have secured the docks, and loaded the ships. All they need right now is us."

"How long have they been there?" Agron exclaimed.

"At least two hours," the gnome replied.

"Let's go!" Tanya announced, and her forces moved down to the bay.

The Stewardess of Dula could not believe that enough boats were docked in the bay and waiting for them. Her greatest fear was what to do with those who would not fit on the boats. Agron had politely chided her noting that it was *all part of the Plan.* He pointed out that if the Adoni wanted them to go to Janadis, then They would have arranged for the transportation.

Laton informed Tanya that there had been fifty guards on duty when the Water People departed from the water. It had been quick work to defeat them. They had learned from captives that most of the navy had just returned from the Bromor Delta. Since it was on the border of Orpha and Bromor, it was an ideal meeting place for the three forces. Word of Gib-ron's taking the throne of Dula caused the three armies to return home and prepare for the invasion. This is why the entire navy was docked here and why they were celebrating.

"I guess they missed the latest memo," Tanya observed to no one in particular.

Although everyone had traveled light, and knew the drill, it still took half an hour to load all the people and supplies onto the boats. As the last minotaurs were boarding, one of the sentries called out, "Guards!" Tanya began to direct the defense of her forces. Those ships that were already loaded were cast off, and began to move out of the docking area. The last six more were almost loaded, but would take another ten or fifteen minutes.

"Leave this to my people," Laton offered. "Leave one ship for us." When Tanya nodded agreement, he motioned, and twenty of his men moved off to form a wall between the in-coming guards, and the escaping refugees. Tanya and Agron climbed a stack of crates on the dock in order to see the battle.

The first wave of troops came out of the darkness, screaming their battle cries, swords lifted high. Agron suddenly realized that none of the Water people sent to defend the docks had any weapons. He scanned his memory, and now recalled that he had never seen a Water Citizen with any sword, knife, spear, or bow. As the attackers fell upon the Water People, the line never moved. As each soldier came close enough, they slashed at the water warriors. To Agron's amazement, the Water People offered no initial resistance. The commander cried out as he saw blade after blade slash through the bodies of their defenders, cutting all the way through. It was going to be a massacre.

Anger flared in Agron's heart at the idea that Laton had sent his men out to die as a diversion to buy them time to escape. They needed warriors, not lambs for the slaughter. The commander was about to order others from the ships to aid in defense of the docks, but Tanya's hand was on his arm.

"Wait," was all she said.

Agron noticed that the Water Warriors did not fall from the blows. It was as if they had never been touched. The attackers were just as shocked as Agron. They slashed a second time, cutting their foes in half again, but they did not fall. When the solders attacked a third time, Agron realized that the Water People were turning their bodies to water so that the blades passed harmlessly through them, but still holding enough form in order to remain standing.

As the attackers raised their swords for a fourth blow, each Water Citizen raised his/her hands, fired their fists into the faces of their attackers. It was more than a blow, because as the fist made contact with the Magarian faces, they exploded into water. The Water People had offered no defense for the first three attacks to draw the soldiers in so they could not escape. The Water People held their hands on the faces of the Magarians who began to drop their weapons, grab at their heads or chests, and scream. Each soldier dropped to the ground writhing in death; drowning where they stood..

"How?" Agron asked turning to Laton who was now beside them.

"Many years ago, our people were taken captive as a race. Many were killed. We vowed that we would never be victims again. We know the ways of war. Each of my people used their control over the water in their bodies to travel up the tear ducts, nose and sinuses, even the mouth. They sent part of their water into the brain, head, or chest, and then expand their water, and turned it hard. The result is a rather painful death from a scrambled brain, exploded sinuses, or crushed heart and lungs."

A second wave of attackers roared their defiance, charged out of the darkness with three times the number of the last wave and met a similar fate. The screams of the dying were almost more than those on the ships could bear. As the second wave lay dead on the docks, thousands of arrows came tearing through the night skies. All the shafts passed through the water bodies. The impact with the liquid drained the arrows of their momentum, and they clattered harmlessly on the ground. The last ship was ready to leave.

"Call them back so we can shove off," Tanya ordered.

"They will stay until we are safe," Laton announced.

"My orders were to leave none behind. That goes for Water People as well," Tanya declared.

"You would risk the safety of others to insure my people are rescued?" The voice of Laton was incredulous.

"When they came with us, they became my people, too," Tanya observed. Laton studied the Knight of Es-Soh-En for a long moment. As he did, another wave of attackers charged out of the darkness.

"I will be the last to board the ship," Tanya replied to Laton's continued stare. "If your warriors are not on the ship when it leaves, then neither will I be on board."

Laton could tell the Child of Earth was determined in her position. He nodded, and made some sound that could only be made by a water creature. It sounded like a blending of a gurgling sound and a whistle. The line of defense began to move back as the attackers came forward. Instead of waiting until the Magarian troops were close enough to reach out and touch; each Water Warrior *fired* small balls of water from their bodies at the attackers. Some of the projectiles were round and hard, crushing skulls or bones when they impacted. Others let the air currents shape them into long sharp points of water that, when hardened by the water citizen's command, pierced the strongest armor when they hit. Even though retreating, the water people took out the entire wave of attackers.

All the ships were out of sight in the darkness except for the last one Tanya was going to be on. There were three other ships left in the harbor that had not been needed. True to her word, Tanya waited at the gangplank for the defenders of the docks to board. She was the last one up, and she kicked the plank into the water as she cleared the railing and bounded onto the deck. An unseen wind caught the sails and moved the ship away from the dock before the Magarians could get close enough to board.

"They're heading for the other ships," Tanya noted. She looked around for a bowman who might fire flaming arrows onto the other decks, but no bowman had come aboard her ship. Laton motioned to three of his warriors. Each one broke open a barrel of water, placed one arm in the barrel, and the other arm pointed at one of the three remaining ships. There came a slurping sound as all the water in the barrel was drawn into the water person's body, then a *fa-foom* sound as the excess water was *fired* at each of the ship. The water bombs struck the main hull of each ship, splintering the wood, and tearing open the hull at the water line. Within seconds, each ship was tilting at a forty-five degree angle or greater, and sinking into the bay.

"Fire arrows!" Laton announced. Tanya's attention was turned back to the docks. They were not far enough away to be safe. She knew that the Magarians had skilled archers, with strong bows, and most of their arrows would make it to her ship. The rest of the Water People lined the aft railings. As the flaming shafts tore through the sky like streaking meteors, each Water Citizen position himself/herself to catch the shaft in their bodies and extinguish the flames. Where the arrow was too high to block, the Water Citizen fired a small burst of water, dousing the flames, and knocking the projectiles out of the air. Before a second round could be mounted to the bows and ignited, the ship was lost in the darkness.

The Magarian archers fired three more volleys just in case one shaft might be lucky enough to make it to the ship. Tanya watched the arrows, like falling stars arching high into the night, and plunging from the sky. The Knight of Es-Soh-En took satisfaction with the *hissing* sound they made as they dropped into the waves, and their flames were snuffed out. Laton joined her on the aft deck. She squeezed his shoulder, smiled and declared, "On to Janadis."

CHAPTER TWENTY-FIVE

THE UNDERSEA CITY

It had been five days that Tanya's fleet had been on the Great Sea. Hentery perched on the aft railing as Tanya stood basking in the sun, her eyes closed; the wind blowing through her hair. It had been a most unusual wind. Once a ship had been loaded in the Bay of Magar, a wind came up, and moved it out of the bay and onto the open sea. The wind did not move any ship that was not fully loaded. When the sun rose over the eastern horizon the following morning, land was nowhere in sight, but the ships still moved in a straight line. With the first light of morning, Tanya was surprised that all the ships were sailing in such close formation, but didn't seem to be in danger of colliding. When she tried to figure some way to lower a life boat and try to go to the other ships, the wind died down. All the ships rested calmly in the water. Tanya took the opportunity to transfer several personnel among the ships to balance out the number of each race and the number of command personnel on each ship. As soon as every one was transferred, and the last life boat back in place on the ship, the wind rose from the west, blowing towards the east and the undersea city of Janadis. This was contrary to normal wind patterns. Several had come to call the strange weather event *the Breath of the Adoni.*

Those familiar with the ways of the sea had no explanation for the unusual weather, but Tanya would simply smile when they tried to find some logical explanation. This would normally be the time of fierce storms on the Great Sea. It was not safe to travel far from land during these months. The Magarian navy had hugged the shoreline when they left for the Bromor Delta. Her fleet had done what seasoned sailors would never have dared. Further, the weather was so warm and calm, that most lounged on the decks, and rested during the journey.

"So if it's really an ocean, why is it called the Great Sea?" Hentery asked after long moments.

"When map makers first began to chart the waters, they believed that on the eastern shore of these waters lay the Kingdom of the Adoni," Tanya replied, still keeping her eyes closed, and savoring the warmth of the late morning sun.

"Is it?"

"It depends. If you are destined to find the Kingdom of the Adoni, you travel east across the sea until you come to a great cloud bank. Things change, and after a while you find yourself in the Lesser Kingdom. That's *if* you're destined to enter the Kingdom." Tanya recalled her second visit to Dula when Teacher had guided them on Gaylord and Yeesha through the clouds to the Lesser Kingdom. Teacher had told them then that if someone had traveled normally, they would never reach the Kingdom.

"If you aren't being called into the Kingdom, you just keep traveling on the sea. But the map makers believed that the Kingdom was on the eastern shore, and that all this water was surrounded by land. Since a sea is a large body of water enclosed by land, it was called the Great Sea. By the time sailors found out otherwise, the use of the name was too common to change."

"So what happens if you keep sailing east on the Great Sea?" Hentery asked.

"You come to the end of the world and fall off," she replied. The sudden squeal of the mouse told her that he did not appreciate her sense of humor. "It's a joke, Hentery."

"Then what does happen?" the mouse asked once his nerves were a little more calm.

"Before the Veil of Darkness appeared, you would come back to Dula. However, since the Veil formed, I don't know. I would guess that you run aground on dry land either in or near the Veil. To be honest, I can't think of anyone who has sailed that far east and came back to tell us. I guess even in this age, it's still a mystery."

"Janadis off the port bow!" came the cry from one of the crow's nests. Tanya opened her eyes, shaded them from the glare on the water, and caught sight of the jewel of the ocean. She had seen it several times before. She had even visited it on more than one occasion. Still, it was a beauty to behold. It was green amid the clear waters of the ocean. It had its own light source, and was carved from a green stone found only in the area where the city had been built. Although the sunlight never got through the water to touch the undersea city, the internal lights gave the effect of sunlight dancing on a great emerald.

Tanya climbed to the bow of the ship to call out the greeting to open the gates to the city. On previous occasions a great tube would rise from the ocean's floor, surround the ship, and pump the waters out of the tube. This way the entire ship would be lowered to the ocean bed, and the passengers could walk directly into the city. As she stood on the bow, arms spread in a gesture of friendship, there was a suddenly lurch, and she had to catch herself. The gusts of wind increased, pushing the ship away from the gates of the city.

"What's going on?" Co-lin asked checking to make sure Tanya had not been injured.

"Something doesn't want us to use the main gates. We're being blown past the city." As soon as they were out of position for the gates of the city, the wind returned to its original strength, still moving the ships to the east.

"Do you think the Dark One has interfered?" asked Ren.

"It doesn't feel like it. I almost get a feeling like this is the way we're supposed to go. The sudden increase in speed was to keep us from doing something we weren't supposed to do."

"Any suggestions?" Agron asked.

"If we cannot enter through the gate, there is the Isle of Morning to the east," Tanya suggested. "We had sent several messengers to Janadis while searching for Queen Dianna. They came back saying that there was no response to their request to enter the city. The Adoni must know we won't get in that way, and are sending us on."

"Why the Isle of Morning?" Co-lin asked.

"There's a tunnel there that leads to the city." Tanya climbed back to the center deck, and called up to the lookout, "When we clear the city, we need to go north-east!" The message was relayed by the lookouts from ship to ship. It took about half an hour for the strong breeze to carry the ships past the under-sea city. Although Tanya had given instructions to each of the ships, when they cleared the city, each ship encountered a slightly different air current, changing the direction for the entire fleet.

"I don't think I'll ever get used to this," Hentery declared.

"It's a good sign. The Adoni are taking greater involvement in the events of Dula. It won't be long now."

"Until what?" Hentery asked.

"Until the return of the Adoni," Tanya replied with a matter-of-fact tone to her voice. When Hentery realized the enormity of what had just been announced, he stood dumb-founded on the railing. He caught his tail in his paws, and played absently with the hair at its tip as he tried to grasp what he was truly involved in.

***

The following morning, the winds died down just before the sun rose.

"What does it mean?" asked Agron, strapping on his sword, and coming out of his cabin to climb to the deck. Tanya was only one or two strides ahead of him.

"If everything keeps the way it has, I'd guess that we are where we need to be. Pass the order to begin preparation to disembark." She mounted the stairs two at a time. She caught the railing next to the doorway that formed the stairs going up to the aft deck, fastened both hands onto it, pulled herself up and flipped over to land half-way up the stairs.

"Show-off!" Agron joked at her as he had to climb the rest of the stairs the hard way.

True to the Knight of Es-Soh-En's prediction, when the first rays of morning lit the seascape, the main Isle of Morning lay before them. The ships had moved into the harbor on their own, and it was simply a matter of dropping the gangplank and wading through shallow water to the shore.

"Now that's what I call service." Tanya joked as she was one of the first down the plank and into the water. Pentra came after her singing one of the older songs of praise to the Adoni. He had spent a great deal of time on the voyage gathering the older songs and learning to sing them. Many times he would be passing time on the bow, singing to himself, and the song would catch on. After a few minutes, all hands working on the deck and in the look out would be singing along.

It took about three hours to unload all the personnel, supplies, and personal possessions. The unicorn had kept the horses with them in hiding. Each ship had to unload, and its passengers move with their supplies further into the interior of the island to make room for the next ship. By the time the last passengers climbed down the gangplanks and into the water, those who were first to disembark had already set up a temporary camp and prepared the mid-morning meal for the others.

"So where do we go from here?' Ren approached the Stewardess as she finished her meal.

"We need to send out scouts. Somewhere on this island is the entrance to a tunnel that will take us into the undersea city."

"Any idea what we should be looking for?" Han asked as he was already signaling his men to prepare for the search.

"I've never used the tunnel entrance before. Each time we came, the gates of the city were opened to us, expect the first time. Even then we sent a gnome to swim to the gates and open them for us. In order to carve a tunnel under the sea, they would need a lot of rock. In fact, according to the stories of how the city was built, the founders found a supply of the green stone when they began to carve the tunnel. It's the same kind of green stone used to build the city. Let's track down a supply of the stone, or some quarry where it was carved from," Tanya suggested.

As soon as she had finished the instructions, the centaurs were spreading out in different directions to search the island. Three came back with possible locations an hour later. The others had covered the rest of the island, and hadn't found anything fitting the description. Tanya, Agron and Han went with the three centaurs who had found possible sites for the tunnel. They coordinated their journey to hit the first site, swing around to the second site more in the center of the island, and then come down the northern shore to check out the last one. The first location had a lot of possibilities, but Tanya couldn't find anything to indicate where the door to the tunnel would be if this were the site. They spent over two hours testing and exploring for any further clue. Finally, they had to abandon the site, and move to the second one.

"Surely they wouldn't have begun digging this far back." Agron noted. "They would have to dig under half the island before they even got to the sea. It would seem like a lot of extra work."

"If you or I were planning the dig, but remember, this city was designed by the Adoni. They gave all the instructions on how and where to build to the prince in a dream. Maybe they needed to begin digging this far back just to get enough support on the tunnel roof before the weight of the ocean began to press down."

The group had spent an hour searching, and when Tanya was about to call off the search and move to the next site, she noticed something on one of the cliffs. As she studied it, she began to laugh.

"Find something?" Han asked, trotting up with the other centaurs.

"This!' Tanya declared.

"It looks like someone carved some kind of sword onto this section of the wall."

"Exactly!" Tanya announced. "Janadis and Dula were joined by the Sword Logos. Dula kept the Sword as their sign of divine right to rule; Janadis was given the hilt jewel as a symbol of their eternal treaty."

"I don't see anything to press or turn." Han observed as he studied the symbol.

"But it is pointing over there." Agron suggested. The group moved in the direction indicated by the position of the sword.

They found another sword carved on rock. The search lasted another half-hour, and took them completely away from the area where the green stone had been found. They finally came upon a small mountain. One side of it had been broken loose.

There was a small rough rock jutting out of it just about at shoulder-level. Here Tanya found another, smaller carved sword. She gripped the rock and pressed it. Nothing happened. She then twisted it. It moved, but nothing happened. She twisted the rock, pressed down, and there came the sound of some kind of mechanism engaging deep inside the face of the rock. A few moments later half the rock cliff opened up, swung back, and inside they found, "The door to Janadis!" Tanya exclaimed.

CHAPTER TWENTY-SIX

THE CRY OF THE EAGLE

Tanya rubbed at her eyes. They were aching from the strain and the dust. It had been three weeks since they had found the tunnel into the undersea city. Once they had actually entered the city, Tanya discovered why no one had answered their previous messages: the entire city was deserted.

"Why is it that every time someone needs to look for you, they always find you in some records chamber?" It was the voice of Co-lin, and he stood at the entrance with a tray of food and two mugs of hot drink.

"This is where I do my best work," she joked.

"At least you aren't maiming or wounding anyone in here. It frightens me as a healer the amount of damage you've trained your body to inflict." He sat the tray of food in front of her, took one of the mugs, and sat down, leaning back. His body language announced he was settling in to relax and visit; and Tanya knew him well enough to know he would not leave until she had taken a break.

"Most people just say, *Let's take a break.*" she offered, sipping from the second mug.

"And you ignore most people," Co-lin noted. "You spend a great deal of time among the books and scrolls. Any success?"

"No," and she let her frustration creep into her voice more than she desired. "When I first came to Janadis, we found the city deserted then, too. But that time it was different. As we walked down the streets, there were items laying everywhere. It was like people had grabbed all they could hold and ran. After running, they got tired, but they were still afraid. They threw less important things away, and ran some more. After another few blocks they were even more tired. The process repeated until they had thrown everything away in order to simply save themselves."

"From the stories I've read, there was a crack in the great dome at that time. The thought of several tons of water collapsing on you do not exactly make one calm or comfortable," Co-lin noted. He sipped from the cup as a signal for Tanya to take up the conversation.

"This time it's strange."

"Coming from you, that is quite a statement. Your whole life has been dealing with the unusual or the strange. Why is this different?"

"This time, it's like..." and she sought for the words to express what she was thinking. She finally found them. "It's like they never left."

"If that's the case, then where is everybody?" Co-lin enjoyed being a sounding board. It didn't take too much energy, and he was enjoying the hot drink and company.

"That's just it. We came into the city, and it was clean. It was like they had just finished with all the daily chores. There was nothing lying in the street. The tunnel was sealed, and the flocks and herds were still grazing in the fields on the Isle of Morning. When we went into the buildings, things were laid out as if people had been working on them, and then walked away for a minute, but had planned on returning. Even in the homes we found meals set out on the tables, books opened to be read.

Except for the food having gone bad and cows in desperate need of milking, everything could have been as if everyone left just moments before we entered."

"And so you have a mystery on your hands."

"Exactly!" Tanya announced.

"This brings you to the record chamber."

"Yes…" Tanya was growing cautious. She had been led down this path once too often by the healer.

"Because you're the only one who can do all this work," Co-lin paused.

And there it is, Tanya said to herself. "I seem to be the only person who can read the ancient records." Tanya defended.

"Perhaps, "but does it have to take your every moment? Think about back in Dula. You spent long hours searching for things in the record chamber. Did you find anything on your own?"

"I found the scroll," Tanya declared.

"Yes, but only because the Adoni showed you where it was. Did you find anything other than the scroll in all your long hours of searching?"

"Well…no," Tanya finally admitted. "But that doesn't mean it isn't here."

"But if it was here, and the Adoni wanted you to read it, don't you think They would call attention to it for you." Tanya was trying to come up with a response, but her mind was too tired.

"My point exactly!" Co-lin thumped the stack of books triumphantly. "You're wearing yourself out. You need to be fresh for when we return. If you were suddenly needed right now, would you be able to perform your role?"

"Why are you so good at what you do?" Tanya teased.

"I guess it's the path that the Adoni have set before me." he joked.

At that point Gort came into the room. He had a book which he had been reading.

"I heard that you were looking for information, Lady Tanya. I found this in one of the buildings while we were searching. It's pretty interesting."

"What's it about?" Co-lin asked for Tanya since he had finally gotten the Child of Earth to set aside her books, and eat the meal he had brought.

"It's all about the people of Janadis being carried off."

"*Carried off*?!" Tanya was out of her chair, and snatching the book out of Gort's hand. Co-lin rolled his eyes knowing that all his careful work to get Tanya to relax had just been undone.

"Well, it's not about being carried off by any enemy. They believed they were going to be carried off by the Adoni."

"Carried off to where?" Co-lin gave up on relaxation, and joined into the discussion."

"My guess is that they believed they were going to be carried into the Greater Kingdom."

"They all were going to die? Then where are all the bodies?"

"No, they thought they were going to go bodily into the Greater Kingdom. This books quotes books that have been here for centuries. The author did quite a bit of research on the subject, and put it all together."

"You cannot go bodily into the Kingdom. You have to die," Co-lin protested.

"Not everyone," Tanya countered as she poured over several pages in a fast scan.

"Then who?" Co-lin challenged.

"Singer!" Tanya countered.

"Anyone else?" Co-lin continued.

"The author listed Pentra – the original Pentra," Gort added.

"Legends say he died in the Veil, and then went to the Kingdom," Co-lin observed.

"No, Queen Dianna told us that she saw what happened in the Veil. Pentra was at the point of death, but Glidon healed him, and then he went bodily into the Kingdom."

"But the *normal* method is for someone to die first, and *then* go into the Kingdom," Co-lin declared.

"Normal, yes. But since when has anything around us been normal recently?" Tanya joked.

"You mean to suggest that everyone went bodily into the Kingdom? They were here one second, and then the next they were all gone?"

The description suddenly sounded familiar and reminded her of her own world. "It would fit the pattern of everything we've found here. It would also be the same thing that happened to Queen Dianna. The Adoni told me that she was in the Greater Kingdom. I saw her once when They were speaking to me, but They insisted that she hadn't died. And if I'm not mistaken..." Here Tanya paused, and fumbled through some papers. She found the report she needed, pulled it from its place in the pile, and stabbed at it with her index finger.

"Exactly!" she declared. "Queen Dianna disappeared when David and I came to Dula. It seemed to have been at the exact same moment. One second she was on the throne, the next she was gone. This report sets the time when everyone disappeared from here, and it's somewhere in the same time frame as when Queen Dianna disappeared and we appeared."

"So you're saying that when the Adoni called you from you world into ours, They took Queen Dianna and the entire population of Janadis all at the same time?"

"That's my point!"

"Must have gotten awfully crowded during the transfer," Co-lin joked.

"Janadis has spent long years studying the writings of Tra and Kal. Books used to be rare in Janadis because trees and paper were scarce; but all that has changed. Janadis found other material that was thin like paper and could be printed on. There are books everywhere now. The New Words and the Teachings of Tra and Kal were an obsession with Janadis. They have collected and copied all the lessons of Teacher and accounts written about His activities, teachings and promises by those who were close to Him. When Teacher came to Janadis and shamed them into changing their entire social structure, they put their entire lives into His teachings." She began to fumble with several scrolls, pulled one out, unrolled it and read, "*When tears appear as loved ones go/Life is empty, hope is low/Lift your hearts unto the sky/Rejoice my friend, Es-Soh-En draws nigh!*" Tanya recited.

"Yes, I've heard that quotation many times. It's used at funerals to comfort us with the loss of a loved one."

"But, it can also tell us about this disappearance. *Loved-ones go* could refer to the disappearance of Queen Dianna and everyone in Janadis. *Hope being low* is what we've had to deal with these last few months. The kingdom has been in an uproar, Magar was attacking, Gib-ron tried to steal the throne, David was killed. It hasn't exactly been a time of rejoicing."

"And so you think that this passage is to encourage us to not give up because all these things point to the return of the Adoni?" Gort asked.

"You seem very interested in this teaching," Co-lin noted.

"It's been a passion with my family for generations. I remember sitting at my mother's feet, and she would tell us that one day the Adoni was going to return, and drive out the Dark One once and for all. It is supposed to be a time of peace," Tanya declared.

"Your mother knew about the Lands of the Adoni?" Gort asked.

"No, but there is a similar teaching concerning my world, just the names are different. How could I have missed all of this?"

"Perhaps because you have been so worried since you got here," the healer suggested. "I would like to believe all this, and there is a lot of evidence for either argument, but this has been anything but a time of peace," Co-lin suggested.

"Actually, it ties in with what Glidon told me when last I saw Him. He said that Cronis is increasing his efforts to meet with the Adoni and challenge what They are doing. The Dark One believes this is a show of power, but Glidon said the Adoni see it for what it really is, a desperate attempt to hold onto power even though he is losing."

Co-lin thought for long moments. "I want to believe – but forgive me for my unbelief. I have heard talk of the Adoni returning for many years. After you hear it for so long, it's not that you stop believing; it just doesn't inspire as it should. I believe in the Adoni. I serve the Adoni, but I am not sure if They really promised to return."

"What about the passage near the end?" Gort asked. He took the book from Tanya, flipped through the pages to the section he wanted, and handed it back to her.

"*When the severed jewel is joined once more/And one returns beyond death's door/Dula shall stand for one more day/Then Cronis shall win and fade away.*"

"*Someone coming back from the dead?* Now that would be something to see. If I saw someone come back from the dead, then I would believe. Think you can pull that off for me?" Co-lin suggested.

***

David burst out of the clear fresh water, throwing himself into the sky. When the momentum of his leap expired, he relaxed, and fell laughing into the waves once more. Beside him Ghandrah, the whale king, mirrored the leap and fell back into the waves. The king of the whales displaced so much water a small tidal wave tossed David several feet from where he had landed. The dolphins laughed with him. Kya was waiting for them as the waters embraced them. She motioned to the deeper section of the ocean, and he swam after her. He drew the water into his lungs, let his new body pull the oxygen out of the liquid, and then exhaled. He enjoyed the feel of the water filling his lungs. Before he had been terrified about the sensation, but now it was natural. He was able to breathe beneath the waves the same as his dolphin pod. When he thought of them, several came darting from beneath, rubbed against him, and then swam away as if trying to draw him into a game of *tag* under the waves.

The Knight of Es-Soh-En flipped around, caught one by the tail, and then swam after Kya. She was already several leagues under the sea. She had found a coral forest on the ocean floor. The plant life was full of colors, and several smaller fishes glowed with their own light. She was treading water waiting for him. He stole a kiss as he swam past, and three dolphins came charging by trying to catch the Child of Earth. David back-flipped in the water; laughed and caught Kya in a passionate embrace. As they hugged and kissed, their bodies floated to the surface, their dolphin brothers and sisters dancing in the waters around them and chattered for them to join them. David splashed at them with one hand.

As their heads broke the surface, two dolphins rose on their tails, and skidded across the waves on their tails, chattering and laughing with the couple. Ghandrah used his mighty tail to splash water in David and Kya's faces. Before the water fight could get seriously started, David heard his name. Everyone stopped in mid-attack. David turned around in the water, and saw the figure of Es-Soh-En, the black lion with the golden mane, waiting for him on the shore.

"Race ya!" he called out, and Kya, David, and the dolphins cut through the water charging for the shore. Ghandrah swam off to rejoin Flotsam. At the last second Kya caught David's foot, and pulled him back, passing him, and reaching the grass covered shore ahead of him. David pulled himself up onto the grass, shook the water out of his eyes, and used his fingers to comb his shoulder-length hair out of his eyes. David noticed that Tra and Kal had come to join them, and that Singer, Reva, Fibbergee and Pentra were standing by the trees that grew right up to the water's edge.

"Greetings Es-Soh-En! Greetings friends." All nodded their welcoming to the other. "So what brings you to this part of the Kingdom today? Care to swim in the fresh-water ocean?"

"Not today, David," Es-Soh-En replied. "I have come because I have a favor to ask of you."

"How can I refuse You? Speak and I will obey." Kya cuddled close to David. He put an arm around her to hold her closer.

"Before you commit yourself, you should hear the favor. I am here to ask you to return to the Lands of the Adoni. I need you to assume your mortal body, lead the army of Dula once more into battle, and prepare that world for the Return of the Adoni." The Hobber's eyes were somber, almost sympathetic.

"Do You know what You're asking me to do?" It wasn't anger in David's voice, more of a desperation; something akin to fear, if such an emotion could be present here. "I'm alive here. This is where I belong. You're asking me to give up all of this. You're asking me to set aside my friends, my loved ones, and take up that mortal body once more. That body is dying. It hurts. It's full of pain, doubts, and insecurities.

"You want me to give up the sweet meats of the Kingdom, and eat the decaying flesh of that world. You want me to give up peace and joy. You want me to live as a mortal. Not to go back to living, but back to dying. Do You know what that's like?" There was no anger in the topaz eyes of the Great Hobber. He simply sat there, looking into David's soul. Suddenly David remembered what the Adoni had done for him. Es-Soh-En knew what He was asking. He knew better than even David knew. Es-Soh-En said no words, but David knew the answer. Es-Soh-En did know. The Knight of Es-Soh-En fell before the Hobber's great paws.

"Forgive me, Es-Soh-En. Let me return. Let me return a hundred times if that is what You require of me." The Adoni leaned over, and licked David on the forehead.

"All was forgiven long ago." As David stood, Kal and Singer embraced him. Tra clasped his hand, and Reva kissed him on the cheek. Pentra embraced him. Kya took him into her arms, and clung to him as if her heart would break.

"I will wait for your return," she promised. Even the dolphins in the water behind them chattered their good-byes.

"The others wish you well. They would have come, but there are preparations to be made. Suffice it to say, our separation this time will not be long."

Es-Soh-En breathed on David, and his attire transformed to the battle garb of the Knight of Es-Soh-En. His sheath hung empty at his side.

"I will go and get Gennerroth," David offered.

"There is no need, my son. Another sword has been provided for you." The Great Hobber breathed once more, and this time the golden mist surrounded him. The clear skies, the fresh waters, soft grass, and good friends were blocked from his view. Somewhere deep in his mind, he thought he heard the cry of the Great Eagle as if coming from some other world, some other life. It sounded three times, and then darkness came over him.

CHAPTER TWENTY-SEVEN

REUNIONS AND TRAVELING COMPANIONS

David opened his eyes as if coming out of a long sleep. He couldn't remember where he had been, how he got here, or even where *here* was. He saw murals adorning the walls around his bed, but the bed was far from comfortable. The murals on the wall were pictures of him and of his sister. He thought they reminded him of the Chamber of Ages in the undersea of Janadis, but his last memories were of the palace in Dula.

Something fell hard on his chest, and he looked up to see Tanya clinging to him as if her grip was needed to save his life. She was also crying. That was something he hadn't seen her do for some time. However, the weeping did not seem to be the kind of weeping he had seen her do in pain or sorrow. She was laughing while she cried. Co-lin, Pentra, Agron, Handar, Gort, Ren, and Han were all around him. At the foot of his hard bed he saw Wil Den and Fin Den. Rolling his head up to see above him, he saw Laton of the Water People.

"Well, it seems like everyone is here," he finally announced.

"Welcome back!" Agron declared, and took him firmly by the hand, and helped him to a sitting position.

"*Back*? Where have I been?" David mumbled, now sure he was in Janadis, but still not remembering what brought him here.

"You're back from the dead!" Co-lin almost shouted. He was bubbling with excitement. David could never remember seeing the healer so out of control, so exuberant before. He had always recalled seeing Co-lin so much more reserved.

"*Dead*?!" David was fully awake now. He sat all the way up, swung his legs over the side, and realized he was lying on a table instead of a bed. He had to swing to the right side of the table because Tanya wouldn't release her hold on him, and this was the only way to move without dragging her across the table top.

"You were killed in ambush in the palace," Ren announced. Suddenly David remembered seeing Tanya sliding across the floor, yelling for him to get down. Everything was hazy after that. He could remember something about clouds, bright lights, dolphins – he loved dolphins. He heard Ghandrah laughing in his mind. And for some reason he thought of Kya. He hadn't thought much about her since they had returned to Dula.

"The scar is gone," Co-lin noticed. David brought his hand to his cheek, and felt the section of skin that had once been scarred. It was now smooth like the rest of the face.

"There's no need for the scar," Tanya declared. She finally stopped clinging to him, looked in his eyes, wiped her tears, and then hugged him that much harder.

"Will someone please tell me what's going on here?" David pleaded. Everyone started to talk at once, and finally the Steward of the Throne held up his hands for silence. "One at a time."

There came the sudden voice in his mind of Deenara. "Welcome back herd-brother."

"So I was dead?" he asked in his mind.

"Very." the unicorn replied. "Since your death, Tanya has become one of us. She, too, now bears the title of *Friend of the Unicorn*."

"You've seen unicorn?" David asked of Tanya.

"Yes!" she said through laughter and weeping. "And I know *the Secret of the Unicorns.*" The conversation between David, Tanya and Deenara had been a silent one as all the information passed back and forth through their minds. Everyone still waited for David to speak aloud. Finally a furry creature scrambled up on the table next to the Steward of the Throne of Dula.

"Since I am used to reporting many things, no matter how emotional they might be, perhaps I can put all of this into order." Hentery took off his hat of office, bowed before David, and waited for his permission to begin.

It took almost two hours with many questions, pauses, and repetitions to complete the story. Everyone had taken turns adding what they felt were the most important bits of detail to the story. For the most part, Hentery carried the tale, but everyone added their versions to it.

"While Co-lin, Gort, and I were talking in the records chamber," Tanya was adding.

"The records chamber? You've been in the records chamber here, too?" David observed.

"Where else? But while we were there, I heard the voice of Glidon. He cried out three times, just like He told me He would. There's no way I could have heard that cry in the city. He wasn't here, and the water would have blocked out His cry, but I still heard it. I ran to the chamber where your body was, put the chain over your head and about your neck, and you started breathing once more." She sat on the table next to him, holding tight to his arm, touching him from time to time to make sure he was real.

"I told Lady Tanya that I could not believe in the return of the Adoni unless someone came back from the dead. I had just said those words, and she jumped up, ran into the chamber with Gort and I following her. If I hadn't seen it with my own eyes, I would never have believed it. I *did* see it with my own eyes, and I'm still having a hard time believing it!" Co-lin exclaimed.

"The return of the Adoni!" Pentra declared. "In our life time! Praise the Adoni!!" he shouted. Everyone joined in with the cheer. Far in the back of his mind, David remembered hearing the cries of Glidon, but they were as an echo from some other world. He rose to his feet, and began to lead the procession out of the chamber. As he moved, the jewel on the chain bounced hard against his chest. He reached up to remove the chain, and Tanya's hands shot out to stop him.

"DON'T!" she cried out. Everyone stopped to see what was happening. She caught her emotions, and continued in a calmer voice, but the tone still told everyone how terrified she was. "Glidon told us that this power could only be used once, and only at the proper time. What if you take it off and you die once more? I couldn't bear to lose you again."

"If the Adoni have sent me back, then They will keep me." He started to undo the chain one more time.

"But what if you die?" Agron asked.

"Then I die," David declared. He suddenly realized that death held no fear for him. Even deep within, where he did not dare to lie to himself, he knew he was not afraid of death. His purpose was to serve the Adoni, either by his life or his death. That was all that was important to him. He pulled the chain from over his head while everyone held their breaths. He held the chain up so that the stone dangled in front of him. "I know this stone."

"It looks familiar to me, too," Tanya admitted, daring to breathe once more.

"It should. This is the hilt jewel of Logos. It was embedded in the throne on our first visit to Janadis. It was given to Teacher by the people of Janadis on our second visit."

"And it went with Him into the Greater Kingdom," Tanya recalled.

"And Glidon brought it back to you in the Forest of Venra," Pentra added.

"Do any doubt it now?" Co-lin challenged. "It is the time for the return of the Adoni." All agreed with the healer.

"This is probably part of that passage you read," Gort suggested to Tanya.

"*Passage?*" David asked.

"There was a passage I was reading just before I heard the cry of Glidon. It went…" and here Tanya had to think for a minute to get the right words. "*When the severed jewel is joined once more/And one returns beyond death's door/Dula shall stand for one more day/Then Cronis shall win and fade away.*"

"This is the severed jewel," David observed.

"And you are the one who has come back from beyond death's door," Co-lin added.

"If only we had Logos to join the stone with," David noted.

"We do!" Tanya beamed. "I was told to bring it with us when we left Dula. It's in my chambers. I'll get it." Suddenly both David and Tanya felt the mind of Deenara in their thoughts.

"No. They will be joined, but not at this time. Both pieces have been given to us, but we need to wait until the proper time to join them." It was strange to feel Deenara and his sister in his mind. Of course, it was probably just as strange for Tanya.

"So what does the rest of the passage mean?" Gort asked. "I just can't see Cronis winning. That part doesn't make any sense. Everything I've read and heard about the return of the Adoni talks about Cronis being broken and driven out."

"If he is driven out, then he must be in power somewhere," Pentra suggested.

"These bits of information rarely make sense until everything is over. It's the kind of information designed to be understood in hindsight. Something we look back on and say, *Yes, this was part of the Plan. The Adoni knew this was going to happen this way.* I believe we will simply have to do what we are told, and trust the Adoni for the results," David suggested. "Now, is there any food around here? I'm famished."

There was a vast banquet. Everyone came forth with their food, drinks, tableware, and deserts they had prepared for private dinners, but now shared with the entire population. The entire gathering wanted to see David for themselves. There were songs of praise, and prayers of thanksgiving. Dancing had a habit of breaking out throughout the city, most of the time before the music even began. It was not uncommon for someone to start singing, and others get up and dance to the song; or people would begin to dance, and others would sing a song that supported the dance. Minstrels took up their instruments and performed, moving throughout the crowd in order to play for all the people. Sometimes a single musician would be playing in one area while a full orchestra would be playing in another. Entertainers juggled, did magic tricks, and performed for groups who had congregated throughout the city square. It was hard to tell how much time had passed during the celebration because the sunlight from above never reached the undersea city. The regular inhabitants had adjusted to life on the ocean floor, and would increase or decrease the lighting in the city to create night and day; but the visitors had left the lights on all the time they had been there. Even though there was no real way of telling time here, the celebrators slowly nodded off, broke up into smaller groups, laid down and slept. All except David and Tanya. They walked the halls of the palace alone, looking at the murals, recalling their adventures, and sharing their hopes and dreams.

"I can't help but get the feeling that this is where it all comes together. Everything we ever did, every battle, victory, lesson, and visit was all preparation for this one," Tanya observed. David smiled. "It's good to see you smile," she replied.

"It's good to smile – to be able to smile," he replied.

"What is that supposed to mean?" she challenged.

"You remember the story in our world? The man who came back from the grave after he had already been buried for four days?" David asked. Tanya nodded. "According to legends, once he came back from the dead, he never smiled again. Those who tell the tale point out that Jesus wept at his grave. They suggest Jesus wept, not because He missed Lazarus, but because He was going to call Lazarus back to this life. The legends grew up because people believed he could never be happy in this world after seeing paradise. He always missed Heaven, and so he never smiled."

"You've smiled several times since you've been back," Tanya pointed out.

"Yes, and I'm glad that I can still smile."

"Do you remember anything about it?" Tanya asked.

"No. It's all very vague. I recall something about clouds surrounding me, a light leading me higher into the sky. I even think I remember something about dolphins."

Tanya told David about what she saw when Es-Soh-En spoke to her in her mind. David somehow knew it was true, but he couldn't actually remember the scene. They found themselves in front of one of the larger murals. This one depicted Es-Soh-En and the Children of Earth.

"Do you remember that visit?" Tanya asked, pointing to it. Suddenly, the portion of the mural displaying the Great Hobber transformed into the actual creature. Es-Soh-En separated Himself from the wall, took on a three-dimensional shape, leaped to the floor between them, and greeted them.

"Things must be serious for you to take such an active part in the affairs of the Lands of the Adoni," Tanya observed.

"These are serious times. Even now Cronis gathers his forces. He will use the armies of Magar, Bromor, and Orpha to move against Dula. You are to leave tomorrow for the Bay of Magar. All military forces are gone, most civilian forces have fled. Retrace your route through the Dulan Alps back to Dula. It is the most direct course. Your new task from this point on is a single task: rescue the city, hold the city. After you have driven off the armies of man, Cronis will bring forth his forces from the Veil of Darkness. There is no place to run. Dula will be the last outpost. Hold the throne for as long as you can; surrender is not an option with the Dark One."

"Is that when Cronis will win?" Tanya asked. Es-Soh-En gave her a look that was both stern, and filled with compassion and sorrow.

"Yes, Child of Earth. He has amassed every ally he has. This is as strong as he can make his army. This will be the day when he seeks victory at all costs. Do not despair. Even as it was in the night you battled the shadow creature in the Valley of Seven Forests, victory can come from defeat."

The Great Hobber blessed them both, then leaped back into the mural, and was soon nothing more that a two-dimensional collection of jewels and precious metals.

***

It was almost noon when the last of the refugees exited the tunnel that led from Janadis to the Isle of Morning. Although it had been a late evening the night before, everyone was up early the next morning. When David and Tanya announced that they were to return to Dula, all the people moved in an organized fashion to gather weapons, supplies, and possessions; and transport them through the tunnel to the isle. When they came on board the ships, they discovered that all the supplies had been replenished while they were in Janadis. As the assembly gathered on the shore of the Great Sea for David to deliver the blessing of the Adoni on their journey, two spots appeared in the eastern sky. At first no one took much notice of them, since they seemed little more than birds. After another few minutes, it became obvious to all that these were too big for birds. Han ordered the bows strung and archers at the ready. David ordered them to hold off until they could see what they were dealing with.

"Those wing spans are too large for birds," Han declared.

"If it were only one, I would believe it might be Glidon, the Great Eagle," Tanya suggested.

"But since when are there two Great Eagles? What else can it be other than an attack of bat things?" Han suggested.

"If they came from the west, I'd agree, but these come from the east. I think we should wait a while longer. I do not feel threatened by what I've seen so far. Hold off a little longer," David recommended.

The figures grew in the sky. Someone further down the beach called out and the word was passed up to David and Tanya, "They look like horses – winged horses."

"Gaylord and Yeesha?" Tanya asked of David.

"That would be my first guess." He shaded his eyes to see better. "But they are the wrong color."

Tanya could now see that one was a pure white, the white of a dove. The other was golden – the same polished gold color of Glidon. Once the Children of Earth had reference points, they could tell how fast the horses were flying. The wings of the horses were easily six feet on either side. They were flexing and pushing against the air in a graceful rhythm. Several times they glided on the air currents. When they were only a little ways off shore, they tilted their wings to cut their speed, dropped from the sky, and back-winged to land just in front of David and Tanya. Everyone crowded around to see the marvel.

"Greeting from the Greater Kingdom," announced the golden steed. "I am Wind Song, son of Gaylord and Yeesha. This is Morning Star," here Wind Song motioned with his head towards the white mare. "She is my sister. We have been sent from the Greater Kingdom by the Adoni to carry you into battle, and to serve you as our parents did." Both horses bowed before the Knights of Es-Soh-En.

"You're the twins who died at birth?" Tanya recalled. She came forward, and stroked the neck of Morning Star. The white fur was as soft as silk. Her long white mane was more glorious than that of a unicorn.

"Your father and mother spoke of their love for you," David added.

"Yes, we have spent many years in the Greater Kingdom with them. Where they had served you before, now we have been given that honor. The Adoni have set aside other tasks for our parents."

"We are honored," David accepted. He stepped forward, and rubbed the neck of Wind Song. The muscles were hard and strong under the soft golden fur. Wind Song's mane and tail were blonde, but the rest of his fur was like a polished gold. David could almost see himself in it. He could see the sunlight reflected off the stallion's firm body.

"We thank you for your service, but are we to leave our army behind?" David asked.

"No, we are to travel with your army. We will journey with you, and carry you into battle." David gripped the mane of Wind Song, pulled himself onto the horse, and hooked his legs under the great wings. Tanya thought about doing the same, but hesitated.

"Do not worry, Tanya. I am to be your horse forever. You cannot harm me. We have gone beyond the realm of pain long ago. Such is the beauty of the Greater Kingdom."

Tanya took a handful of mane into her hand, half-leaped, and half-pulled herself onto Morning Star. Once she sat astride of the graceful mare, she was amazed at how natural it felt. "It's like I belong here," she noted.

"Because you do. We are joined. Just as you and the unicorn have been joined, so you and I have been joined. This will help us to understand each other, and to work better as a team in battle."

At the mention of the unicorns Tanya suddenly thought of her herd-brothers. She tried not to acknowledge it, but Wind Song and Morning Star were so much more beautiful, so much more graceful than the unicorn. She had thought there could be nothing else as majestic, as awe-inspiring as the horned steeds; even after she had been joined to them. Now they seemed pale by comparison. In her heart she grieved for the loss of such glory and beauty. Deenara was in her mind.

"Do not grieve my sister," Deenara spoke aloud for all to hear. "This is the way that things should be. This is what we have known since the beginning of time. We chose to remain untouched by the world. We retained our original condition. This is why we seemed so impressive to you. All you had to compare us to were shadows of what the Adoni had created, and these shadows were flawed by the rebellion of Ish and Issha. Everything in this world was tainted, tarnished by the Fall. We are the Untarnished. We chose to remain untainted, to keep our first state. It only follows that since the price of our creation was so much less than the price of your redemption, the result would also be so much less. Here you see what the Adoni have in store for you all. As we were above you these many years, so you will eventually be greater than us. It is not a reason for sorrow, but for rejoicing. This is what we have kept ourselves pure to attain for you all."

David pronounced the Blessing of the Adoni upon the army gathered before him. When he finished cheers and applause broke out along the shore. Songs of praise filled the air as David and Tanya, astride Wind Song and Morning Star led their forces onto the waiting ships where the Breath of the Adoni would carry them back to the Lands of the Adoni and the destiny that waited for them there.

CHAPTER TWENTY-EIGHT

THE DELIVERANCE OF DULA

As the returning army camped in the Forest of Venra, Tanya took David to the Grove of Three Oaks to meet Gantra, Bendora, and Wodin. David remembered Bendora from their visit long ago, and enjoyed the opportunity to renew the friendship. Gantra was glad for the chance to learn all that happened while Tanya's forces were in Janadis. Even though the Tree Druids were able to gather some information from the plant life in the sea, it was only a scrap or two. Rarely could they hear about Janadis because it was so deep in the water, and cut off to sea plants by the dome.

"I shall put this on the root," Gantra declared as soon as Tanya had finished relaying the details.

"*On the root?*" David asked.

"Oh, that's just a plant expression. We transfer so much information back and forth. We used to say put it on the *leaf*, but several plants complained since they had needles, thorns, or blades instead of leaves. We finally all agreed to call the process *putting it on the root* because everyone had a root."

Bendora cleared his trunk with a sound much like clearing the throat. "Okay, there are one or two who don't have roots, but we can't make everyone happy," Gantra responded.

"So what is happening back in Dula?" Tanya asked.

"Grave tidings," Wodin began. "Magar has moved its entire army to the Bromor Delta, met with Orpha and Bromor's forces, and even now have surrounded Dula. All the population has moved supplies, livestock, and people behind the city walls, but they have been under siege for a week now."

"How long until we get back to Dula?" David asked Tanya.

"It took us two weeks coming this way last time. I don't see how we can cut it down much more than that."

"Can the city hold for that long?" David asked of Wodin.

"It would tax their supplies, but the walls are good. Magar and its allies have been trying to break through, but the Adoni are with Dula. The Tree Druids can move their forces among them, and try to hinder their efforts. That should make sure they can't get through for a while."

"Good!" David declared. "Put this *on the root* as well. Instruct the Tree Druids to move in and around the camp. At night, remove as many supplies and weapons as they can. Travel only at night. If they can, have some of the Tree Druids transfer the food and weapons into the city so that Dula can hold out longer. Do we still have talking animals?"

"Talking animals?" Gantra retorted. "There are a few species, but the larger ones have passed into the Kingdom, or forgotten the power of speech. A few mice, birds and other small ones."

"We may need to send Hentery and Beech to the city via birds to help them prepare a defense," David suggested.

"Wait a minute!" Tanya exclaimed. "Why can't one of us fly to the city? We have winged horses. On Morning Star I could make it in one or two days."

The Children of Earth gathered what additional information the Tree Druids had to help them. The Tree Druids knew all the locations of the attacking armies. They knew where supplies were, how many horses, how much food, and where the command staff was staying. Gantra even promised to have the plants inside the camps, and inside the commanders' tents keep track of the battle plans and transfer them ahead.

"I'll have Airron meet you at the city of Dula. She can interpret the messages from the plants," Bendora promised. The Knights of Es-Soh-En thanked the Tree Druids for their support, and rejoined the army. David announced that Tanya would be flying ahead, and the main force would move as quickly as they could to rescue the city.

It was early morning when Tanya and Morning Star sighted the city. The crops and fields had been burned and scraped away. The ground had been slowly stacked against the wall trying to form a ramp that would let Magar and its allies breech the city's defenses. It had been a slow process, and the ramp only reached a fourth of the way up the wall. Great pits dotted the landscape where the dirt had been dug up for the ramp. What she could see of the wall showed signs of wear from catapults slamming boulders against it. There were a few cracks, sections showed chips knocked out of the blocks, Areas where the top of the wall had been hit during the catapult attacks showed the greatest damage, but for the most part the city was secure.

She had flown over the enemy forces in the night in order to avoid detection. The campfires were like fireflies below them in the darkness, but it looked like thousands of fireflies. Now in the morning light, lookouts would spot her and Morning Star. She asked Morning Star to put on an extra burst of energy to get them over the city walls before archers could be summoned.

Those manning the city walls were nearly scared out of their wits when they looked out over the battlefield and saw something so large flying with such speed from the direction of the enemy camp. One or two shafts were fired before Tanya was close enough for the watchmen to recognize the flying creature as a winged horse and not some shadow creature. Morning Star had been able to bank or dive out the path of the arrows. A few moments later they were landing in the marketplace inside the city walls.

"Lady Tanya!" the leaders exclaimed as they came out to investigate the miracle. The Child of Earth dismounted, and introduced Morning Star to the group. The officer of the day went with Tanya and Morning Star through the streets of the city to the castle. Here the moat which once flowed around the structure was dry.

"They've dammed up the river. I think they were trying to cut off our water supply." Jekson reported.

"How is the city's water supply?" Tanya asked as they crossed the drawbridge. Inside the walls was the courtyard. Where once it had served as an additional meeting and market place for the palace staff, it now was a warehouse for food and supplies.

"We have seven wells throughout the city. There are another two inside the castle itself. They haven't been able to sabotage these."

As the threesome came into the palace, guards snapped at attention, yet tried to see the wonder of the winged horse as they strode past. When they came to the throne room, the commanders were already up and making plans. Tanya noted that the throne had been blocked off so none would sit on it.

"My lady!" several of the officers exclaimed when she came through the door. There were then gasps or exclamations of surprise and wonder when Morning Star entered one or two steps behind.

The Stewardess brought the group to order, and began relaying what information she had. She told of their journey to Janadis, the return of Sir David, the size of the forces coming to their aid, and what she had seen flying over the enemy camp. There was a sudden disturbance in the hall, and Tanya went out to see what was causing it.

There was a Tree Druid trying to explain to the guards that she had been summoned by Lady Tanya.

"It's alright!" Tanya called out to the guards blocking the Tree Druid's path. "I take it that you are Airron?"

"Yes," replied the tree druid. "I received word on the root that I was supposed to meet you here." Tanya ushered their new ally into the throne room, and explained to the others how the Tree Druids could speak with the plants and serve as information-gathering sources for the city. Once Tanya had brought the others up to speed on the events outside the city, the officers made their reports to bring Tanya current on the state of Dula.

***

A week-and-a-half later, David stood at the head of his army astride Wind Song as the first rays of morning light warmed his back. He had sat there in the false dawn watching Magar and its forces scramble to find their weapons and armor. There had been a rash of thefts lately, and anyone who left anything unattended would find it missing come the morning. David had used his contact with the unicorns to keep in communication with Tanya. She had relayed his request to the Tree Druids through Airron so that during the night, the Tree Druids moved, stole or misplaced as many items in the Magarian camps as they could. Since Magar and the other kingdoms had forsaken the way of the Adoni, they had not had any communication with Tree Druids for centuries. They were all but a forgotten legend to most. For this reason, no one took notice of trees in the compound. Ten minutes ago, David had sounded the call to arms. His troops were already spread out in formation behind him. The trumpet sound had been more to warn the forces of Magar, and to send them into disarray when they found any army ready for battle and their own weapons now missing.

As the sun created the true dawn, David prepared to give the signal. His forces would charge out of the sunrise. The sleeping camps would be disjointed. With the sun behind David's back, the Magarians would have to fight looking into the sun. Since David held the higher ground, his attack would have greater momentum charging down the hill, while the enemy had to use the greater effort to charge up the slope.

David had sent word to Tanya the night before. She had her forces ready inside the city gates. When David drove Magar to the west, the enemy would find themselves blocked by the city walls. Tanya's forces could then attack from the above, or meet the enemy on the battlefield. Now David could tell that the sun was in the right position behind him. He raised Logos high over his head. In the presence of the entire army, he snapped the link holding the hilt jewel about his neck, and slammed the legendary stone into the socket where it belonged.

The sudden thunderclap would have knocked David off of Wind Song had he not been prepared. A bolt of lightning erupted from the blade into the air, lighting the early morning landscape brighter than the noon-day sun. Several bolts of lightning spat out in the direction of the Magarian camp and set tents and supplies on fire. David had been warned by the unicorn as to what to expect when the Sword and Jewel were reunited. David had cautioned his troops to look away when the event took place. Several of the horses jolted at the sound, but were not blinded by the flash since their riders had turned them around so the flash was behind them. David's forces held fast, while Magar and its allies broke and ran before them. With the Sword and

Jewel joined once more, the Knight of Es-Soh-En dropped the blade down to signal the attack.

As David's men charged down the hill into the enemies' camps, over a third of the enemy forces tried to flee. Hundreds were crushed by their own comrades as man and horse became tangled in the wave of deserters. The other two-thirds of the armies took what weapons they had protected through the nights and charged. Still others found clubs or other make-shift weapons with which to defend themselves.

David was at the front of the battle. His men had urged him to stay behind and direct his forces from behind the lines, but he had refused to listen. "I am a leader, not a commander. Therefore, I lead."

The minotaur and centaur grunted their approval. It was the way of their race, and they were glad David had chosen to honor their traditions of the commander being the first into battle. It would inspire all of their warriors to give as much as the Knight of Es-Soh-En.

Although David was the first into the battle, Pentra and Agron were immediately behind him. The Tree Druids would stand watch on the hills above the battlefield. Several unicorn stayed with them to keep the attacking army informed of any sudden movements, shifting of forces, or attacks from unseen positions. A unicorn had been positioned in each section of troops so David could communicate with them during the battle, or they could hear warnings from the unicorns on the hill. The Tree Druids, kept constant contact with the plant life to make sure there weren't other surprises waiting for David's forces.

As David came to the first warrior who had dared to stand before him instead of running, the Knight of Es-Soh-En brought Logos down with all the force of his body behind it, and the full momentum of his charge. Inches away from contact with the enemy sword, sparks exploded, shattering the Magarian blade. Logos continued the blow, erupting more lightning that tore at the Magarian's armor, driving its wearer to the ground, dead before the enchanted blade could make contact. The power of the attack caught David off-guard for a second. Three more Magarian's – these belonged to the Black Heart sect according to their markings – sprang to attack from their hiding place; but David recovered, and lashed out without missing more than half-a-beat. Again lightning spewed from Logos, charring the enemy where they stood. The unicorn blade never made contact directly with any weapon or enemy soldier. Nothing touched or tainted the immortal sword. All those coming at Sir David died before contact could be made.

The battle continued. Most of the delay was climbing over the dead bodies of the Magarian, Bromor, and Orpha troops. When Logos sprayed lightning bolts before them, they lashed out in blind panic, striking anything around them with a weapon. In most cases they cut down their own allies.

The unicorns warned David of a wedge trying to move forward and cut him off from his troops. He repositioned his soldiers, and the wedge found centaur arrows cutting their forces to ribbons before they could move an additional ten feet. When the wedge broke ranks, the minotaurs moved in to finish them off.

Four hours after the initial attack, the enemy forces were pressed between the city walls, and David's army. Tanya's forces attacked from the ramparts. After a brief show of force, the Magarian troops and allies broke, and tried to flee around the city and to the west. Tanya's cavalry erupted from the western gates, and pursued them until the deserters were defeated or driven off. Those who had survived fled all the way to the Veil of Darkness.

The battle had lasted a little over five hours. Not that Magar or its allies had put up that much of a fight, but there were that many of the enemy between them and the city. Once it was clear that there was no opposition left, David contacted Deenara who was in communication with all the unicorn.

"How many lost?" he asked.

"None," Deenara replied.

"None?!" David echoed. "No one was killed from among the entire army?"

"Not a single life was lost from among our forces. There were some wounds, but nothing major. The enemy had no stomach to fight. They were broken before you even attacked."

"*None lost*," David muttered.

"What was that?" Pentra asked. He sat astride his horse next to the Knight of Es-Soh-En.

"Deenara says that none of our people were killed in the battle. All we suffered were some injuries, but nothing major."

"Praise be to the Adoni!" Pentra shouted and thrust his sword in the air. The troops around him echoed the cry, and it spread across the battlefield. Soon it was a chant from thousands of throats. Those inside the city took up the cry.

There came the sound of metal grinding on metal, screaming as if in pain as the main gates of the city were opened. The doors had been knocked off balance during the early days of the war. Those inside the city thronged behind Tanya as she and Morning Star rode out to meet her brother and Wind Song. The chanting had turned to singing, and from there into a celebration.

In the evening hours, after a great feast, David and Tanya met with the leaders, captains and section commanders. They assigned everyone a task. The first order of business was to clear away the ramp; the tons of dirt were used to fill in mass graves to bury the dead. The enemies had unknowingly dug their own graves. David would not let the land be further polluted by leaving unburied bodies around. While one group sought out all the bodies and brought them to the pits where the dirt had been removed, the other half worked to dig away the ramp, and carry it back to the pits where the bodies of the dead now waited to be buried.

The next task was to repair any damage to the walls. Here David took a lesson from the Words of the Adoni in their world, and ordered that each family and neighbor living along the wall were to repair the section closest to their own home.

"It is a good idea," Ren noted as he moved fresh-hewn blocks into position. David had ordered the waterways where the river had flowed into and out of the city bricked up. If Magar had been cunning enough, they would have followed up on damming the river with an invasion using the river's entrance and exit points in the city as a breech in the wall. "The wall will be more secure now than before. If you're working to keep a neighbor safe, you grow tired and do not make a full effort. If you are building the wall to protect you and your family, you always put in that extra effort."

As the wall was being repaired, the rest of the city set out to gather all the weapons left on the battlefield. Others collected food and supplies from the Magarian campsites or from other sources outside of the city. David and Tanya worked side-by-side with the people. Those who were commanders or nobility joined in the tasks with those who had tilled the soil, swept the floors or baked the bread. True to Tanya's dream, the women now were seen as warriors, as much as the men. They had earned the respect of those who had once scoffed at such an idea.

Within five days, the city was as great as it had ever been, and the storerooms were filled to capacity. That night, the Children of Earth ordered a celebration to give thanks to the Adoni for their deliverance.

CHAPTER TWENTY-NINE

THE DARK LORD AT THE GATES

The celebration had been going for three hours, when Dayton made his way to the head table where David, Tanya, Agron, Pentra, and the leaders of the various races sat to eat. With Dayton were his wife and three children: one son, and two daughters. He carried a rather bulky package that he sat before the Children of Earth.

"We wanted to thank you for all that you did for our city, and our family. This is a gift that is precious to us, and which we have used to make this gift for you. I'm sorry we did not have the ability to make more than one, but when you open it, you will see why." Dayton then stepped back, and amid the applause, David slid the package over to Tanya to open. She snapped the ribbons, peeled back the wrapping, and the room was suddenly flooded with a brilliant blue light. Gasps and exclamations erupted from around the room as Tanya pulled out a silver shield. Etched on the steel oval was the image of Glidon, the Great Eagle. Embedded in the chest of the Eagle was the Eye of Suma.

Tanya hefted the work of art on her arm, and the blue glow lit up the faces of those in front of her.

"We are honored," David began. "This is a gift which was given to you and your family by Teacher. It could not be stolen or taken by force. It must mean a great deal to you."

"We will try to be worthy of your faith in us," Tanya added. David rose, and clasped Dayton's hand, and hugged Dayton's wife and each of the children. Tanya passed the shield on to David, and likewise thanked the family for the magnificent gift. They had chairs brought to the head table for Dayton and his family, and spoke for long hours about the history of the jewel, the background of Dayton's family, and the workmanship that went into the shield. People lined up and waited for hours to pass by and get a closer look at the eagle-shield.

David was roused from his sleep before the first rays of light had cleared the Dulan Alps. The pounding was urgent, and he pulled his tunic and pants on as he stumbled toward the door. He often wished that the Adoni would give him the ability to change clothes instantly like his sister. It would have made mornings like this much easier.

"My lord!" came the worried voice of the guard as the door opened. "There's trouble." David snatched his clothing, and dressed as they headed down the hall toward the throne room.

"Where is Lady Tanya?" he asked, pulling on his boots and hopping down the hall at the same time.

"She has been summoned. As they rounded they corner where the hallways met, Tanya almost ran into David. The pair then put on more speed to get to their destination.

"Our patrols were out last night, guarding the area west of the city. This morning, Meep was seen staggering toward the gate. He says that his entire squad was wiped out in the night. He alone survived. He was ordered by his commander to ride back with the warning. He rode until his horse dropped dead under him, and then ran until he could run no more."

The Children of Earth burst into the throne room. Co-lin was already administering medication to the soldier. He was suffering from dehydration and extreme exhaustion. Once David was sure the messenger was being tended, he turned and ran toward the stairs that led to the castle wall. Tanya and several advisors were right behind him. As he reached David's Perch, he nearly cried out from the sight.

"Has the Veil of Darkness grown?" Pentra asked, coming to his side. The entire sky before them was black in the early morning light. David looked at the edges where the darkness met the sky. He scanned the ground where the blackness grew closer and covered the grass. He did not need Deenara to tell him.

"No, the Veil of Darkness has not grown, but Cronis has brought all his forces to us."

"All that is the army of Cronis?" Agron gasped. Tanya looked with her enhanced vision and could see that the black cloud moving towards Dula was comprised of shadows creatures flying so close and so thick that they blotted out the sun. The ground forces swarmed over the rocks and ground like an evil spreading stain, keeping in the shadow of the air creatures.

David called out for all the leaders to meet with him in the courtyard, and shouted for all the supplies, weapons and civilians to be moved inside. Within minutes the city was mobilized. Han, Ren, and Laton were the first leaders to meet. Fin Den and Wil Den were sending messages to their people to move everything underground, and seal off the windows and doors. David ordered the gnome warriors to return to their village to protect their civilians, but the gnome leaders protested.

"If the Dark Lord gets past us, your women and children will be defenseless," David urged.

"If the Dark Lord gets past us, then it will be too late for all the Lands of the Adoni," Wil Den declared.

"This will be the final battle, Sir David," Fin Den noted. "If you were to survive this day against the attacks of the Dark One, and we were somewhere else, how do you think it would look in the legends? Let us stand this day with you." The Knight of Es-Soh-En nodded, and began to pass out instructions.

"Han, we can expect an attack from the air as the Dark Lord's first move. We need all the archers on all the walls. We need another wave of archers hidden so they are protected. We have fifty archers among the humans; I need you to help deploy your best where they can do the most damage." Han nodded, never thinking to ask about the chances for survival of his warriors. Within moments, the centaurs were in all the key positions. Those who did not have the war bow strung stood along side those who did in order to keep the supply of arrows coming, and to protect the centaurs with the bows.

David began to assess the strengths of each of the races available to him. The minotaurs were the fiercest in hand-to-hand combat. They would be one of the last lines of defense inside the buildings. The Water People would be the most difficult to pass since it was almost impossible to hurt them. Their weakness laid in their life stones. David had to work out some place for them to fight where their strengths were enhanced, and their weaknesses reduced. He chose to place them in the pools and river banks inside the city, and just outside the castle. In the river banks, their life stones would be hard to distinguish from other smooth stones in the waters.

The gnomes were placed in all the small and tight places to fight. Having the shorter bodies, they were able to maneuver better than most in such areas. The tree druids could not move quickly. They were poor fighters, and so David placed them in secure positions where they could oversee the battle. Deenara was already placing his unicorn in key positions. He had sworn that there would always be a ring of unicorn around the Knights of Es-Soh-En.

"We cannot hide." Tanya insisted. "We are the Knights of Es-Soh-En. We must be in the battle."

"You are also the Steward and Stewardess of the Throne of Dula. You must be protected at all costs," Deenara countered.

"Then keep by our sides, but do not keep us from battle. We fight for Es-Soh-En. We fight for the Adoni!" David passed the eagle shield to Tanya to use with Sy-lar. Wind Song and Morning Star stood in reserves to attack those shadow creatures that would eventually break through the hail of arrows. Heart Company took up positions inside and outside the castle, making sure they took full advantage of the layout of the castle to do the most damage.

Barely ten minutes after placing all the troops, and securing the civilians and supplies, there came the roaring sound of thousands of leather wings beating the air. They flew high and close with their heads down. Their first purpose was to provide a cloud cover from the sunlight for those on the ground. Han's archers were instantly alert. The great war bows of the centaurs were fitted with arrows, drawn, aimed, and released. Hundreds of shafts tore through the screen. Just as many shadow creatures wailed, screamed, thrashed at arrows protruding from vital organs, and dropped from the sky. Before the first screams were even echoing in the castle, the second wave of shafts was hurtling towards their targets.

The centaurs wrecked havoc with the shadow creatures. Because they had been flying so high to blot out the sun, the man-horses had enough time to sight their targets, and drive the projectiles home. After several waves of attack, the shadow creatures broke their formation, and abandoned the ground troops to deal with the full light of day. Within moments the bat things were diving into the courtyard, slashing and attacking the centaurs. Those protecting the archers were in fierce combat with wings, talons, and fangs. Wind Song and Morning Star were attacking those who had taken out archers in different areas, giving the ground forces time to replace their fallen comrades.

After half-an-hour the attention was divided between the assaults from the air, and the screams of battle outside the gates. Heart Company manned the walls, and began to fire on the ground forces just before they made contact with the Water People. Hundreds of Cronis' subjects died in the first few moments of the attack. Row after row of demon things fell to the ground, their comrades crawling over their bodies to get at the enemy.

When the ground forces were close enough, Laton led the charge, springing to life out of the river beds. His entire race joined the assault, crushing internal organs, exploding heads with their unique method of battle. The terror they created in the hearts of Cronis' forces caused a major section to stop in their tracks. As more of their fellows screamed and died in horror, the ground forces actually fell back.

Instantly Cronis turned those in the back of the lines against those in the front lines. Anyone who had tried to turn and flee, or those who did not move forward, was attacked by their own allies. Soon it became a question of terror from ahead or death from behind.

In the midst of all the carnage and battle, David and Tanya moved from point to point. When centaurs needed protection from bat creatures, Tanya and David were there lending assistance. When shadow creatures fell wounded into the courtyard, the Knights of Es-Soh-En and others would finish them off so they couldn't pose any additional threat. Several times, David and Tanya found the bat creatures had faked injury to drop into the court, and when the Knights of Es-Soh-En approached, it turned into a battle for their lives.

Tanya found that the eagle shield with the Eye of Suma embedded in it made an excellent offensive weapon as well as defensive. Most of the creatures who served Cronis could not stand light, and when the Eye of Suma blinded them with its light, they fell to the ground in pain, or turned and ran.

The battle had been going for hours. David noted that the sun was beginning to drop behind the horizon. He ordered torches brought to flood the walls and courtyard with light. He doubled the guards at all the dangerous points. Although they had held their own during the daylight, with the coming night, exhaustion, and darkness began to play against them.

Within an hour of sunset, David ordered the troops off the walls, and into the castle, abandoning the walls and courtyard to Cronis. The Water Warriors pulled back inside the castle through water ways. Tanya and David worked with the other leaders trying to work out a schedule where some of the forces could sleep while the others carried the fight. After another few hours, the forces of Cronis stormed every door, every window, trying to break in. When these proved futile, there came the sounds of large rocks being dropped on the roofs. Han sent his archers to the upper levels, used the broken sections of the roof to fire their bows through, and tried to sight the enemy flying overhead. In most cases it was a dark shape moving against the stars in the sky. They would fire their shafts, and would hit some of the creatures, but not as many as they would have liked.

The civilians had begun to move around the insides of the buildings, bringing food and drink to the warriors, caring for those who were injured in the attacks, and keeping a fresh supply of arrows for the archers. They had quadrupled their supply of arrows from those left behind by Magar and its allies. The unicorn kept in constant contact with the Knights of Es-Soh-En, and Airron stayed with one or the other so the Tree Druids could report on what was happening outside.

"How are we doing?" David asked Han as he made the rounds about midnight. He could tell that the long hours had worn everyone down, even the centaurs.

"Our concern is that we are running low on arrows. We have probably ten thousand more left."

"How many have you fired today?" David asked. He had believed that an additional ten thousand arrows should be adequate to hold for several days.

"I don't have an exact number, but somewhere about two hundred thousand shafts have been spent this day."

"Make arrangements for the civilians to try and recover those shafts in the bodies we have in the courtyard. We will move out at day break and try to reclaim it and the walls."

It was a long night, and the morning gave David's forces what they needed to move out. The sunlight drove many of Cronis' forces back. The Dark One eventually slaughtered hundreds to force his army forward, but by then, David's forces held the courtyard and the walls. Many took up the grisly task of recovering arrows from the bodies, and trying to dispose of the dead before they filled the entire courtyard. Several points along the wall had been damaged during the night while Cronis held the outer perimeter. David had to send additional troops to hold those positions. He knew that if they retreated at sunset, there would be no wall or courtyard to retake the next morning. Cronis already recognized his mistake in leaving the defenses in place during the first night.

Again, in the middle of the night, shadow creatures flew overhead and dropped great rocks on the roofs, trying to break in from above.

"Where are they getting the rocks? There weren't that many rocks outside the city," Agron asked as Tanya made her rounds.

"I suspect that when the sun comes up tomorrow, the walls will be gone. My guess is they are breaking the walls apart and using the blocks from it to drop on the roofs." True to the Child of Earth's prediction, when the light of morning drove most of the forces back, those looking out of the courtyard, found it difficult to recognize it as the courtyard from the day before.

"Should we try to retake the area?" Ren asked.

"It would take a lot of our forces to drive them back; it would take even more to hold it. Even then, we could only hold it for one more day. We should work reinforcing what we have." David set up squads to move out into the courtyard area, and recover what arrows they could, and to gather rock and timbers left strewn by the Dark Lord's forces. As soon as they moved out of the main building, the shadow creatures began their attack. David had anticipated the lull in the battle being nothing more than a ruse; and his archers were already in position, driving the bat things from the skies. His forces were able to hold off Cronis' army long enough for David's troops to complete their task in the courtyard area. Even with cover from the higher points of the building, those in the square suffered numerous injuries and several losses.

When darkness fell, this time the attack was not only to the roof, but at several points on the palace walls. The soldiers inside the fortress poured flaming oil on those below with the battering rams. Archers fired through the broken roof at the shadow creatures. For all their efforts, the Knights of Es-Soh-En knew that it was a losing battle.

"Move the civilians to the center of the castle. Reinforce doors, walls and ceilings. We will layer the forces inside the castle. The Evil One will have to fight each step of the way to get to those we protect."

The rearrangement of the castle took most of the night; the attacks continued, but the boiling oil and random discharge of arrows gave occasional pauses in the bombardment. By the following morning Han came to David.

"We are just about out of shafts for the bows."

"Can we recover any more?" David asked.

"Not enough to make any difference. The time has come to sever the bow strings," the centaur declared. David knew exactly what Han was referring to. The war bows of the centaur were made of steel, and only the strongest could hope to draw them. In addition to being a bow, when the strings were cut, the bow straightened out and formed the double-edged, double-bladed swords that could do a great deal of damage in close quarter combat. Han wanted to cut the bow strings, use the swords, and attack Cronis' forces.

"I know your heart. It is full of honor. There is no greater calling than to die in combat serving another. But we must cool our hearts. It is not just us we must care for. There are women and children deeper in the castle who are counting on us to last as long as we can. We are their only defense. If the forces of the Dark One breech the inner walls, then it will be the time to sever the bow strings."

Han nodded to acknowledge the instructions. It would be hard for them to stand by and wait for battle; just as it had been hard for the minotaur to stand by and let the others carry the attack using the bows.

Half-an-hour before the dawn, there came the terrifying sound of mortar and stone cracking and then crumbling. The relentless pounding was taking its toll. Han and Ren moved their forces to the chamber inside the collapsing wall. The centaur severed the bow string, and began whirling the bows around them so rapidly that David could not even see the blades. As the army of Cronis poured through the breech in the wall, they were cut to ribbons by the spinning blades. Cronis was behind them, in the courtyard, shrieking orders, and driving them to their deaths. As some slipped past the centaur's blades; the minotaur moved in to attack. Within minutes, the entire chamber was a mass of bleeding and dying bodies on both sides. The Water People and gnomes guarded the passageways. Those who made it past the chamber, found the gnomes all but impossible to pass. The unicorn formed the final ring between the civilians and the forces of darkness.

As the sun began to climb back into its position in the sky, David studied the scene before him. He had to act fast or Dula would fall. Already Cronis was at the door of the castle.

The Knight of Es-Soh-En began to bound up the stairs to the upper chambers where Heart Company now stood guard over any attacks from the air. As he cleared the steps two at a time, Deenara was suddenly in his mind.

"You can't do that!" the unicorn called out.

The urgency of the unicorn's message caught Tanya's attention. "What's going on?"

"I know what I'm doing," David replied, trying to navigate the rubble on the stairs.

"What are you doing?!" Tanya came back even stronger.

"He's going to attack Cronis directly!" came Deenara's reply.

CHAPTER THIRTY

AND CRONIS SHALL WIN...

"That's suicide!" Tanya cried out in her mind. She was working her way toward the upper level to confront her brother. By the time she got there, David was already mounting Wind Song.

"Look," David insisted. "We can't stop all these creatures. For every one we kill three more take its place. The key to this war is Cronis. We have to take him out."

"And how do you propose to do that?" Tanya demanded.

"His attention is on the battle. If Wind Song can get me close enough, I can drop on him from above. With some luck, I can even take him out." Tanya was about to protest, but she knew it was their only option.

"Then give me the chance to give you the diversion you need. We need to push back with all our forces. If there's a full scale counter attack, then he will give that his full attention."

"You'll be cut down." David told her.

"No more than you. Like you said, it's our last chance." Turning to Heart Company she cried out, "I need volunteers!"

The entire company came forward, and Tanya had to choose a handful to stay behind and guard the roofs. "In all likelihood, we won't be coming back. You understand that, don't you?"

The entire company voiced their agreement. Handar, Pentra, and Agron stood at the forefront.

"It's what I've waited for," Handar declared. "My entire life has been in preparation for this one moment. I have no intention of selling my life cheap." As he spoke, Handar hefted his ax to emphasize his words.

"So say we all. Though we go to our deaths, we go for the Adoni. There can be no greater honor," Pentra added.

"Then let's do it. Wait for our diversion," Tanya told David as she led her forces down the stairs. When she came to the chamber where the battle still raged, she found Ren, wounded, but still fighting. Han had already fallen.

"We're going to make one great charge," Tanya told Ren. Even though he was in great pain from several major wounds, a smile broke out on his bull-face.

"To die in battle with you? The Adoni have granted my prayers." Tanya gave quick orders for the gnomes and the Water People to fill in behind them. She, Heart Company, Ren and the remaining minotaurs would drive the wedge and lead the attack. When the army reached the breech in the wall, the gnomes and the Water People were to hold the line while the rest went forward. If their action failed, then it would be up to Wil Den, Fin Den and Laton to take command, and hold the castle for as long as they could.

Once everyone was in position, the gnomes led the charge. The smaller bodies caught the demon creatures off-guard as the attacks came from the waist down. As the small warriors tore through the throng, screams erupted as they cut their enemies down. Tanya was at the point of the wedge, Ren and Handar directly behind her. Immediately behind them came Agron, Pentra and Gort. Heart Company then formed most of the wedge, and minotaurs fell in as the wedge passed through the chamber to add what strength they could to the attack. At the last moment, the gnomes parted on either side of the breech in the wall, revealing Tanya with the eagle shield at the head of the attack. The brilliant glow from the Eye of Suma caused most of the enemy to fall back in pain. Cronis now had to give his full attention to the charge and to force his troops back into battle.

The first few minutes of the charge pushed Tanya further than she had believed possible. Handar carved his way through the demons, taking extra care not to let any of them throw themselves on top of his ax-blade like before. Sy-lar slashed to the left and right as Tanya pressed forward. There came a motion from the right, and Handar went down. Instantly twenty demon creatures were on him. Though he swung and killed many of his attackers, it was too late for him. Tanya knew, as did everyone in the wedge, that if someone fell they were on their own. No one would offer more than passing aid because it would slow the momentum of the wedge. Everyone, even herself, was expendable. No one cried out for help as they were brought down, and others filled in the position the fallen had just held. The Knight of Es-Soh-En steeled herself for the task ahead. Pentra moved to the point behind her to protect her back. The wedge moved deeper into the sea of Cronis' forces.

The rising sun and the glow from the Eye of Suma gave Tanya an added advantage. She could see Cronis several yards ahead. His full attention was on her and her forces. She doubled her efforts. There came a burning pain as something slashed her left side. Her hip and leg were instantly wet. She did not need to look to know she had been wounded. She twisted to protect that side, swung with Sy-lar, and cut down two more creatures trying to follow up on the previous attack. Another press from the right charged. Ren threw himself on them, even as he died; his horns gored another creature and sent it to its death.

As Tanya continued to move and cut down those in front of her, she looked back and saw that only twenty or thirty of

Heart Company was still standing. The wedge had been all but destroyed. Instead of trying to cut a retreat back to the castle, the Knight of Es-Soh-En knew her life was forfeit. She prepared herself for her *Dance of Death*. She turned to face the demon god, fire in her eyes, determined that she would reach him even if it was her last breath. Cronis caught sight of her, and for one brief moment, the Dark Lord knew terror. He motioned for his personal guards to leave him and attack her. That was the moment David had been waiting for.

Wind Song knew what David was looking for. The moment Cronis was alone, the golden steed exploded from the broken section of the roof. David pressed close against Wind Song to keep from striking the edges of the opening. The winged stallion dropped from the sky, swooping at the Dark Lord. It was only a second before David leaped off the back of Wind Song that Cronis even became aware that something was happening overhead. Before Cronis could even move, David slammed into the Dark One, driving him to the ground.

The savagery of David's attack was taking its toll on him. He swung, kicked, butted, slashed, and pummeled the figure beneath him. He had to stop Cronis before the demon god's forces had time to know that their leader was under attack. In response to David's brutal pounding, Cronis used fang and claw to counter. The chain mail David wore had been snapped or torn in a dozen places. Blood was flowing from several wounds. If victory was going to be won, it had to be in the next few moments.

A sea of creatures slammed into David from behind, tearing him off of their master. Try as he might, the Knight of Es-Soh-En could not regain his footing, nor gain any ground through the sea of attackers. Logos was torn from his grasp, and he was driven to the ground. As he fell, David saw Tanya had lost the eagle shield and was overwhelmed by another wave of creatures.

Agron and Pentra were going down as well. As the followers of Cronis pinned David and Tanya to the ground, the Dark Lord strode over to where David lay, placed his foot on the Knight's neck, raised one hand and shouted to the world, "Victory!"

"You may have us, but you haven't taken the kingdom!" Tanya shouted trying to snatch the pleasure of victory from the Dark One.

"On the contrary," he gloated. "You are the Steward and the Stewardess of Dula. I have you both. I have the kingdom." His voiced trailed off as his eyes caught something in the eastern sky. Suddenly his cry of success turned into a screaming wail, "NOOOOO...!!"

David turned his head to see what Cronis was screaming at. There, at the head of the sunrise was a great white billowing cloud. Even from this distance, David could tell that the cloud was rolling towards them at an incredible speed. As the cloud expanded, unfolded, came into position David and Tanya could suddenly see that it wasn't a vast cloud bank spreading across the entire horizon and being driven by some unseen storm. This was no cloud. It was an army dressed in pure white. The lightning which flashed among them was the sun shining off of swords and armor. Millions of winged horses beat the air carrying their riders across the sky. At the head of the attack was Es-Soh-En, bearing down on the castle where Cronis stood trembling. The Adoni had returned!

CHAPTER THIRTY-ONE

"...AND THEN FADE AWAY"

Tanya had a sudden sensation flooding her body. She could think of no other way to describe it other than she suddenly felt *more real*. It had been similar to the time they had entered the Kingdom of the Adoni, only this was more intense. Her senses sharpened, enhanced, and focused all at the same time. She could make out the features of those in the sky; but before she could recognize any of them, her nostril caught the faint and sudden hint of Jasmine. There was only one person she had known who had a love for the fragrance.

Even as she turned, three of the demon creatures who were frozen in their tracks by terror and had not released their hold on her were cut down. As the Child of Earth looked up to see her rescuer, she already knew who it was.

"Jensen!" she cried out. Although he was an older, more mature Jensen than the one she had known years ago, she knew him instantly. His black flowing hair still had its streak of grey down the left side. He wore a short beard, and his green eyes glistened as he looked upon the Singer of the Lesser Song and smiled with his whole heart.

Although Cronis trembled where he stood, he had not taken his foot off of David's neck. Something slammed into the Dark Lord's mid-section, causing him to double over, remove his foot, and step back. In an instant David rolled out of the demon god's reach. He, too, had experienced the change when Tanya was transformed. In addition to the new body, he recalled all the events in the Kingdom of the Adoni. As he drew his feet under him to stand, a slender, well-tanned hand reached out to help him.

"Kya!" he exclaimed, and noted that she held her shepherdess staff that had obviously been the weapon she had used to drive Cronis back. All around them, those who had fallen in the service of the Adoni were healed, revived, and transformed. Ren and Han came forward to stand beside Tanya. Agron, Gort, Pentra, and Handar were at the ready and beside David. Those who had not died began to transform. Laton, Wil Den, Fin Den and others came swarming through the breech in the wall to join those already in the remnants of the courtyard.

The cry of the Great Eagle sounded above them, and when the forces of Cronis broke to run, Heart Company, centaurs, minotaurs, gnomes, and Water People pursued them. As soon as the servants of the Dark Lord were clear of the courtyard, hundreds of Tree Druids blocked their paths. When the deserters fled around the Tree Druids, the ground itself cracked, split, and rose to form a sheer cliff to cut off the demons' escape. Already the forces of the Adoni had encircled Cronis and all of his troops.

A section of the eastern wall assembled itself, and Es-Soh-En lighted on the rampart over-seeing the entire operation. Glidon dropped from the sky to perch next to Him. From among the assembly, David spotted Tra and Kal, now coming to join Han and Ren. Singer and Reva were there. Pentra, Flotsam and each of the Knights of Es-Soh-En were moving toward them. Wilton and the Knights Inkling were among them. Dig Gen, Brig Gen, Trig Gen, Ton Kin, and Mig Gen joined with Wil Den and Fin Den at the head of the gnome community. Those of the gnomes who had been in the Gen Forest when the Adoni returned had also been transformed, and then transported to the castle. A tall warrior and his beautiful lady also stood among the gnome population. David recognized him as Gen transformed into a man along with Leah the Water Citizen. Even among the unicorn David spotted Lendara, his horn still gone, but welcomed back by his entire herd.

The names and faces were almost endless. Tanya noted that there were more people among the followers of Es-Soh-En than had been accounted for by the army of the Adoni and those in the castle. She also saw that those among the forces of Cronis had grown as well. She knew then that all those who had still been alive at the return of the Adoni had been brought to this place, and assigned to one of the two camps. The Children of Earth could have taken weeks to meet and greet all those who had been a part of their many visits to the Lands of the Adoni.

The faces which David noted were not here were Queen Dianna, and Yeesha. Gaylord hovered in the air at the head of the herd of winged horses. Wind Song and Morning Star had joined them.

Those on the ground, and those hovering in the air, drove all the followers of Cronis into one section. The number was so vast it filled the entire city and fields beyond. When everyone was in place, Es-Soh-En nodded, and new walls, far greater and stronger than those before, grew from the ground, blocking any chance of escape for the Dark Lord or his legions. The millions of followers of the Adoni stood on the walls, or hovered in the air. The millions who served Cronis huddled below.

"Cronis!" came the voice of the Great Hobber. Tanya realized that she had never heard the voice of the Adoni spoken without mercy until now. "Centuries ago in the Veil your power was broken. At that time judgment was passed, but the sentence was suspended. This day shall that judgment come upon you and your followers.

"The sentence was not carried out then, not because I lacked the will, nor the ability; nor because of anything you had done to hold off that judgment. The sentence was held off to give all who were tainted by you the chance to turn from you to Me. Now all seeds of rebellion have taken root, grown into death and destruction. Those who sought to rebel have been allowed to rebel. Those who sought mercy have been given mercy. All that is left is judgment."

A maimed figure burst from among the ranks of Cronis. It took Tanya several moments to recognize the man who had changed and distorted so much. It was Gib-ron.

"Spare me my Lord," came the cry. All eyes both inside the courtyard and around the courtyard walls were focused on the figure. "I have served You all along. I sought to bring Cronis to You. He has held me captive all this time. He has made me do things I did not want to do. Have mercy my Lord."

"Had this been any other time, then mercy would have been granted, but there is no mercy on this day. All mercy which was available has already been given out. This is the Day of Judgment. Those who have not obtained the mercy of the Adoni will now know only the judgment for their crimes. You have followed Cronis willingly, and now you will join him in his judgment. Depart from Me Gib-ron. In truth, I never knew you!" Snarls and hisses marked the exit of Gib-ron as he slithered his way deeper into the crowd of servants of the Dark Lord in hopes to hide when the moment came.

"Now that you have been broken, stripped of your power, and taken prisoner, Cronis; will you at last give Me the honor due the Adoni?"

"What?" screamed the Dark One. "Honor You? Even if this were my last breath, I would never honor You. Let this be my final response to You." The Dark One spat upon the ground. Instantly Es-Soh-En began to glow. He grew so bright that all those in the courtyard screamed in pain, covering their eyes, and cowering away from the source.

"Even now, you would seek to rebel?"

"You are Lord because You created me. You are Lord because You have won this day. You are Lord, but I will never praise you," Cronis snarled. He crouched on the ground, cowering from the intense light. It was obviously taking everything he had to keep control over his own terror.

"It is not your praise that I seek, nor would I accept any praise from you because it would be as false as your own heart. You have, however acknowledged and called me *lord*. It is that acknowledgement that I sought," Es-Soh-En bellowed.

"What?!" cried Cronis, trying to take back the words he had spoken.

"Kneel before me, and hear your punishment," the Great Hobber commanded.

"Never!" Cronis shouted, and then a long string of vulgarities spewed from his mouth as he sought to bolster his own withering confidence.

"It was not a request, but an order. KNEEL!" As Es-Soh-En spoke the command once more, His light increased in intensity. Those who were of the Adoni's camp were not affected by the radiance, and could see through the light, and observed as the followers of Cronis scrambled to bow, and hide their eyes from the brilliance. Cronis fought all the while, but the light burned his eyes, and some unseen force was driving him to his knees. He roared and screamed in protest, but his body obeyed its Creator. His entire kingdom knelt before the Adoni; not out of respect, but because they no longer had the power to stand or resist.

"You shall be banished from My presence. You shall be cast into that place reserved for you and your followers. It is a place of eternal fire and torment. It is a place from which there is no escape." Even as Es-Soh-En spoke the judgment, millions of servants of Cronis began to scream, and weep, and wail concerning their fate. None sought forgiveness for their deeds or attitudes. The Great Hobber gave one last look into the souls of those before Him. There was no spark of repentance among them, only regret for not winning this day. Finally the Adoni shouted, "Be gone!"

The entire collection of Cronis and his servants disappeared from view, fading like snowflakes caught in a blast furnace. One second they were assembled in the courtyard, the next they were less than a vapor. Just as those who served the Adoni had become more real, those who followed Cronis became so much less real that they were no longer part of this world. All those in the courtyard, those who had fallen in battle over the last few days, and those who had fallen in service to Cronis over the long centuries and their souls had been reserved in a waiting place for this day now experienced the final judgment in only an instant. The wail of each lost soul tore through the air as the entire gathering of Cronis' forces were cast from this world, and into outer darkness, amid the fires which could never be quenched.

Had those present heard with their old ears, grasped with their old minds, they would have pitied the doomed souls; but now they saw all as Es-Soh-En saw. They understood as

Es-Soh-En understood. There was no pity for those cast away, for they had rejected every offer of salvation given to them in their lifetimes. As the screams were snuffed by the closing of the door between where the followers of Cronis agonized, and where the followers of Es-Soh-En cheered, David realized that all were where they had chosen to be.

CHAPTER THIRTY-TWO

RESTORATIONS

As soon as the judgment was over, Es-Soh-En rose on His hind legs. He continued to rise until He stood upright like a man. His shape and appearance began to transform until it was no longer the Great Hobber that stood before the gathering, but Teacher. This was now the true form of Es-Soh-En, ever since His incarnation into human form so many years before. Now that the battles were finally over, all knew that He would never assume His Hobber form again. He was, for now and always, the Godman: God who had become man – the Kinsman Redeemer. His attire also changed. The simple robes and garments once worn by Teacher were now replaced with dark pants, turned-down knee boots of black leather. He wore a silk shirt the color of topaz. The shirt had a wide collar, opened at the throat, and bellsleeves fastened at the cuffs. Over this was a black tunic, and over this was a polished metal breastplate. On either side of the breastplate were embedded six precious stones – a total of twelve stones all together. Embossed on the center of the breastplate was a work of art. When Teacher stood at one angle, the golden image of a lion's head and full mane was clearly visible. As He turned, and the angle changed, the image shifted to silver and the lion transformed into that of a lamb.

"Come, for all things are now complete!" He called out to the gathering. David and Tanya noticed a kind of over-lapping as if one world were superimposed upon another, and another. All worlds blended together into this one place. From where they stood, David and Tanya saw great throngs from each world standing around the Adoni. At the head of one throng, the Children of Earth saw their father and mother. Teacher smiled when the recognition was visible on the Knights of Es-Soh-En's faces. "It's just as Gaylord said, *All worlds are the same; only the names are different.*"

The Children of Earth held off the desire to run and greet their parents. They had wanted to tell them for years what had happened to them. They had tried the first time they came back from Dula. David went to his mother, and tried to explain why they had been gone for so long, only to discover that Es-Soh-En had returned them only moments after they had left. Several times Tanya wanted to bring up the subject, but each time all evidence of their having been to Dula was gone. Without something to support their claims, the brother and sister finally resigned themselves to keeping it secret from their father and mother. Now it would be secret no longer, but other matters demanded their attention.

Once the joining of all worlds was complete, and all worlds were now part of this world, Teacher stepped back, and Glidon leaped into the air. The Great Eagle breathed the golden mist upon the area, and everyone knew to step back, and how far. All present knew what was expected of them without any instructions being given. When they had cleared a large enough area, the golden mist settled. It lay thick on the ground like a morning fog, but unlike the morning fog instead of dissipating, it rose from the ground. Once it was hovering above the ground, the former structure of the walls and courtyard where the judgment of Cronis had taken place was gone, and a completely different structure was visible underneath. As the golden cloud rose, so did the structure. After several minutes, a great castle, two hundred times larger than the palace of Dula stood in the midst of the gathering. The golden mist rose still higher, and faded from view. There before the throng of countless followers of all worlds and all ages stood a castle like none had ever seen before. Twelve platforms formed the perfectly square foundation supporting the entire castle. Each platform rested on the one beneath it, and was a little smaller; thus creating steps leading up to the actual edifice. The stairway to the castle was the entire length of the building, and serviced all four sides of the structure. Thus, anyone could approach and enter the building from any side. David noted that the stairs were made of the same precious stones that were on the breastplate Teacher wore, and were even in the same order. The first level was made of ruby. The second level was sapphire; the third was amethyst, the fourth topaz. Each level was an entire single precious stone with the final level being carved out of a single diamond. The stairway created a visual image: *Though your sins be as scarlet; they shall be as white as snow.* The bottom stone was blood-red and the top stone was clear or pure.

On the upper level, the edge of the diamond platform was not cut at a straight ninety-degree angle as were the previous levels. Where the sharp ninety-degree cut should have been was a row to inverted triangles, cut at a forty-five degree angle to the stair and the floor. The facets caught the sunlight and rainbows erupted from the diamond; rainbows that danced and sparkled as someone would walk up to the castle. The rainbows were ever shifting and swirling so long as a visitor was in motion towards the palace. If an observer was still, the light splintering on the diamond edges created a pool of rainbow light in the air around the upper level.

Resting on the multiple platforms were columns carved of polished marble easily two hundred feet tall. The columns were set back from the edge of the last step in order to create a vast porch all around the palace. The pillars stood evenly spaced every fifty feet. There were so many columns along all fours sides that it gave the illusion of a forest of marble trees. The base and the cap of each column was golden, pure gold; engraved with grape vines. Between the marble and the gold was a ring of ivory. From a distance the ring of ivory appeared small compared to the massive gold base or caps and the shaft of the marble column, but when David and Tanya later climbed the stairs, the ivory ring was easily three or four feet tall.

Along the caps of the columns rested massive beams, twenty to thirty feet thick. The beams were carved from cinnamon trees, and the fragrance of cinnamon welcomed each visitor. Across the top of the cinnamon beams, and laced back and forth forming the entire roof of the edifice were emeralds carved like various leaves from each tree known from each world. There was no indication how the millions of emeralds were joined together, and if one thought about it, the dome roof appeared too vast to be able to support the weight of so many jewels, but the jewels were fitted in such a way that they supported each others' weight, and there was no danger of collapsing.

There were no actual walls to the castle, and any visitor could approach from any direction, climb the stairs at any point, and pass between the columns to enter the only room of the castle: the throne room.

The floor of the throne room was the smooth surface of the diamond of the upper level. In the center of the throne room, a smaller replica of the castle's foundation formed the twelve-stepped dais on which twin thrones sat. Here the upper step, still carved out of a single diamond, was cut in such a way as to create thousands of facets encircling the throne. As the light struck the multiple facets, it shattered into rainbow colors which continually danced around the throne. Anyone sitting on the throne would be surrounded by an ever-changing rainbow of light.

The thrones were not harsh, stiff, or straight, but of a sloping, comfortable design. There were no legs for the thrones, but a platform made of twelve discs of the same precious stones that formed the castle's foundation and the throne's dais. Unlike other thrones which could face only one direction, both of these swiveled to allow the personage sitting on the throne to turn and face visitors as they approached from any direction. Where the throne of other kingdoms forced visitors to come from only one direction, and made it clear that the visitor had to adjust for royalty; these thrones created the impression that those sitting upon these thrones wanted to meet visitors, and welcomed them into the throne room.

The arm rests were of gnome wood and as you approached the thrones you would smell cinnamon, cloves and nutmeg. Each throne had red padding attached to make the thrones comfortable for those who sat there. Where the hands would rest at the end of the arm rest were the carved heads of the Great Hobber; black onyx for the face, topaz for the eyes, and gold for the mane. Whoever would sit on these thrones would rest their hands on the heads of the Hobber. The seat of each throne was a thick, comfortable red cushion, and the back had a similar red cushion attached with a separate pad for the head to rest against. Engraved in silver and gold above the pad for the head, was the same design of the lion and lamb insignia found on the breastplate of Teacher. Circling in a half-circle above the image of the lion and lamb, like a rainbow adorning the sky, were the twelve precious stones found on the breastplate of Teacher, and the stairs of the palace. The two thrones were identical, on the same level, and sitting side-by-side.

Teacher motioned, and all the followers of all the worlds and all the ages moved forward, climbing the stairs, standing on the diamond surface around the throne, and filling the great porch. When this area was filled, those outside stood on the stairs. No one noticed at first because the curve of the ground was so subtle it first appeared to be level, but the ground on all sides of the castle sloped slowly up so that those who were standing outside the castle could see over those in front, and look directly into the throne room. It was like a giant amphitheater.

Following instructions, which seemed almost an instinct, the throng parted at the center of the eastern wall. David and Tanya left their parents, Kya and Jensen with their friends, and climbed the staircase before them. They climbed in unison, moving to a tune no one heard, but all knew. They made their way up the dais to the left-hand throne, and stood on either side. Once they were in place, Teacher began to follow after them. When He came to the foot of the dais, He stopped, looked up at the Knights of Es-Soh-En, and waited. Both David and Tanya knew the words that needed to be spoken.

"Dear Jesus," David began, and discovered that the structure and shape of the throne room was designed to amplify his voice so that by the time it reached the columns, a whisper was as loud as a shout. The voice would increase as it drifted out of the castle and to the sea of people outside. Thus, even if one spoke softly, everyone could hear clearly.

"Dear Jesus," David repeated, "for such is how I first knew You. Dear Es-Soh-En, Teacher, Adoni, Creator of all the Lands of the Adoni, Savior, Redeemer," and here David suddenly knew the titles by which this One was known and identified in all worlds. David flashed back to the conversation with the Great

Hobber when Ish was formed about how none were names, but all were titles. Only the Unnamed Adoni knew Teacher's true name, and it would be revealed by the Unnamed Adoni when the time was right. David smiled with the memory; Teacher looked at David understanding the reason for the smile, and smiled back. The Child of Earth recited all of Teacher's titles for all to hear. When he had completed the list, he continued. "I present you with Your throne. As Steward of the Throne of Dula, this has been placed under my care these last few months. I surrender it now back to You, the Rightful King. The One, and only One who is truly worthy to sit upon it."

"As Stewardess of the Throne of Dula, I surrender now to You, this throne, entrusted to me these past few months. As with David, I, too, surrender it now to You, the Rightful King. The One, and only One who is truly worthy to sit upon it," Tanya added.

Teacher climbed the steps up to the throne, turned around, and was seated for all to see. Once He was enthroned, the Knights of Es-Soh-En descended the steps, came to the diamond floor, turned to face each other, and then turned once more to face Teacher upon His throne. Both Children of Earth knelt before the King, and pledged their eternal loyalty and undying love. Teacher then motioned for David and Tanya to ascend the steps. Kneeling before Him there on the top step, He rose, placed a hand on each of their heads, and pronounced a blessing that had been especially designed for them and the service they had performed for the Adoni. He then motioned for the Children of Earth to rise, and stand on either side of Him during the remainder of the ceremony.

Out of the sea of people came Singer. Reva walked beside him, and carried Singer's staff. Singer carried a velvet box in his hands. At the foot of the throne both Singer and Reva stopped, knelt, and pledged their eternal love and loyalty. When Singer and Reva rose, Singer spoke for all to hear.

"This is from Your Father," Singer announced, climbing the stairs of the throne. When the sage reached the throne, he opened the case, and drew out a crown of gold. It was not a thick solid band, but a delicate weaving of gold strands with setting for jewels made of white gold. The front of the crown held a large red ruby, full of life. On either side of the ruby were six smaller stones identical to the twelve precious stones which served as the foundation for the castle. "The Unnamed Adoni has prepared this crown for You to be used on this, the day of Your coronation. The center stone is ruby, the color of blood, for though all worlds may seem different, they are all the same. Though the redemption of each world may be unique for that world, the price has always been the same: the price of Your life, of Your blood."

Here Singer held up the crown for all to see. He then came directly before the throne, and as he placed the crown on Teacher's head he announced, "I have been given the honor to crown You, and to declare that You are truly Lord of all lords, King of all kings, Creator of all worlds, and Savior of us all!"

Singer then turned towards the crowd, raised both hands and declared, "Let all present hear and acknowledge. All titles have been restored to the Rightful Owner!" The sea of people erupted into a song of praise; strong, powerful and awesome in the blending of billions of voices. It was a new song – one that had never been sung, or even thought of before. But all now knew the words, the tune, and the melody. The entire gathering knelt before Teacher, lifting their hands in worship, and singing this new song.

When the song was complete, Singer motioned for Reva to join him before the throne. She climbed each step with the alluring grace of the Water People. As she came to stand beside

Singer, she bowed to Teacher, and handed the staff to her beloved. Singer took the staff, and raised it for all to see.

"This is my staff," Singer declared presenting the treasure to Teacher. "It was carved from a branch of the Tree of Unending Life when I was commissioned by You and Your Father to serve You all of my days. Although it was cut from a tree that could not die, could not know death, the staff came to know death. Thus, that which could not die, knew death." As Singer spoke, everyone understood that He was not speaking of just the staff by this observation. "That which could not die, died for us all. Here is the staff that could not die, but which did die. Here is the staff that was broken but restored. It has been the sign of my office all these many years. I now return it to You with my pledge of allegiance."

Teacher rose from His throne, took the staff from Singer, embraced the sage, and the Reva. As the pair knelt before Him, He placed a hand on each of their heads, and pronounced a blessing upon them which was unique to them.

After Singer and Reva descended, and returned to their place among the crowd, Ish and Issha approached, joined by Tra, Kal, and Dig Gen who followed three abreast one pace behind the first Father and Mother. These three had formed the Clan of Sword-keepers, and it was into their care that the Sword had been placed upon its return. Ish and Issha walked side by side, with all the royalty and dignity of the First Father and Mother of their world. Ish was on the left and Issha on the right. They clasped their hands between them; Ish's right hand with Issha's left. The clasped hands were raised high for all to see, and held in those hands was Logos, the Talking Sword.

The First Couple ascended the stairs, standing before Teacher, Tra, Kal, and Dig Gen stood on the step below and behind the first Father and Mother.

"This is the blade, Logos, forged from the horn of Lendara, an innocent who gave his life so that we might not die for our sins," Issha declared. "It has been placed into our care as the First King and Queen of the Lands of the Adoni. It is the Sword which pierced Your heart to save us. Its stain reminds us of the price You paid for us. It has always been a symbol of our divine right to rule, the right which You alone can claim. On behalf of all our sons and daughters for all ages who were blessed to sit in Your stead upon the thrones of our world, we return it now to You, and swear our eternal love and allegiance." Teacher rose, took the sword offered Him by Ish and Issha.

"And how speaks the Sword-keeper Clan?" He asked.

"The Sword-keeper clan is honored that the blade can be returned to You after having been entrusted into our keeping," Kal declared. Teacher stepped forward and hugged Ish and Issha. They knelt before Him as He placed a hand on each head of the First Couple and blessed them. When they stepped aside, Kal came forward, knelt and was blessed by Teacher. After him came Tra, and then Dig Gen.

When the Keepers of the Sword descended the dais. David and Tanya knew that they were to descend the steps as well, and join the group that now approached. At the head of the gathering was Trayton. Next to him was the last of his line, Dayton who had given the Eye of Suma to David and Tanya. David stood on one side of Trayton, while Tanya stood next to Dayton. Behind them were all the children of the family of Trayton who had cared for the Eye of Suma through the centuries. Before the throne, Trayton held up the eagle shield with the Eye of Suma still glowing for all to see.

"This was the price You paid for my immediate sin. It was not as great a price as the one You paid for all our sins, but it was precious to us all. It showed the depth of love You had for one who was guilty, and could never atone for the death he had caused. Although worthy of slavery, You sacrificed this to set me and my family free." He then passed the eagle shield to Dayton who handed it to Tanya.

"This is the Shield of the Eagle, entrusted to us by the descendants of Trayton. As the last to care for it, and to carry it into battle, and on behalf of Trayton and his heirs, we present it now to You." Tanya handed the eagle shield to Teacher as He rose to greet them all. David and Tanya returned to their place on either side of the throne while Teacher blessed each one of Trayton's line who came to kneel before Him, and swear their allegiance.

The ceremony continued in this fashion for many weeks. None were tired, bored, or weary. Each one came before Teacher, and no matter how great or small a role the follower had played in the over-all Plan, Teacher knew him or her by name, remembered the efforts he or she had made. Each one came with some gift, or offering which Teacher gratefully accepted. Teacher would then pronounce a blessing especially designed for the one who knelt before Him. No two blessings were the same despite the vast throng that came before the throne, because no two services were ever the same. Each follower was unique with his or her own strengths and weaknesses. The Adoni had used those strengths and weakness to fulfill some part, some role in the greater Plan.

The gnomes came before him. The Water People came to worship and proclaimed Him to be the *God Who Breathes Gold.* The talking animals, the tree druids, the minotaurs, the centaurs – every race of the Lands of the Adoni came to pay homage.

What stood out most from all the other parts of the ceremony was the procession of Queen Selena. Her people had given her the name *Queen Yola* – which means kindness – because she had created Yola Province in Dula. She had been the queen who had begun charity in her kingdom by providing food, clothing and housing for the poor. Long after she had passed into the Kingdom, others took up her cause and continued her work.

From the very back of the throng of followers came a single, sweet, pure sounding of a golden trumpet. When all turned to see, the trumpet hung in the air, suspended by hands not connected to a body. These had been the same hands the Children of Earth had seen on previous occasions when they were served meals from the Kingdom. The crowd parted, and Queen Selena stood at the very back. As she began to make her way towards the throne, applause broke out, cheering followed, and then laughter, singing and exclamations of joy and praise filled the entire kingdom. Those who had begun the cheering started to chant *Queen Yola* as they broke away from the others in the crowd. It was like a sea of its own moving among the population of the New Kingdom of the Adoni. They separated themselves to surround Queen Yola, singing her praises. They called her by her nickname for her true name had been lost among the ages.

Although all had now been redeemed, there was that special quality of the citizens of the New Kingdom that people could see them in their new state, and also recognize them from their old. Each of these people had been an outcast of society. They had been poor, drunks, prostitutes, thieves, addicts, and the list went on. Each one had been touched by the caring of Queen Yola, both during her life, and in the many years after she had entered the Kingdom. They had all been the debris of acceptable company, but Queen Yola had not forsaken them. Her love, her care, and her work changed each one; brought them to the point of giving their lives, their pain, and their problems to the Adoni. Through her care, they had forsaken their old ways, and now stood with the redeemed of the Kingdom; a place which polite society had refused to believe any of these could ever attain.

Tanya had no idea that there had been so many, but a full fourth of all those in the Kingdom, praised their Queen Yola, and attributed their coming to the Adoni to her care and efforts. They were all her *children of the heart*. She stood there, tears flowing down her cheeks, tears of joy as each came to thank her, praise her, and celebrate with her. They formed a great procession, following her, singing for her, and rejoicing in all that she had done for them. At her side was the midwife who had first aided the queen, and was the inspiration for Queen Selena's work.

Of all the procession for kings, priests, and warriors, none had a procession like unto this one. Teacher left the throne, came down the stairs, and exited the palace to meet her more than half-way. There He embraced her, kissed her tears away, and drew forth a crown like none had ever seen. Its jewels, one for each soul she had touched, were countless. The gold was more pure than any would have thought possible. The praise given to her by the Adoni and by her children was more rewarding than any spoken in the long years of the Kingdom of the Adoni. She had been all but forgotten in the later history of Dula, but Teacher produced great volumes for all to see, and written on the pages of each volume was a careful record of all her honest prayers, her sleepless nights, her tears for the poor, and her work to ease their suffering.

And so the procession came into the palace, Queen Selena on Teacher's right arm, the midwife on his left. Her children spread out behind her. They sang with voices that would have been hoarse from coughing, weak with drink, off-key from sadness; but in the New Kingdom, their voices were more pure and sweet than any song sung of man.

When this procession of Queen Yola had finally been spent, and all had given the thanks and praise they sought of the great woman; another throng formed at the back. David and Tanya descended the stairs and met the procession half-way, turned and led this procession before Teacher.

These were the Knights of Es-Soh-En – all one hundred and forty-four of them. Added to their ranks were the Knights Inkling. Each Knight wore a breastplate of pure gold bearing the lion and lamb symbol of Teacher. The small army came to the base of the stairs and spread out on either side of David and Tanya. As a single unit they knelt and swore allegiance and love to the one they were named for. Here, Teacher stood to do honor for their years of service. The Knights Inkling sang the many songs of their deeds and sacrifices. And now after all these generations, the Battle of the Line was restored to memory. The Knights Inkling sang this song for the first time for all to hear.

When all the processions were complete, one last procession remained. The last one to approach was Lendara, King of the Unicorns. He had once been the greatest – the first; and now he came last, but there was no shame in this steed. He had chosen along with his race to keep their first state. Once they had been above all the creations of the Adoni in their majesty, purity, and power. They had chosen to remain untouched by the Fall of the world, and so the price of their creation was so much less than the price of the others' redemption. As Lendara came before the throne, the rest of the unicorn herd filled in behind him – including David and Tanya as *Friends of the Unicorn*. Lendara stopped at the foot of the dais, bowed, and if he had still had a horn, it would have touched the floor in front of him, the greatest sign of respect a unicorn could give. Those of his herd followed his example.

"Dear Es-Soh-En, for such is how I and my race always knew You. I have given my horn, my life in Your service, and even that is not enough to honor You who chose to create us, to give us life, and free will. There is little that I can give which has not already been given, but allow us to give this gift to You."

So saying, Lendara, and all the unicorns threw back their heads, and sang a song such as had never been heard before. By it, all other songs of praise paled. When the song was complete, Teacher rose with tears in His eyes, descended the stairs from the throne to meet Lendara and the herd on the floor of the palace.

"Tears, my Lord?" Lendara asked.

"There is always a place for tears of joy," Teacher replied. So saying, Teacher turned to the herd, "Dear friends, for such is how I have always known you. I now have something to give to you. This is a time of restoration. A time to restore the Kingdom, a time to restore titles, a time to restore what was lost." Teacher then touched Lendara on the forehead, where the scar of his lost horn was. Instantly a change began to take place. It was not painful for Lendara, but a new horn began to sprout and to grow to full size at an incredible rate. It spiraled higher, and was more beautiful than any horn in the entire herd, and was far more beautiful than the one given in service to the Adoni. What made this horn so much different was that instead of the traditional silver horn of the unicorn, this one was pure gold. Lendara's hooves also transformed from silver to gold. Teacher smiled, and hugged His friend and said, "I always keep my promises."

When Teacher released Lendara, there were tears in the eyes of not just Lendara, but of the entire herd. Even David and Tanya as herd-brother and herd-sister, found their eyes filling with tears as the shame Lendara had born quietly all these centuries was removed.

"Tears, dear unicorn?" Teacher joked.

"*There is always a place for tears of joy,*" Lendara quoted. Thus began the procession out of the palace. As Teacher led His followers out of the castle, down the stairs, and to another place that had been prepared by the Unnamed Adoni, He would stop and speak or visit with some follower. As before, He recalled the name of each follower, and their service to Him, no matter how small. All who sought to speak with Him, or walk with Him, were given the opportunity.

As the procession came to the gnomes, Teacher sought out Brig Gen from among all the others. Teacher came to the gnome, knelt down to his level, and hugged his friend. After the embrace Teacher asked with a twinkle in His eye, "Well friend gnome, now will you praise me?"

Those had been the exact words spoken by Glidon to Brig Gen in the Dark Woods when the Great Eagle had delivered them from the Moving Trees. Brig Gen had refused to praise that day until the trees were gone. Once Glidon had passed judgment on the trees for their rebellion, the Great Eagle had turned, and asked that question of the stubborn gnome. It had been the turning point of his life. Now Brig Gen broke out into laughter, and hugged Teacher once more.

Teacher stood up, and began to recite the poems Brig Gen had written concerning Es-Soh-En and the Adoni during the years after the Quest for the Sword was complete. At some point Teacher transformed the presentation from reciting poetry to singing the poems. As He sang the songs of praise written by the greatest poet of the gnome race, He held His hands palm-up before Him, and a disturbance rippled in the air. As the songs continued; the rippling effect transformed into a silver crown, growing with each verse. Teacher had saved the greatest works by the gnome for last, and as Teacher sang these final poems, a jewel or pure emerald grew to fill the numerous settings prepared in the crown. As the last poem was sung, Teacher held a crown of silver and emeralds, designed especially for Brig Gen.

"Let these emeralds remind you always that it was in the green of the Dark Woods that your faith was born, and your faith grew like the trees of the Gen Forest: always beautiful, and always pleasing to Us." Teacher placed the crown of Brig Gen's head, positioning the traditional gnomish cap to pass through the crown and hang over the back of the work of art. The two embraced once more, and Brig Gen fell into line with the parade as it wound through several green sloping hills and bubbling brooks.

As they came to the final rise, before them stood a vast gathering of trees. They formed a counter-part to the castle, but this was made of grass, trees and leaves. There was no throne inside this structure, but a platform rose in the center. Gaylord came to be by Teacher's side; and Wind Song and Morning Star came to be with David and Tanya. Singer came to the head of the procession, pointed to the sky, and cried out for all to hear as he spoke to Teacher, "Behold Your bride!"

CHAPTER THIRTY-THREE

THE BRIDE OF ES-SOH-EN

In response to the announcement of Singer, all eyes turned unto the sky. There a single star burned in the heavens; glowing brighter all the while it descended from the sky. After a few moments, it was as brilliant as the sun, and an image became visible at the center and as the source of the glow. It was Queen Dianna, riding on Yeesha. The Queen of Dula wore a wedding gown, pure as snow, white and spotless, flowing behind her in the air like the tail of a comet. Yeesha hovered on the air currents, slowing their descent so that all could see her passenger. The entire gathering, with the exception of Teacher, David, Tanya, Gaylord, Wind Song and Morning Star moved down to the hall of trees, filling the inside, and spreading out around the structure. Just as with the palace, the ground sloped slowly up so that everyone could see into the edifice. The throng opened a space for Teacher and Dianna to pass and enter the hall for the wedding.

The unicorn broke forth in a wedding song as Dianna and Yeesha came to rest on the soft green grass before Teacher. Teacher had mounted Gaylord, and Tanya and David had mounted Wind Song and Morning Star. The four humans sat astride the four winged horses as the mares and stallions carried their charges down the slope to where the crowd had parted. They moved in time to the song of the unicorns. When the procession came to the outer edge of the crowd, the song shifted, began a new movement, and the unicorns held silent as the trees and plants took up the next stanza.

When the song shifted, David, Tanya and Dianna held back, as Gaylord carried Teacher with pride down the aisle way to the center of the gathering upon the raised platform. The horse held his head high, filled with the excitement at having been chosen for this great honor. Gaylord carried Teacher to the area where the wedding ceremony was to be held. Once there, Teacher slipped off of Gaylord, hugged the steed, patted his neck, and turned to look back down the aisle.

This time it was David and Wind Song's turn to come forth. Again there was another shift in the singing, and where the plants had accompanied Teacher, now they fell silent and the mountains took up the sound in deep bass tones. When David was next to Teacher, he slipped off of Wind Song. The two winged horses stood side-by-side just as David and Teacher stood side-by-side, looking down the aisle.

As Tanya and Morning Star began their journey down the path, the mountains fell silent, and the stars began to sing. When Morning Star came to the section where Teacher and David stood, she turned to the left, and waited for Tanya to dismount. Now all had their attention on the bride.

The moment Dianna and Yeesha began down the aisle the stars continued to sing, but were joined by the plants, trees, mountains, and the unicorn all singing of the love Teacher had for Dianna. Water Citizens broke from the crowd, danced in front of Yeesha as she carried the Bride of the Adoni down the aisle. As they danced, the Water People sprinkled flower petals along the path. As they came to the wedding area, the Water People broke off, and joined the crowd. Yeesha came up the platform, waited and Queen Dianna dismounted.

Once all were in place, Glidon swooped to the platform area to stand as witness to the ceremony. The structure was suddenly filled with the glow of the Unnamed Adoni. His voice was rich and sweet, and the smell of cinnamon and cloves filled the edifice, the vale where all stood to witness the wedding, and beyond.

"My Son," sang the voice of the Unnamed Adoni. The tones He created were so pure, so filled with the emotions and feelings of the moment that it sounded like its own symphony. The tones blended upon themselves like a choir even though it was only one voice – but oh that single voice! It filled all those present so full of joy that they could not contain the emotion, and were overflowing, basking in the pleasure they experienced.

"You have paid a great price to redeem this bride. Your love and Your life have been sacrificed for her. Will You now accept her as Your bride for all of eternity?"

"I do!" Teacher sang in reply.

"And do You join her to You, becoming One flesh, One mind, One heart? Offering all that You are, all that You have, all that You will be to her?"

"I do" Teacher sang once more.

"And do You promise to love her with all of Your heart? To love her with all of Your mind? To love her with all of Your soul? Caring for her? Living for her?"

"I do!" Teacher sang the third time.

"Dianna, my daughter," the Unnamed Adoni now sang to the Queen, focusing His attention upon her. "Do you accept the love that My Son has offered to you?"

"I do!" Dianna declared for all to hear.

"Do you accept Him as your husband, your friend, your companion for all of eternity?"

"I do!" Dianna repeated.

"And do you accept what He now offers of Himself, His kingdom, all that He possesses, to live with Him, work with Him, share with Him, and love with Him?"

"I do!" Dianna replied.

"Then by these three vows which you have made willingly this day, I now pronounce you husband and wife, King and Queen, friend and friend, both for now, and for all eternity. Let this union last until the vanishing point of thought can pass away and then beyond. So be it! You may now kiss Your bride!"

Teacher took Dianna into His arms; they clung to each other with all the love their hearts could hold. They kissed, long and deep, a kiss filled with all the passion that eternity would hold for them.

"Allow me to present to you your King and Queen," the Unnamed Adoni declared. Teacher and Dianna turned to face the throng. The Unnamed Adoni spoke the Name of names, the One Name, the True Name of Teacher, revealing it for all time. It was a good name, the right name. All who heard it found the name filled them with joy, with peace, and with security. The Unnamed Adoni introduced Teacher by this new name and Dianna as His bride. The Royal Couple stood before the gathering as all the followers of all the worlds and all the ages, cheered, wished them well, and sang of their praises.

As the Couple stepped down from the platform, and onto the grass, flowers began to spout where their feet touched. As they walked down the aisle, they laughed with the joy of the moment. Well-wishers called to them, cheered for them, applauded for them. The sun, moon and stars began the Song of Exodus as the King and Queen left the structure. The mountains added their voices for the bass tones. The trees clapped their branches together for the beat, and sang in their own voices. Even the rocks found voice to cry out in praise of their Creator. The plants, birds, animals, and all the followers joined in singing their songs of praise as the bride and groom led everyone to the great wedding feast that had been prepared for them, and for which all had been called and invited since before the worlds were first sung. There they sang, and ate, and toasted their King and Queen. Now, after all the long centuries, the endless battles, the sacrifices and dedication, the Son of the Adoni had finally come into His own.

CHAPTER THIRTY-FOUR

EPILOGUE

How long the celebration, dining, dancing, and singing lasted, no one could really tell. Had it been days, weeks, months, years or even centuries? It really didn't matter. Suffice to say, it had been adequate to express all the love, joy, and happiness the bride and groom, and all their guests experienced.

Now the King and Queen set court in the palace of marble and precious gems. As the new age in the New Kingdom of the Adoni dawned, The Bride and Groom sat side by side on their thrones, among the dancing rainbows that would always decorate their palace. They sat greeting all who came. They sat side-by-side, holding hands, and stealing glances, smiles and kisses. They met with all who came to visit. Those who wanted to thank the Adoni personally for bringing them through the dark periods of their lives, or those who simply wanted to recall their times together in the other worlds were given as much time as they desired or needed to be with their King and Queen.

When the King and Queen mounted the dais as a couple, and sat upon the thrones, the palace was filled with light, a light that flooded the entire kingdom.

Four humans and two winged horses watched from a distance as the light danced amid the emerald leaves of the dome and glowed like the Eye of Suma from this distance. David sat astride Wind Song, Kya resting against his chest as she sat in front of him. He held her with one arm, and kissed her sweet hair from time to time. Tanya sat astride Morning Star. Jensen sat behind her, and hugged her, holding her close as if he would never let go.

"So now what?" David asked of the group.

"What do you mean, *Now what*?" Tanya quipped back. "We have all eternity. We have all we want. We have all the time to do whatever we want. What do you want to do?"

"I know a place…" he began.

"A fresh water sea?" Kya suggested.

"With a grass-covered shore and trees that grow right down to the waters' edge?" Jensen continued.

"And let me guess, a pod of dolphin is waiting for us to join them for a swim."

"Don't forget Flotsam and Ghandrah," Morning Star added.

"Well, it seems like a good place to start." David laughed. Wind Song leaped into the air, flexing his wings, and catching the currents. Morning Star was only a beat behind him as they raced through the air to the fresh-water sea, laughing all the while, and now hearing the dolphins who called for them to come and join them.

HERE ENDS THE DULAN ARCHIVES

AND THE KINGDOM OF THE ADONI BEGINS

THE RETURN OF THE ADONI

GLOSSARY

[AUTHOR'S NOTE/SPOILER ALERT: As this is the final book of the Dulan Archives, this glossary is probably the most comprehensive I have put together. For this reason I must caution the reader that some entries may contain information about the final outcome of the Return of the Adoni, or inside information from other books of the Dulan Archives. If you don't want to have the story line spoiled, the reader should finish the entire book and the other works before referring to entries in this glossary.]

ADONI, THE – In the ancient Dulan tongue, this is the word for *Lords*. On a grammatical note, in all of the ancient manuscripts where this word is used, it is used in the singular tense as if speaking of a single entity, but the structure of the rest of the sentence used the plural tenses as if speaking of more than one entity. This is because those following the Adoni have the creed, "*The Adoni are Three, the Adoni are One.*" The Adoni are a collective, three distinct and separate personalities and forms. However, They are so joined that one cannot study any One of the Adoni without referencing the other two. In response to teachings which sprang up at the time of *The Return of the Adoni*, David James, the Child of Earth took great care to point out that the Adoni were Three, yet the Three were only One.

He also stressed that there were not more than three who made up the Adoni. The Adoni is made up of Es-Soh-En the Great Hobber who is also known as the Son of the Adoni, Glidon the Great Eagle; and the Unnamed Adoni who is so great, and so powerful that no name or form can ever do Him justice. After *The Battle of Es-Soh-En* a fourth entity was accepted to be part of the Adoni. This was Teacher. This is why some claimed the Adoni was more than three, and sought to add additional names to the list. According to the followers of Teacher, and the Children of Earth, Teacher is not a separate fourth member of the Adoni even though His claim to be one of the Adoni is true. He is Es-Soh-En, the Adoni made human when He was born into the human race to redeem His creation. The Adoni are recognized by Dula as the One who created the Lands of the Adoni. Teacher is simply the identity and form Es-Soh-En became when He was incarnated as a human to comply with guidelines set down for the Battle of Es-Soh-En.

AGRON – An officer who was demoted by the Council for daring to speak in favor of going to war with Magar. He was ordered to serve in the dungeons until Sir David found him, and discovered that Agron was a loyal follower of the Adoni. When David later discovered that Agron had secretly trained an army known as the Heart Company in preparation for the war with Magar, Sir David promoted him to second-in-command of the armies of Dula just below Pentra the Lesser.

AGRON, CAPTAIN – Ancestor of Agron who came to lead Heart Company. Captain Agron served briefly with David James during a previous visit. He was remembered by Sir David for his dedication to the Adoni, and his devotion to duty in the service of Queen Dianna.

AIRRON – Young Tree Druid who was contacted by Gantra of the Grove of Three Oaks to serve the Children of Earth during the final battles of Dula. Airron served to keep communications opened between plants and other races of the Lands of the Adoni.

AIR WALKER – One of the titles given to Sir David by Es-Soh-En when David was knighted as a Knight of Es-Soh-En. This title refers to an event which took place on the Mountain of the Sky while David was on the Quest for the Sword. Es-Soh-En was teaching the party about trust by carrying them over a vast chasm on His back. David asked Es-Soh-En for the opportunity to walk across the chasm on the air. Es-Soh-En granted the request, and David began to walk. David did not feel as if he had reached the edge of the ground he had been on, and took his eyes off of Es-Soh-En to look down. When he did, he discovered he was already half-way across the chasm. He lost his faith, and began to fall. Es-Soh-En leaped into the chasm, caught David, and carried him to join the others. When Es-Soh-En was listing David's various titles during his knighting, Es-Soh-En added the title of "Air Walker" to commemorate the event.

BAND OF BETROTHAL – A special band a husband-to-be gives to his wife-to-be as a promise of the intention to wed. The band of betrothal given by Teacher to Queen Dianna depicted a heart pierced from behind by a sword to illustrate the price He paid to redeem her.

BARRIS – One of the twin moons of the Lands of the Adoni. Its name comes from Dulan mythology which told how the night was actually husband and wife, and their child was the morning sun. Barris is the husband of the legend.

BAT THING – There are two kinds of creatures which bear this title. They appear to be of the same species, but have different characteristics. The more common species is a large man-like creature that lives in the Forest of Venra and has great leather wings. According to legends, they were once a race of bird creatures, but through a deal with Cronis were transformed into their current form. This species is brutish, with no real power of thought or consciousness. They attack anything that comes into their territory. If anyone is cut or bitten by one of these creatures, and the skin is broken, a deadly disease gets into the bloodstream. If untreated, the disease will produce a coma and then death. The second species is identical to the first other than its size is bigger, the eyes glow red as a sign of their service to Cronis, and they have some limited intelligence. This second species is not actually of the Lands of the Adoni, but came from the world beyond when Cronis gained partial claim to the title deed to the Lands of the Adoni. This second species has difficulty functioning in bright light because it has lived all of its life in darkness. It makes its home in the Veil of Darkness. This second species which serves Cronis is also known as a shadow thing or demon thing/creature.

BATTLE OF ES-SOH-EN, THE – This is the name given to the confrontation between Es-Soh-En and Cronis for the purpose of determining ownership of the title deed to the Lands of the Adoni. The confrontation was first promised to Ish and Issha when they were expelled from the Garden of Tangar. The actual Battle of Es-Soh-En took place many centuries later. Instead of Es-Soh-En actually being the one to confront Cronis, Es-Soh-En had to set aside all of His power and authority as one of the Adoni. In order to do this, He incarnated, being born human, raised human, and then complied with all the laws governing the Battle of Es-Soh-En. Those of the Lands of the Adoni did not recognize the confrontation as the Battle of Es-Soh-En at first because in His human incarnation Es-Soh-En went by the name *Teacher*. The battle took place in the Veil of Darkness. At the time of the Battle of Es-Soh-En the power of Cronis was broken, and the title deed restored to the Adoni when Cronis broke one of the laws of the Battle, by using Logos to strike Teacher down from behind, killing Him.

BAY OF MAGAR – This is a natural bay on the Great Sea in the kingdom of Magar. It is the main port for Magar, and from time-to-time the navy of Magar is docked here.

BEECH – One of the talking mice of Dula. He was a boyhood friend of Hentery and nearly died as a young mouse when tunnels they were playing in collapsed. Hentery went back in, and risked his life to save his friend. After the rescue, Beech vowed to spend his entire life repaying the debt. Hentery tried to discourage Beech from this and to have a life of his own; but after several years, Hentery finally gave up, and let Beech be with him the rest of his life.

BENDORA – A Tree Druid who set down roots in the Forest of Venra and came to be part of the Grove of Three Oaks. Before he *plant*ed, he traveled all over the Lands of the Adoni collecting samples of plants with healing properties. While he traveled, he met David and Tanya the Children of Earth. From them he learned a great deal about plant lore, and the proper use of plants, roots, leaves, and herbs to treat wounds or illnesses. Bendora is attributed for taking scarce and rare healing plants, and spreading their seeds and cuttings throughout all the Lands of the Adoni so they would be available when and where they were needed.

BENTAR – According to Dula tradition, only the greatest of swords are given scabbards with names of their own. Such was the case with Gennerroth the sword given to David at the time he was made a Knight of Es-Soh-En by Es-Soh-En on the Mountain of the Sky. Bentar is the scabbard for Gennerroth. Where the name *Gennerroth* is from the Old Dulan tongue meaning *He who is worthy*, *Bentar* is from the same tongue, but means *One who is redeemed*.

BLACK HEART(S) – A caste of warriors in Magar. They are the most sadistic and cruel of all of Magar's forces. They used torture and slow death as a form of entertainment, and they are feared by those inside Magar as well as outside. Inside this caste is an elite sub-caste called the Blood Troops which protect the royal family of Magar. This sect obtained their name because in order to show their dedication to Cronis and the royal family of Magar they would kill their first-born child by slow torture, and then use the child's blood to paint the image of the demon-god on their shields.

BLADOE – A strong narcotic which when absorbed by the body makes the user unable to focus their thoughts, remember basic information or control voluntary motor activities. It does not affect involuntary motor activity. If taken in strong enough doses, it can create a forced coma.

BREATH OF THE ADONI, THE – A weather phenomena that occurred when Lady Tanya took her forces to Janadis during the winter months after the death of Sir David. The air currents controlled the ships in her fleet, bringing them to the right location at the right time. When the ships needed to stop, they came to rest due to a sudden lack of breeze. When they needed to speed up; the wind velocity increased. When a course correction was needed, the winds shifted. The winds even moved one ship while not moving others which were not ready to sail. The Child of Earth attributed this strange weather activity to the control of the Adoni, and thus the occurrence was called *the Breath of the Adoni*. (Note: if the reference is not to the escape by Lady Tanya from Dula to Janadis, then it is in reference to a golden mist/fog which is created by the Adoni to accomplish miracles or empower their followers). (Also see *Golden Mist*).

BRIG GEN – A gnome of the Gen Family. He was alive at the time Queen Dianna went on the Quest for the Sword. He was one of the factions which stayed behind to guard Dula while the Queen was on her quest. He was known for his stubborn nature, short temper, and his complete lack of faith in anything he could not touch or see. This made it difficult for him to believe in, or trust the Adoni. During a failed rescue attempt, his party was trapped by the Moving Trees, and Glidon came to rescue the party. This was the turning point for the gnome. He came to be a great warrior, and was the first of his race to write poetry. His later years were marked by his extreme devotion to the Adoni.

BRILL LEAF – a short tree whose leaves released a soothing fragrance, and would calm anyone who drank it in a warm mixture. Some people would add honey while others drank it straight. It was reported to have healing properties.

BROMOR – One of six kingdoms which make up the Lands of the Adoni [Dula, Magar, Orpha, Bromor, Janadis and the Cantile Islands]. It is the southern-most kingdom. It has three main points of historical reference. These are: the Valley of Seven Forest, the Lightning's Scar, and the Grey Castle of Bromor. While Dula remained faithful to the Adoni while all others turned away, Bromor was the one kingdom that, although professing a belief in the Adoni, sought only to use the name of the Adoni to lay legal claim to the throne of Dula.

BROMOR DELTA – An area along the southern coast of Bromor which has a natural harbor used as a port by both Bromor and Orpha.

CANTILE ISLANDS – One of the kingdoms of the Lands of the Adoni [Dula, Magar, Orpha, Bromor, Janadis and the Cantile Islands]. A large island in the northern section of the Great Sea, and several smaller islands which surround the main island. It is known for its mountains and fields which are ideal for raising herds or flocks. Because it was not part of the main continent, it has been spared from most of the wars which beset the Lands of the Adoni. Due to a lack of ocean skills or strong ocean crafts, the Cantile Islands went undiscovered for several centuries. As it took a certain amount of skill to navigate the northern waters, few ever traveled there, and so the population was very sparse. Since its location could serve no strategic position for any kingdom, it was all but ignored in any aggressions, and later it was declared a neutral country, and pretty much left to its own. It was to this island that David fled when he had committed an act of disobedience to the Adoni. It is the home of Kya.

CAVE OF WHISPERS, THE – A cave where Pentra the Greater was directed to when Es-Soh-En called him to serve as a Knight of Es-Soh-En. During the Quest for the Sword, its location was revealed to Queen Dianna by the Adoni, and it became a base of operations for the resistance during the Magar occupation.

CENTAURS – One of the races in the Lands of the Adoni. They are half-human and half-horse. They have the body of a horse which actually is an entire horse's body except for the neck and head. However, they have the body of a human from the waist up where the horse's neck normally is located. This gives the centaur four legs and two hands. They were created by Tanya when she sang the Lesser Song, in the Garden of Tangar with Glidon. After Ish and Issha broke the Law of the Adoni, the centaur race denied sanctuary to the First Father and First Mother. When Cronis sent a Demon Cloud after the couple for the purpose of killing them both, the centaur was one of two races that refused to help. Tanya shamed and disowned both races before she went to battle with the Demon Cloud. This shame prompted both races to dedicate their entire lives to becoming warriors worthy of Tanya's praise. They are skilled with the bow, and the war bow of the centaurs also serves as a double-edged, double-bladed sword. As a test for man-hood, young centaurs must capture a fire bird, and use its flame-proof feathers as fletching for their first quiver of arrows. Once man-hood is bestowed upon a young centaur in this fashion, the status cannot be taken away. In earlier generations, growth of a beard was another sign of man-hood, and to shame those of the race who would not fight, those being shamed would be forced to keep their face clean-shaven. After Tra endured the shaming, and while still shamed became one of their greatest warriors, the lack of a beard no longer brought shame to a centaur.

CHAMBER OF AGES, THE – This is a vast room in the palace of Janadis the undersea city. Because the city was beneath the ocean, and trees were not plenteous to use for paper manufacturing, the artists of Janadis sought other forms of artistic expression which did not involve canvas or paper. One such technique was the creation of murals to decorate walls in homes and public buildings. In the palace, the king and queen had commissioned artists throughout the ages to create murals made of precious stones and metal to adorn the walls of the largest chamber in the palace. The theme of these murals was to be great moments in history which showed the unity of Janadis with Dula. Along the upper section of the wall in the Chamber of Ages is carved these words: *United in History, United in Destiny.* The kings and queens sought to represent this philosophy in their decorating the palace. For this reason the murals depicted events involving the Adoni and the Children of Earth. Later, as more room was needed, an entire wing was opened up and decorated with newer murals. Both the original chamber and the new wing were referred to as the Chamber of Ages. One area which is separate from the other murals depicts the scenes from the Battle of Es-Soh-En. Although grouped with the others when referred to as the Chamber of Ages, it is also known separately as the Chamber of Battle.

CHAMBER OF RECORDS, THE – Although most cities or castles had a room which was referred to as a chamber of records or records chamber, this title specifically refers to the Chamber of Records in the palace of Dula. The reason for this is that it was the most complete collection of all records, documents, and historical facts in all the Lands of the Adoni. The reason why this collection of records was so vast and used by all the great scholars of the Lands of the Adoni was that the royal line of Dula had to keep careful records of their lineage to prove their right to ascend the throne. When Queen Dianna was given Unending

Life by the Adoni, she continued the practice. However, instead of collecting data to prove her divine right to rule, she sought news items which would help prove that one day Teacher would return as the Rightful King of Dula.

CHILDREN OF EARTH, THE – This is a title given to David and his sister, Tanya. These are two people who have been transported by the Adoni from Earth into the Lands of the Adoni at various points in the history of this world. When first brought to Dula, David and Tanya thought the reference was to their age as they were not yet legal adults in their world. At the creation of the Lands of the Adoni, David discovered that the title actually refers to the fact that David and Tanya's race was formed of the earth. For this reason, David and Tanya had no problems with the people of the Lands of the Adoni referring to them by this title, even though they were later fully-grown adults. The title used collectively refers to the brother and sister together. The title used singularly (Child of Earth) can refer to either David or Tanya depending upon the reference.

CLAN OF SWORDKEEPERS, THE – (See Swordkeepers Clan)

CLAN OF TRA, THE – Although Tra was a member of the Swordkeepers Clan, he also created a separate clan for centaurs which provided other centaurs the opportunity to serve the Adoni without becoming warriors. By the time of the Return of the Adoni, this clan had risen to honor among the other centaur clans, and actually became the leading clan with members setting aside the non-violence criteria of the clan, and going into battle for the Adoni. This clan kept their faces clean shaven.

CO-LIN, THE HEALER – Co-lin is one of a profession called *healers*. His skill was in illnesses and injuries to the head and mind. His personal hobby was the study of body language to see what the person was actually saying when they spoke. He was a long-time follower of the Adoni, but his close association with the study of the mind made him an extremely practical thinker. For this reason, even though he believed in and followed the Adoni, he had difficulty with those teachings concerning the Adoni where the natural order was set aside, and the supernatural took over. He had spent long years serving Queen Dianna as healer, counselor, and friend. It was his skill which gave Tanya information she needed to resist Gib-ron, and it was his quick thinking which helped other followers of the Adoni escape Dula.

COUNCIL, THE – This is not to be confused with the Council of Ancients. Where the Council of Ancients was a gathering of great minds to gather more knowledge, the Council at the time of the Return of the Adoni was a governing body in Dula. It had initially been a single post in the castle – the Post of Protocol – that counseled royalty and the kingdom on customs and traditions of other races. It grew into a counsel of experts who could counsel the king and queen on matters of importance to the kingdom. During the years after the Battle of Es-Soh-En, the people sought greater self-rule, and Queen Dianna granted this to her people. Over the years it was abused, and a Council was created of various city leaders to address the special interests of factions in the kingdom. Through abuse of the rights Queen Dianna had granted to the people, the Council eventually took away most of her power. Once her power was weakened, the Council then led the kingdom in a direction away from the worship of the Adoni and more for the gathering of wealth and power.

CRONIS – Cronis is known by many titles both in and outside of the Lands of the Adoni. Although scholars believed
he was equal to the Adoni it was revealed that he was only a
created being. Another misconception is that he is exclusive
to the Lands of the Adoni. The Adoni revealed to the Children of Earth that Cronis once led the praises to the Adoni
in the Kingdom of the Adoni. After thousands of centuries,
he sought to rebel, and claim the throne for himself. He is
credited with recruiting to his cause over a third of the hosts
who served the Adoni in the Kingdom of the Adoni. A great
war broke out in the Kingdom of the Adoni. After the initial
blow to knock Cronis back from the throne, the Adoni did not
take personal action in the war, but allowed Their followers to
defeat Cronis, and to banish Cronis and his followers from the
Kingdom. Cronis has sought to corrupt, steal, and destroy all
worlds created by the Adoni. Because he never met the Adoni
in personal combat, he always believed he was strong enough
to defeat the Adoni given the chance. The Battle of Es-Soh-
En provided Cronis with that opportunity, and it was shown
that even without the power and authority which is part of the
make up of the Adoni, Cronis was still doomed to lose. He used
lies and deception in the Lands of the Adoni to mislead Issha,
and through her to gain some legal claim to the title deed of
the Lands of the Adoni, even though the actual claim to the
title deed was in question. To resolve the issue of his claim
to the title deed, the Battle of Es-Soh-En was fought in the
Veil of Darkness, and the power of Cronis was broken when
he violated the rules of the Battle of Es-Soh-En and stabbed
Teacher from behind with Logos. At that time, judgment was
pronounced on Cronis, but it was suspended to allow the seeds
of rebellion he had planted to take root, grow, and produce the
actual fruit of rebellion. Those of the Lands of the Adoni have

been cautioned not to speak the actual name of Cronis as use of his name can sometimes give him power over the one speaking the name. For this reason titles are used to refer to Cronis. Some of these titles are: The Dark One, The Dark Lord, The Evil One and The Demon-god. Although banished from the Kingdom of the Adoni for his rebellion, Cronis is permitted to return from time to time to present legal arguments as a way of gaining additional power or authority.

CRYSTAL EYE, THE – This refers to a clear, round sphere made of polished crystal. In and of itself, it is little more than a ball of glass, but it has been associated with the worship of Cronis. It is not the sphere, but the mentality and attitudes of those using the crystal eye which opens them up to direct control and influence of Cronis. For this reason, its use is banned by the Words of the Ancient, and those using this device are to be sentenced to death. The ball is a focus point where those using it open their minds to any outside influence. Cronis and his servants are always seeking such subjects, and will inhabit the minds and bodies of such users. The ball acts as a connection for Cronis and his followers to enter the Lands of the Adoni, and so although the crystal eye is nothing more than glass, Cronis draws the minds which are opened to him into the ball, and uses his influence over them. The more a person uses the ball, the greater the influence Cronis can exert. Because Cronis draws the mind into the ball to exert his influence, if the ball is shattered or damaged while the user is in mental contact with the crystal eye, it can cause damage and even death. The information obtained from such a joining with Cronis and his followers through the crystal eyes is not always accurate, and in some case is intentionally misleading. There is only enough truth presented by Cronis and his followers to the user of the crystal eye to entrap the user and encourage future use. The crystal eye is known by other titles. They are: the Seeing Eye and the Eye of Cronis.

CURSE, THE – This is a title to refer to judgment the Adoni passed on the Lands of the Adoni because of an abuse in using Logos the Talking Sword. The Talking Sword would sing songs of praise to the Adoni for various events such as the sunrise, sunset, rainfall, harvest, etc. When the Sword was not singing the songs of praise to the Adoni, it was available to answer any questions someone may have. Asseem created a Council of Ancients that was made up of the wisest men in all the Lands of the Adoni, and they took turns asking questions about their areas of expertise when the Sword was not singing. It was during the Song of Morning that one of the members of the Council of Ancients grew impatient, and sought to distract the Sword from its song of praise in order to obtain an answer to his question. He demanded that the Sword answer the question *in the name of the Adoni*. The Song of Morning stopped abruptly, in mid-sentence; and the voice of the Unnamed Adoni spoke. The Unnamed Adoni rebuked the Ancient for using His name to deny Him the honor due the Adoni. Because the Council of Ancients sought the voice of the Sword instead of the Adoni, the Sword would continue to sing it's praises as before, but all the ears in all the Lands of the Adoni would forever be deaf to the sound of the Sword's voice. Only David and Tanya, the Children of Earth, could still hear the voice of the Sword since they came from Earth and not the Lands of the Adoni. After the Quest for the Sword, Tra and Kal had the Curse lifted from their ears. It was the fact that the Ancients had made knowledge their true god, and this idolatry brought about the Curse, that the Lands of the Adoni never progressed beyond the Medieval Ages in technology. Whenever someone produced some new technology, he or she was attacked by the people fearing an even greater Curse. Thus people with new ideas gave up seeking technology, and as a result, the Lands of the Adoni remained at the level of technology it had when the Curse was pronounced even until the Return of the Adoni.

DANCE OF DEATH, THE – A strategy used by the Knights of Es-Soh-En when they know that escape or survival is no longer an option. They spin, dive, swing and give up all attempts to protect themselves, but to inflict as much death and damage to their foes before they fall.

DANCER IN/OF THE GARDEN OF TANGAR – This is a title bestowed upon Lady Tanya. The title commemorates the fact that she was the first to dance in the Garden of Tangar during the creation of the Lands of the Adoni. With Glidon empowering her as they both sang the Lesser Song, whatever Lady Tanya touched in her dance came to life. This is how the centaurs, minotaurs, gnomes and tree druids were created.

DARK LORD, THE – (See Cronis)

DARK ONE, THE – (See Cronis)

DARK WOODS, THE – This is the previous name for the Gen Forest. When the Demon Cloud failed in its attempt to kill Ish and Issha, and was wounded by its battle with Lendara, it came back to the place where it had entered the Lands of the Adoni. The opening between worlds was closed by the Adoni, and so it used its ability to join with plant life and become part of the forest for its own protection. Unfortunately, the cloud creature was so weakened by its battle with Lendara it could no longer separate itself from the plants, and so this area of woods was always influenced by the cloud creature's personality. Because of the sacrifice of Lendara, the forces of Cronis could only affect humans or other races which had close ties to humans. Because of this, humans would not settle in the Dark Woods, and so it became home to the gnomes, centaurs, minotaurs, and Water People. After the Quest for the Sword, Es-Soh-En drove the evil out of the Dark Woods as a reward to the Gen family of gnomes, and set them up as the ruling family of the gnome community. At that time the Dark Woods came to be known as the Gen Forest.

DAVID JAMES – One of the two Children of Earth. He is brother to Tanya. Together he and his sister were drawn from Earth into the Lands of the Adoni, at various points in its history to provide some service to the Adoni. He was granted several titles by the Adoni during the Quest for the Sword. Among these titles were: Knight of Es-Soh-En, Friend of the Unicorn, Steward of the Throne of Dula. When he asked to walk on the air between two cliffs on the Mountain of the Sky, he made it half-way across before taking his eyes off of Es-Soh-En and falling. Es-Soh-En caught him, and returned him to the other side of the chasm. At his knighting, Es-Soh-En also granted him the title of *Air Walker*. David James is also addressed as David, Sir David, and on some occasions with those close to him, D.J.. He is also the only one other than the unicorn who knows *The Secret of the Unicorn*. He is *herd brother* to the unicorn and is joined to them mentally.

DAVID'S PERCH – A section of the western wall of the palace of Dula which was given this name because this is where Sir David waited for Teacher to return from the Veil of Darkness.

As he came here often to meditate, it came to be called David's Perch. Farmers in the surrounding area would send messengers to inquire if the Children of Earth had returned if they ever saw anyone standing for any length of time on this section of the wall.

DAYTON – Last of the line of Trayton. It was to his family that the Eye of Suma had been given. Dayton was grateful to Tanya for freeing him and his family from the dungeon where Ki-el had been torturing them trying to learn the location of the Eye of Suma. To show his gratitude, he had the Eye of Suma mounted in an oval shield which had the image of Glidon etched onto its face. His family presented the eagle shield to Tanya and her brother David at a feast of thanksgiving in Dula.

DEENARA – A unicorn of the Kingdom of the Adoni. One of the Untarnished. At the death of Lendara Deenara was named as Steward of the Unicorns to serve in Lendara's stead. Over the centuries he served to guide the herd as Lendara desired. He was joined with Lendara at the moment of Lendara's death, so his mind was in constant contact with Lendara even though Lendara was already in the Kingdom of the Adoni. He was also the *second* for Lendara in the battle with the Demon Cloud which had come to kill Ish and Issha. Had the Demon Cloud not fled, Deenara was ready to sacrifice his life to save Ish and Issha, the same as Lendara had already done.

DEMON CLOUD – At the Fall of the Lands of the Adoni under the control of Cronis, one of the demon things had managed to enter the Lands of the Adoni through a small portal in the north. The other demon things still trapped outside of the Lands of the Adoni sent their strength and mass through the portal to the Demon Thing. This caused the demon thing to continue to increase in size until it became a Demon Cloud. Cronis sent this to kill Ish and Issha before the issue over the title deed to the Lands of the Adoni could be resolved. The Demon Cloud trapped Ish and Issha on one side of the River of Warning. Lendara, the king of the unicorns, warned the Demon Cloud to leave or die. When it chose to attack, Lendara send lightning into the heavily charged sky and used his horn to draw it down as a lightning bolt hundreds of times more powerful. The lightning killed Lendara, shredded the Demon Cloud and created the Lightning's Scar. What was left of the Demon Cloud returned to the portal to escape; but could not. It then joined with the plants around it creating the Dark Woods. The intelligence of the Demon Cloud floated off into the sea and many generations later revived enough to steal mass from other demon things to heal itself and replace what had been lost in the battle with Lendara. It had developed an ability to draw light from the sky to gain strength. In a battle with Cronis, this ability was discovered, and Cronis used the Demon Cloud to create the Veil of Darkness. The last of the Demon Cloud died when it battled Pentra in the Ring of Fire inside the Veil of Darkness.

DEMON GOD, THE – See Cronis

DEMON CREATURE/DEMON THING – Also known as Shadow Thing, Shadow Creature or Bat Thing. [See Bat Thing]

DIANNA, QUEEN – Last of the royal family of Dula. She had lost her throne to Dragnock when vital papers which could prove her lineage and right to rule were lost in a fire. Dragnock came forward with his documentation, and Dianna was forced to abdicate the throne to him. In order to prove she was the rightful Queen of Dula, she announced she was going on a quest to recover the long-lost Logos the Talking Sword. Dragnock ordered Dianna tied to a tree throughout the night as a test to see if the Adoni had blessed her quest. Although Dragnock had intended on killing Dianna during the night, Es-Soh-En gave His approval to the quest by sending the Children of Earth to free her. Dianna then went on her quest, and recovered the lost Sword. She returned to Dula, and reclaimed her throne. At the end of the Quest for the Sword, Dianna was given the Gift of Unending Life. Over the two hundred years after the Quest for the Sword, she came to be a target of Cronis who finally convinced her that she could hear the voice of the Sword. Through lies, Cronis took control of Dianna. When Teacher came to be tested as the Rightful King of Dula, Dianna was completely under the influence of Cronis. In order to break the control Cronis had on Dianna, Teacher went into the Veil of Darkness, and took part in the Battle of Es-Soh-En. Teacher returned Logos to Dianna, but she was not yet ready to set it, or all that it stood for, aside. Teacher and Dianna performed the Ceremony of Betrothal announcing their intention to marry. Teacher then left to await the time when Dianna would be ready to be His bride.

DIG GEN – One of the four gnome brothers who sided with Queen Dianna at the time of the Quest for the Sword. He is the third youngest of the gnome brothers in the Gen Family of gnomes. He was first known for his lack of skill with the sword, and was constantly afraid of dying. He was one of the two gnomes who actually went on the Quest for the Sword. Their adventures took them through the Valley of Seven Forests where Dig Gen was the first and only gnome to ever kill a demon plant. While protecting Queen Dianna from bat creatures, he was inflicted with a fatal disease and died. He was returned from the dead by

Es-Soh-En and made a Knight of Es-Soh-En. At the end of the Quest for the Sword, he was named to the Sword-Keepers clan. He was the last of the Sword-Keepers clan, and the only member who did not have the ability to hear the voice of Logos. Queen Dianna, beginning to fall under the influence of Cronis, spread rumors that he had not actually died on the Quest for the Sword, nor had he actually been made a Knight of Es-Soh-En. She used the rumors to take back the Sword from the Sword-Keepers clan. Dig Gen continued his vigil in front of the palace, and eventually died of a broken heart. At the Battle of Es-Soh-En when Dianna was freed of the influence of Cronis she repented of her actions, and restored the honor due Dig Gen. Because of his courage in battle, even though he was fighting his own fear of dying, Es-Soh-En gave him the title *Knight Without Fear* at the time Dig Gen was knighted as a Knight of Es-Soh-En.

DOCUMENTS OF HERITAGE – Whenever a member of the Royal Family is born, a special scroll is created. This scroll would contain copies of his/her lineage. It would be a complex family tree showing ancestors, siblings and children. It was passed down from one generation to the next and an official notary would document that the information was true and correct by examining the original document presented to him at the time of the child's birth and taking testimony of the child's parent or guardian. Once the parent passed away, the eldest child could keep his/her copy of the document, or claim the parent's documents as their own after paying a notary to document the transfer of ownership. These were used to trace the family lineage should a title be called into question.

DRAGNOCK – Known as *Dragnock the Usurper* for his actions in trying to steal the throne of Dula. He was a distant member of the royal family of Dula, but had been raised in Orpha because his family was in disgrace at the court. When he grew to manhood, he arranged for a fire to destroy the documents Queen Dianna needed to prove her lineage and her claim to the throne. He then declared a challenge to the right of leadership, presented his own documents, and forced Queen Dianna off the throne. When she voiced her intention to seek Logos to prove her right to rule, Dragnock set up a test designed to give him the opportunity to have her killed. When this failed, and Dianna went on the Quest for the Sword, he made a pact with Magar to declare war against them, and then surrender so that they controlled Dula, and would allow him to continue as its ruler even if Dianna did return with the Sword. Those loyal to Dianna rose up in rebellion led by Kal and Glidon, and drove Dragnock from the throne, and Magar from the kingdom. Dragnock returned with a greater army to seize the throne by force when Dianna returned. Dragnock, and all the army of Magar with him, were destroyed when Es-Soh-En passed judgment on them, and they all burst into flames. His name, even at the time of the Return of the Adoni was used as another name for *traitor*.

DRAGON'S TEETH – A name for a row of mountains in Southern Magar. They got their name because all were volcanoes, most inactive, but some still belched fire and smoke. The broken craters of the mountains looked like a row of sharp teeth, and the fire gave the impression of a dragon breathing fire.

DULA – One of the kingdoms in the Lands of the Adoni [Dula, Magar, Orpha, Bromor, Janadis and the Cantile Islands]. It was chosen as the ruling kingdom of all the Lands of the Adoni when the people could still hear the voice of Logos the Talking Sword. When the Curse came upon the Lands of the Adoni, other kingdoms broke away, forsaking the worship of the Adoni. It was through this kingdom that Es-Soh-En came to establish Himself as the Rightful King, not only of Dula, but of all the Lands of the Adoni. Dula, and its sister kingdom Janadis were the only kingdoms to remain loyal to the Adoni. It is the north-western kingdom of the Lands of the Adoni.

DULAN ALPS – A mountain range which creates a natural boarder between Dula and Magar. It is at the southern end of this mountain range that the Mountain of the Sky is located.

EL-TON – Servant in the palace of Dula. He was sent to the edge of the Veil of Darkness to inform David that Lady Tanya had been injured in the records chamber. He was not a strong follower of the Adoni, and so did not escape when Tanya led the others to freedom. It is reported that he died when Magar and its allies attacked Dula in her absence.

ES-SOH-EN – Title for the second member of the Adoni. His form is described as a great black lion, with golden mane, and topaz blue eyes. Although He appears to be a black lion, the actual name of the creature He resembles is called a Hobber. He is the only one of His kind. His name in the Lands of the Adoni came from a misunderstanding between David and Ish. David sought to explain the difference between the *sun* up in the sky, and a *son* who is born. To show the difference, David spelled both words. When he spelled *S-O-N*, Ish accepted that as the name for Es-Soh-En. Es-Soh-En is also referred to as the Great Hobber, the Son of the Adoni, and the Creator of the Lands of the Adoni. In order to fulfill the requirements of the Law, and an agreement between Es-Soh-En and Cronis to resolve a dispute over the title deed to the Lands of the Adoni, Es-

Soh-En agreed to set aside His power and authority, and meet Cronis in the form of a human man. To accomplish this, Es-Soh-En was physically born as a human, grew to manhood, and presented Himself to Queen Dianna for testing to prove that He was the Rightful King. While as a human His title was Teacher. It was Teacher who fought Cronis in the Battle of Es-Soh-En in the Veil of Darkness. Although Es-Soh-En is now human, and Teacher is His true form, using the Power of the Adoni He transforms Himself back into the Great Hobber when going into battle as this previous form is better designed for combat.

ES-TRA – Greeting in the centaur battle language. The battle language of the centaur is designed to take minimal sounds of a phrase and condense it down. The full phrase here is: *May the peace of Tra's Es-Soh-En be with you.* In the battle language it uses the first syllable of Es-Soh-En and the name of Tra to form the term Es-Tra.

EYE OF CRONIS, THE – Another name for a crystal eye or seeing eye. [See Crystal Eye]

EYE OF SUMA, THE – The name given to one of the twin blue jewels which served as eyes for the figure head on the sky ship Suma. At the time of the Battle of Es-Soh-En, Teacher presented one of the jewels to Trayton in order to pay his debt for accidentally killing his neighbor, Giban. Queen Dianna sought to obtain the jewel, but Teacher had placed a curse on the stone to protect it from being stolen. The only way the ownership could be transferred was a voluntary and intentional transferring of the jewel to another. If the stone was taken by force, duress, treachery or threat; the new owner would be punished until the jewel was returned to the rightful owner. Trayton kept the jewel in his family for generations. The last of Trayton's line was Dayton, and before the final battle for Dula had the jewel used to create an eagle shield which was presented to the Children of Earth at a feast of thanksgiving.

FALL, THE – This is a reference to the disobedience of Ish and Issha. After the creation of the Lands of the Adoni, Ish and Issha were declared the First Father and First Mother of this world. They were also the King and Queen of all the Lands of the Adoni. When creation was complete, and all societies ready to begin; Es-Soh-En gathered all the races together to recognize Ish and Issha as the rightful rulers of all creation. He declared that they held the title deed to all the Lands of the Adoni. With the transferring of the title deed from Es-Soh-En as the Creator to Ish and Issha, Es-Soh-En set down several Laws to guide the races in their conduct with the Adoni, and their conduct with each other. The primary of these Laws was that *the Adoni are Three, the Three are One.* Secondary in this Law was that the Unnamed Adoni was so great and so powerful that no name or form could ever do Him justice. For this reason no name or titles were to be assigned to Him, and He was to remain known simply as the Unnamed Adoni. Cronis began to weave a web of lies and misrepresentations, first with Issha, and then later using her influence, with Ish. Cronis convinced them that it was possible to know the Unnamed Adoni's name, and that knowing His name would give them power over the Adoni. He convinced them that Es-Soh-En had been lying when He gave them the Law. Finally, Ish and Issha challenged Es-Soh-En, ordered all their subjects to call on the true name of the Unnamed Adoni, and then spoke the name of Cronis. To further add to their rebellion, Ish and Issha transferred the title deed of their world into the hands of Cronis. Es-Soh-En was able to provide some protection to Ish and Issha, and the Lands of the Adoni through a clause He added with their permission to the transferal of the title deed. Later He kept Cronis from personally killing Ish and Issha as was his right. When Lendara gave his life to save Ish and Issha from a Demon Cloud Cronis had sent to kill Ish and Issha, Cronis' power was further limited. Es-Soh-En convinced the Unnamed Adoni that the title deed could not be transferred through deceit since it was the intent of Ish and Issha to return the title deed to the Unnamed Adoni, and Cronis had misinformed them concerning the proper name. As there was dispute over the ownership, and transferal of the title deed, the issue was suspended until the dispute could be resolved. The resolution of the dispute was to come at the Battle of Es-Soh-En. The transferal of the title deed from Ish and Issha to Cronis, and then the suspension of the title deed were called the *Fall* by the inhabitants of the Lands of the Adoni. The loss of the idyllic kingdom established by Es-Soh-En for Ish and Issha is also referred to as the Fall by the inhabitants of the Lands of the Adoni. In the later days before the Return of the Adoni, the inhabitants of most kingdoms, and even some in the kingdom of Dula questioned if there ever was such a Fall, or the need for the Battle of Es-Soh-En. In Dula, the presence of Queen Dianna who had been present at the Battle of Es-Soh-En, made it difficult for those trying to dismiss both the Fall and the Battle of Es-Soh-En to gain much credibility. Those who believed and taught the Fall, identified it as the time period from the meeting in which Ish and Issha ordered their subjects to called on Cronis as the Unnamed Adoni, to the point where Es-Soh-En presented Logos to Ish and Issha as the actual "Fall."

FEAST OF THE SWORD, THE – A yearly celebration established by Es-Soh-En to commemorate the return of Logos at the end of the Quest for the Sword It was to be a feast where all were fed freely, and wares given without cost to celebrate the establishment of Queen Dianna's throne by her presenting Logos to the kingdom as a sign of her divine right to rule.

FEL DOR – During one of the early visits to Dula, David James spent several years among the gnomes. He was befriended by Fel Dor, of the Dor family of gnomes. Under Fel Dor's guidance, David James was educated in all the ways of the gnomes, and taught their greatest secrets and lore. Fel Dor was later captured by Magar, but gave his life to expose an invasion attempt. He is honored as one of the great warriors of the gnome community. David said of him, "If he had lived, he would have been worthy to be a Knight of Es-Soh-En."

FENRA – One of the twin moons of the Lands of the Adoni. According to mythology, the pair was looked upon as a couple. Each morning they gave birth to their child, the sun. Fenra was the wife in the myth.

FEN-TON – Member of the Council at the time of the Return of the Adoni. He was the head of the farmer's guild, and spoke out against Gib-ron and his recommended use of the Crystal Eye. He was later killed in the siege of Dula by Magar and its allies.

FIBBERGEE – A talking mouse at the time of the Quest for the Sword. He was known for his elaborate spy network, and information gathering skills which aided the underground resistance during the occupation of Magar. His service to Queen Dianna brought him recognition at the court, and he was made the royal messenger. The title was transferred down from generation to generation. The last of Fibbergee's line was Hentery who served at the time of the Return of the Adoni.

FIN DEN – One of two leaders of the gnomish community at the time of the Return of the Adoni. He had a twin brother named Wil Den. According to gnomish law, the eldest of the clan was to lead the entire community. The age of a gnome was determined by the date of the birth, and the hour of the birth. Gnomish law did not allow for any further distinction to determine age. As Fen Den and Wil Den were born on the same day, and during the same hour, they shared leadership of the clan, and the community.

FIRST MOTHER – This term is normally in reference to Issha, however when spoken by either the minotaur, centaur, gnome, or Tree Druid community, it is actually a reference to Lady Tanya as she is seen as the mother of their races when she called them into creation through the singing of the Lesser Song, and the dancing in the Garden of Tangar.

FLENDA POD – A pod produced by the flenda plant. These pods are produced year round, but in small numbers per bush. While the pod is ripe, it is filled with a thick juice which is used to treat burns. The juice clings to the injured skin, and reduces pain, promotes skin regeneration, and restores vital nutrients which are lost due to exposure to heat. They normally grew only in Orpha, but due to the passion of Bendora the Tree Druid, they are now found in all Lands of the Adoni.

FLOTSAM – A young boy found on the beach outside a fishing village in Dula after a great storm on the Western Sea the night before. He did not know who he was. He grew up without family and was the first to discover the Western Sea had receded and vanished due to that battle between Cronis and the Shadow Thing. While on the Western Sea floor looking for valuables, he came across Ghandrah the king of the whales who had been wounded in the battle between Cronis and the Shadow Thing. He entrusted Flotsam to sing his death song to the whales. It was later discovered Flotsam was Prince Terra of Janadis who was believed drown when his ship went down in a storm.

FOLLOWER/THE FOLLOWING – A title which came into use at the time of the Quest for the Sword to identify those who followed the Adoni. The underground movement at that time identified those who followed the Adoni as a *follower*. The collection of all the followers was called the *Following*. When Teacher came to be recognized and accepted as the incarnation of Es-Soh-En, the term was also used to identify those who followed Teacher.

FOREST OF VENRA – The greatest forest in all the Lands of the Adoni was in the center of the land mass. A range of mountains cut through the forest and formed a natural border between Dula and Magar. The forest on the western side of the mountain range was in Dula, and was called either the Dark Woods or the Gen Forest. The portion of the forest on the eastern side of the mountain range was under Magar's domain, and called the Forest of Venra. The Forest of Venra is home to the bat things, and the Grove of Three Oaks.

FRIEND OF THE UNICORN – Title given to David at the creation of the Lands of the Adoni. When Es-Soh-En paused in the Song of Creation, just before the creation of Ish, a portal opened between the Lands of the Adoni and the Kingdom of the Adoni. Through this portal came the unicorn led by Lend-ara. The unicorns were constantly in contact with each other through a "bonding" of the minds and spirits. David was bonded with the herd, and could hear their thoughts, and speak with them at any time. This bonding gave David the title of Friend of the Unicorn since he was the only non-unicorn to be considered a member of the herd. At the Return of the Adoni, with the death of David, Deenara revealed the unicorns to humans for the first time since the Fall, and then bonded Lady Tanya to the herd, making her a Friend of the Unicorn.

GANDRA – Citizen of Janadis who came to present a message to Sir David during one of the early visits by the Children of Earth to the Lands of the Adoni. The message was to tell David that Lady Tanya was alright, and had survived an attack to her while she was visiting the undersea city of Janadis. Gandra had actually been the negotiator to try and work out the details of Tanya's release, but he was unable to meet the demands of the kidnappers before the deadline. David had come to believe that his sister had died at their hands, but Gandra arrived in the city to give the good news that Tanya was alive, though injured, while the kidnappers were either dead or completely disabled. Tanya had asked David to wait for her to recover, and then she would join him in Dula, but David and Gandra traveled to Janadis to meet her.

GANTRA – Tree Druid who came to "put down roots" in the Forest of Venra. He is one of the three Tree Druids who make up the Grove of Three Oaks. He is the youngest of the three, and spoke to Tanya when she arrived in the grove. He is also the one who spoke to Queen Dianna when she came there on the Quest for the Sword, and gave her instructions on how to treat the illness caused by wounds from the bat things. While still a young tree druid, and before putting down roots, Gantra traveled more widely than most Tree Druids throughout the Lands of the Adoni. Bendora held the record prior to Gantra due to his travels to find and plant healing plants throughout the Lands of the Adoni. He has a collection of tales which he enjoys sharing. For this reason he is prone to speak to visitors before the proper length of time has transpired in which a tree druid gets to know visitors before speaking to them. He excuses this rash behavior by saying that he still has "a little bit of itchy bark left."

GAR – Last minotaur born to the race before the Return of the Adoni. He was the son of Ren, the leader of the minotaurs, and his wife Zon. Ren had been forced to leave before the birth had taken place, and his birth was relayed to Ren by the unicorn.

GARDEN OF TANGAR – Area of land set aside by the Adoni as a place for Ish and Issha to live. It was different from all the other sections of the Lands of the Adoni in that every tree, plant, bush, and flower found in all the Lands of the Adoni were planted here. When Ish and Issha rebelled against the Adoni, it was sealed off, and no longer available to the First Father or First Mother.

GAYLORD – One of the talking horses of Dula. He was present in Dula at the time of the Quest for the Sword. Prior to the Quest for the Sword, Gaylord had traveled to Bromor where he was mistaken for a normal horse, and placed into service in the Bromorian cavalry. After years of serving as a war horse, he overheard plans to kill all the horses for food after a failed battle. That night he killed his rider, and fled to Dula. He arrived in Dula nearly dead, and was found by Kal who nursed the horse back to health, and taught him about the Adoni. As Gaylord had spent so many years not speaking to keep his identity safe, he now made up for the lost time by speaking with anybody and everybody about his love for the Adoni. He and his wife, Yeesha, were set aside by the Adoni for special service, and given long life to allow him to survive until their service to the Adoni was complete. He and Yeesha traveled into the Veil of Darkness at the time of the Battle of Es-Soh-En, and they became the Witnesses to the conflict. Both Gaylord and Yeesha gave their lives protecting Teacher's body in the Veil of Darkness from the attacks of Cronis. They were resurrected by Teacher, and transformed into the First of the Redeemed. Their transformation changed them into winged horses. Gaylord became the horse chosen to carry Teacher to His wedding with Queen Dianna.

GEN – According to gnomish tradition, the youngest in the clan is given just the clan name. Thus Gen was the youngest of the Gen clan of gnomes. When a new child is born into the clan, the gnome bearing the clan name selects his or her new name and announces it at the birthing ceremony. After the birthing ceremony, the now second youngest gnome is known and addressed by his or her new name, while the new-born is given only the clan name. Gen was one of four gnome brothers who served Queen Dianna at the time of the Quest for the Sword. He and his brother Dig Gen traveled with Queen Dianna on the actual quest. While on the quest, Gen fell in love with a Water Citizen named Leah. Their love was impractical as they were from different races. At the end of the Quest for the Sword, Es-Soh-En transformed them so they could marry and produce children. Gen was made human, and chose to retain the clan name, even though another was later born to the gnome clan. To avoid the confusion of names, the gnomes would refer to Gen as "Gen, the human gnome."

GEN FAMILY – One of the clans of the gnomes which inhabited the Gen Forest. Although all the clans supported Queen Dianna when her claim to the throne was challenged at the time of the Quest for the Sword, the Gen family sent their leaders to physically aid the queen. Because of the sacrifice and service of these four gnome brothers, Trig Gen was promoted to the head of the gnome community by Es-Soh-En. Many years later, at the time of the Battle of Es-Soh-En the Gen clan was split between those abusing the status, and those tired of leading the community. Eventually the Gen Family retired from active service in the community, and other families took turns as head of the community. The name of the Dark Woods was changed to the Gen Forest by Es-Soh-En to honor the Gen clan for their service.

GEN FOREST – Once known as the Dark Woods, it is the forest between Dula and the Dulan Alps. It serves as home for the gnome community, the centaur and minotaur camps, and the Water People community. Some farmers had tried to settle there, but farming never really developed, and so they moved on.

GEN WOOD – Wood from a tree grown only in the Gen Forest. It is cultivated for its fragrance that gives off several spices blended together. Although it is used in some building of the gnomes' homes, it is especially fragrant when burned. The gnomes promised Queen Dianna a supply of the wood for her fireplaces for as long as she sat on the throne. After she had gone to the Kingdom, the gnomes continued to provide the wood to Sir David and Lady Tanya as Lady Tanya was considered the First Mother of the race.

GENNERROTH – Sword given to Sir David when he was made a Knight of Es-Soh-En on the Mountain of the Sky by Es-Soh-En. It is an unbreakable Adoni blade, and the ball of its hilt has the carved image of Es-Soh-En. It was forged for Sir David by the craftsmen of the Kingdom of the Adoni, and its name means *One Who Is Chosen*. It was given a scabbard named Bentar. The name *Bentar* means *one who is redeemed*.

GHANDRAH – King of the Whales at the time of the Battle of the Veil. He was a free spirit and had not chosen a wife, nor produced an heir. He was deep in the Western Sea when the battle began between the Shadow Thing and the Dark Lord. He went to investigate and was fatally wounded by the energy bursts. He tried to make it to the shores of Dula to sound a warning, but the water evaporated too quickly, and he was stranded several miles off shore. There he met Flotsam, who learned his whale song, and went forth to share it with the whale community.

GIBAN – Rancher at the time of the Battle of Es-Soh-En. He was constantly using his neighbor's fields and crops to feed his livestock, and then denying it when Lydel confronted him. He was found dead from an arrow wound, and Lydel was accused of the murder. Teacher conducted an investigation as part of His testing to be the Rightful King of Dula. At the investigation, Teacher proved that Trayton, a different neighbor had caused Giban's death by accident while hunting for food. Queen Dianna ordered Teacher to pay the debt of Trayton, or go to prison in his place. In response, Teacher gave Trayton the Eye of Suma to pay off the debt the death had incurred.

GIB-RON – Member of the Council of Dula at the time of the Return of the Adoni. His family had been positioned in

Dula by Magar to spy for Magar. Gib-ron rose in status in the community, and became one of the leaders of the Council, but used his power to complete his own agenda to weaken Queen Dianna's power, and prepare the country for take-over by Magar. He became interested in the black arts which opened him to the influence of Cronis, and gave himself completely to Cronis in exchange for power. He was wounded by Tanya on two occasions. The first time she shattered his elbow, the second time she shattered the Crystal Eye while he was in contact with it. This resulted in his being blind in his right eye, and his right arm being limp and useless. Gib-ron rose to power in Dula through trickery, but when the Crystal Eye shattered, he was exposed, and driven out. He was driven into the Veil of Darkness where he further negotiated with Cronis for sanctuary, and while Cronis led his entire army against Dula for the final assault, Gib-ron remained behind in the Veil of Darkness. When Cronis' army was defeated at the Return of the Adoni, Gib-ron was transported from the Veil of Darkness to the site where Es-Soh-En held court over Cronis. Even though he tried to deny involvement with Cronis, he was cast out with Cronis and his followers.

GLIDON – The Great Eagle. The third member of the Adoni. It has traditionally been His role to watch over the followers of the Adoni and to intercede when help from the Adoni is needed. He took a much less active role in the affairs of the Lands of the Adoni after the disappearance of Queen Dianna. Once Tanya shattered the Crystal Eye used by Gib-ron, Glidon appeared physically to Lady Tanya, and took a more active role. He is the One who aided in the creation of the other races in the Lands of the Adoni when He inspired Tanya, and sang with her the Lesser Song.

GLIDONITES – At the time of the Return of the Adoni, this was a sect of the Following which believed that the Adoni were taking an active role in the affairs of the Lands of the Adoni. They held fast to the belief that Glidon, the Great Eagle, was still present in their lives, and working miracles. Because they focused on Glidon in all their teachings, they came to be known as *Glidonites*. Their teachings were met with such resistance, that they met with Queen Dianna, and obtained permission to move to Janadis where their teachings were more widely accepted. The movement of the Glidonites from Dula to Janadis is called the *Migration of the Glidonites*.

GOLDEN EAGLE, THE – Another term for Glidon. [See Glidon]

GOLDEN MIST, THE – Also known as *the Breath of the Adoni*; however, this is not in reference to the weather phenomena encountered by Lady Tanya when she took her followers to Janadis. This is in reference to a golden mist or fog which had been seen coming out of the mouth of Es-Soh-En and Glidon in order to work a miracle or empower a follower with the Power of the Adoni. It is also the same golden mist/fog which appears to transport Sir David and/or Lady Tanya from Earth to Dula.

GORT – A member of the Heart Company. One of the followers of Teacher who was arrested by Gib-ron. He escaped with Tanya and was the one who found books in Janadis discussing a possible answer to why everyone in Janadis had disappeared.

GNOMES – One of the races in the Lands of the Adoni. They were created when Tanya and Glidon sang the Lesser

Song at the creation of the Lands of the Adoni. Unlike gnomes of Earth, this race of gnomes is about three to four feet talk. They are tightly knit through family and clans. They make their home in the Gen Forest. Their homes are underground, using large tree trunks for doors, windows, passageways, and smoke stacks from the lower levels. They are skilled in wood crafts, legends, cooking, and wood working. A gnomish home will have the floors, walls, ceiling and furniture made through using songs to select the trees, cut the trees, and join the wood. The result is that the wood used in manufacturing the homes and furnishings vibrate and carry certain notes or sounds when those present sing, speak, or snore. When singing or music is present, the entire room will echo the songs. The sleeping chambers will respond to sounds as well, and an old gnomish proverb is: *A gnome who snores is truly blessed.* The gnomes are also the most meticulous in preserving and translating legends. The credibility of the gnomish community is of the highest caliber when it comes to the legends and stories they relate to others. Traditionally, the gnome men wear clothing which is natural colors and allow them to blend into the forest land-scape. They wear shirts with bell sleeves and wide collars, with a vest laced up in the front. The vest and shirt hang down to the top of the thighs. The men wear pants with turned-down knee-high boots. Each male gnome also wears a cap. Although the cap is traditionally pointed, it is made from soft material so that the point lies down on the head. Gnomes wear their hair long, normally about shoulder length, and it is a disgrace for a gnome to have short hair. Their skill in cooking is famous throughout the Lands of the Adoni, as they take great care, patience, and creativity in preparing even the simple meals of the gnome community. The Gen Family had the claim that their food was the cooking the Adoni praised. This was in response to a meal made by Brig Gen and Trig Gen, and served to the underground resistance during the occupation of Magar. As Glidon was present to prepare them to regain the throne of Dula, He ate the meal, and praised it as being as good as those served in the Kingdom.

GREAT EAGLE, THE – A reference to Glidon. [See Glidon]

GREAT SEA, THE – An ocean to the east of the Lands of the Adoni. It was called the Great Sea because early map makers believed that the Kingdom of the Adoni lay on the eastern shores. This belief led many to insist that the body of water, no matter how large, would be enclosed by land, and therefore, be a sea. Long after the name *the Great Sea* had been in common use, travelers claimed the Kingdom of the Adoni was not on the eastern shore, and that it was an actual ocean, and not a sea. By this time the use of the word "sea" was too firmly in use to change. It is under this ocean that Janadis was built.

GREATER KINGDOM, THE – See Kingdom of the Adoni.

GREY CASTLE, THE – Palace for the kingdom of Bromor. It was here that Logos the Talking Sword was hidden from the royal family of Dula when it was stolen by a thief. The thief came to the castle on his way to the Lightning's Scar to destroy the Sword, and free himself of the curse he had incurred in stealing the Sword. While at the Grey Castle, the king of Bromor switched the real Sword for a copy in their collection. The next day, they sent the thief on his way with a map which was designed to lead to his death in the Valley of Mist. The castle was designed by the royal family which was prone to murder, thefts, deceptions, and mistrust. For this reason the castle was a massive maze of hidden doors, passageways and traps built into the castle when it was first constructed.

GROVE OF THREE OAKS, THE – A grove in the Forest of Venra. It takes its name from the fact that three Tree Druids – all oaks – came to put down their roots here. The three Tree Druids are Wodin, who is the oldest of the three, came first and selected the best location. The second tree druid in age and second to come to the grove was Bendora. He brought with him a collection of seeds and cuttings from healing plants which he planted around him before putting down roots. The last to join was Gantra. He is the youngest, and has a tendency to speak to passer-bys before a proper length of time has passed to know the visitor.

HAN – Leader of the centaur race at the time of the Return of the Adoni. He took great pride in the fact that he could trace his ancestry all the way back to Tra, and is the first ancestor of Tra to rise to the head of his race.

HANDAR – a descendant of Gen. He was a young officer at the time of the Return of the Adoni. He had little actual battle experience, but convinced David to let him go with him and Pentra the Lesser into the Veil of Darkness because of his ancestry. He was honored for this service, and this honor went to his head, causing him not to follow the disciplines a soldier would normally follow. He used his honor to associate with the heads of the military and the Children of Earth, when his rank would have required him to keep his distance. His pride in his new-found honor made him reckless, and so he never became the great warrior he sought to be. He was known for his skill with the ax, and chose to use it in battle over a sword. His rash approach to battle caused him to be the first to fall when he followed Tanya in her wedge-attack on Cronis.

HEALER(S) – By the time of the Return of the Adoni, this was most commonly used to refer to those who were skilled in the healing arts. Originally, it referred to the Council of Ancients – those who were experts in all fields of knowledge. When the Council of Ancients abused the opportunity to question Logos the Talking Sword, their abuse brought the Curse upon all the Lands of the Adoni. In an effort to "heal" the damage done by their abuse, and the loss of communication with Logos as a source of information and knowledge, the Council of Ancients changed their name to *Healers*. Thus, in ancient manuscripts, a healer was one who had been a member of the Council of Ancients. As the word changed in its usage, it then referred to one who was knowledgeable, and skilled in a single subject or craft. As the Lands of the Adoni became more opposed to technology and technological advancements because such search for knowledge brought the Curse on the Lands of the Adoni, such experts became more rare, and eventually sought privacy for their work, and would no longer claim the title. Thus, by the time of the Battle of Es-Soh-En, it had come to mean one skilled in the art of healing.

HEART COMPANY – Title given to an underground army of about four to five hundred soldiers trained by Agron in preparation for an eventual war with Magar. They were given their name because each was a Follower, and to show their dedication to Teacher they had displayed the symbol of a sword-pierced heart on each of their shields. When Sir David discovered Agron had been secretly preparing for war, he made Agron second-in-command of the army of Dula. To Agron's credit, whenever any of the army was tested, Heart Company always emerged as the best of the best.

HEART OF THE SUN, THE – A jewel which fell from the sky and struck the ground on the border between Magar and Dula. The battle to gain possession of the jewel is called the Border War or the Battle for the Heart. Neither is spoken of in Dula as they forsook any desire to win the jewel when it was believed that the jewel was sent by Cronis. The Magarians called the jewel the Heart of the Sun, and used it in a yearly celebration. Over the years, the jewel was nearly stolen several times, and so to protect the jewel, the king created a plan which took three generations to accomplish. The king ordered a mountain carved away until it was naught but a high tower. The ground was dug away from the base of the tower creating a valley. The Heart of the Sun was placed in a box, and carried by the current king and his son to the top of the tower where the king stayed to die, and his son buried the stairs under tons of rubble. At the base of the tower stands an honor guard who never unlink their arms except when their shift changes. As part of His second test to prove that Teacher was the Rightful King, He had to obtain the Heart of the Sun for Queen Dianna without causing a war with Magar. When Teacher returned with the Heart of the Sun, Queen Dianna's greed destroyed the jewel and left it a smolder, charred rock.

HENTERY – Last of the line of Fibbergee. He is a talking mouse who served Queen Dianna by traveling to Magar to spy on their plans. When Queen Dianna disappeared, Hentery and his close friend, Beech, returned to Dula to offer their services to the Children of Earth.

HISSEN – Scabbard for Sy-lar the eagle blade of Tanya. As Sy-lar was one of the great Adoni blades, its scabbard was also given a name. *Hissen* in the Old Dulan tongue mean *a musical pause*. It is a musical notation which calls for the singer of the song to pause, and for the people who are listening to meditate upon what had just been sung.

HOBBER – A species of large wild cats found only in the Lands of the Adoni. The Hobber is described as a large black lion, with topaz blue eyes. The mane and the tip of the tail are a soft golden fur. Although a Hobber is a species unto itself, there is only one actual Hobber. This is the second member of the Adoni, Es-Soh-En. This is the form Es-Soh-En assumed for Himself in the Lands of the Adoni prior to His incarnation as Teacher. Since He is the only Hobber in all the Lands of the Adoni, reference to the *Hobber* or *Great Hobber* is understood to be a reference to Es-Soh-En.

HONOR OF THE GREAT, THE – Ceremony for the royal family of Dula. Whenever a member of the royal family dies, their body is prepared for burial, and then placed on display in the palace for the population to come and pay their respects. After this ceremony is over, the body is then buried.

HOOFA – A gnomish drink made from beans grown on the Hoofa Tree. The beans are roasted, ground and mixed with hot water. It is a morning drink that wakes the drinker up so that they can function for the day.

ISH – First Father of the Lands of the Adoni. He was created by Es-Soh-En. As Es-Soh-En sang the last portion of the Song of Creation, Ish was formed from the dust of the ground, and

Es-Soh-En then breathed life into him. He was given dominion over all the Lands of the Adoni. He broke the Law of the Adoni by attempting to know and speak the name of the Unnamed Adoni. In the process, Ish transferred his claim of the title deed of the Lands of the Adoni to Cronis. As the transfer was the result of deception by Cronis, the transferring of the title deed was called into question. Cronis claimed the right to kill Ish and his wife, Issha, but lost that right when an innocent, Lendara died in their place.

ISLE OF MORNING, THE – A body of six small islands which lie to the east of Janadis in the Great Sea. It serves as farmland and grazing land for the citizens of Janadis. The larger of the islands contains a tunnel which leads to the undersea city. This tunnel is used to bring herds out to graze, transport crops to Janadis, and in case of an emergency it also serves to evacuate the undersea city.

ISSHA – First Mother of the Lands of the Adoni. She is the wife of Ish. She was created by Es-Soh-En by putting Ish into a deep sleep and calling her forth from him. She was approached by Cronis when she first became pregnant, and Cronis used the deception that others would not understand what they understood since they had not created life as she had, to keep her from telling anyone that he had contacted her. In this way he continued to mislead and deceive her into thinking that he was the Unnamed Adoni. Once she believed this, he began using her to gain influence with Ish. Cronis requested that Issha transfer the title deed of the Lands of the Adoni back to him. He then encouraged both Ish and Issha to call upon him, and to place themselves under his authority. This was in direct violation of the Laws set down by Es-Soh-En. Once he had caused them to disobey, he then claimed the right to kill them both for that disobedience. Es-Soh-En stopped Cronis from carrying out his effort personally. The servant Cronis sent ended up killing Lendara instead. The shedding of the innocent blood barred Cronis from his right to kill either Ish or Issha.

JANADIS – One of the kingdoms of the Land of the Adoni [Dula, Magar, Orpha, Bromor, Janadis and the Cantile Islands]. In the ancient Dulan tongue, this means *dream city*. It was given this name because the Prince of Dula had given up his right to a portion of the throne to his twin brother in order to prevent the kingdom from being split. As a reward for his sacrifice, Es-Soh-En came to him in a dream, and provided him with all the plans, information, and skills needed to build his own city underneath the Great Sea. The prince then left Dula with all of his followers to build the city, and establish a kingdom of his own. As he left Dula, his brother gave him the hilt jewel from Logos as an eternal treaty between their two kingdoms. In the palace of Janadis the message: *United in history, United in destiny* is carved as a reminder that they are still a single kingdom in the eyes of Es-Soh-En. The hilt jewel was mounted on the throne of Janadis, but when the city was visited by Teacher after the Battle of Es-Soh-En, they gave it to Him to show their love for the Adoni. Prior to this visit, the city was under a strict caste system based completely upon titles and honors. Through Teacher's example, they were shamed, and shown the folly of their system, and after the Battle of Es-Soh-En, no caste was ever in use in Janadis again.

JENSEN – One of the great poets of Dula. He had already passed into the Kingdom by the time of the Return of the Adoni, but during one of her visits to the Lands of the Adoni by Tanya he fell in love with her. Although they were never to be married because she had to return to Earth after her mission was complete, he refused to love any other; and spent his entire life writing poems in honor of her. The story of Jensen and Tanya's love grew to be one of the great love stories in Dulan history.

JEKSON – Officer of the day on duty in the courtyard of Dula when Lady Tanya landed on Morning Star during the siege of Dula by Magar, Bromor and Orpha. He had been one of Heart Company who had been ill when Heart Company rode into battle, and so he was left behind. He had been the one to tell others that the Sir David *killed* by Lady Tanya was missing the scar on his cheek, and that Gennerroth should not have broken in battle. It was his efforts which led the kingdom to believe that Lady Tanya had killed an imposter brought in by Gib-ron.

JEN-TAR – Member of the Council of Dula at the time of the Return of the Adoni. He was the head of the construction guild.

JOL-DAR – Scholar of Dula at the time of the Return of the Adoni. His only notoriety was that he was the first scholar to enter the record chamber when Lady Tanya had been injured. He was not the first person to enter as Unter the Healer was already there. Jol-Dar was known for his constant babbling, and his rambling about the precision of speech as communication. It was due to his inability to recognize situations around him as he lectured which found him many times speaking to empty rooms, or empty market places. It was during one such lecture, that Magar attacked, and everyone fled to avoid boulders hurled by catapults. Jol-Dar was still speaking, unaware of the attack when he was killed.

KAL – Minotaur who was loyal to Queen Dianna at the time of the Quest for the Sword. He stayed behind to protect Dula while Queen Dianna was on the quest. His efforts saved numerous followers, and prepared an underground army which was used to take the throne of Dula from Dragnock. Because of his loyalty to the Adoni he was granted his most fervent prayer: having the Curse lifted from him so he could hear the voice of Logos. At the end of the Quest for the Sword, Es-Soh-En placed him in charge of a new clan called the Sword-Keepers Clan. He, Tra and Dig Gen were given physical possession of the Sword, and questioned the Sword regarding many issues. The Sword-Keepers Clan wrote down all the new information obtained from Logos, and published it in a work which came to be known as the New Words or Words of the Clan. He had previously been disgraced in the minotaur clans for his seeking to take his own life without the permission of the Adoni. He had done this because he believed he had lost his honor after accidentally killing his brother. For years he was an outcast, and after the Quest for the Sword, he was accepted back into the minotaur community, and given great honors for his efforts to preserve the kingdom of Dula.

KENDERY – Father of Hentery. He was growing too old to serve as the Queen's messenger, but Queen Dianna did not have the heart to relieve him of duty. Thus she approached Hentery, the next in line; to serve her without his father being aware of it. Hentery went to Magar to spy for the Queen, while Kendery continued to serve for another six months. Finally, when he found he could not climb the steps of the palace, he had to admit that he was too old to be of service and retired. To help him maintain his dignity, and his sense of self-worth, Queen Dianna, delegated him to the information center, where all bits and pieces of information brought by various sources was compiled and then delivered to Queen Dianna. It was Kendery who initially put together the pieces to prove to Queen Dianna that Magar was waging a war of the mind through sponsoring various books, plays and other works of art.

KENDAR BUSHES – Small shrubs noted for their wide leaves. The leaves had a healing property which would prevent infection, and actually stimulate cell growth. Its leaves were used as bandages for wounds to promote healing.

KEEPERS OF THE SWORDS, THE – Not the same as the Swordkeepers Clan. This title referred to all who had the Sword Logos entrusted to their care. This would identify all the kings/queens of Dula up to the point where the Sword was stolen. It would then continue with Queen Dianna who brought the Sword back to Dula. It would then include the Swordkeepers Clan, as well as Teacher, Sir David and Lady Tanya as all had possession of the Sword. Those who would not be included would be the kings/queens of Bromor from the time the Sword was stolen up to the reign of Lord Mondule, and Gib-ron. These, although in possession of the Sword, were not legally entitled to possess the Sword and would not be listed among the Keepers of the Sword.

KI-EL – Member of the Council at the time of the Return of the Adoni. He represented the stonecutter's guild on the council. He was obsessed with obtaining the Eye of Suma, and this obsession caused him to act against the best interests of Dula, and to physically attack David. He was imprisoned for his actions, but when Gib-ron resumed power, he was released and arrested Dayton and his entire family, torturing them in an effort to learn the location of the Eye of Suma. When Tanya shattered the Crystal Eye, and Gib-ron was exposed as a servant of Cronis to the people of Dula, Ki-el was captured, and executed as the city tried to cleanse itself of any influence of Cronis.

KINGDOM OF THE ADONI, THE – Whenever someone dies in the Lands of the Adoni, and they are a Follower they are *taken to the Kingdom*. Before the Battle of Es-Soh-En this was a place known as *the Lesser Kingdom*. It served as a waiting place until the power of Cronis was broken. After the Battle of Es-Soh-En, all the inhabitants of the Lesser Kingdom were transported to the Greater Kingdom. Where the Lesser Kingdom served only the Lands of the Adoni, the Greater Kingdom joins all worlds together. Both of these Kingdoms were later replaced by the New Kingdom of the Adoni at the Return of the Adoni.

KNIGHTS OF ES-SOH-EN – This is the title given to special servants of the Adoni. Es-Soh-En selects those who will be knighted. Before the Quest for the Sword, there were only nine knights listed in a book obtained by Sir David: Dairus, Hinton, Jarra, Fepar, Pentra, Singer, Vera, Meln and Gar. During the Quest for the Sword three other knights were added: David James, Tanya, and Dig Gen. Between the Quest for the Sword and the Battle of Es-Soh-En one more knight was added: Tendar. In reality, there were 144 Knights of Es-Soh-En. They came from all time periods, lands and races of the Lands of the Adoni. During the time of Pentra the Greater, the Knights Inkling began to collect and preserve the achievements of the various Knights. Unknown to all – because the Adoni removed all memory of their service – all 144 knights participated in Pentra's battle in the Ring of Fire. While Pentra entered the Veil of Darkness via Suma; the other 143 Knights of Es-Soh-En fought the Battle of the Line where they fought the forces of Cronis at the eastern edge of the Veil of Darkness. Many Knights were killed in this battle; but Es-Soh-En restored all to life, healed all wounds; and returned them to their own time with no memory of the Battle of the Line until such time as they entered the Kingdom of the Adoni. After Pentra's battle in the Veil, some scholars suggested that the Adoni had completed Their involvement with the Lands of the Adoni, and had now abandoned the Lands of the Adoni to those fates now pre-ordained. Singer had been made a Knight of Es-Soh-En during this period of time; but he served mostly behind the scenes and only occasionally identified himself as a Knight of Es-Soh-En. The lack of interest in the Knights of Es-Soh-En resulted in many of the Knights being forgotten or having served without public recognition. The continued appearances of David James and Tanya caused many to challenge this belief that the Adoni no longer involved Themselves in the affairs of the Lands of the Adoni. Tanya remains the only woman to be chosen as a Knight of Es-Soh-En. For a complete listing of all 144 Knights of Es-Soh-en, their exploits and Adoni blades see the Appendix for *The Ballad of Pentra*.

KNIGHTS INKLING, THE – This was a group of people during the time of Pentra the Greater who sought out and collected the various accounts of the Knights of Es-Soh-En. The members collected bits of stories and legends, preserved songs and even performed some of the accounts as skits and song during festivals in Dula. They put all their information into a book. At the time of the Battle of the Veil the members of the Knights Inklings were: Pentra [Pen], Wilton [the oldest of the group], Sam from Vintar, Glen of the Lower Lake centaurs, Aston from Southfork and Grill of the Kess Clan of gnomes rounded out the regulars. Others were given honorary membership [Jon Gen, Ven, Belta, and Deka], but the originals formed the core, and when the last one went to the Kingdom, the title was never claimed by any others, out of respect for their dedication to the craft.

KYA – A young shepherdess from the Cantile Islands who befriended David James on his previous visit. Sir David was struggling with a disobedience to the Adoni which he had committed, and had exiled himself as far from Dula as possible. This brought him to the Cantile Islands where he gave up on life. Kya found him, worked with him, and fell in love with him. It was through her care and compassion that Sir David came to heal the emotional wounds which had led to his act of rebellion. She never married after Sir David returned to Earth, but had spent her entire life remaining true to her love for him.

LANDS OF THE ADONI, THE – This is the collective title of all the kingdoms created by the Adoni. At the creation of Ish and Issha, this entire world was seen as one kingdom and called the Lands of the Adoni. The reference to *lands* had nothing to do with kingdoms or other countries, but to the diversity of the geographic make up of the land. Many generations after the Fall, the children of Ish and Issha began to spread out and settle in these many areas. After several more generations, they set up communities, and then cities. As they were so far removed from each other, the collection of cities eventually sought one to rule over them, and meet their needs as a community. This was the creation of the kingdoms of the Lands of the Adoni. In later years, these kingdoms were referred to collectively as the Lands of the Adoni. These kingdoms are: Dula to the North West, Orpha to the South West, Bromor to the South, and Magar to the East. When Janadis was built and the Isle of Morning was discovered, they, too, were added to the reference of the Lands of the Adoni. When the Cantile Islands were discovered, they, too, were added to the reference.

LAKE GEN – A lake in the Gen Forest. It is fed by the Nyson River, a smaller branch of the Tandur River which flows from the east, through the city of Dula, and then to the Dulan Alps. It was at this lake that Sir David camped with Heart Company in preparation for the battle with Magar. It was at this site that Sir David chose to cut his forces before going into battle against Magar. He used the lake as the final test of which warriors to keep, and which to send back to Dula. The test was to have each soldier drink from the lake. Those who knelt were sent home, those who lay on their stomachs were kept for the battle. Sir David said that he did this to follow orders given to him by the Adoni.

LATON – Leader of the Water People community at the time of the Return of the Adoni. Since the near genocide of the Water People community at the time of the Quest for the Sword, the Water People had kept very distant contacts with humans. Further, they had trained in a unique form of war designed to take full advantage of their ability to transform from human to water and back once more. Laton had been a Follower, and initially faced strong opposition to joining the Water People with the other races who were supporting the humans in their war against Magar. When his people saw the dedication of Sir David in cutting his forces even though outnumbered several times over simply because the Adoni instructed him to do so, the race reconsidered. After observing Sir David further, they eventually chose to ally themselves with Sir David, and became strong supporters of his campaigns. After the death of Sir David, the Water People gave the same support to his sister, Lady Tanya.

LEAH – A female of the Water People community at the time of the Quest for the Sword. She was the first of her race to seek to worship Es-Soh-En because of His teachings even though all the Water People community worshipped *the God Who Breathes Gold*. She was betrayed by her sisters when they tried to rescue David from the dungeon where Dragnock had imprisoned him. The betrayal caused Leah to weep, something very rare of among the Water People. Later, she was the one who saved her entire race from genocide by posing as a drunken human, and stumbling against the tank which contained all their life stones. The life stones fell into the Tandur River, and allowed the entire Water People community to escape Dragnock's men. She traveled beyond the Dula Alps, and encountered Queen Dianna on the Quest for Logos. Leah went with Queen Dianna, and fell in love with Gen the gnome. At the city of Janadis she sacrificed herself to save him. Glidon saved her. At the end of the Quest for the Sword, Leah discovered that Es-Soh-En was *the God Who Breathes Gold* worshipped by her race, and became instrumental in bringing her race to the worship of the Adoni. In reward for her service, she was transformed by Es-Soh-En so she and Gen could be married and have children.

LENDAR – Council member who represented the silversmith's guild. He was known for his many affairs with women, but his refusal to honor any promise to marry them. It was later learned that he was one of three Council members who had been put into power by Magar to discredit the throne of Dula, steal the power from Queen Dianna, and prepare the kingdom for the coming of Magar.

LENDARA – King of the unicorn at the time of the creation of the Lands of the Adoni. He was close to Ish and Issha, but the deception of Cronis caused them to stay away from him. Later, when Cronis sought to kill Ish and Issha, Lendara confronted the Demon Cloud sent by Cronis to kill them. The Battle took place at the River of Warning in Southern Bromor. The Demon Cloud thought it was safe attacking Lendara because it believed that Lendara was one of the creatures of the Lands of the Adoni. However, Lendara and all the unicorn were created in the Kingdom of the Adoni. This meant that Lendara's horn could injure the cloud creature. To press the advantage, Lendara collected electricity throughout the night before confronting the cloud creature. When Lendara released the electricity into the sky and it came back hundreds of times more powerful as a lightning bolt. Lendara used horn to draw lightning from the sky and into the Demon Cloud. The blast of the lightning struck both Lendara and the Demon Cloud, and split the ground beneath them down to the molten core. The Demon Cloud was wounded, and fled. Lendara's horn was torn off by the blast of lightning, and the unicorn was fatally wounded. Before dying, he named Deenara as his steward. Lendara was the only unicorn to ever taste of death. His horn was taken by Es-Soh-En and forged in the fires of the Lightning's Scar to make the Sword Logos. After the final judgment of Cronis, Teacher replaced his lost horn with a horn of gold.

LESSER KINGDOM, THE – See Kingdom of the Adoni.

LIFE STONE(S) – A Water Person is made up completely of water with the exception of a single stone worn as an ornament around the neck. This is the stone the Water Person's parents would polish and use from the lake or river bed in their mating ritual, and transfer some of their own essence into the stone. The blending of the two lives is bound to the stone, and a new Water

Citizen is born. The water of the Water Person can be replaced by any fresh water, but if the life stone is damaged, broken, or completely dried out; then the Water Person will die. The secret of the life stones was kept hidden from other races, but during the Quest for the Sword Dragnock discovered the secret, and used it to attempt genocide of the entire Water People race. The actions of Leah saved her race. Since that time the Water People have taken great care to learn the ways of war, and to protect their life stones from any similar attack by the other races.

LOGOS – This is the Talking Sword, given to Ish and Issha when they were judged for their disobedience. Es-Soh-En had forged this Sword in the fires of the Lightning's Scar, and only in the Lightning's Scar could it be destroyed. It was given as a reminder that an innocent, Lendara, had sacrificed his life to save the guilty. This was to be a symbol of the coming Battle of Es-Soh-En. The Sword had a spiraling bone handle grip, with a ruby the color of blood in the end of the hilt. If the Sword was held in a certain position, the cage that protected the user's hand would appear to be the shape of a heart. The blade would be piercing the heart; and the stone would represent the blood shed when the heart was pierced. This was a prophecy, hidden in plain sight, of what Es-Soh-En would do in the Battle of Es-Soh-En to free the Lands of the Adoni. The hilt jewel was removed by one of the kings of Dula and given to his twin brother who was traveling to the Isle of Morning in order to build Janadis. The hilt jewel was to serve as a reminder and a treaty that the two kingdoms were *United in History, United in Destiny.* The cross piece was white metal shaped like the locks of hair from a unicorn's mane. The blade itself was silver, long and tapered to a point. It was also known as the Talking Sword because it would sing songs of praise to the Adoni for the sunrise, sunset, harvest, rain and other events. When the Sword was not singing songs of praise, it would be possible for those near it to ask questions, and the Sword would answer. Because this questioning process was abused by the Council of Ancients, the Curse came upon all the Lands of the Adoni. The Sword was never to be carried except in its sheath. It was never to be carried into battle because if the Sword ever shed innocent blood, its power would be broken. It belonged to the royal family of Dula, and none but the royal family could claim it, or touch it. It was protected by a curse that anyone trying to steal the Sword would be turned over to Cronis to torment until the Sword was returned, and the thief repented. Several generations after the Curse, a thief did steal the Sword, and Cronis offered only a token of torment in order to frighten the thief, and drive him to Bromor. The thief carried the Sword to Bromor where it was taken by Justin, the King of Bromor and replaced with a copy. King Justin had a servant make the actual transfer and touch the Sword and place it in hiding. When the servant began to be tormented, King Justin killed him. As long as King Justin or others never touched the Sword, Cronis chose not to exercise his right to torment them as it served his own purpose to have Logos lost to Dula. The Sword had been the one to select the next ruler of Dula before the Curse. After the Curse, possession of the Sword was evidence of the divine right of the owner to rule in Dula. After the Sword was stolen from Dula, careful records had to be kept to prove lineage as a person's right to rule. When Queen Dianna lost her throne to Dragnock, she set out on the Quest for the Sword in order to recover Logos, and prove she was the rightful ruler. The Sword was discovered, and Queen Dianna brought it back to Dula to reclaim her throne. At the end of the Quest for the Sword, Queen Dianna was given the Gift of Unending Life by Es-Soh-En, and the care for Logos passed into the hands of the Sword-Keepers clan, which was made up of Kal, Tra and Dig Gen. Tra and Kal had the Curse removed from their ears, and were able to speak with the Sword and obtain additional information which they shared with the people in the form of a new book called the New Words or Words of the Clan. When Dig Gen was rumored not to have been a true Knight of Es-Soh-En, Queen Dianna, under the influence of Cronis, reclaimed the Sword. Through the Sword, Cronis eventually took greater and greater control of Queen Dianna. Teacher came to claim His place as the Rightful King, and Queen Dianna put Him to the test. At the end of the testing Cronis stole the Sword, and took it into the Veil of Darkness where Teacher went to compete in the Battle of Es-Soh-En to recover the Sword, and claim the title deed for all the Lands of the Adoni. During the Battle of Es-Soh-En Cronis used Logos to kill Teacher from behind. Because Cronis had worked for so many years to gain control of the Sword – and through the Sword control over Queen Dianna – he was the power of the Sword at the time it shed Teacher's innocent blood; and so it was the power of Cronis that was broken. At the end of the Battle of Es-Soh-En Teacher freed the spirit who had lived in the Sword and sang praises to the Adoni all those centuries. He returned Logos, stained with His blood, to Queen Dianna. It remained with Queen Dianna, over the centuries, and she came to depend on it less and less. At the Return of the Adoni, it was revealed that the Sword was not just a symbol of a unicorn's sacrifice, but it was the actual horn of Lendara re-shaped in the fires of the Lightning's Scar. This information was called the Secret of the Unicorn, and Sir David was the only human to know this secret. At the Return of the Adoni, Sir David joined the hilt jewel to Logos, and it became an unbeatable weapon used by Sir David as the Steward of the Throne of Dula to battle Magar and its allies, and then later the armies of Cronis.

MAGAR – Eastern kingdom of the Lands of the Adoni [Dula, Magar, Orpha, Bromor, Janadis and the Cantile Islands]. It was the first to break away from serving the Adoni, and openly worship Cronis. The kingdom became so corrupt and so twisted that it produced such groups as the Blood Troops and the Black Hearts. The kingdom has tried on several occasions to conquer Dula and on several occasions Es-Soh-En has punished this kingdom for it evil.

MEEP – Soldier who was on patrol along the western area of Dula at the time of the Return of the Adoni. His patrol was destroyed by the forces of Cronis as they came to attack Dula. He was ordered to flee the battle by his commanding officer and carry the warning back to Dula. He rode his horse until it dropped dead under him; he then ran until he nearly died of exhaustion himself to get the message to Sir David and Lady Tanya. He recovered from the strain, and fought against the army of Cronis. He was the only non-Heart Company soldier to be part of the wedge Tanya used to attack Cronis. He was one of the few still alive when Es-Soh-En returned to defeat Cronis.

MIG GEN – Gnome at the time of the Battle of Es-Soh-En. He was a descendant of Brig Gen, and had collected all of his ancestor's poetry for others to read. Where other members of the Gen Family of gnomes abused the praise given them by the Adoni, shaved their heads, and rebelled against traditional gnomish ways, Mig Gen refused to follow his family's practices, and was basically cast out by his family. He was one of the first followers of Teacher prior to the Battle of Es-Soh-En.

MIGRATION OF GLIDONITES – Sect among the Following who believed that the Adoni still took an active part in the affairs of the Lands of the Adoni. Their teachings caused controversy in Dula, and so they sought permission from Queen Dianna to move all of their followers to Janadis which held beliefs similar to their own. The mass exodus of these Glidonites nearly drained the kingdom, and caused the Council to seek new laws to forbid the movement and stop the exodus. As the followers of this movement focused on Glidon the Great Eagle, they were called *Glidonites*. Since birds were known to migrate, it was mostly as a joke the term came to be applied to their exodus from Dula.

MINOTAUR – One of the races of the Lands of the Adoni. From the neck down, a minotaur has a human body, but from the neck up they have the head of a bull. Although their appearance might mislead an observer, the minotaur is a highly intelligent and articulate race. However, instead of turning their efforts to inventions or sciences, they have worked for centuries to perfect the art of war, and more important to them, hand-to-hand combat. The reason for this obsession with combat is that Tanya disowned and shamed the entire race when they refused to offer aid to Ish and Issha when their lives were threatened by the Demon Cloud sent by Cronis to kill them. They have spent centuries trying to atone for this by learning the ways of war. This is one of the races which were created when Tanya and Glidon sang the Lesser Song. Fay was the first male minotaur created when Tanya sang and touched one of two large rocks. Leen was the first female minotaur and had been the second rock Tanya touched during her song. Fay and Leen married and headed the first clan. Their descendants became the Fayleen Clan – the fiercest of all the minotaur clans. When Gret sought to lead the Fayleen Clan into service to Cronis, the Adoni sent Singer to defeat Gret in battle and reveal the deception. Singer became the head of the Fayleen Clan and entrusted the clan to be ruled by Krel. Singer returned several generations later when Kor was leading the clan. Singer reestablished his leadership of the clan and instructed the clan how to deal with Kal who had undertaken Sharahka without the permission of the Adoni.

MORNING STAR – One of the twins born to Gaylord and Yeesha after the Quest for the Sword and before the Battle of Es-Soh-En. Both she and her brother died at a young age. The cause of their deaths was never revealed by Gaylord and Yeesha as it was too painful for the parents to speak of it. At the Return of the Adoni, She was sent from the Kingdom of the Adoni to bond with Tanya and served her as her parents did.

MOUNTAIN OF THE SKY, THE – A large mountain in the southern end of the Dulan Alps. It is so tall, that its peak is lost from view. According to those who have been to the top, the Mountain of the Sky forms one side of a great chasm. The other side of the chasm is also known as the Mountain of the Sky, but this other side of the chasm is part of the Kingdom of the Adoni, and its base is not in the Lands of the Adoni. It is impossible to cross this chasm unless Es-Soh-En carries one across. Those reaching the peak must enter a tunnel beneath the mountain. This tunnel will bring travelers to the *Chamber Beneath the Mountain*, as it is called. This chamber forms the base of the Mountain of the Sky. The walls of the chamber are encrusted with silver, gold, and precious stones. Once in the center of the *Chamber Beneath the Mountain*, a rock can be moved aside, and then a great wind will fill the chamber and carry the travelers to the top of the Mountain of the Sky where they can go no further, nor climb back down until they met Es-Soh-En. It was on this mountain that David and Tanya were knighted as Knights of

Es-Soh-En, and given their swords: Gennerroth and Sy-lar. It is also on this mountain top that Suma the sky ship is stored by the Adoni. It is also here that the Portal of Ages is located.

MOVING TREES, THE – At the time of the Fall, Es-Soh-En had given a forest of trees the power to move in order to enclose the Garden of Tangar to keep Ish and Issha – or any others – from every returning to the Garden of Tangar. Cronis came to the trees, and promised to transform them into complete Tree Druids if they would desert the Adoni and serve him. The trees abandoned their post, later Sinta (who came to be known as Singer) found the location, but not the Garden as the Adoni had removed it from the Lands of the Adoni. At the time of the Quest for the Sword the trees obeyed Cronis, and encircled the rescue party in the Dark Woods. The rescue party had been led by Kal and they had tried to rescue David from the dungeon where he had been imprisoned by Dragnock. Kal instructed his rescue party to sing songs of praise to the Adoni while they were trapped. Brig Gen refused to sing, but sat with his back to the others, facing the trees. The stubborn gnome kept mumbling that he would not praise the Adoni until the trees were gone. Glidon broke through the trees from above, and informed the trees that Cronis did not have the power to make them Tree Druids, and they had sold themselves for a lie. The Great Eagle then pronounced judgment on the moving trees, and they burst into flames. When the trees were nothing more than piles of ash, Glidon turned to Brig Gen and said: *The trees are gone. Now will you praise Us?*

MUSIC OF THE GROUND – Although communication between humans and plants was lost with the Fall, Tree Druids can still converse with all plant life. This creates an instantaneous communication and news can spread through the plant kingdom from the Veil of Darkness to the shores of Magar in just a little over an hour. If you can speak to a Tree Druid, you can tap into this communication.

NEW FOREST, THE – When Es-Soh-En destroyed the army of Magar with fire outside the gates of Dula after the Quest for the Sword, the Adoni gave the ground the power to heal itself of the evil which had tainted it. In response, a vast forest, like the forests seen in the Garden of Tangar before the Fall sprang up in only a few hours. It held all the majesty, purity, and innocence of an untarnished world. People would come from miles to walk through the forest. When Sir David and Lady Tanya first saw it, they made reference that in comparison to the New Forest (as it was coming to be called) the great trees and forests of their world were nothing more than giant weeds. Over the centuries, the glory of the New Forest faded until it was like any other forest. It eventually was dug up and used for expansion of the city. At the time of the Return of the Adoni all that remained of the New Forests were those works of art depicting the scene.

NEW KINGDOM OF THE ADONI, THE – Not to be mistaken for the Lesser Kingdom, nor the Greater Kingdom; this is an entirely new Kingdom. Here all worlds were joined together, and all titles were properly restored. What sets this Kingdom apart from the Lesser Kingdom or the Greater Kingdom was that Teacher rules openly, and has taken a bride to rule at His side. No additional citizens will be entering the New Kingdom because all works of creation, guidance and redemption are now complete, and so this is the complete kingdom, a New Kingdom of the Adoni. To quote a prediction found in the revelations of the Adoni recorded in all worlds: *All things are passed away.*

NEW WORDS – A collection of teachings, quotations, and instructions recorded by Tra and Kal as they learned from Logos when the Curse was lifted from their ears, and they were given the care of the Sword. (Also see the Words of the Ancients and Words of the Clan).

NIGHT THE TWIN MOONS KISS, THE – this is a cycle of the twin moons. They form a near eclipse and appear to be touching. Then they spread apart during the night skies – fifty days later, they come back and touch once more, and repeat the cycle.

OLD WORDS – See Words of the Ancients.

ORPHA – Kingdom to the south of Dula [Dula, Magar, Orpha, Bromor, Janadis and the Cantile Islands]. It was one of the kingdoms to fall away from the Adoni, but not to the degree as Magar. During the coming of the Veil of Darkness, this was the only Kingdom to join with Dula to invade the Veil and try to keep it from spreading. During the Battle of Three Armies, all soldiers who trusted the Adoni were protected and did not die. Unfortunately, there were many among the Orphan army that refused to believe in or trust the Adoni. They died in the battle. Due to the fact that none of the Dulan troops died; and all fatalities involved Orphan troops who did not trust the Adoni, relations were strained and eventually broken between the two kingdoms.

PAVA LEAVES – a treatment for someone with a head injury. The leaves will reduce swelling and infection in case the head injury causes the brain to swell.

PEARLS OF ES-SOH-EN, THE – During the Children of Earth's third visit to the Lands of the Adoni, they were present for the Creation of the Lands of the Adoni. Cronis sought to deceive Ish and Issha into worshipping him rather than the Adoni. Es-Soh-En was in the Western Sea where He wept over the coming Fall of the Lands of the Adoni. He shed eight tears, and the Unnamed Adoni transformed those eight tears into a chain of islands. They were not in existence when the Adoni gave all the Lands of the Adoni to Ish and Issha, and they were created from material that was not part of the Lands of the Adoni. For this reason, they were never placed under the control of Ish and Issha. They were never part of the Lands of the Adoni, and they were never touched by the Fall of the Lands of the Adoni. No human has ever seen or visited these islands except for the Knights of Es-Soh-En. Their name was given to them by Sir David when he liked them to the pearls created by oysters as they suffer. Es-Soh-En suffered and grieved over the Fall, and it produces the eight tears that became the islands. It is here where Suma the Starship was built in secret, waiting for Pentra to be ready for his calling. It is here that the Knights of Es-Soh-En were gathered after the Battle of the Line.

PENTRA THE GREATER – (Also known as Pentra of Suma at the time of the Return of the Adoni) Knight of Es-Soh-En who was called by the Adoni to fly Suma into the Veil of Darkness. Pentra battled with a demon creature given the power to create and to expand the Veil beyond the Western Ocean. The battle lasted days, and Pentra was fatally wounded before killing the demon creature. Before he could die, Glidon came to the Veil and healed him. Pentra was offered the choice of returning to the Lands of the Adoni or of entering the Kingdom of the Adoni bodily. He chose to go bodily into the Kingdom of the Adoni. The site of his battle with the demon creature was called the Ring of Fire, and later became the site for the Battle of Es-Soh-En.

PENTRA THE LESSER – A distant descendant of Pentra the Greater. Although Pentra died without children, a cousin of Pentra had come to help care for Pentra' parents after his death. Pentra the Lesser can trace his line back to this cousin. He was a member of the Council of Dula at the time of the Return of the Adoni. He represented the military on the Council. Although a Follower he had compromised his beliefs for political convenience, and job security. At the time of the Return of the Adoni, he went into the Veil of Darkness the same as his ancestor. Although a great warrior, this experience, and other experiences taught him that he had traded away what was most important to him. By the time he returned from Janadis with Lady Tanya, he had rededicated his life to the service of the Adoni. He was one of the last to die in battle before Es-Soh-En returned to defeat Cronis.

PLAN, THE – Reference to the fact that the Followers believed that each event, each detail of their lives was all planned out by the Adoni. This was not a teaching of predestination, as those professing the teachings of The PLAN all readily insisted it must be understood with the concept of free choice. The events were set (this is The PLAN), the response of each individual was still their own choice (this is free choice). It was taught that when all events had taken place, then the world would turn out the way the Adoni had intended. Thus the term "PLAN" could refer to the individual plan for a believer, or the over-all "PLAN" the Adoni had for the Lands of the Adoni.

PORTAL OF AGES, THE – This refers to the back wall of a chamber at the top of the Mountain of the Sky. Those looking into this portal could see the past, present or future. The back side of this same portal was located in the Lesser Kingdom of the Adoni, and it had an additional property that it could also show "*what if*" scenarios for those gazing into its depths.

POWER OF THE ADONI, THE – The Adoni place a small portion of Themselves into each Follower as an anointing that serves as a *down payment* or a guarantee that the Adoni will work in their lives and accomplish what was promised to them. Thus all Followers have the Power of the Adoni to some degree in their lives. However, there is a greater anointing of the Power of the Adoni which is given to those called to greater service, and this anointing is much more visible. When a great leader, or a Knight of Es-Soh-En, is granted this special anointing, their entire body is immersed in a golden mist which will cover them completely, and permeate every pore. Once any Follower has been given either source of the Power of the Adoni-whether the unnoticed anointing, or the complete emersion, they can tell what the Adoni desire them to do. They are also given additional strength, wisdom, or abilities as needed to fulfill their calling by the Adoni. Once this power is given, it cannot be taken away.

QUEST FOR THE SWORD, THE – When Queen Dianna was forced to surrender her throne to Dragnock she vowed to recover the long-lost Sword Logos to prove her divine right to rule Dula. Her quest took her to numerous places in the Lands of the Adoni as the Adoni sought to teach her and the Children of Earth the importance of trusting the Adoni and obeying Them completely. On the quest, Queen Dianna went to the Mountain of the Sky and was taken to see the Portal of Ages. She was given Suma the sky ship, and sent to Janadis. From Janadis, they were instructed by the hilt jewel of Logos to travel to the Grey Castle of Bromor. While flying there on board

Suma, they were attacked by a swarm of bat things when they were over the Forest of Venra. Queen Dianna was separated, and came to the Grove of Three Oaks. There Gantra instructed her in the use of healing pods needed to cure those infected by the bat things. There were not enough pods to treat all of those with her, and so she chose to refrain from the treatment for herself so another could live. As a result, she died after delivering the pods. Es-Soh-En met her in the next life, and returned her and Dig Gen back to the Lands of the Adoni. The Quest continued through the Valley of Mists to the Lightning's Scar. From there, Singer brought them back to the Grey Castle where it was discovered that Lord Mondule, the ruler of Bromor had tried to replace Suma with a copy, and that Logos was hidden in the castle. Queen Dianna recovered the Sword, and returned with it to Dula. While she had been gone, Dragnock, had surrendered to Magar, been driven out by Kal, and an underground army, and the castle was under siege from the forces of Magar. Queen Dianna mounted the walls to display the missing Sword, and called upon the Adoni to aid her kingdom. In response, Es-Soh-En and Glidon came and destroyed the invading army. A great feast was held to celebrate, and Es-Soh-En rewarded those who had served faithfully on the Quest for the Sword. The Adoni ordered an annual feast to be held to commemorate the Quest for the Sword. This came to be known as the Feast of the Sword. Although the actual Quest for the Sword is seen by some scholars as the point where Queen Dianna left the kingdom of Dula and concludes with her return, more serious scholars of Dulan history claim the proper time frame for the Quest of the Sword would be from the moment the Children of Earth appeared in the Lands of the Adoni until the point where Es-Soh-En returned the Children of Earth back to their own world.

RAYTON – Servant of Gib-ron at the time of the Return of the Adoni. He had been entrusted with the scroll discovered by Lady Tanya in the Chamber of Records and stolen by Gib-ron. He was identified by Beech and captured. Once the scroll was returned, Rayton was imprisoned. When Gib-ron learned that Rayton had failed to deliver the scroll, he had him put to death.

REN – Head of the minotaur community at the time of the Return of the Adoni. He allied his race with Sir David when Dula went to war against Magar. After the death of David, Ren offered his loyalty and service to Lady Tanya. Although severely wounded, he led the charge of his race in the wedge-attack by Tanya against Cronis. He died in battle, taking one last enemy with his horns as he did.

RENTARA – Unicorn who was a close friend of David. The two fought the Demon Cloud that was sent by Cronis to kill Ish and Issha. The battle Rentara and David waged against the Demon Cloud lasted all night, and resulted in the creation of the Valley of Seven Forests. Although David was Friend of the Unicorn, and bonded to the entire herd, this event drew the two of them closer, and David would think of Rentara as his own personal unicorn. Even when Lendara had died, the unicorn mourned, but never shed tears. When David died, Rentara became the first of his race to shed tears in grief.

REVA – A Water Citizen at the time the Curse was placed on the Lands of the Adoni. She had been in love with Asseem [later known as Sinta, and then Singer]. When their love became public knowledge, Reva took the Vow of a Lifeless Stone to keep Asseem from being killed. She spent the rest of her life serving the *God Who Breathes Gold*. Reva took her love for Asseem and refocused it into charity work for the community. She was one of the first Water People to come and live inside of Dula, and her actions eventually led to a Water People community living in Dula. This community continued to grow until a vast majority of the Water People lived in the Dulan Community at the time of the Quest for the Sword. With the near genocide of the Water People race at the hands of Dragnock, the Water People moved into the Gen Woods where they had originally lived and separated themselves from humans. When the Quest for the Sword was completed, Singer's task was also complete. He was taken bodily into the Kingdom of the Adoni and there reunited with Reva.

RIGHTFUL KING, THE – Although the right king will always sit on the throne of Dula, there is only one Rightful King. The title of Rightful King is in reference to the Adoni assuming human form, and coming to rule His kingdom, and all the kingdoms in the Lands of the Adoni in person. Those seeking this title must pass several tests, but none were successful until the coming of Teacher who passed all the tests to prove He was qualified to be the Rightful King, and then claimed the title by sacrificing Himself to break the power Cronis held over the Lands of the Adoni. Although Teacher proved He was qualified to be the Rightful King, and had earned the title of Rightful King, He did not assume His position after the Battle of Es-Soh-En, but held off for several centuries until all the seeds of rebellion planted by Cronis in the hearts of the citizens of the Lands of the Adoni had either taken root and blossomed into rebellion, or had been crushed by those who chose to follow the Adoni. At the Return of the Adoni, Teacher assumed the title, the role and the throne of the Rightful King; and fulfilled His vow to marry Queen Dianna and make her His bride.

RING OF FIRE, THE – A place deep inside the Veil of Darkness. The Veil of Darkness was originally the site of the Western Ocean. When Lendara sacrificed himself to destroy the Demon Cloud that had been sent by Cronis to kill Ish and Issha the Demon Cloud exploded into thousands of pieces. Some of the pieces reformed and moved to the area where it had entered the Lands of the Adoni and joined with the vegetation there and came to be known as the Dark Woods. However, the one piece of the Demon Cloud that held its intelligence was caught in the River of Warning and washed from there into the Cove of Faces and then into the Southern Sea. Currents carried it into the Western Ocean. Here in the Western Ocean its consciousness returned and it began the slow process of drawing power off of Shadow Things the way it had drawn off of them to grow into the Demon Cloud initially. It was several centuries before Cronis noticed the loss of power. He tracked the source back to the former Demon Cloud – now Shadow Thing. He and the Shadow Thing waged a war beneath the Western Ocean which boiled away the entire Western Ocean. Cronis could not learn the secret of drawing power from others, but he was able to defeat and imprison the Shadow Thing through a Ring of Fire on the dried ocean bed. Through pain and torture Cronis was able to work through his imprisoned foe to draw light from the sky, create the Veil of Darkness and then to extend the Veil of Darkness. The Veil of Darkness spread to the shores of Dula, and began to claim the Kingdom of Dula before Pentra came to battle for the Lands of the Adoni. The Ring of Fire is where the flames held the Shadow Thing captive. It was the site of the battle between Pentra the Greater and the demon creature which had expanded the Veil of Darkness. It was later the site of the Battle of Es-Soh-En. It gets its name from the fact that whenever one of these events took place, flames of fire shot up high around it, making it impossible for anyone else to enter while the conflict between Pentra the Greater and the demon creature, or Teacher and Cronis took place. After the Battle of Es-Soh-En it became one of the few places in the Veil of Darkness which gave off any light. The center of the Ring of Fire is stained with the blood of Teacher, and it is this stain which continued to glow and give off light, no matter what Cronis does to try and stop it. It is a reminder to Cronis of his defeat by Teacher.

SALADON CANYON – A canyon in Magar where a massive mountain range of pure crystal cracked and was split open during the singing of the Greater Song. The entire area was a single massive crystal. As Es-Soh-En sang the final note of the Song of Creation, the Greater Song, the note was so rich, so pure, and so powerful that it cracked the jewel and exposed its surface for the entire world to see. The canyon is made of sheets of pure crystal which catch the rays of the sun and the twin moons, and provide a constant dance of rainbow light. The crystal is so hard, that nothing can break it or chip it away. Thus, although Magar has the greatest wealth in all the Lands of the Adoni, it is worthless to them since they cannot remove it or access it.

SECRET OF THE UNICORN, THE – Until the secret was revealed by Deenara to Lady Tanya, this was known only to Sir David. The secret was created at the death of Lendara, and kept hidden for centuries because it would add to Lendara's shame if others outside the unicorns or the Kingdom of the Adoni knew. The secret was that Logos was actually the horn of Lendara reshaped by Es-Soh-En in the fires of the Lightning's Scar. Lendara entered the Kingdom of the Adoni upon his death without his horn, and his horn was never replaced until the day Teacher was crowned.

SEEING EYE, THE – Reference to the Crystal Eye or the Eye of Cronis.

SELENA, QUEEN – One of the forgotten queens of Dula. She was ruler of the kingdom with her husband King Anon. She was the first of the Royal Family to give birth to twins. She had been barren for a number of years, and went to a midwife to obtain certain herbs which could help in child-bearing. In order to find the midwife, she had to travel to the poorer section of Dula, and was deeply touched by the poverty and conditions her subjects were forced to live in. When the herbs were successful, and she gave birth to twins, Queen Selena made a vow to repay the kindness the midwife had shown her in easing her suffering by easing the suffering of the midwife and her neighbors. She approached her husband, King Anon, with plans to help the poor, but he refused. He informed his wife that if she had money of her own, she could use it any way she desired, but the money in his treasury would be used as he dictated. Queen Selena then took several jewels she had owned since before she was married, and sold them. She had a keen mind for business, and had advised her husband for many years. Now she stopped advising her husband and focused her attention on her own business affairs. While her wealth increased until some claimed it was more than could be counted, her husband's dealing nearly drove the kingdom into bankruptcy. King Anon finally came to realize his folly, repented of his harsh words to his wife, and turned the finances of the kingdom over to her. Under her care, the kingdom became wealthy once more. She used her own personal wealth to set up programs to help the poor, the sick, and the outcast. Her subjects came to call her Queen Yola after the Dulan term *yola* which means *kindness*. She rebuilt poor sections of the kingdom, and they came to be known as the Yola Province after the queen's nick name. Ironically, it is this nickname: *Queen Yola* by which she was remembered.

SHADOW THING – Another name given to bat things. However, this specifically refers to that species of bat things that serve Cronis. They live in the Veil of Darkness, and have difficulty dealing with sunlight or any bright light. Some of the older shadow creatures have been so drained by their service to Cronis that they have little substance left, and are little more than shadows. These bat things were drained of their substance in order to prepare them to operate outside the Veil of Darkness.

SINGER – Singer was the first of the Ancients – although still very young when the Council of Ancients was formed. The title of *Ancient* was initially given to those who had spent their entire lives dedicated to mastering all knowledge concerning a single subject. He had approached Octavous III, the King of Dula, for permission to form a Council of Ancients – others like himself who had dedicated their lives to the gathering of wisdom. The Council of Ancients would be allowed by the King of Dula to question Logos and increase their wisdom and knowledge. The king granted permission, and Singer (then known as Asseem) gathered those who desired knowledge, and set up a schedule for questioning the Sword. The Council grew frustrated because they had to share their times with others, and with those times when the Sword broke off answering questions in order to sing songs of praise to the Adoni. It was during one session that one of the Ancients became frustrated when the Sword stopped answering his questions to sing the Song of Morning. The ancient tried to distract the Sword from the song, and then demanded an answer to his question in the *name of the Adoni*. The Song of Morning broke off in mid-verse, and the voice of the Unnamed Adoni spoke, placing the Curse on all the Lands of the Adoni. Because Asseem had fallen in love with Reva a Water Citizen, he blamed himself for the Curse in that he did not monitor the questioning more carefully. Too late he realized that the Council had made knowledge their god instead of the Adoni. It was an idolatry which had brought the Curse upon the Lands of the Adoni. Asseem left Dula to seek an audience with the Adoni and ask them to remove the Curse and place it only on him. He came to live among the gnomes and was given the name of Sinta. With the loss of his clan among the gnomes, Sinta came to the Garden of Tangar after the Moving Trees had abandoned their post and the Garden of Tangar had been removed from the Lands of the Adoni. Sinta was met by the Children of Earth and they led him into the Garden of Tangar, where he was confronted by the Unnamed Adoni. Sinta was given to eat of the fruit from the Tree of Unending Life. A branch from the Tree of Unending Life was cut, and shaped into a staff for Sinta. He was then knighted as a Knight of Es-Soh-En, his name changed to Singer, and he was given the task of securing the throne which would eventually be held by the Rightful King. To this end, Singer served the Adoni for many centuries in various ways. He went with Queen Dianna on the Quest for the Sword. With the granting of the Gift of Unending Life to Queen Dianna, the return of Logos, and the promises of Es-Soh-En, the throne was established for the coming of the Rightful King. At that point, Singer flew Suma for Es-Soh-En to the Kingdom of the Adoni where Singer became one of the two to bodily enter the Kingdom of the Adoni without dying. In the Kingdom of the Adoni he was reunited with Reva, the Water Citizen he had loved and had been forced to leave behind in his service to the Adoni.

SINGER OF THE LESSER SONG, THE – This is a reference to Lady Tanya. After Es-Soh-En had completed the Song of Creation, the Greater Song; and while its power still vibrated in the creation, Glidon guided Tanya in another song, playing off of the Greater Song. The song was called the Lesser Song because it did not actually create, but it took the creative power still lingering in the Lands of the Adoni, and allowed parts of the creation to transform into centaurs, minotaurs, gnomes and Tree Druids. Lady Tanya's voice was focusing the power found in the echo of the Song of Creation, and as she touched an object, she transferred that power to the object so that it transformed into one of the four races previously mentioned. Thus her dancing made her touch various objects transferring the ability to change, while her singing (with the power of Glidon) generated the ability for objects to change. This is also a title granted to Lady Tanya by Es-Soh-En when she became a Knight of Es-Soh-En on the Mountain of the Sky.

SHIELD OF THE EAGLE, THE – Name given to a steel shield, polished like fine silver and crafted for Dayton. The shield is an oval, and etched into its otherwise polished surface is a likeness of the Great Eagle, Glidon. In the chest of the Great Eagle, and in the center of the shield is embedded the Eye of Suma. This shield was then given to Sir David and Lady Tanya by Dayton and his family. The Eye of Suma had a curse placed on it by Teacher that it could only change ownership by voluntary agreement of the original owner; otherwise the new owner would be tormented by Cronis to return the stone. The fact that the shield passed from Dayton to the Children of Earth proved the entire family was willing and in agreement to the giving of the gift.

STEWARD OF THE THRONE, THE – Title given to Sir David on the Mountain of the Sky when he was made a Knight of Es-Soh-En.

STEWARD OF THE UNICORNS, THE – Title given to Deenara upon the death of Lendara. Deenara was to rule the herd of unicorns in place of Lendara who was the only unicorn to taste of death. Upon the Return of the Adoni, and the restoration of all titles, Deenara transferred leadership of the herd back to Lendara.

STEWARDESS OF THE THRONE, THE – Title given to Lady Tanya when she was made a Knight of Es-Soh-En on the Mountain of the Sky.

SUMA – The sky ship created from trees cut down by Pentra and used to build Suma. It was first presented to Pentra the Greater to fly into the Veil of Darkness. Once Pentra had completed his task, it was stored on the Mountain of the Sky, until it was made available to Queen Dianna on her Quest for the Sword. After that it was not seen again until the Battle of Es-Soh-En when Teacher used it to pass one of the tests to prove He was the Rightful King. As part of the testing of Teacher, He gave one of its twin blue jewel eyes to Trayton to buy him and his family out of debt for the accidental killing of his neighbor. The ship floats upon the air currents by the Power of the Adoni. It is carved to look like a great eagle, with the spread wings serve as the stairs to board the ship. It has three sails made of spun gold with the image of the Great Hobber embroidered on the main sail. The figure head is a carved eagle's head, and the eyes of the figure head are twin blue jewels filled with life. Whenever the ship is used, all supplies are replaced as they are used by the crew.

SWORD-KEEPERS CLAN, THE – Created at the end of the Quest for the Sword. As both Tra and Kal had been disowned by their clans because they had forsaken the war-like ways of their people to serve the Adoni, Es-Soh-En created a new clan for both of them and Dig Gen. This was called the Sword-Keepers Clan, or Clan of Swordkeepers; and it was to this clan that Logos was entrusted. The creation of this clan allowed others of the centaur and minotaur races to forsake war and seek after the Adoni without becoming an outcast to their community. Although the clan continued under other titles it remained the Sword-Keepers Clan until the death of its last founding member, Dig Gen.

SY-LAR – The eagle-sword of Lady Tanya when Tanya was made a Knight of Es-Soh-En, Es-Soh-En gave her this sword. This Adoni blade was forged in the Kingdom of the Adoni and cannot be broken. Its hilt is shaped like an eagle, with the wings forming the cross piece of the sword. Its sheath is called Hissen which refers to a musical pause. Both Hissen and Sy-lar have the ability to appear whenever Tanya summons them. If she has no need of them, they disappear to a waiting place until they are needed once more.

TAKARD – A very pungent herb made from crushing the roots of the takard plant. It is used to treat lung infections, but if applied too often, can cause spasms in the lungs restricting the flow of oxygen, and can produce a deep sleep similar to a coma. The plants are very rare, and it takes a number of plants to create a small amount of takard. This is because the takard plant has very small and very few roots per plant.

TALKING SWORD, THE – Reference to Logos, the Talking Sword. It was able to speak for the Adoni, sing songs of praise, and instruct those who could hear its voice prior to the Battle of Es-Soh-En. At the Battle of Es-Soh-En, Teacher freed the voice from the Sword and returned the empty shell back to Queen Dianna.

TANDUR RIVER – A river that flows from its source east of Dula through the city. Part of the river is diverted to fill the moat around the castle. When the river passes out of the city of Dula, it flows to the Gen Forest. In the Gen Forest, the river forks with part flowing into Lake Gen and the other flowing into the Dula Alps.

TAN-CEPTS – A phrase in the centaur and minotaur battle language. It is taught to young warriors, but never spoken. The phrase means that Lady Tanya has forsaken her rejection of the centaur and minotaur race spoken at the time of the Fall, and now accepts the races as her children. It is made by combining the two key words in the phrase: *Tanya* and *Accepts*. The words are then abbreviated into *Tan-Cepts*.

TANYA – One of the two Children of Earth. She is sister to Sir David. She is the only female to be made a Knight of Es-Soh-En. She was made a Knight of Es-Soh-En with her brother on the Mountain of the Sky while on the Quest for the Sword with Queen Dianna. At that time she was given Sy-lar the eagle sword, and the ability to change into battle attire with only a thought. She is also known by the titles of Dancer of the Garden of Tangar, and the Singer of the Lesser Song. Both of these titles refer to her visit to the creation of the Lands of the Adoni. At that time, she was with Glidon and began to sing with Him, and dance through the Garden of Tangar. Whenever she touched a rock, tree, or bush; a Tree Druid, gnomes, minotaur, or centaur was created. Thus she was viewed as the mother of all these races. Later during the Fall she disowned the minotaur and centaur for their refusal to protect Ish and Issha when their lives were threatened by a Demon Cloud sent by Cronis to kill them. She attacked the cloud creature herself, falling in battle. One minotaur and centaur chose to give their lives to rescue her, and when they drove the Demon Cloud away instead of dying, they began the life style of their races, learning the ways of war in order to redeem themselves to Lady Tanya. Tanya met Jensen on one of her visits to Dula, and fell in love. The story of Jensen and Tanya became the talk of the court, and later one of the great love stories of Dulan history. Tanya returned to Earth at the end of that mission, and did not return until long after Jensen was dead. He had spent his entire life expressing his love for Tanya through poetry. At the time of the Return of the Adoni, Tanya assumed the role of Stewardess of the Throne of Dula, and she and her brother ruled in Queen Dianna's stead. From her long association with the centaur and minotaur races, she was a fierce warrior, and deadly in hand-to-hand combat. She was believed to be unbeatable in battle, and only when attacked by over-whelming numbers could she be brought down.

TEACHER – Title Es-Soh-En assumed when He was incarnated into human form. Teacher was Es-Soh-En the Great Hobber, the Son of the Adoni. As part of an agreement with Cronis, Es-Soh-En agreed to set aside all His power and authority as a member of the Adoni and meet Cronis in battle to determine ownership to the title deed to the Lands of the Adoni. In order to accomplish this, Es-Soh-En placed Himself into a woman's womb, became a baby, was born into the race of Ish, and grew to manhood all as a normal human. He had to be born of woman and human in order to be related to the human race as required under the Laws of the Adoni to redeem a relative. He could not be fathered by a man as the rebellion of Ish was passed through the blood line. Thus, in order to be qualified to redeem the human race, He had to be human, but a human born of woman and not of man; thus a virgin birth. Throughout his entire incarnation, and up through the Battle of Es-Soh-En He was in constant communication with the other Adoni, but never had any of His previous power or authority. He presented Himself to Queen Dianna as the Rightful King who had been predicted would come to claim the throne of Dula and all the Lands of the Adoni. She put him through three tests, the first was to see if He could dispense justice, the second was to test His compassion, and the third tested His resourcefulness by pitting a desire to be fulfilled against the protection of the kingdom. He proved to be successful in all areas. At the end of the testing Cronis stole Logos from the throne, and carried it to the Veil of Darkness. Teacher then had to enter the Veil of Darkness, travel to the Ring of Fire, and confront Cronis in mortal combat. During the battle, Cronis used Logos to strike Teacher from behind, driving the blade through Teacher, and piercing His heart. The action was in violation of the rules set down for the conflict, and so Cronis lost the Battle. Further, Cronis had become the power behind the Sword, and when Logos shed innocent blood, it was the power of Cronis which was broken. Teacher's body was carried away from the battle by Gaylord and Yeesha who served as the two appointed Witnesses to the Battle. Gaylord and Yeesha protected the body from the hoards of Cronis for three days. At that point Gaylord and Yeesha fell in battle. As Gaylord died, Teacher was resurrected. Since the Battle of Es-Soh-En was complete, and the power of Es-Soh-En was needed for the confrontation with Cronis, Teacher was resurrected as Es-Soh-En the Great Hobber. Since the incarnation, Teacher is the proper form for Es-Soh-En, but when there is a need to battle; Teacher transforms Himself into the Hobber as this form is more formidable in battle.

TE-FAR – Council member who represented the writer's guild. His guild reproduced books and scrolls. They also printed and bound various written works. His guild was also responsible for collecting news and dispersing it to the general population. He was known for his many spies. Anyone who was at court was never truly alone.

TONDOR – Dulan soldier at the time of the Return of the Adoni. He was one of the soldiers sent to drive the band of thieves out of the Gen Forest. His entire company was wiped out, and he alone made it back to Dula, although badly battered and wounded. Before the city gates could be opened, he was killed by and pinned to the gates with Magarian arrows. Agron was a close friend, and used this event to illustrate to the Council the need for Dula to prepare for war with Magar. Agron's actions resulted in his being removed from command and assigned to guard the dungeons.

TON KIN – Gnome at the time of the Battle of Es-Soh-En. He was a loyal Follower of Teacher. He was the first to learn of the coming Battle of Es-Soh-En through the Children of Earth. It was his privilege to introduce the Children of Earth to the population of Dula attending the two hundredth anniversary of the Quest for the Sword, and to announce that now was the time for the Battle of Es-Soh-En.

TONRU – Shopkeeper at the time of the Quest for the Sword. He was a loyal Follower of the Adoni, and when Magar took over Dula, he gave supplies to Kal and his group without charging them for the provisions. His store was also set up as the beginning point for Followers to come in order to escape Dula before Magar could capture and kill the Followers of the Adoni.

He and his wife Yeema had always wanted children, but were barren. Even though they were past the age of childbirth, Es-Soh-En granted them children as a reward for their service during the Quest for the Sword.

TOWER OF THE SUN, THE – This was once the highest mountain in all of Magar. When Magar won possession away from Dula of a jewel that fell from the sky, there was always the danger of the jewel being stolen. To prevent this one of the kings of Magar ordered the mountain carved into a lone tower. He then ordered the base of the mountain dug away until it became a great valley. The jewel, called the Heart of the Sun, was sealed in a box, carried to the top of the tower, and the stairway sealed with tons of debris. The top of the tower is opened to the sky so that Cronis could look down from the constellation of the Dragon each night, and see that his gift had been given great care. The tower carved out of the mountain came to be called the Tower of the Sun because it housed the Heart of the Sun.

TRA – (Also known as Tra the Skeptic). This is a centaur at the time of the Quest for the Sword. He was skeptical concerning the Adoni and Es-Soh-En. Tra had left the war-like ways of his race, and was ordered to shave his beard – a sign of manhood among the centaurs. He was ordered to keep his beard shaven until he was willing to return to war. Tra accepted the punishment of his race, and dedicated himself to reading and poetry. He became good friends with Kal the minotaur who spoke often of the Adoni. The two were close friends, but had numerous debates concerning the Adoni and Es-Soh-En .When Queen Dianna was tested by Dragnock to determine if her quest for the Sword was of the Adoni, Es-Soh-En sent the Children of Earth to save her. The appearance of the Children of Earth is what finally convinced Tra that the Adoni were real, and Es-Soh-En was all that the legends said of Him. Once convinced, Tra became a dedicated Follower. His skill at war made him perfect to aid Kal in protecting Dula from the attacks of Magar, and to lead the attack which drove Dragnock from Queen Dianna's throne. He was wounded in the battle, and at the end of the Quest for the Sword, Es-Soh-En healed his wound, and opened his ears to the voice of Logos the Talking Sword. He was made part of the Sword-Keepers Clan, and given charge of caring for Logos. He and Kal spent many hours recording all the lessons, information, and teachings of the Sword, and published them in a work which came to be called the New Words or Words of the Clan. Although he was now permitted to grow his beard by his race, he chose to keep his face clean-shaven to prove that manhood comes from within, and not from without. A movement among the centaurs grew from this belief, and all its members refused to grow beards.

TRAYTON – Citizen of Dula at the time of the Battle of Es-Soh-En. There was a murder where Giban was found dead from an arrow. Giban's neighbor, Lydel was accused of the killing because there had been previous threats by Lydel for Giban sending his herds into Lydel's crops. Queen Dianna ordered Teacher to determine who was guilty, and try the case as part of his testing as Rightful King. Teacher conducted his own investigation, called forth several people during a public gathering before Queen Dianna, and proved that Trayton had killed Giban. Trayton confessed, and begged for forgiveness. He claimed he had been hunting, and the killing was an accident. Under Dulan Law, Trayton would have to provide for Giban's family or be sold into slavery to help support the family. Trayton was too poor, and begged Teacher to help him. Teacher produced the Eye of Suma and gave it to Trayton and his heirs to help them meet the added financial obligation.

TREE DRUIDS – One of the races of the Lands of the Adoni. When Tanya sang the Lesser Song with Glidon in the Garden of Tangar, whenever she touched a tree, or a rock, or a bush, it transformed into a Tree Druid, centaur, minotaur or gnome. The Tree Druids came from the trees that were touched by Lady Tanya. They assume tree form, but can transform into human form. While in human form, they are slow, and their skin is dark like the bark of a tree trunk. They live for centuries, and after a few thousand years will find a location and *put down roots*. Once the roots are put down, the Tree Druid gives up the ability to transform back to human form or to move. The Tree Druid can still communicate and think as it did when in the human form. Gantra joked that the reason younger tree druids were always changing form and moving around was because they had *itchy bark*. Once a Tree Druid has *planted* he or she will not speak with others unless they have known them for three or four years or unless the person follows proper Tree Druid etiquette or is a friend of another Tree Druid. As Tanya pointed out to Gantra, since humans would not wait three or four years for someone to speak to them, this might be why few people visit with older Tree Druids.

TRIG GEN – Head of the Gen Family of gnomes at the time of the Quest for the Sword. He stayed behind with Brig Gen while his brothers Dig Gen and Gen went with Queen Dianna on the Quest for the Sword. His devotion and service in Dula at this time was recognized by the Adoni, and They granted him his heart's desire: to have the evil driven out of the Dark Woods. This was a battle led by Es-Soh-En as He took the gnomes into battle allowing them to purge the evil from their woods. Once the woods were clean, Es-Soh-En pronounced the woods safe for all, and renamed it the Gen Forest.

UNICORNS – Although unicorns are found in the Lands of the Adoni, they are not of the Lands of the Adoni. Unicorns were originally of the Kingdom of the Adoni. When Es-Soh-En sang the world into creation, and before Ish was formed from the dust of the ground, a portal opened between the Lands of the Adoni and the Kingdom of the Adoni so that the unicorns could enter the new world. Once they had entered, the unicorns – then led by Lendara – bonded with David making him one of the herd, and fulfilling one of his titles as Friend of the Unicorn. Although David was able to see and communicate with the unicorns, when Ish and Issha rebelled and brought about the Fall, all communication between humans and unicorns ceased with the exception of David. The unicorn chose to remain separate and untouched by the Lands of the Adoni and the corruption which had taken root in the Lands of the Adoni. For this reason they worked behind the scenes to serve the Adoni. This separation from the Lands of the Adoni earned the unicorn the title of the *Untarnished*. They had stated that the price of their creation was so much less than the price of the redemption of others, thus when redemption was bestowed upon the inhabitants of the Lands of the Adoni, the unicorns seemed pale by comparison. The unicorn told Tanya that they knew this was the price, and not to grieve that they had kept their original state. After the death of David, the unicorns, now led by Deenara bonded with Tanya, making her a Friend of the Unicorn. From that point on, the unicorn operated openly in preparation for the Return of the Adoni.

UNNAMED ADONI, THE – Very little is actually known concerning the Unnamed Adoni except for what He has revealed concerning Himself. He, and the other Adoni, have referred to Him in the masculine sense, and so it is assumed that He is masculine. He is so great and so powerful that no name or form can do Him justice, which is why He has remained without name or form. When He appears, it is in the form of warm brilliant light. When He is present, or when He speaks, those present are flooded with a sense of joy, peace, and security.

UNTARNISHED, THE – Title for unicorn.

UNTER THE HEALER – At one time Unter was a good and honest man, truly seeking to undo the damage caused by the Curse. He studied healing of the body, but as a hobby he spent a great deal of time studying the ways of Cronis. It was through these studies that he was eventually seduced, and approached by Cronis to serve the Dark Lord in exchange for power and position. From that point on Unter began the downward path that led him to the point where he had tried to kill Lady Tanya by mis-administering medication to her while she was injured. Later, when he tried to contact others through the powers of Cronis, a Shadow Thing was dispatched to kill him.

VALLEY OF THE SEVEN FORESTS, THE – At the time of the Fall, this was a valley in southern Bromor. As the Demon Cloud sent by Cronis to kill Ish and Issha, traveled south to hunt its prey, David and Rentara the unicorn blocked its path at the entrance to the valley. Following instruction from Cronis, the Demon Cloud took some of its own essence and evil, and exerted influence on the plant life in the valley. David fought every step of the way, and the battle took all night for the Demon Cloud to make it through the valley. At the break of day, the Demon Cloud used plants to capture and hold David and Rentara fast so it could get past, and continue its search for Ish and Issha. The energy and evil used by the cloud creature created the Valley of Seven Forests. Each forest is known for a different color, or condition. The forests are individually called the Forest of Blood, the Forest of Gold, the Forest of Sleep, the Forest of Green, the Forest of Illusion, the Forest of Death, and the Forest of Fur. Some of the forests have had more than one name over the centuries, such as the Forest of Blood was also known as the Forest of Fire, and the Forest of Passion. It was in the Valley of Seven Forest that Dragnock sent an ambush for Queen Dianna. Queen Dianna was separated from Singer and the Children of Earth. The Queen, Dig Gen, and Gen were tricked by Cronis into entering the Forest of Death. There the party was captured and nearly killed by demon plant. Dig Gen attacked the demon plant and killed it – something no gnome had ever done before.

VEIL OF DARKNESS, THE – At one time the area west of Dula was a vast ocean called the Western Ocean – or by some: the Golden Ocean. The intelligence of the Demon Cloud that had survived the attack of Lendara was washed out to sea where it drifted into the Western Ocean. Once there it began to use the ability it had developed to become the Demon Cloud and draw sustenance and substance away from the Show Things that served Cronis. It recreated itself into a full-sized Shadow Thing. When Cronis discovered the ability of the former Demon Cloud, he attacked the Shadow Thing to learn its secret. The battle resulted in the entire Western Ocean being boiled away. As the battle continued, the Shadow Thing adapted its ability to draw from other Shadow Things and began to draw light out of the sky. It had created the beginning of the Veil of Darkness before being defeated and captured by Cronis. Using torture, Cronis caused the Shadow Thing to expand the Veil of Darkness all the way to the former Shores of the Western Ocean along Dula. The Veil of Darkness expanded into Dula and Orpha, which led to the alliance of the two kingdoms and their invasion to drive back the forces of Cronis. This was the Battle of Three Armies. Dula and Orpha were driven out of the Veil. Eventually, Es-Soh-En ordered all 144 Knights of Es-Soh-En to invade the Veil in what came to be called the Battle of the Line. This was to draw off the forces of Cronis while Pentra the Greater flew Suma into the Veil of Darkness. At the Ring of Fire, where Cronis imprisoned the Shadow Thing, Pentra fought the creature to the death. With the death of the Shadow Thing Cronis lost the ability to expand the Veil any further. The Battle of the Line was removed from all memories – including the Knights of Es-Soh-En who were returned to various time periods unaware the battle had taken place. Cronis was able to inhabit the Veil with all of his followers who had previously been forbidden to enter the Lands of the Adoni, and had to wait in a limbo world. Once his servants filled the Veil of Darkness, this became the Dark Lord's base of operations in the Lands of the Adoni. It was difficult and painful for Cronis, or any of his followers, to leave the Veil; but whenever someone spoke of Cronis by either title or name, it gave Cronis the legal authority to send one or more of his servants into the Lands of the Adoni to operate until they were driven out. At the time of the Battle of Es-Soh-En it was the site of the conflict between Teacher and Cronis.

WATER PEOPLE/ WATER NYMPHS – One of the races of the Lands of the Adoni. They were the last race created by Es-Soh-En, and He breathed a golden mist over the Pools of Shiva. The golden mist and the song called the life stones to life on the bottom of the pools. Es-Soh-En gave one last look at the pools before leaving. This caused the first Water People to see blue eyes staring down at them, through a golden breath. The Water People had been a shy race, and never came out of hiding all the time Es-Soh-En was present with Ish and Issha. After the Fall, they eventually communicated with Ish and Issha, but always believed that they had been created by someone other than the Adoni. For centuries they simply referred to their creator as *the God Who Breaths Gold*. The Water People Community kept themselves separate from the other races due to their religious beliefs in *the God Who Breathes Gold*, few people ever encountered Water People, and most encounters were women who were performing various tasks near the rivers and lakes. For this reason, the other races began calling them Water Nymphs. At the time of Asseem, the men of the Water People began to interact with the citizens of Dula, and Asseem instructed many to refer to them as the Water People or Water Citizens. When Asseem left after the Curse came upon the Lands of the Adoni, most resorted back to use of the term Water Nymph in referring to the Water People. At the end of the Quest for the Sword, they became aware that their creator and Es-Soh-En were the same. Also, at the time of the Quest for the Sword, the entire Water People community was captured by Dragnock and nearly wiped out. The Water People community was saved by the actions of Leah. After the Quest for the Sword, they separated themselves once more, and learned the ways of warfare, applying their own unique abilities to hand-to-hand combat. A Water Citizen can transform from water to human, and back once more; thereby avoiding injury by any weapon. The only part of their bodies which cannot change is the life stone. If the life stone is broken, destroyed, or damaged, the Water Person will die. Water People mate in lakes, rivers or streams, giving of themselves to other polished stones on the water bed. When the couple adds some of themselves to the polished stone, it becomes a life stone, and a new Water Person is created. The water of a Water Person can be replaced, but the life stone never can. All Water Citizen names begin with either an "R," an "S," or an "L" to identify if they were formed in a river, stream or lake. The first Water People all had names which began with a *P* or an *SH* since they had been called to life in the Pools of Shiva. Water People are part of a very close community and have very strong family ties.

WEN-GAR – Captain of the gates on the day when Sir David came to review the troops. He had been a member of Heart Company, and had served as second-in-command of Heart Company while it trained in secret. He was forced to choose between allowing Sir David in before he was sure of Sir David's identity, or of jeopardizing his career by offending the Steward of the Throne. He chose to make Sir David wait until he could be identified. Sir David praised his caution, and when Heart Company was revealed, Wen-Gar became third in command of the army under Agron.

WESTERN OCEAN, THE – [Also referred to as the Western Sea on some maps.] This was once a great ocean, it was boiled away to a vast desert with bodies of millions of sea life during the battle between Cronis and the Shadow Thing. It also became the location of the Veil of Darkness.

WIL DEN – Twin brother of Fen Den and leader of the gnome community at the time of the Return of the Adoni. According to gnomish law, the eldest of the clan was to lead the entire community. The age of a gnome was determined by the date of the birth, and the hour of the birth. Gnomish law did not allow for any further distinction to determine age. As Wil Den and Fen Den were born on the same day, and during the same hour, they shared leadership of the clan, and the community.

WILARA – When Lendara died saving Ish and Issha at the Fall, Deenara was moved to the Steward of the Unicorn. Where Deenara had served as second-in-command of the herd under Lendara, Wilara was promoted to second-in-command under Deenara.

WILTON – At the time of Pentra the Greater, Wilton unofficially organized and led a group of writers and performers called the Knights Inkling. He created the title because they loved the Knights of Es-Soh-En and they worked in ink. They sought to collect and preserve as many stories, songs and plays about the Knights of Es-Soh-En as possible. These were eventually collected into a single book.

WIND SONG – Brother of Morning Star. He and his sister were twins born to Gaylord and Yeesha, but died shortly after birth. They were sent by the Adoni from the Kingdom of the Adoni to bond with the Children of Earth. Wind Song bonded with David, and served him in the same manner that their parents had served in previous years.

WODIN – The first Tree Druid to put down roots in the Grove of Three Oaks. He was the oldest, and claimed to have been *a mere sapling* back when Tanya called him to life while singing the Lesser Song with Glidon. His fondest memory was of his dancing with Tanya in the Garden of Tangar, and he wished he was able to dance when he and Tanya were reunited at the Return of the Adoni. During the Kingdom of the Adoni, Tanya would come to visit him and he would transform back into human form and dance with her, and she would *tussle* his leaves.

WORDS OF THE ANCIENTS, THE – After the Curse was placed on the Lands of the Adoni, Asseem sought to undo the damage the Council of Ancients had caused. He collected all the information recorded by the Ancients from their time of questioning Logos, and published them in a work. The collection came to be known as the Words of the Ancients. When Kal and Tra had the Curse lifted from their ears, and could hear the voice of the Sword once more, additional collections were published of new teachings, lessons, and bits of information obtained from Logos. This new collection came to be known as the New Words or Words of the Clan. The original collection, previously known as the Words of the Ancients, came to be called The Old Words.

WORDS OF THE CLAN, THE – This is in reference to the Clan of Swordkeepers writings. Both Tra and Kal had the Curse lifted from their ears, and they were able to hear the voice of the Sword Logos for the first time in centuries. They spent hours with the Sword, writing down everything that Logos revealed to them. These writings were collected and published for all to read. They were called the New Words or the Words of the Clan.

YEESHA – One of the Talking Horses in Dula at the time of the Quest for the Sword. She and her husband, Gaylord, served Queen Dianna. At the end of the Quest for the Sword, Es-Soh-En blessed both she and her husband with long life, and set them aside for a special task. At the time of the Battle of Es-Soh-En, she and Gaylord became the Witnesses for all the Lands of the Adoni, and returned from the Veil of Darkness to share what they had seen. Both Yeesha and Gaylord fought to protect the body of Teacher in the Veil, and were killed by the forces of Cronis. When Teacher resurrected them both, they were transformed into flying horses. They traveled to Janadis with Teacher, and recited the story of the Battle of Es-Soh-En to the entire city. From there they flew Teacher and the Children of Earth to the Lesser Kingdom. At the Return of the Adoni, Yeesha carried Queen Dianna to her wedding with Teacher.

YEEMA – Wife of Tonru. She and her husband owned a small market at the time of the Quest for the Sword. This market provided supplies to the underground resistance of Followers, and was the starting point for an escape route for Followers who were fearful of being captured by Magar. She and her husband wanted children, but they were past the age of childbearing. Because of their dedication and service, Es-Soh-En gave them children in their old age. When Yeema first met Tonru, he was not a Follower of the Adoni, but as they dated, her logic, dedication, and information won him over before they were married.

YOLA, QUEEN – Nickname for Queen Selena.

YOLA PROVINCE – Section refurbished by Queen Selena in the poorer section in Dula. It was designed as housing and care for the poor, the sick, and the outcast. It was funded by Queen Selena's personal wealth and business dealings, and continued for many generations after her death. Unfortunately, when the funding ran out, it became even poorer. At the time of the Quest for the Sword only the most poor would still live there as it had fallen into a terrible state of disrepair. It was named for the nickname the people had given Queen Selena of Queen Yola. In the Dulan tongue *yola* means *kindness*.

ZON – Wife of Ren, head of the minotaurs. She gave birth to Gar, the last minotaur born before the Return of the Adoni. In the minotaur clan, the wife of the leader must be as great a warrior as the husband, and she ruled the minotaur community during the absence of her husband who had taken the others into battle.

Review Requested:

If you loved this book, would you please provide
a review at Amazon.com?

CPSIA information can be obtained
at www.ICGtesting.com
Printed in the USA
BVHW071531120819
555662BV00001B/55/P